The Editor

RAE GREINER is associate professor of English at Indiana University and coeditor of the flagship journal *Victorian Studies*. She is the author of *Sympathetic Realism in Nineteenth-Century British Fiction* (Johns Hopkins University Press, 2012). Her current project is a study of affect in relation to the concept of stupidity.

NORTON CRITICAL EDITIONS
Age of Sensibility & Romanticism

For a complete list of Norton Critical Editions, visit
wwnorton.com/nortoncriticals

A NORTON CRITICAL EDITION

Jane Austen

PERSUASION

AUTHORITATIVE TEXT
BACKGROUNDS AND CONTEXTS
CRITICISM

THIRD EDITION

Edited by

RAE GREINER
INDIANA UNIVERSITY

W. W. NORTON & COMPANY
Independent Publishers Since 1923

W. W. Norton & Company has been independent since its founding in 1923, when William Warder Norton and Mary D. Herter Norton first published lectures delivered at the People's Institute, the adult education division of New York City's Cooper Union. The firm soon expanded its program beyond the Institute, publishing books by celebrated academics from America and abroad. By mid-century, the two major pillars of Norton's publishing program—trade books and college texts—were firmly established. In the 1950s, the Norton family transferred control of the company to its employees, and today—with a staff of five hundred and hundreds of trade, college, and professional titles published each year—W. W. Norton & Company stands as the largest and oldest publishing house owned wholly by its employees.

Copyright © 2025, 2013, 1995 by W. W. Norton & Company, Inc.

All rights reserved
Printed in the United States of America

ISBN: 978-1-324-07074-0 (pbk)

W. W. Norton & Company, Inc., 500 Fifth Avenue, New York, NY 10110
www.wwnorton.com
W. W. Norton & Company Ltd., 15 Carlisle Street, London W1D 3BS

1 2 3 4 5 6 7 8 9 0

Contents

Introduction

"This peace will be returning all our rich Navy Officers ashore." So says Mr. Shepherd at the start of *Persuasion*'s Chapter III, laying down the newspaper he has just been reading to broach with Sir Walter Elliot the hard necessity of letting Kellynch-hall: "Many a noble fortune has been made during the war. If a rich Admiral were to come our way . . ." (14). But here Shepherd is interrupted by Sir Walter, who interjects that such a man would be "very lucky," for "a prize indeed would Kellynch-hall be to him; rather, the greatest prize of all, let him have taken ever so many before." Offering up this specimen of "wit," a punning wordplay that Shepherd, as his employee, is obliged to reward with a laugh, Sir Walter's joke (such as it is) plays on the multiple meanings of the word "prize," in particular the prize-money awarded to navymen on the capture of enemy ships.

As the reader soon learns, this practice of capture and reward has enriched men like Captain Frederick Wentworth and his navy friends Benwick and Harville, as it had enriched Jane Austen's naval brothers, Francis (Frank) and Charles Austen, who sent prize-money, and presents purchased with it, back to their sisters at home. Where Wentworth's promotion to commander follows his success in the Battle of San Domingo on the island now called Haiti, which took place against French forces in February 1806, so the prizes awarded to Frank for his valor in that same action enabled him finally to marry Mary Gibson in June of that year. Given the centrality of the British navy to the Austen family's fortunes during the French Revolutionary and Napoleonic period, and to the "False Peace" of 1814–15 during which *Persuasion* is set, it is perhaps unsurprising that Anne Elliot, the novel's long-suffering protagonist, remarks in the same chapter: "The navy, I think, who have done so much for us, have at least an equal claim with any other set of men, for all the comforts and all the privileges which any home can give. Sailors work hard enough for their comforts, we must all allow" (15). These words—on what is owed the navy for their labor and sacrifice—are the first she speaks in the book.

As Patricia Meyer Spacks made clear in her preface to the Norton Critical Edition of *Persuasion* that preceded this one, Jane Austen had good reason for so thoughtfully considering the extent of the sailors' sacrifice and discomfort. Yes, Austen was suffering from the disease that would take her life just one year after she completed the revisions for *Persuasion*, and there can be little doubt that physical pain and thoughts of mortality affected both the conception and the writing of her last completed novel. But it is also true that *this* novel, arguably more than her earlier works, prompts readers to contemplate shared, collective suffering, especially the painful effects of wartime: "to think complexly about Austen in the context of her contemporaries—not only her literary peers, but all the other men and women living through the Napoleonic Wars on the Continent and their political repercussions in England," as Spacks puts it. *Persuasion* "speaks of more than life in a village, or even in Bath," Spacks continues, in that it "ironizes Austen's well-known profession to her brother about 'the little bit (two Inches wide) of Ivory on which I work with so fine a Brush,'" directing our attention beyond the local, and binding individual lives to the vicissitudes of history and society, "the life of personal feeling" to "the navy's symbolic connection with private as well as public virtue."[1] The materials excerpted in the Backgrounds and Contexts and Criticism sections of the present volume were selected so as to illuminate such connections between private and public concerns, as well as the wider global perspective that *Persuasion* encourages us to take in reading it.

Indeed, it is hardly possible to take in Anne's story of multiplied griefs and acts of self-sacrifice—to the needs and demands of her family, to her father's vanity, and to Lady Russell, whose part in Anne's life's most bitter disappointment was in judging her engagement to Wentworth "a wrong thing"—or even to comprehend her faded looks and low spirits in isolation from the economic and political events that have shaped her fortunes in her twenty-seven years of life. Describing Anne and Wentworth's earliest days of youthful acquaintance with something of the comedy that readers familiar with her other novels may have come to expect, Austen writes that the two fell in love quickly, "for he had nothing to do, and she had hardly any body to love" (20). But *Persuasion* is not a comic novel, nor is it preoccupied with first romance: "A short period of exquisite felicity followed, and but a short one.—Troubles soon arose" (20). These words refer of course to the pair's brief happiness in the summer of 1806 and to the unhappy end of their union that just as quickly follows. But they also describe a time that would become widely recognizable— though only later, only in retrospect—as painfully short-lived.

The False Peace, as the period soon would be called, represented at the time during which Austen was writing and revising *Persuasion*

1. Patricia Meyer Spacks, Preface, in Jane Austen, *Persuasion*, Norton Critical Edition, 2nd ed. (New York: W. W. Norton & Company, 2013), pp. vii–xi.

(ca. 1815–17) a welcome respite from the alarms of war, but also a pause doomed not to last, shattered as it would be by the return of an unvanquished Napoleon Bonaparte and the resumption of troubles between England and France. As Mary A. Favret writes in *War at a Distance: Romanticism and the Making of Modern Wartime* (2009), excerpted in the present volume, "When, in her last complete novel, Jane Austen, that great historian of the ballroom, attempts something 'not unlike' a history of war, she does so precisely by calling the reader's attention to a negative sort of history, a lost history, a history of what seems unable to be told."[2] In setting the novel's action amid a temporary, uneasy peace between formal wars, Austen reminds readers not only of the near-perpetual wartime during which her own, retrospectively short life was lived, but also of the pains endured by all of the other ordinary people living in it: from women like herself, who wrote to and received letters from their naval brothers, to those simply at home, reading of battle after battle in newspapers and perhaps thinking, as *Persuasion's* Mr. Shepherd had done, of displaced men and families in need of temporary homes. The novel stresses the fact that the military service of men like Captain Wentworth indexes a historical first: the first time that ordinary men, not "battle-trained elites," comprised the bulk of the British armed forces. Favret reminds us that it was during the Napoleonic period that "the term 'noncombatant' as well as the popular understanding of 'civilian' as nonmilitary first emerged in English; and the notion of 'wartime' as a distinct category emerged with them."[3] Wartime is the temporality in which *Persuasion* happens, including the temporary lull in combat during which the main events of the plot take place.

With this in mind, we might revise our understanding of the loss of what the novel calls "bloom." If Anne when we first meet her seems to epitomize the dreaded fate of spinsterhood that animates the marital striving of her elder sister, Elizabeth, we cannot be too quick to designate her an old maid. Despite her twenty-seven years— Anne is old only in relation to the period's *ideal* of marriage, not its actuality—it is not so easy to say with certainty what is or isn't finished, washed up. From her father's vain obsession with maintaining his youthful good looks and revulsion at freckles, to his outraged sense of bombardment by "the wreck of the good looks of every body else [around him] . . . Anne haggard, Mary coarse, every face in the neighborhood worsting; and the rapid increase of the crow's foot about Lady Russell's temples [that] had long been a distress to him" (6), there is throughout the novel a feeling of time

2. Mary A. Favret, *War at a Distance: Romanticism and the Making of Modern Wartime* (Princeton, NJ: Princeton UP, 2009), p. 148.
3. Favret, *War at a Distance*, 13.

distempered, of young faces "wrecked" by life or time and older ones, like Sir Walter's, somehow unharmed. Unnatural beginnings and endings, to be sure, but also hard questions about the passage of time—especially wartime—and the ways in which the experiences of one's life manifest on one's face and skin. Falsely attributing the improvement of Anne's looks during the family's sojourn at Bath to the use of Gowland's Lotion, Sir Walter relates: "I should recommend Gowland, the constant use of Gowland, during the spring months," adding, "Mrs. Clay has been using it at my recommendation, and you see what it has done for her. You see how it has carried away her freckles" (104). Advertisements for Gowland's Lotion—a real product sold at the time—promised to "[remove] every kind of coarseness, eruption, and unpleasant appearance, and [render] the skin clear, smooth, and transparent," but also functioned like a chemical peel, stripping away the top layer of skin by way of corrosive ingredients, "a solution of mercurie chloride 1, ammonium chloride 1, in emulsion of bitter almonds 480 parts."[4] And yet, despite Sir Walter's near-constant complaining about "deplorable-looking personage[s]" like Admiral Baldwin (another navy man)—"his face the colour of mahogany, rough and rugged to the last degree, all lines and wrinkles" (16)—the association of freckles with the sailing life suggests that they might signify something other than ruined good looks. They might instead be emblematic of a kind of freedom, one that England's near-constant wartime had made newly available to young women like Anne.

Consider Mrs. Croft—wife of Admiral Croft, sister to Wentworth, and newly arrived tenant of Kellynch-hall—as she is presented to us, focalized through Anne's perspective:

> Mrs. Croft, though neither tall nor fat, had a squareness, upright-ness, and vigour of form, which gave importance to her person. She had bright dark eyes, good teeth, and altogether an agreeable face; though her reddened and weather-beaten complexion, the consequence of her having been almost as much at sea as her husband, made her seem to have lived some years longer in the world than her real eight-and-thirty. Her manners were open, easy, and decided, like one who had no distrust of herself, and no doubts of what to do; without any approach to coarse-ness, however, or any want of good humour. (36)

In Mrs. Croft's "reddened and weather-beaten complexion" Anne finds neither ugliness nor unwanted evidence of the passage of time, but instead the imprints of an adventurous life. Indexing her

---

4. Oliver Farrar Emerson, "Two Notes on Jane Austen," *Journal of English and Germanic Philology* 18.2 (1919): 217–20, at 217.

experiences of global travel, these signs of weathering correlate quite directly to Mrs. Croft's open, honest manner and pleasing sensibility. Anne slides easily from observing one set of qualities to the other, from apprehending the redness of her face to appreciating the lively qualities of her character. If her time at sea makes Mrs. Croft appear older than "her real eight-and-thirty" years, her experiences of and in "the world" have altered her in ways that Anne, contemplating the heavy penalties of her own youthful decisions, considers well worth the cost of beauty: "no distrust of herself, and no doubts of what to do."

If *Persuasion* is unique in offering so sympathetic a view of sun-damaged complexions, it is not without likeness. *Portrait of a Lady with Freckles*, an 1853 painting by the French painter Victor Favier (1824–ca. 1889), offers a rare, uncritical pictorial rendering of a freckled female subject. While earlier painted depictions of freckled persons exist, such as the image of Judas appearing in *The Lamentation of Christ* (ca. 1520), a panel in an altarpiece by the Dutch painter Joos van Cleve (1485–1541), the appearance of freckles often signified sinfulness and, as is true in *The Lamentation*, conveyed antisemitic meaning. (Andrei Oişteanu has found Romanian folk idioms that refer to freckles as *"Judas' Dreck"* ["Judas dirt"], citing a versified legend purporting to explain "how the Yids came to be freckled."[5]) Favier's portrait is different. Seated is a woman richly dressed in a black gown with delicate lace trim, a sumptuous green shawl and gold earrings, with several golden rings on her fingers, each item conveying a wealth and ease that are reflected in the calm expression and slight smile that adorn her face. Like Mrs. Croft, whose first name, Sophia, comes from the Greek word for wisdom, the woman in Favier's portrait is confident, her gaze direct and her attitude relaxed, unperturbed by the freckles dotting her slender hands and clustering around her nose, cheeks, and chin. While such appreciations remain rare in the nineteenth century, we might place her alongside Austen's Mrs. Croft in an aesthetic lineage that would lead, nearer to the century's end, to the "dappled things" celebrated by the British poet Gerard Manley Hopkins (1844–1889) in his 1877 poem of praise, "Pied Beauty":

> Glory be to God for dappled things—
>   For skies of couple-colour as a brinded cow;
>   For rose-moles all in stipple upon trout that swim;
> Fresh-firecoal chestnut-falls; finches' wings;
>   Landscape plotted and pieced—fold, fallow, and plough;
>   And áll trádes, their gear and tackle and trim.

---

5. Andrei Oişteanu, *Inventing the Jew: Antisemitic Stereotypes in Romanian and Other Central-East European Cultures* (Lincoln: U of Nebraska P, 2009), p. 58.

All things counter, original, spare, strange;
  Whatever is fickle, freckled (who knows how?)
  With swift, slow; sweet, sour; adazzle, dim;
He fathers-forth whose beauty is past change:
            Praise him.[6]

Here, freckled things are not just beautiful but vibrantly, verbally alive: swimming, winging, adazzle. Their very variety individuates even as it synthesizes, compressing enormities into small, original objects and moments—not two inches of ivory here, but perhaps not unlike it, these rose-moles stippling the fishes, the brindle hues streaking across the sky.

At the same time, as the skin-bleaching power and attractiveness of Gowland's Lotion to men like Sir Walter make clear, such appreciations were not often extended to persons born with dark skin. In this respect, *Persuasion*'s interest in the British navy, and by extension the British Empire, affords readers an opportunity to gain insight, however oblique, into Austen's attitudes toward race and the British imperial project. Several of the paratexts included in this volume encourage readers to position *Persuasion* in relation to global events for which questions of racial identity, geopolitics, and national belonging are explicit and paramount. Not included here, but recommended for anyone interested in these topics, are Gayatri Chakravorty Spivak's pivotal essay "Three Women's Texts and a Critique of Imperialism" (1985) and Edward W. Said's *Culture and Imperialism* (1993), two early postcolonial critiques that remain influential in shaping how readers attune themselves to these issues in British writings of the period, many of which either ignore racial meaning, and even slavery, altogether or portray racialized subjects in entirely negative, racist terms. Spivak opens by proclaiming as self-evident an idea that was also a provocation: "It should not be possible to read nineteenth-century British literature without remembering that imperialism, understood as England's social mission, was a crucial part of the cultural representation of England to the English."[7] Understanding well that reading nineteenth-century British novels "without remembering" empire was not only possible but had long been standard practice, Spivak turns to Charlotte Brontë's *Jane Eyre* (1847) and to feminist readings of that novel which celebrate Jane's fiercely won self-fashioning, while in the process either forgetting or allegorizing away the character (and significance) of Bertha Mason, Rochester's "mad" Creole wife, the "other woman" with

---

6. Gerard Manley Hopkins, *Poems of Gerard Manley Hopkins*, ed. Robert Bridges (London: Humphrey Milford, 1918), p. 30.
7. Gayatri Chakravorty Spivak, "Three Women's Texts and a Critique of Imperialism," *Critical Inquiry* 12.1 (1985): 243–61, at 243.

whom the novel must dispense in order to reward Jane with the happy resolution of her courtship plot. Appraisals of that novel that render Bertha a "dark double" of Jane's own psyche, as Sandra Gilbert and Susan Gubar provided in their pathbreaking feminist text *The Madwoman in the Attic* (1979), interpreted as psychological and individualizing what was instead, in Spivak's view, political and nationalistic: a project of differentiating "Europe [from] its not-yet-human Other."[8] In similar fashion, Said in *Culture and Imperialism* looked to the novels of Austen, especially *Mansfield Park* (1814). Austen's decision to place the Bertram family estate "at the center of an arc of interests and concerns spanning the hemisphere, two major seas, and four continents," he argues, links events taking place "at home," including frivolous entertainments like the home-staged play, to events occurring far away and elsewhere—specifically Antigua, the site of a second, highly profitable Bertram family possession, a sugar plantation that would without question have been powered by enslaved people's labor.[9] "More clearly than anywhere else in her fiction," Said writes, *Mansfield Park*

> synchronizes domestic with international authority, making it plain that the values associated with such higher things as ordination, law, and propriety must be grounded firmly in actual rule over and possession of territory. [Austen] sees clearly that to hold and rule Mansfield Park is to hold and rule an imperial estate in close . . . association with it. What assures the domestic tranquility and attractive harmony of the one is the productivity and regulated discipline of the other.[1]

Whether or not one shares his fairly damning conclusions about Austen's attitude toward the project of empire—at once alarmingly "casual" in reference to the colonies and endorsing the colonial enterprise as a national good—it is hard to disagree with Said's demand that readers work better to understand even seemingly offhanded references to spaces outside Britain: "we should try to understand *what* [Austen] referred to, [and] why she gave it the importance she did."[2]

Said's framework provokes readers to see beyond the "3 or 4 families in a country village" that had long served as the narrow perimeter past which one needn't travel in understanding Austen's fictional worlds.[3] Doing so enables us to ask different questions about even the

---

8. Spivak, "Three Women's Texts," 247.
9. Edward W. Said, *Culture and Imperialism* (New York: Knopf, 1993), p. 84.
1. Said, *Culture and Imperialism*, 87.
2. Said, *Culture and Imperialism*, 89. On the choice of the name "Mansfield," see the editorial notes to John Bicknell and Thomas Day's "The Dying Negro" (1775) in the present volume.
3. Jane Austen, "Letter LX, Chawton, 9/18 Sept. 1814," in *The Letters of Jane Austen*, ed. Edward, Lord Brabourne, and Sarah Chauncey Woolsey (Boston: Little, Brown, and Co., 1908), pp. 268–69.

most well-considered features of her works, including the sources of the funds on which such families relied for their fine clothing, furnishings, and carriages. In this light, we might ask what makes Wentworth a good match in 1814 in a way that he hadn't been in 1806. Readers will recall Anne's early conviction that she ought to have married Wentworth regardless of his lack of inheritance and uncertain income, her conviction that, despite "every disadvantage of disapprobation at home, and every anxiety attending his profession, all their probable fears, delays and disappointments, she should yet have been a happier woman in maintaining the engagement, than she had been in the sacrifice of it" (23). Much misery follows, and is compounded when she is made to regret anew all that she has lost: Wentworth "had, very soon after their engagement ceased, got employ," had "distinguished himself, and early gained the other step in rank—and must now, by successive captures, have made a handsome fortune" (23). However glancing this description of Wentworth's naval career may be, it correlates Anne's personal regret with the fortunes of the British navy, just as Wentworth's "handsome fortune" has an untold history of its own.

As C. L. R. James explains in *The Black Jacobins: Toussaint L'Ouverture and the San Domingo Revolution* (1938), excerpted in this volume, the fierce battles waged over control of San Domingo reflected the staggering wealth that the island was capable of producing: in 1754, "there were 599 plantations of sugar and 3,379 of indigo"; in 1767, it "exported 72 million pounds weight of raw sugar and 51 million pounds of white, a million pounds of indigo and two million pounds of cotton, and quantities of hide, molasses, cocoa and rum." If, as James continues, "on no earthly spot was so much misery concentrated as on a slave-ship, then on no portion of the globe did its surface in proportion to its dimensions yield so much wealth as the colony of San Domingo."[4] That the skirmish enabling Wentworth's naval promotion, which in turn increases his share of the profits for each "successive capture" of enemy ships, was the 1806 Battle of San Domingo suggests, in its very specificity, Austen's certainty that such recent history would not pass by her readers unnoticed. This island, with its disproportionate share of immense and concentrated misery, is a portion of the globe on which Anne and Wentworth's future successes (on another little island: England) are built.

That Austen expects her readers to notice, and treat as meaningful, such details is reflected in Susan Morgan's claim that "to read *Persuasion* as simply about a couple rather than about a couple and a country is to fall back on an approach that would leave out much

---

4. C. L. R. James, *The Black Jacobins: Toussaint L'Ouverture and the San Domingo Revolution*, 2nd ed. (New York: Vintage, 1989), pp. 45–46.

of Austen's achievement."[5] Moving beyond explanatory frameworks that depend upon the biographical facts of Austen's life, Morgan maintains, does not require us to forget that Austen had two naval brothers whom she loved and whose experiences at sea inform so much of this book. Morgan shows that the navy's success in the Battle of San Domingo was linked in the minds of the British public to the successful uprising against the French led by Toussaint L'Ouverture, the subject of C. L. R. James's book. A Black man of African parentage, born into slavery[6] and later serving in the French military, L'Ouverture ignited public imagination for his role in the island's revolt against France, a response to Napoleon's 1802 order to reinstate enslavement in the French territories—the first time that any country had resumed the legal practice of slavery after having previously abolished it. British enthusiasm for his rebel army's unprecedented defeat of the mighty French can be seen to reflect growing abolitionist sentiment at home (L'Ouverture's army was comprised of formerly enslaved Black and mixed-race persons as well as white French colonists opposed to Napoleon's action); or, it might signify admiration among disenfranchised Britons for those fighting for freedom against tyranny "at home." England's desire to conceive of its protracted battle with France as similarly waging war against outside oppression no doubt occluded Britain's own crimes and hypocrisies, but that doesn't diminish the fact that, as Morgan writes, Britain's liberatory self-image "was enhanced starting in 1806 when Parliament abolished the foreign slave trade," and buttressed by the navy's charge, from 1806 on, "not only to beat the French but to enforce the ban on foreign ships and, starting in 1807, British ships carrying slaves."[7] To judge Wentworth's coldness toward Anne on his return to England in 1814 as entirely the product of a bruised ego or a broken heart may therefore be to overlook the geopolitical forces shaping his outlook during his time abroad. Likewise, Austen encourages readers to see Wentworth's vehement defense of the value of a firm and unyielding personal character—with "not a puncture, not a weak spot anywhere," as he says in comparing this ideal to (of all things) a fallen tree nut—as more than a personal preference. Wentworth's inaction when Louisa Musgrove, his would-be paramour, falls from the Cobb, a stone breakwater, requiring immediate care that he is too stunned to render, might

5. Susan Morgan, "Captain Wentworth, British Imperialism and Personal Romance," *Persuasions* 18 (1996): 88–97, at 88–89.

6. L'Ouverture was likely born enslaved circa 1739–46 on the plantation of Bréda at Haut de Cap on the northern coast of San Domingo. His father, Gaou Guinou, was the son of the king of Benin in West Africa and his mother, Pauline, was Guinou's second wife. "Toussaint Louverture: Haitian revolutionary leader," The National Museum of African American History & Culture, Washington, D.C., online.

7. Morgan, "Captain Wentworth," 91.

be seen as "the fate of a too rigid perspective confronting the complexities and ambiguities of a peacetime world," Morgan writes. "Without the clarity of an external enemy, Wentworth is paralyzed."[8]

Because the collection of readings gathered together here provides nineteenth-century as well as twentieth- and twenty-first-century perspectives on a variety of themes, they are best read transtemporally and in conjunction with one another. Excerpts from two autobiographical accounts of naval life, Robert Hay's *Landsman Hay: The Memoirs of Robert Hay, 1789–1847* (unpublished until 1953) and Olaudah Equiano's *The Interesting Narrative of the Life of Olaudah Equiano* (1789), depict experiences aboard British navy and merchant ships from the vantage of the volunteer, then later impressed, sailor (Hay) or the enslaved sailor forced into service (Equiano). These accounts might profitably be read alongside the reflections on British naval prowess by the American naval officer Captain A. T. Mahan in his 1892 *The Influence of Sea Power upon the French Revolution and Empire, 1793–1812*, an interesting companion piece to Edmund Burke's *Reflections on the Revolution in France* (1790) and to George Gordon, Lord Byron's 1814 poem "The Corsair." Likewise, John Bicknell and Thomas Day's abolitionist poem "The Dying Negro" (1775) and James Stephen's *The Crisis of the Sugar Colonies* (1802) pair with Devoney Looser's recent research into the Austen family's connections to colonial profit, providing readers opportunity for considering a range of methodological techniques and approaches—poetic, rhetorical, sentimental, political, descriptive—for addressing difficult topics like the history and practice of enslavement. Following Mary Favret's example in calling attention to the experiential, felt qualities of wartime registered in the writings of those who remained at home, especially women, I have also included a selection of writings by Charlotte Dacre (1771/72–1825) and Anna Laetitia Barbauld (1743–1825) that reflect on political themes like war and peace, the struggle for independence, political sovereignty, and abolition, as well as on traditionally female or private topics, including first love and the pain of missing one's beloved (a combining of the political and the sentimental that is present also in "The Dying Negro"). The excerpt from Barbauld's "On the Origin and Progress of Novel-Writing" (1810) represents what may be *the* earliest attempt at producing a canon of British novels, one that, in Barbauld's hands, contained eight women. Barbauld might productively be paired with other assessments of the period's fiction, especially Ian Watt's landmark *The Rise of the Novel: Studies in Defoe, Fielding, and Richardson*, published in 1957. Austen is the only female

8. Morgan, "Captain Wentworth," 94–95.

novelist Watt considers at any length in his canon of British novelists, as his book's subtitle attests.

The present volume allows, in other words, for synchronic and diachronic ways of reading that stress differences among contemporaneous accounts of the same or similar topics, and demonstrate how objects of scholarly fascination and attention change across time. One topic recurring in the selected readings in this volume is the concept of theory of mind, with its focus on how humans think and how we can begin to grasp the inner workings of the minds of others. In the excerpt from "Lost in a Book: Jane Austen's *Persuasion*" (1997), for instance, Adela Pinch compares the influence of books and, specifically, of reading novels on one's own mind to the influence that one person's mind—her beliefs and judgments, likes and dislikes—can have over another's, an experience of which, in *Persuasion*, Lady Russell's act of persuasion is but one, albeit a prominent and powerful, instance. Pinch situates Austen vis-à-vis the gothic and sentimental novelists of her time—against whose extravagant, "unreal" fictions Austen's tamer, more mundane novels so often have been approvingly compared—as well as in relation to philosophical and literary debates regarding aesthetic taste, including the tasteful exercise and control of the passions. As Pinch demonstrates, *Persuasion* tracks the problem and practice of emotional management in a world riddled with opportunities for harm. Readers follow Anne Elliot as she learns to modulate her feelings in relation to external stimuli around her, from daily irritants like children's noisy chatter to more painful events, like the gutting sensation of overhearing one's former beau flirt with a pretty new companion from one's hiding place under the hedgerow. At issue here is the mind's ability to minimize bombardment by life's agitations, its ceaseless bangs and buzzing—a problem that will remind readers familiar with *Middlemarch* (1871) of the famous passage in which George Eliot imagines the deadly assault that the everyday noises around us—the sound of grass growing, the squirrel's beating heart—would be to us, were we unable to block them out. When Deirdre Lynch, in "Jane Austen and the Social Machine" (1998), examines the same basic concepts—the crowded tangle of opinions rubbing about inside one's head, the voices of others preventing us from being alone with our thoughts—she comes at the topic from another angle, that of the exploding world of print and commercial culture that became a defining feature of nineteenth-century life. A prevailing issue for Lynch is the idea of the copy, whether in the form of plagiarism and book piracy (rampant problems in bookselling culture throughout the period in both Britain and America) or in relation to questions of personal identity and selfhood. What might it mean, for instance, to conceive of individual people as interchangeable with one another, as is arguably the case with character types, such as the golden child, the good mother, or the no-good sot? Lynch notes the ways in which Austen clusters individuals into deindividuated groups: "young ladies of nineteen and twenty," for example, with "their usual stock of accomplishments . . . like thousands of other young ladies, living to be fashionable, happy, and merry" (31). This is how readers of *Persuasion* are introduced to the sisters Henrietta and Louisa Musgrove, who are presented as typical instances of a recognizable group, and as easily replicable rather than distinctive or unique. Noise, buzz, and hum in this analysis show Austen neither rejecting the values of romantic individualism nor rehabilitating dangerous passions in order to tame and naturalize them, but instead demonstrating the skill with which the period's new form—the novel—marries the personal with the impersonal. Lynch shows the novel instructing readers in how best to read it, by giving readers both a sentimental "inside view"—of the sort afforded by free indirect discourse (FID),[9] a technique masterfully wielded by Austen, for peering into the hearts and minds of others—and also a view from the outside, as exemplified in the banal clichés and inside jokes that comprise so much sociable table talk in any given day (including our own). This combining of the private and public, inside and outside, gives the novel its special power.

In closing, I offer some additional pairings of materials in this volume, though I must stress that the works collected here are in conversation with one another beyond what this introduction has space to consider. Barbara Benedict's commentary on two perennial subjects in Austen scholarship, gender and the marriage market, emphasizes the commercialization of the process by which unmarried women marketed themselves to prospective husbands by showing off feminine talents such as drawing, piano-playing, or singing. The metaphorical business of marriage is literalized in the new consumer economy in which Austen was writing, where advertisements for a suitable wife might be placed in newspapers (including, in an example Benedict examines, by a clergyman) and where novel readers are trained in how best to shop for a suitable spouse. Robert D. Hume's contribution helps to make sense of Austen's penchant for naming precise sums of money, enabling readers to comprehend the very different styles of living afforded to her novels' characters by detailing the fiscal realities that shaped Austen's own life in years marked by financial uncertainty and change. The bank failure of 1816 that devastated the finances of Austen's favorite brother, Henry Austen,[1] and the end of the Napoleonic campaign that forced

---

9. FID occurs when a third-person narrator takes on and inhabits the perspective and speech patterns of characters.
1. Henry's bankruptcy was precipitated by his debt to the Crown for £44,445 in taxes, which he had collected in his role as Receiver-General of Taxes for Oxfordshire. See

Frank and Charles into half-pay, meant that she could no longer rely on her brothers' yearly allowances. This in turn put added pressure on Austen to publish in a climate that was exceedingly hostile to women novelists, especially those of the genteel classes, whose profit-seeking (and profit-making) linked them to prostitution. When Barbauld writes in "On the Origin and Progress of Novel-Writing," that "a Collection of Novels has a better chance of giving pleasure than of commanding respect," she addresses a prevailing attitude at that time: that the enormous popularity and marketplace success of the novel genre were attributable to its immaturity and inelegance, the bad taste on which it capitalized and inculcated in readers, and its inherent immorality. Barbauld's insistence that the "dignity" of the author should not depend on "the pleasure he affords his readers" is a sharp reminder that the very enjoyment of novel-reading might be taken as evidence of that novel's moral or aesthetic badness.[2] Efforts to mitigate the stigma of female authorship were a feature of early novel criticism, as in Maria Jane Jewsbury's 1831 *Athenaeum* review, which portrays Austen as an "unambitious" author for whom novel-writing was a "delightful occupation" but "not a profession": "she passed unscathed through the ordeal of authorship," Jewsbury writes; "in society, she had too much wit to lay herself open to the charge of being too witty; and discriminated too well to attract notice to her discrimination."[3] As Charles Beecher Hogan's 1950 essay "Jane Austen and Her Early Public" makes clear, this nexus of pleasure, money, and vice was not confined to the nineteenth century. Even as he shows Austen to have been more popular among ordinary readers than had heretofore been appreciated by scholars and literary historians, he takes pains to paint Austen as "unostentatious" and "modest," shunning the publicity and fame that her novels achieved, as if despite herself.

This image of Austen as an unassuming maiden living in shy retirement from the glare of public notice has not entirely faded, prompting efforts to take stock of Austen's knowledge of and engagement in worldly matters. Where Margaret Oliphant would describe Austen, in 1882, as finding "enough in the quiet tenor of life which fell under her own eyes to interest the world," without having ever to "[step] out from the shelter of home, or [call] to her help a single

John Avery Hones, "Henry Austen: The Eventful Earlier Years as Receiver General of Taxes for Oxfordshire." *Persuasions Online* 44.1 (2023).

2. Anna Laetitia Barbauld, "On the Origin and Progress of Novel-Writing," in *The British Novelists; with an Essay; and Prefaces, Biographical and Critical*, vol. 1 (Rivington, 1810), pp. 14–15.

3. [Maria Jane Jewsbury], "Literary Women No. II. Jane Austen," *Athenaeum* 200 (August 27, 1831): 553–54.

incident that might not have happened next door,"[4] scholars today tend to take a far more expansive view of Austen's imaginative vantages. In her contribution to the edited collection *Romantic Climates* (2019), for example, Clara Tuite considers Romantic-era writing in relation to catastrophic events more geological and ecological than political, including the eruption of Mount Tambora (in present-day Indonesia) in the spring of 1815, an event that led to the 1816 "Year Without a Summer." Tuite's analysis reveals how the poems of Byron, for example, can be seen to reflect the deranged temporalities that emerged in the discourses of the period's new earth sciences, including "the newly dissident science of geology," and in arguments like that of the comparative anatomist Georges Cuvier, who claimed that "the world had been destroyed several times before the creation of man" (113).[5] Where Byron's "catastrophist writing" of 1816–17 in particular "mediates [the] emotional disturbance" caused by his separation from Lady Byron (Annabelle Milbanke), so too does *Persuasion* link "environmental geography" to "emotional geography" in ways that register the "perfect storm of Romantic catastrophes" affecting Austen's own life in 1816 (114). For Tuite, the novel's thematization and experimentation with an especially unruly time—"through the form of the backward romance; in the novel's concern with 'futurity'; in the figure of 'the ruins of the face' that both delineates Anne's premature widowhood and indexes the famous fossil ruins on the shores of Lyme Regis, by the Cobb and one of 'its old wonders'; and in the 'general air of oblivion'"—function as a way of "telegraphing . . . geological discussions of deep time" (133–34). In a different vein, William H. Galperin sees the deranged temporalities of *Persuasion*—from premature loss and faded youth to false peacetime and other unnatural endings and beginnings—as a feature of what he calls Austen's "uncanny alignment with her romantic contemporaries in locating horizons of possibility in quotidian life."[6] In *The Historical Austen* (2003), excerpted in the present volume, Galperin treats Austen's historicism not as inadvertent or casual (as it was for Said) but rather as evolving and developing across the compositional life of her novels. In Galperin's view, *Persuasion* differs from

---

4. Margaret Oliphant, *The Literary History of England in the End of the Eighteenth and Beginning of the Nineteenth Century*, vol. 3 (London: Macmillan & Co., 1882), p. 205.
5. Clara Tuite, "When the Earth Moves," in *Romantic Climates: Literature and Science in an Age of Catastrophe*, ed. Anne Collett and Olivia Murphy (London: Palgrave Macmillan, 2019). Georges Cuvier (1769–1832), French anatomist, paleontologist, and proponent of the catastrophist theory of geology, which established extinction as a historical fact. Catastrophism proposes that the Earth's history is marked by sudden, violent, and catastrophic episodes of change; it is contrasted to uniformitarianism (or gradualism), which privileges slower processes, such as erosion, that have the capacity to produce massive changes over long periods of time.
6. William H. Galperin, *The Historical Austen* (Philadelphia: U of Pennsylvania P, 2003).

its predecessors in that FID no longer serves the social regulatory function it had, for example, in *Emma* (1815), where the narrator's harsh judgment of her heroine is at odds with the novel's demand for readerly sympathy for her. The ending of *Persuasion*, by voicing "perplexity over the subject's fate," proves a powerful index of all that falls, in Austen's final novel, outside the boundaries of narrative and authorial, or personal, control: the "dread of future war" looming on an unseen horizon, the "tax of quick alarm" that may yet, may always, "dim [Anne's] sunshine," the perhaps perpetual cost of "being a sailor's wife."

The Text of
PERSUASION

Persuasion

Chapter I

Sir Walter Elliot, of Kellynch-hall, in Somersetshire, was a man who, for his own amusement, never took up any book but the Baronetage;[1] there he found occupation for an idle hour, and consolation in a distressed one; there his faculties were roused into admiration and respect, by contemplating the limited remnant of the earliest patents;[2] there any unwelcome sensations, arising from domestic affairs, changed naturally into pity and contempt. As he turned over the almost endless creations[3] of the last century—and there, if every other leaf were powerless, he could read his own history with an interest which never failed—this was the page at which the favourite volume always opened:

ELLIOT OF KELLYNCH-HALL

Walter Elliot, born March 1, 1760, married, July 15, 1784, Elizabeth, daughter of James Stevenson, Esq.[4] of South Park, in the county of Gloucester; by which lady (who died 1800) he has issue Elizabeth, born June 1, 1785; Anne, born August 9, 1787; a still-born son, Nov. 5, 1789; Mary, born Nov. 20, 1791.

Precisely such had the paragraph originally stood from the printer's hands; but Sir Walter had improved it by adding, for the

1. *The Baronetage of England with a List of Extinct Baronets* (1808), 2 vols., by English publisher John Debrett (1753–1822). A hereditary rank and the highest possible for a commoner.
2. Titles (of nobility).
3. New peerages. The indebted King James Stuart IV of Scotland (James I of England) had begun the practice of raising funds by creating and selling titles. In 1618 the standard price of an English barony was £10,000; sales of peerage under James added roughly 2,600 knights bachelor and 126 Knights of the Bath. After the English Civil War (1642–51), King Charles II awarded titles (which cost nothing to bestow) to landed families who had remained loyal to the king, as well as lowborn men who had performed military service. The latter group would later include figures repugnant to Sir Walter, such as British naval hero Lord Horatio Nelson, whose father was a mere Anglican clergyman. Notably, the name Elliot is of Scottish derivation.
4. Jennifer Fitzgerald describes the opening paragraph as "presenting the reader with a hypothetical Debrett entry," a reference to John Debrett's *Correct Peerage of England, Scotland and Ireland*, first published in 1769 and still active today ("Jane Austen's *Persuasion* and the French Revolution," *Persuasions* 10 [1988]: 39–42, at 40). The term "esquire," originally a title relating to the battlefield, evolved into an informal honorific for gentlemen, sometimes designating someone in the legal profession.

information of himself and his family, these words, after the date of Mary's birth—"married, Dec. 16, 1810, Charles, son and heir of Charles Musgrove, Esq. of Uppercross, in the county of Somerset,"—and by inserting most accurately the day of the month on which he had lost his wife.

Then followed the history and rise of the ancient and respectable family, in the usual terms: how it had been first settled in Cheshire; how mentioned in Dugdale[5]—serving the office of High Sheriff,[6] representing a borough in three successive parliaments, exertions of loyalty, and dignity of baronet, in the first year of Charles II.,[7] with all the Marys and Elizabeths they had married; forming altogether two handsome duodecimo[8] pages, and concluding with the arms and motto: "Principal seat, Kellynch hall, in the county of Somerset," and Sir Walter's hand-writing again in this finale:

"Heir presumptive, William Walter Elliot, Esq., great grandson of the second Sir Walter."[9]

Vanity was the beginning and the end of Sir Walter Elliot's character; vanity of person and of situation. He had been remarkably handsome in his youth; and, at fifty-four, was still a very fine[1] man. Few women could think more of their personal appearance than he did; nor could the valet of any new made lord be more delighted with the place he held in society. He considered the blessing of beauty as inferior only to the blessing of a baronetcy; and the Sir Walter Elliot, who united these gifts, was the constant object of his warmest respect and devotion.

His good looks and his rank had one fair claim on his attachment; since to them he must have owed a wife of very superior character to any thing deserved by his own. Lady Elliot had been an excellent woman, sensible and amiable; whose judgment and conduct, if they might be pardoned the youthful infatuation which made her Lady Elliot, had never required indulgence afterwards.—She had humoured, or softened, or concealed his failings, and promoted his

5. Sir William Dugdale, *The Ancient Usage in Bearing of Such Ensigns of Honour as Are Commonly Call'd Arms, with a Catalogue of the Present Nobility of England . . . Scotland . . . and Ireland* (1682).
6. An unpaid office as the sovereign's judicial representative in a county. The honor dated from the 10th century.
7. Austen's readers would have recognized parallels between the political situation of England in 1660, "the first year of Charles II," marking the restoration of the monarchy after an eleven-year period of republicanism under Oliver Cromwell (1599–1658), and that of contemporary France: the failure of the French Revolution and subsequent Reign of Terror, and the restoration of the Bourbon constitutional monarchy (with King Louis XVIII) following the abdication of Napoleon Bonaparte in 1815.
8. A small book, about the dimensions of a modern popular paperback, with pages made from sheets folded twelve times.
9. Kellynch-hall is entailed and must be passed to the closest male relative ("heir presumptive"), however distant, if Sir Walter bears no son ("heir apparent") before death.
1. In his physical appearance.

real respectability for seventeen years; and though not the very happiest being in the world herself, had found enough in her duties, her friends, and her children, to attach her to life, and make it no matter of indifference to her when she was called on to quit them.—Three girls, the two eldest sixteen and fourteen, was an awful[2] legacy for a mother to bequeath; an awful charge rather, to confide to the authority and guidance of a conceited, silly father. She had, however, one very intimate friend, a sensible, deserving woman, who had been brought, by strong attachment to herself, to settle close by her, in the village of Kellynch; and on her kindness and advice, Lady Elliot mainly relied for the best help and maintenance of the good principles and instruction which she had been anxiously giving her daughters.

This friend, and Sir Walter, did *not* marry, whatever might have been anticipated on that head by their acquaintance.—Thirteen years had passed away since Lady Elliot's death, and they were still near neighbours and intimate friends; and one remained a widower, the other a widow.

That Lady Russell, of steady age and character, and extremely well provided for, should have no thought of a second marriage, needs no apology to the public, which is rather apt to be unreasonably discontented when a woman *does* marry again, than when she does *not*; but Sir Walter's continuing in singleness requires explanation.—Be it known then, that Sir Walter, like a good father, (having met with one or two private disappointments in very unreasonable applications) prided himself on remaining single for his dear daughter's sake.[3] For one daughter, his eldest, he would really have given up any thing, which he had not been very much tempted to do. Elizabeth had succeeded, at sixteen, to all that was possible, of her mother's rights and consequence;[4] and being very handsome, and very like himself, her influence had always been great, and they had gone on together most happily. His two other children were of very inferior value. Mary had acquired a little artificial importance, by becoming Mrs. Charles Musgrove; but Anne, with an elegance of mind and sweetness of character, which must have placed her high with any people of real understanding, was nobody with either father or sister: her word had no weight; her convenience was always to give way;—she was only Anne.

To Lady Russell, indeed, she was a most dear and highly valued god-daughter, favourite and friend. Lady Russell loved them all; but it was only in Anne that she could fancy the mother to revive again.

2. According to Samuel Johnson's *Dictionary of the English Language* (1775), that which strikes with awe or fills with reverence.
3. Sometimes printed as "dear daughters' sake." If intentional, the singular "daughter's" is an ironic indication that Sir Walter sacrifices remarriage not for the sake of his daughters (plural) but for his favorite daughter in particular.
4. Social distinction.

A few years before, Anne Elliot had been a very pretty girl, but her bloom[5] had vanished early; and as even in its height, her father had found little to admire in her, (so totally different were her delicate features and mild dark eyes from his own); there could be nothing in them now that she was faded and thin, to excite his esteem. He had never indulged much hope, he had now none, of ever reading her name in any other page of his favourite work. All equality of alliance must rest with Elizabeth; for Mary had merely connected herself with an old country family of respectability and large fortune, and had therefore *given* all the honour, and received none: Elizabeth would, one day or other, marry suitably.

It sometimes happens, that a woman is handsomer at twenty-nine than she was ten years before; and, generally speaking, if there has been neither ill health nor anxiety, it is a time of life at which scarcely any charm is lost. It was so with Elizabeth; still the same handsome Miss Elliot that she had begun to be thirteen years ago; and Sir Walter might be excused, therefore, in forgetting her age, or, at least, be deemed only half a fool, for thinking himself and Elizabeth as blooming as ever, amidst the wreck of the good looks of every body else; for he could plainly see how old all the rest of his family and acquaintance were growing. Anne haggard, Mary coarse, every face in the neighbourhood worsting;[6] and the rapid increase of the crow's foot about Lady Russell's temples had long been a distress to him.

Elizabeth did not quite equal her father in personal contentment. Thirteen years had seen her mistress of Kellynch-hall, presiding and directing with a self-possession and decision which could never have given the idea of her being younger than she was. For thirteen years had she been doing the honours, and laying down the domestic law at home, and leading the way to the chaise and four,[7] and walking immediately after Lady Russell out of all the drawing-rooms and dining-rooms in the country. Thirteen winters' revolving frosts had seen her opening every ball of credit which a scanty neighbourhood afforded; and thirteen springs shewn their blossoms, as she travelled up to London with her father, for a few weeks annual enjoyment of the great world. She had the remembrance of all this; she had the consciousness of being nine-and-twenty, to give her some regrets and some apprehensions. She was fully satisfied of being still quite as handsome as ever; but she felt her approach to the years of danger, and would have rejoiced to be certain of being properly solicited by

5. Loss of color and health, and/or the beauty of youth. Bloom could be verbal, as in "A Defence of Women Painting" (1755) by Irish poet Samuel Derrick (1724–1769): "To please thy eye, she adds to ev'ry grace, / And with vermilion blooms her tempting face" (lines 11–12) (*A Collection of Original Poems* [London, 1775]).
6. Worsening.
7. A light, open carriage seating three or four passengers. The use of four horses signals Sir Walter's extravagance, as two horses were sufficient to pull so light a conveyance.

baronet-blood within the next twelve-month or two. Then might she again take up the book of books with as much enjoyment as in her early youth; but now she liked it not. Always to be presented with the date of her own birth, and see no marriage follow but that of a youngest sister, made the book an evil; and more than once, when her father had left it open on the table near her, had she closed it, with averted eyes, and pushed it away.

She had had a disappointment, moreover, which that book, and especially the history of her own family, must ever present the remembrance of. The heir presumptive, the very William Walter Elliot, Esq. whose rights had been so generously supported by her father, had disappointed her.

She had, while a very young girl, as soon as she had known him to be, in the event of her having no brother, the future baronet, meant to marry him; and her father had always meant that she should. He had not been known to them as a boy, but soon after Lady Elliot's death Sir Walter had sought the acquaintance, and though his overtures had not been met with any warmth, he had persevered in seeking it, making allowance for the modest drawing back of youth; and in one of their spring excursions to London, when Elizabeth was in her first bloom, Mr. Elliot had been forced into the introduction.

He was at that time a very young man, just engaged in the study of the law;[8] and Elizabeth found him extremely agreeable, and every plan in his favour was confirmed. He was invited to Kellynch-hall; he was talked of and expected all the rest of the year; but he never came. The following spring he was seen again in town, found equally agreeable, again encouraged, invited and expected, and again he did not come; and the next tidings were that he was married. Instead of pushing his fortune in the line marked out for the heir of the house of Elliot, he had purchased independence by uniting himself to a rich woman of inferior birth.

Sir Walter had resented it. As the head of the house, he felt that he ought to have been consulted, especially after taking the young man so publicly by the hand: "For they must have been seen together," he observed, "once at Tattersal's,[9] and twice in the lobby of the House of Commons." His disapprobation was expressed, but apparently very little regarded. Mr. Elliot had attempted no apology, and shewn himself as unsolicitous of being longer noticed by the family, as

---

8. Likely studying to become a barrister, considered a genteel profession. Barristers were legal specialists in court proceedings, having the credentials to approach the bar. Unlike solicitors, who worked with and were paid directly by clients, barristers acted as court advocates and were often hired by solicitors for their expertise in legal codes.
9. Located near Hyde Park, Tattersall's pedigree and bloodstock horse auction, founded by Richard Tattersall in 1766 and described as a "grand mart for everything connected with the sports of the field, the business of the turf and equestrian recreations" (in Rudolph Ackermann, *The Microcosm of London; or, London in Miniature*, vol. 3 [1810]).

Sir Walter considered him unworthy of it: all acquaintance between them had ceased.

This very awkward history of Mr. Elliot, was still, after an interval of several years, felt with anger by Elizabeth, who had liked the man for himself, and still more for being her father's heir, and whose strong family pride could see only in *him*, a proper match for Sir Walter Elliot's eldest daughter. There was not a baronet from A to Z, whom her feelings could have so willingly acknowledged as an equal. Yet so miserably had he conducted himself, that though she was at this present time, (the summer of 1814,)[1] wearing black ribbons for his wife,[2] she could not admit him to be worth thinking of again. The disgrace of his first marriage might, perhaps, as there was no reason to suppose it perpetuated by offspring, have been got over, had he not done worse; but he had, as by the accustomary intervention of kind friends they had been informed, spoken most disrespectfully of them all, most slightingly and contemptuously of the very blood he belonged to, and the honours which were hereafter to be his own. This could not be pardoned.

Such were Elizabeth Elliot's sentiments and sensations; such the cares to alloy, the agitations to vary, the sameness and the elegance, the prosperity and the nothingness, of her scene of life—such the feelings to give interest to a long, uneventful residence in one country circle, to fill the vacancies which there were no habits of utility abroad, no talents or accomplishments for home, to occupy.

But now, another occupation and solicitude of mind was beginning to be added to these. Her father was growing distressed for money. She knew, that when he now took up the Baronetage, it was to drive the heavy bills of his tradespeople, and the unwelcome hints of Mr. Shepherd, his agent,[3] from his thoughts. The Kellynch property was good, but not equal to Sir Walter's apprehension of the state required in its possessor. While Lady Elliot lived, there had been method, moderation, and economy, which had just kept him within his income; but with her had died all such right-mindedness, and from that period he had been constantly exceeding it. It had not been possible for him to spend less; he had done nothing but what Sir Walter Elliot was imperiously called on to do; but blameless as he was, he was not only growing dreadfully in debt, but was hearing of it so often, that it became vain to attempt concealing it longer, even

---

1. A period of national celebration, with visits by national dignitaries and events marking the (apparent) end of the Napoleonic Wars, and a Grand Jubilee marking the one-hundredth anniversary of the accession of George I, the first Hanoverian king. The False Peace, as it later became known, was the period between the Treaty of Paris (May 1814), ending the war with France, and Napoleon's escape from exile and return to power in February 1815.
2. Tokens of mourning: his wife had died recently.
3. Property manager.

partially, from his daughter. He had given her some hints of it the last spring in town; he had gone so far even as to say, "Can we retrench? does it occur to you that there is any one article in which we can retrench?"—and Elizabeth, to do her justice, had, in the first ardour of female alarm, set seriously to think what could be done, and had finally proposed these two branches of economy: to cut off some unnecessary charities, and to refrain from new-furnishing the drawing-room; to which expedients she afterwards added the happy thought of their taking no present down to Anne, as had been the usual yearly custom. But these measures, however good in themselves, were insufficient for the real extent of the evil, the whole of which Sir Walter found himself obliged to confess to her soon afterwards. Elizabeth had nothing to propose of deeper efficacy. She felt herself ill-used and unfortunate, as did her father; and they were neither of them able to devise any means of lessening their expenses without compromising their dignity, or relinquishing their comforts in a way not to be borne.

There was only a small part of his estate that Sir Walter could dispose of; but had every acre been alienable,[4] it would have made no difference. He had condescended to mortgage as far as he had the power, but he would never condescend to sell. No; he would never disgrace his name so far. The Kellynch estate should be transmitted whole and entire, as he had received it.

Their two confidential friends, Mr. Shepherd, who lived in the neighbouring market town, and Lady Russell, were called on to advise them; and both father and daughter seemed to expect that something should be struck out by one or the other to remove their embarrassments and reduce their expenditure, without involving the loss of any indulgence of taste or pride.

Chapter II

Mr. Shepherd, a civil, cautious lawyer, who, whatever might be his hold or his views on Sir Walter, would rather have the *disagreeable* prompted by any body else, excused himself from offering the slightest hint, and only begged leave to recommend an implicit deference to the excellent judgment of Lady Russell,—from whose known good sense he fully expected to have just such resolute measures advised, as he meant to see finally adopted.

Lady Russell was most anxiously zealous on the subject, and gave it much serious consideration. She was a woman rather of sound than of quick abilities, whose difficulties in coming to any decision in this instance were great, from the opposition of two leading

---

4. Sellable (i.e., not prevented by legal restriction from being sold).

principles. She was of strict integrity herself, with a delicate sense of honour; but she was as desirous of saving Sir Walter's feelings, as solicitous for the credit of the family, as aristocratic in her ideas of what was due to them, as any body of sense and honesty could well be. She was a benevolent, charitable, good woman, and capable of strong attachments; most correct in her conduct, strict in her notions of decorum, and with manners that were held a standard of good-breeding. She had a cultivated mind, and was, generally speaking, rational and consistent—but she had prejudices on the side of ancestry; she had a value for rank and consequence, which blinded her a little to the faults of those who possessed them. Herself, the widow of only a knight, she gave the dignity of a baronet all its due;[5] and Sir Walter, independent of his claims as an old acquaintance, an attentive neighbour, an obliging landlord, the husband of her very dear friend, the father of Anne and her sisters, was, as being Sir Walter, in her apprehension entitled to a great deal of compassion and consideration under his present difficulties.

They must retrench; that did not admit of a doubt. But she was very anxious to have it done with the least possible pain to him and Elizabeth. She drew up plans of economy, she made exact calculations, and she did, what nobody else thought of doing, she consulted Anne, who never seemed considered by the others as having any interest in the question. She consulted, and in a degree was influenced by her, in marking out the scheme of retrenchment, which was at last submitted to Sir Walter. Every emendation of Anne's had been on the side of honesty against importance. She wanted more vigorous measures, a more complete reformation, a quicker release from debt, a much higher tone of indifference for every thing but justice and equity.

"If we can persuade your father to all this," said Lady Russell, looking over her paper, "much may be done. If he will adopt these regulations, in seven years he will be clear; and I hope we may be able to convince him and Elizabeth, that Kellynch-hall has a respectability in itself, which cannot be affected by these reductions; and that the true dignity of Sir Walter Elliot will be very far from lessened, in the eyes of sensible people, by his acting like a man of principle. What will he be doing, in fact, but what very many of our first families have done,—or ought to do?—There will be nothing singular in his case; and it is singularity which often makes the worst part of our suffering, as it always does of our conduct. I have great hope of our prevailing. We must be serious and decided—for, after all, the person who has contracted debts must pay them; and though a great deal is due to the feelings of the gentleman, and the head of a house, like your father, there is still more due to the character of an honest man."

5. A knight ranks immediately below a baronet. Knighthoods are not hereditary.

This was the principle on which Anne wanted her father to be proceeding, his friends to be urging him. She considered it as an act of indispensable duty to clear away the claims of creditors, with all the expedition[6] which the most comprehensive retrenchments could secure, and saw no dignity in any thing short of it. She wanted it to be prescribed, and felt as a duty. She rated Lady Russell's influence highly, and as to the severe degree of self-denial, which her own conscience prompted, she believed there might be little more difficulty in persuading them to a complete, than to half a reformation. Her knowledge of her father and Elizabeth, inclined her to think that the sacrifice of one pair of horses would be hardly less painful than of both, and so on, through the whole list of Lady Russell's too gentle reductions.

How Anne's more rigid requisitions might have been taken, is of little consequence. Lady Russell's had no success at all—could not be put up with—were not to be borne. "What! Every comfort of life knocked off! Journeys, London, servants, horses, table,—contractions and restrictions every where. To live no longer with the decencies even of a private gentleman! No, he would sooner quit Kellynch-hall at once, than remain in it on such disgraceful terms."

"Quit Kellynch-hall." The hint was immediately taken up by Mr. Shepherd, whose interest was involved in the reality of Sir Walter's retrenching, and who was perfectly persuaded that nothing would be done without a change of abode.—"Since the idea had been started in the very quarter which ought to dictate, he had no scruple," he said, "in confessing his judgment to be entirely on that side. It did not appear to him that Sir Walter could materially alter his style of living in a house which had such a character[7] of hospitality and ancient dignity to support.—In any other place, Sir Walter might judge for himself; and would be looked up to, as regulating the modes of life, in whatever way he might choose to model his household."

Sir Walter would quit Kellynch-hall;—and after a very few days more of doubt and indecision, the great question of whither he should go, was settled, and the first outline of this important change made out.

There had been three alternatives, London, Bath,[8] or another house in the country. All Anne's wishes had been for the latter.

6. Speed.
7. Reputation.
8. Renowned for its mineral-rich hot springs, believed to have medicinal and healing properties, the spa city of Bath became a fashionable destination in the 18th century, in part through the efforts of the English dandy Richard "Beau" Nash (1674–1762), who built up its theaters and public buildings and became Master of Ceremonies, granting access to balls and setting the rules for dress, dance, and behavior etiquette. The heavy costs of the Napoleonic Wars contributed to the diminishing fortunes of Bath at the time of the novel.

A small house in their own neighbourhood, where they might still have Lady Russell's society, still be near Mary, and still have the pleasure of sometimes seeing the lawns and groves of Kellynch, was the object of her ambition. But the usual fate of Anne attended her, in having something very opposite from her inclination fixed on. She disliked Bath, and did not think it agreed with her—and Bath was to be her home.

Sir Walter had at first thought more of London, but Mr. Shepherd felt that he could not be trusted in London, and had been skilful enough to dissuade him from it, and make Bath preferred. It was a much safer place for a gentleman in his predicament:—he might there be important at comparatively little expense.—Two material advantages of Bath over London had of course been given all their weight, its more convenient distance from Kellynch, only fifty miles, and Lady Russell's spending some part of every winter there; and to the very great satisfaction of Lady Russell, whose first views on the projected change had been for Bath, Sir Walter and Elizabeth were induced to believe that they should lose neither consequence nor enjoyment by settling there.

Lady Russell felt obliged to oppose her dear Anne's known wishes. It would be too much to expect Sir Walter to descend into a small house in his own neighbourhood. Anne herself would have found the mortifications of it more than she foresaw, and to Sir Walter's feelings they must have been dreadful. And with regard to Anne's dislike of Bath, she considered it as a prejudice and mistake, arising first from the circumstance of her having been three years at school there,[9] after her mother's death, and, secondly, from her happening to be not in perfectly good spirits the only winter which she had afterwards spent there with herself.

Lady Russell was fond of Bath in short, and disposed to think it must suit them all; and as to her young friend's health, by passing all the warm months with her at Kellynch-lodge, every danger would be avoided; and it was, in fact, a change which must do both health and spirits good. Anne had been too little from[1] home, too little seen. Her spirits were not high. A larger society would improve them. She wanted her to be more known.

The undesirableness of any other house in the same neighbourhood for Sir Walter, was certainly much strengthened by one part, and a very material part of the scheme, which had been happily engrafted on the beginning. He was not only to quit his home, but to see it in the hands of others; a trial of fortitude, which stronger

9. Anne's school years at Bath, from 1801 to 1803, correspond with the period during which Austen resided there.
1. Away from.

heads than Sir Walter's have found too much—Kellynch-hall was to be let.[2] This, however, was a profound secret; not to be breathed beyond their own circle.

Sir Walter could not have borne the degradation of being known to design letting his house.—Mr. Shepherd had once mentioned the word, "advertise;"—but never dared approach it again; Sir Walter spurned the idea of its being offered in any manner; forbad the slightest hint being dropped of his having such an intention; and it was only on the supposition of his being spontaneously solicited by some most unexceptionable applicant, on his own terms, and as a great favor, that he would let it at all.

How quick come the reasons for approving what we like!—Lady Russell had another excellent one at hand, for being extremely glad that Sir Walter and his family were to remove from the country. Elizabeth had been lately forming an intimacy, which she wished to see interrupted. It was with a daughter of Mr. Shepherd, who had returned, after an unprosperous marriage, to her father's house, with the additional burthen of two children. She was a clever young woman, who understood the art of pleasing;[3] the art of pleasing, at least, at Kellynch-hall; and who had made herself so acceptable to Miss Elliot, as to have been already staying there more than once, in spite of all that Lady Russell, who thought it a friendship quite out of place, could hint of caution and reserve.

Lady Russell, indeed, had scarcely any influence with Elizabeth, and seemed to love her, rather because she would love her, than because Elizabeth deserved it. She had never received from her more than outward attention, nothing beyond the observances of complaisance;[4] had never succeeded in any point which she wanted to carry, against previous inclination. She had been repeatedly very earnest in trying to get Anne included in the visit to London, sensibly open to all the injustice and all the discredit of the selfish arrangements which shut her out, and on many lesser occasions had endeavoured to give Elizabeth the advantage of her own better judgment and experience— but always in vain; Elizabeth would go her own way—and never had she pursued it in more decided opposition to Lady Russell, than in this selection of Mrs. Clay; turning from the society of so deserving a sister to bestow her affection and confidence on one who ought to have been nothing to her but the object of distant civility.

2. Rented.
3. Works like *The Art of Pleasing in Conversation* (1691) and Lord Chesterfield's *Letters of Advice to His Son, on Men and Manners* (1774) offered advice for being agreeable company, including the suggestion to "speak less of ones self than any thing else" (*Art of Pleasing*, 9). (*The Art of Pleasing in Conversation*, first attributed to Cardinal de Richelieu, is now attributed to Pierre d'Ortigue Vaumorière.)
4. Obligingness, courtesy, politeness.

From situation, Mrs. Clay was, in Lady Russell's estimate, a very unequal, and in her character she believed a very dangerous companion—and a removal that would leave Mrs. Clay behind, and bring a choice of more suitable intimates within Miss Elliot's reach, was therefore an object of first-rate importance.

Chapter III

"I must take leave to observe, Sir Walter," said Mr. Shepherd one morning at Kellynch-hall, as he laid down the newspaper, "that the present juncture is much in our favour. This peace will be turning all our rich Navy Officers ashore.[5] They will be all wanting a home. Could not be a better time, Sir Walter, for having a choice of tenants, very responsible tenants. Many a noble fortune has been made during the war. If a rich Admiral were to come in our way, Sir Walter—"

"He would be a very lucky man, Shepherd," replied Sir Walter, "that's all I have to remark. A prize indeed would Kellynch-hall be to him; rather the greatest prize of all, let him have taken ever so many before—hey, Shepherd?"[6]

Mr. Shepherd laughed, as he knew he must, at this wit, and then added,

"I presume to observe, Sir Walter, that, in the way of business, gentlemen of the navy are well to deal with. I have had a little knowledge of their methods of doing business, and I am free to confess that they have very liberal notions, and are as likely to make desirable tenants as any set of people one should meet with. Therefore, Sir Walter, what I would take leave to suggest is, that if in consequence of any rumours getting abroad of your intention—which must be contemplated as a possible thing, because we know how difficult it is to keep the actions and designs of one part of the world from the notice and curiosity of the other,—consequence has its tax—I, John Shepherd, might conceal any family-matters that I chose, for nobody would think it worth their while to observe me, but Sir Walter Elliot has eyes upon him which it may be very difficult to elude—and therefore, thus much I venture upon, that it will not greatly surprise me if, with all our caution, some rumour of the truth should get abroad—in the supposition of which, as I was going to observe, since applications will unquestionably follow, I should think any from our wealthy naval commanders particularly worth attending to—and beg leave to add, that two hours will bring me over at any time, to save you the trouble of replying."

5. A reference to the False Peace (see n. 6, p. 317).
6. See *Landsman Hay*, n. 3, p. 244 in this volume.

Sir Walter only nodded. But soon afterwards, rising and pacing the room, he observed sarcastically,

"There are few among the gentlemen of the navy, I imagine, who would not be surprised to find themselves in a house of this description."

"They would look around them, no doubt, and bless their good fortune," said Mrs. Clay, for Mrs. Clay was present; her father had driven her over, nothing being of so much use to Mrs. Clay's health as a drive to Kellynch: "but I quite agree with my father in thinking a sailor might be a very desirable tenant. I have known a good deal of the profession; and besides their liberality, they are so neat and careful in all their ways! These valuable pictures of yours, Sir Walter, if you chose to leave them, would be perfectly safe. Every thing in and about the house would be taken such excellent care of! the gardens and shrubberies would be kept in almost as high order as they are now. You need not be afraid, Miss Elliot, of your own sweet flower-garden's being neglected."

"As to all that," rejoined Sir Walter coolly, "supposing I were induced to let my house, I have by no means made up my mind as to the privileges to be annexed to it. I am not particularly disposed to favour a tenant. The park would be open to him of course, and few navy officers, or men of any other description, can have had such a range; but what restrictions I might impose on the use of the pleasure-grounds, is another thing. I am not fond of the idea of my shrubberies being always approachable; and I should recommend Miss Elliot to be on her guard with respect to her flower-garden. I am very little disposed to grant a tenant of Kellynch-hall any extraordinary favour, I assure you, be he sailor or soldier."

After a short pause, Mr. Shepherd presumed to say,

"In all these cases, there are established usages which make every thing plain and easy between landlord and tenant. Your interest, Sir Walter, is in pretty safe hands. Depend upon me for taking care that no tenant has more than his just rights. I venture to hint, that Sir Walter Elliot cannot be half so jealous for his own, as John Shepherd will be for him."

Here Anne spoke,—

"The navy, I think, who have done so much for us, have at least an equal claim with any other set of men, for all the comforts and all the privileges which any home can give. Sailors work hard enough for their comforts, we must all allow."

"Very true, very true. What Miss Anne says, is very true," was Mr. Shepherd's rejoinder, and "Oh! certainly," was his daughter's; but Sir Walter's remark was, soon afterwards—

"The profession has its utility, but I should be sorry to see any friend of mine belonging to it."

"Indeed!" was the reply, and with a look of surprise.

"Yes; it is in two points offensive to me; I have two strong grounds of objection to it. First, as being the means of bringing persons of obscure birth into undue distinction, and raising men to honours which their fathers and grandfathers never dreamt of; and secondly, as it cuts up a man's youth and vigour most horribly; a sailor grows old sooner than any other man; I have observed it all my life. A man is in greater danger in the navy of being insulted by the rise of one whose father, his father might have disdained to speak to, and of becoming prematurely an object of disgust himself, than in any other line. One day last spring, in town, I was in company with two men, striking instances of what I am talking of, Lord St. Ives, whose father we all know to have been a country curate, without bread to eat; I was to give place[7] to Lord St. Ives, and a certain Admiral Baldwin, the most deplorable looking personage you can imagine, his face the colour of mahogany, rough and rugged to the last degree, all lines and wrinkles, nine grey hairs of a side, and nothing but a dab of powder at top.—'In the name of heaven, who is that old fellow?' said I, to a friend of mine who was standing near, (Sir Basil Morley.) 'Old fellow!' cried Sir Basil, 'it is Admiral Baldwin. What do you take his age to be?' 'Sixty,' said I, 'or perhaps sixty-two.' 'Forty,' replied Sir Basil, 'forty, and no more.' Picture to yourselves my amazement; I shall not easily forget Admiral Baldwin. I never saw quite so wretched an example of what a sea-faring life can do; but to a degree, I know it is the same with them all: they are all knocked about, and exposed to every climate, and every weather, till they are not fit to be seen. It is a pity they are not knocked on the head at once, before they reach Admiral Baldwin's age."

"Nay, Sir Walter," cried Mrs. Clay, "this is being severe indeed. Have a little mercy on the poor men. We are not all born to be handsome. The sea is no beautifier, certainly; sailors do grow old betimes; I have often observed it; they soon lose the look of youth. But then, is not it the same with many other professions, perhaps most other? Soldiers, in active service, are not at all better off: and even in the quieter professions, there is a toil and a labour of the mind, if not of the body, which seldom leaves a man's looks to the natural effect of time. The lawyer plods, quite care-worn; the physician is up at all hours, and travelling in all weather; and even the clergyman—" she stopt a moment to consider what might do for the clergyman;—"and even the clergyman, you know, is obliged to go into infected rooms, and expose his health and looks to all the injury of a poisonous atmosphere. In fact, as I have long been convinced, though every profession is necessary and honourable in its turn, it is only the lot

7. Yield precedence.

of those who are not obliged to follow any, who can live in a regular way, in the country, choosing their own hours, following their own pursuits, and living on their own property, without the torment of trying for more; it is only *their* lot, I say, to hold the blessings of health and a good appearance to the utmost: I know no other set of men but what lose something of their personableness when they cease to be quite young."

It seemed as if Mr. Shepherd, in this anxiety to bespeak Sir Walter's goodwill towards a naval officer as tenant, had been gifted with foresight; for the very first application for the house was from an Admiral Croft, with whom he shortly afterwards fell into company in attending the quarter sessions at Taunton;[8] and indeed, he had received a hint of the admiral from a London correspondent. By the report which he hastened over to Kellynch to make, Admiral Croft was a native of Somersetshire, who having acquired a very handsome fortune, was wishing to settle in his own country, and had come down to Taunton in order to look at some advertised places in that immediate neighbourhood, which, however, had not suited him; that accidentally hearing—(it was just as he had foretold, Mr. Shepherd observed, Sir Walter's concerns could not be kept a secret,)—accidentally hearing of the possibility of Kellynch-hall being to let, and understanding his (Mr. Shepherd's) connection with the owner, he had introduced himself to him in order to make particular inquiries, and had, in the course of a pretty long conference, expressed as strong an inclination for the place as a man who knew it only by description, could feel; and given Mr. Shepherd, in his explicit account of himself, every proof of his being a most responsible, eligible tenant.

"And who is Admiral Croft?" was Sir Walter's cold suspicious inquiry.

Mr. Shepherd answered for his being of a gentleman's family, and mentioned a place; and Anne, after the little pause which followed, added—

"He is rear admiral of the white.[9] He was in the Trafalgar[1] action, and has been in the East Indies since; he has been stationed there, I believe, several years."

"Then I take it for granted," observed Sir Walter, "that his face is about as orange as the cuffs and capes of my livery."[2]

Mr. Shepherd hastened to assure him, that Admiral Croft was a very hale, hearty, well-looking man, a little weather-beaten, to be

8. Court sessions held four times a year by justices of the peace.
9. The navy consisted of three squadrons, Red, White, and Blue. Anne's display of knowledge here reveals her special interest in naval affairs, soon to be accounted for.
1. The Battle of Trafalgar (October 21, 1805) was a major victory for the British navy against France.
2. The distinctive apparel provided for and worn by a household's servants—in effect, a uniform—usually characterized by particular colors and design.

sure, but not much; and quite the gentleman in all his notions and behaviour;—not likely to make the smallest difficulty about terms;—only wanted a comfortable home, and to get into it as soon as possible;—knew he must pay for his convenience;—knew what rent a ready-furnished house of that consequence might fetch;—should not have been surprised if Sir Walter had asked more;—had inquired about the manor;—would be glad of the deputation,[3] certainly, but made no great point of it;—said he sometimes took out a gun, but never killed;—quite the gentleman.

Mr. Shepherd was eloquent on the subject; pointing out all the circumstances of the admiral's family, which made him peculiarly desirable as a tenant. He was a married man, and without children; the very state to be wished for. A house was never taken good care of, Mr. Shepherd observed, without a lady: he did not know, whether furniture might not be in danger of suffering as much where there was no lady, as where there were many children. A lady, without a family, was the very best preserver of furniture in the world. He had seen Mrs. Croft, too; she was at Taunton with the admiral, and had been present almost all the time they were talking the matter over.

"And a very well-spoken, genteel, shrewd lady, she seemed to be," continued he; "asked more questions about the house, and terms, and taxes, than the admiral himself, and seemed more conversant with business. And moreover, Sir Walter, I found she was not quite unconnected in this country, any more than her husband; that is to say, she is sister to a gentleman who did live amongst us once; she told me so herself: sister to the gentleman who lived a few years back, at Monkford. Bless me! what was his name? At this moment I cannot recollect his name, though I have heard it so lately. Penelope, my dear, can you help me to the name of the gentleman who lived at Monkford—Mrs. Croft's brother?"

But Mrs. Clay was talking so eagerly with Miss Elliot, that she did not hear the appeal.

"I have no conception whom you can mean, Shepherd; I remember no gentleman resident at Monkford since the time of old Governor Trent."

"Bless me! how very odd! I shall forget my own name soon, I suppose. A name that I am so very well acquainted with; knew the gentleman so well by sight; seen him a hundred times; came to consult me once, I remember, about a trespass of one of his neighbours; farmer's man breaking into his orchard—wall torn down—apples stolen—caught in the fact; and afterwards, contrary to my judgment, submitted to an amicable compromise. Very odd indeed!"

After waiting another moment—

3. The right to shoot game on the property.

"You mean Mr. Wentworth, I suppose," said Anne.

Mr. Shepherd was all gratitude.

"Wentworth was the very name! Mr. Wentworth was the very man. He had the curacy[4] of Monkford, you know, Sir Walter, some time back, for two or three years. Came there about the year —5, I take it. You remember him, I am sure."

"Wentworth? Oh! ay,—Mr. Wentworth, the curate of Monkford. You misled me by the term *gentleman*. I thought you were speaking of some man of property: Mr. Wentworth was nobody, I remember; quite unconnected; nothing to do with the Strafford family.[5] One wonders how the names of many of our nobility become so common."

As Mr. Shepherd perceived that this connexion of the Crofts did them no service with Sir Walter, he mentioned it no more; returning, with all his zeal, to dwell on the circumstances more indisputably in their favour; their age, and number, and fortune; the high idea they had formed of Kellynch-hall, and extreme solicitude for the advantage of renting it; making it appear as if they ranked nothing beyond the happiness of being the tenants of Sir Walter Elliot: an extraordinary taste, certainly, could they have been supposed in the secret of Sir Walter's estimate of the dues of a tenant.

It succeeded, however; and though Sir Walter must ever look with an evil eye on any one intending to inhabit that house, and think them infinitely too well off in being permitted to rent it on the highest terms, he was talked into allowing Mr. Shepherd to proceed in the treaty, and authorising him to wait on Admiral Croft, who still remained at Taunton, and fix a day for the house being seen.

Sir Walter was not very wise; but still he had experience enough of the world to feel, that a more unobjectionable tenant, in all essentials, than Admiral Croft bid fair to be, could hardly offer. So far went his understanding; and his vanity supplied a little additional soothing, in the admiral's situation in life, which was just high enough, and not too high. "I have let my house to Admiral Croft," would sound extremely well; very much better than to any mere *Mr.*——; a *Mr.* (save, perhaps, some half dozen in the nation,) always needs a note of explanation. An admiral speaks his own consequence, and, at the same time, can never make a baronet look small.

4. The curacy refers to the office and parish responsibilities of the curate, who either assists the vicar or rector whose supervision he is under, or performs the duties of the clergy in the Church of England.

5. Wentworth was the family name of the Earls of Strafford. For Austen's readers the name would have held additional associations, including the abolitionist Anne Isabella Noel Byron, the Baroness Wentworth (1792–1860), recently separated from her husband, the poet Lord Byron, in January 1816; and Lady Henrietta Wentworth (1660–1686), the mistress of the Duke of Monmouth (1649–1685), the illegitimate son of King Charles II. Monmouth was a celebrated figure in Taunton (where he declared himself king) and Lyme, where the Monmouth Rebellion of 1685 occurred. His original name was James Crofts.

In all their dealings and intercourse, Sir Walter Elliot must ever have the precedence.

Nothing could be done without a reference to Elizabeth; but her inclination was growing so strong for a removal, that she was happy to have it fixed and expedited by a tenant at hand; and not a word to suspend decision was uttered by her.

Mr. Shepherd was completely empowered to act; and no sooner had such an end been reached, than Anne, who had been a most attentive listener to the whole, left the room, to seek the comfort of cool air for her flushed cheeks; and as she walked along a favourite grove, said, with a gentle sigh, "a few months more, and *he*, perhaps, may be walking here."

Chapter IV

He was not Mr. Wentworth, the former curate of Monkford, however suspicious appearances may be, but a captain Frederick Wentworth, his brother, who being made commander in consequence of the action off St. Domingo,[6] and not immediately employed, had come into Somersetshire, in the summer of 1806; and having no parent living, found a home for half a year, at Monkford. He was, at that time, a remarkably fine young man, with a great deal of intelligence, spirit and brilliancy; and Anne an extremely pretty girl, with gentleness, modesty, taste, and feeling.—Half the sum of attraction, on either side, might have been enough, for he had nothing to do, and she had hardly any body to love; but the encounter of such lavish recommendations could not fail. They were gradually acquainted, and when acquainted, rapidly and deeply in love. It would be difficult to say which had seen highest perfection in the other, or which had been the happiest; she, in receiving his declarations and proposals, or he in having them accepted.

A short period of exquisite felicity followed, and but a short one.— Troubles soon arose. Sir Walter, on being applied to, without actually withholding his consent, or saying it should never be, gave it all the negative of great astonishment, great coldness, great silence, and a professed resolution of doing nothing for his daughter.[7] He thought it a very degrading alliance; and Lady Russell, though with more tempered and pardonable pride, received it as a most unfortunate one.

6. San Domingo, now Haiti, was a French colony and the site of a successful rebellion by enslaved persons led by Toussaint L'Ouverture, beginning in 1791 and ending in 1804 with the establishment of an independent republic governed by nonwhites and the formerly enslaved. Austen's brother Frank took part in the Battle of San Domingo on February 6, 1806.
7. Giving her no dowry.

Anne Elliot, with all her claims of birth, beauty, and mind, to throw herself away at nineteen; involve herself at nineteen in an engagement with a young man, who had nothing but himself to recommend him, and no hopes of attaining affluence, but in the chances of a most uncertain profession, and no connexions to secure even his farther rise in that profession; would be, indeed, a throwing away, which she grieved to think of! Anne Elliot, so young; known to so few, to be snatched off by a stranger without alliance or fortune; or rather sunk by him into a state of most wearing, anxious, youth-killing dependance! It must not be, if by any fair interference of friendship, any representations from one who had almost a mother's love, and mother's rights, it would be prevented.

Captain Wentworth had no fortune. He had been lucky in his profession, but spending freely, what had come freely, had realized[8] nothing. But, he was confident that he should soon be rich;—full of life and ardour, he knew that he should soon have a ship, and soon be on a station that would lead to every thing he wanted.[9] He had always been lucky; he knew he should be so still.—Such confidence, powerful in its own warmth, and bewitching in the wit which often expressed it, must have been enough for Anne; but Lady Russell saw it very differently.—His sanguine temper, and fearlessness of mind, operated very differently on her. She saw in it but an aggravation of the evil. It only added a dangerous character to himself. He was brilliant, he was headstrong.—Lady Russell had little taste for wit; and of any thing approaching to imprudence a horror. She deprecated the connexion in every light.

Such opposition, as these feelings produced, was more than Anne could combat. Young and gentle as she was, it might yet have been possible to withstand her father's ill-will, though unsoftened by one kind word or look on the part of her sister;—but Lady Russell, whom she had always loved and relied on, could not, with such steadiness of opinion, and such tenderness of manner, be continually advising her in vain. She was persuaded to believe the engagement a wrong thing—indiscreet, improper, hardly capable of success, and not deserving it. But it was not a merely selfish caution, under which she acted, in putting an end to it. Had she not imagined herself consulting his good, even more than her own, she could hardly have given him up.—The belief of being prudent, and self-denying principally for *his* advantage, was her chief consolation, under the misery of a parting—a final parting; and every consolation was required,

8. Gained. Captain Wentworth, spending freely, had been left with no profits from his naval success.
9. He expected to be given command of a ship and assigned to a part of the world that would allow him to capture many enemy vessels.

for she had to encounter all the additional pain of opinions, on his side, totally unconvinced and unbending, and of his feeling himself ill-used by so forced a relinquishment.—He had left the country[1] in consequence.

A few months had seen the beginning and the end of their acquaintance; but, not with a few months ended Anne's share of suffering from it. Her attachment and regrets had, for a long time, clouded every enjoyment of youth; and an early loss of bloom and spirits had been their lasting effect.

More than seven years were gone since this little history of sorrowful interest had reached its close; and time had softened down much, perhaps nearly all of peculiar attachment to him,—but she had been too dependant on time alone; no aid had been given in change of place, (except in one visit to Bath soon after the rupture,) or in any novelty or enlargement of society.—No one had ever come within the Kellynch circle, who could bear a comparison with Frederick Wentworth, as he stood in her memory. No second attachment, the only thoroughly natural, happy, and sufficient cure, at her time of life, had been possible to the nice[2] tone of her mind, the fastidiousness of her taste, in the small limits of the society around them. She had been solicited, when about two-and-twenty, to change her name, by the young man, who not long afterwards found a more willing mind in her younger sister; and Lady Russell had lamented her refusal; for Charles Musgrove was the eldest son of a man, whose landed property and general importance, were second, in that country, only to Sir Walter's, and of good character and appearance; and however Lady Russell might have asked yet for something more, while Anne was nineteen, she would have rejoiced to see her at twenty-two, so respectably removed from the partialities and injustice of her father's house, and settled so permanently near herself. But in this case, Anne had left nothing for advice to do; and though Lady Russell, as satisfied as ever with her own discretion, never wished the past undone, she began now to have the anxiety which borders on hopelessness for Anne's being tempted, by some man of talents and independence,[3] to enter a state for which she held her to be peculiarly fitted by her warm affections and domestic habits.

They knew not each other's opinion, either its constancy or its change, on the one leading point of Anne's conduct, for the subject was never alluded to,—but Anne, at seven and twenty, thought very

---

1. The phrase means that Wentworth had left the area or region (of Somersetshire), but his naval career would subsequently send him once more out of England, in command of HMS *Asp* and, later, HMS *Laconia*.
2. According to Johnson's *Dictionary*, scrupulous and exacting.
3. Financial independence.

differently from what she had been made to think at nineteen.—She did not blame Lady Russell, she did not blame herself for having been guided by her; but she felt that were any young person, in similar circumstances, to apply to her for counsel, they would never receive any of such certain immediate wretchedness, such uncertain future good.—She was persuaded that under every disadvantage of disapprobation at home, and every anxiety attending his profession, all their probable fears, delays and disappointments, she should yet have been a happier woman in maintaining the engagement, than she had been in the sacrifice of it; and this, she fully believed, had the usual share, had even more than a usual share of all such solicitudes and suspense been theirs, without reference to the actual results of their case,[4] which, as it happened, would have bestowed earlier prosperity than could be reasonably calculated on. All his sanguine expectations, all his confidence had been justified. His genius and ardour had seemed to foresee and to command his prosperous path. He had, very soon after their engagement ceased, got employ; and all that he had told her would follow, had taken place. He had distinguished himself, and early gained the other step in rank—and must now, by successive captures, have made a handsome fortune. She had only navy lists[5] and newspapers for her authority, but she could not doubt his being rich;—and, in favour of his constancy, she had no reason to believe him married.

How eloquent could Anne Elliot have been,—how eloquent, at least, were her wishes on the side of early warm attachment, and a cheerful confidence in futurity, against that over-anxious caution which seems to insult exertion and distrust Providence!—She had been forced into prudence in her youth, she learned romance as she grew older—the natural sequel of an unnatural beginning.

With all these circumstances, recollections and feelings, she could not hear that Captain Wentworth's sister was likely to live at Kellynch, without a revival of former pain; and many a stroll and many a sigh were necessary to dispel the agitation of the idea. She often told herself it was folly, before she could harden her nerves sufficiently to feel the continual discussion of the Crofts and their business no evil. She was assisted, however, by that perfect indifference and apparent unconsciousness, among the only three of her own

4. Austen's use of the term "case" suggests the dilemma for ethical judgment between case-based (or casuistic) reasoning and reasoning based on adherence to abstract principles. The *Oxford English Dictionary* defines casuistry as "that part of Ethics which resolves cases of conscience, applying the general rules of religion and morality to particular instances in which 'circumstances alter cases,' or in which there appears to be a conflict of duties."

5. Records of naval officers and related information, including the names of officers who had recently died while serving, the names and condition of ships, and pay scales, published in official venues and in cheap pamphlets like *Steel's Original and Correct List of the Royal Navy* (see p. 193 in this volume).

friends in the secret of the past, which seemed almost to deny any recollection of it. She could do justice to the superiority of Lady Russell's motives in this, over those of her father and Elizabeth; she could honour all the better feelings of her calmness—but the general air of oblivion among them was highly important, from whatever it sprung; and in the event of Admiral Croft's really taking Kellynch-hall, she rejoiced anew over the conviction which had always been most grateful[6] to her, of the past being known to those three only among her connexions, by whom no syllable, she believed, would ever be whispered, and in the trust that among his, the brother only with whom he had been residing, had received any information of their short-lived engagement.—That brother had been long removed from the country—and being a sensible man, and, moreover, a single man at the time, she had a fond dependance on no human creature's having heard of it from him.

The sister, Mrs. Croft, had then been out of England, accompanying her husband[7] on a foreign station, and her own sister, Mary, had been at school while it all occurred—and never admitted by the pride of some, and the delicacy of others, to the smallest knowledge of it afterwards.

With these supports, she hoped that the acquaintance between herself and the Crofts, which, with Lady Russell, still resident in Kellynch, and Mary fixed only three miles off, must be anticipated, need not involve any particular awkwardness.

Chapter V

On the morning appointed for Admiral and Mrs. Croft's seeing Kellynch-hall, Anne found it most natural to take her almost daily walk to Lady Russell's, and keep out of the way till all was over; when she found it most natural to be sorry that she had missed the opportunity of seeing them.

This meeting of the two parties proved highly satisfactory, and decided the whole business at once. Each lady was previously well disposed for an agreement, and saw nothing, therefore, but good manners in the other; and, with regard to the gentlemen, there was such an hearty good humour, such an open, trusting liberality on the Admiral's side, as could not but influence Sir Walter, who had besides been flattered into his very best and most polished behaviour

---

6. Gratifying.
7. The presence of wives and children aboard naval ships is presented as controversial, but it was a common practice for officers and sailors alike. Charles Austen's wife, Fanny Palmer, and their children lived with him aboard HMS *Namur* from 1812 to 1814. Fanny died aboard the ship.

by Mr. Shepherd's assurances of his being known, by report, to the Admiral, as a model of good breeding.

The house and grounds, and furniture, were approved, the Crofts were approved, terms, time, every thing, and every body, was right; and Mr. Shepherd's clerks were set to work, without there having been a single preliminary difference to modify of all that "This indenture sheweth."[8]

Sir Walter, without hesitation, declared the Admiral to be the best-looking sailor he had ever met with, and went so far as to say, that, if his own man[9] might have had the arranging of his hair, he should not be ashamed of being seen with him any where; and the Admiral, with sympathetic cordiality, observed to his wife as they drove back through the Park, "I thought we should soon come to a deal, my dear, in spite of what they told us at Taunton. The baronet will never set the Thames on fire, but there seems no harm in him:"—reciprocal compliments, which would have been esteemed about equal.

The Crofts were to have possession at Michaelmas,[1] and as Sir Walter proposed removing to Bath in the course of the preceding month, there was no time to be lost in making every dependant arrangement.

Lady Russell, convinced that Anne would not be allowed to be of any use, or any importance, in the choice of the house which they were going to secure, was very unwilling to have her hurried away so soon, and wanted to make it possible for her to stay behind, till she might convey her to Bath herself after Christmas; but having engagements of her own, which must take her from Kellynch for several weeks, she was unable to give the full invitation she wished; and Anne, though dreading the possible heats of September in all the white glare of Bath, and grieving to forego all the influence so sweet and so sad of the autumnal months in the country, did not think that, every thing considered, she wished to remain. It would be most right, and most wise, and, therefore, must involve least suffering, to go with the others.

Something occurred, however, to give her a different duty. Mary, often a little unwell, and always thinking a great deal of her own complaints, and always in the habit of claiming Anne when any thing was the matter, was indisposed; and foreseeing that she should not have a day's health all the autumn, entreated, or rather required her, for it was hardly entreaty, to come to Uppercross Cottage, and bear her company as long as she should want her, instead of going to Bath.

8. Customary language in tenancy agreements.
9. Personal attendant, manservant.
1. September 29, the feast day of Saint Michael the Archangel and one of the four quarter days on which leases began, rents were collected, and servants were hired.

"I cannot possibly do without Anne," was Mary's reasoning; and Elizabeth's reply was, "Then I am sure Anne had better stay, for nobody will want her in Bath."

To be claimed as a good, though in an improper style, is at least better than being rejected as no good at all; and Anne, glad to be thought of some use, glad to have any thing marked out as a duty, and certainly not sorry to have the scene of it in the country, and her own dear country, readily agreed to stay.

This invitation of Mary's removed all Lady Russell's difficulties, and it was consequently soon settled that Anne should not go to Bath till Lady Russell took her, and that all the intervening time should be divided between Uppercross Cottage and Kellynch-lodge.[2]

So far all was perfectly right; but Lady Russell was almost startled by the wrong of one part of the Kellynch-hall plan, when it burst on her, which was, Mrs. Clay's being engaged to go to Bath with Sir Walter and Elizabeth, as a most important and valuable assistant to the latter in all the business before her. Lady Russell was extremely sorry that such a measure should have been resorted to at all—wondered, grieved, and feared—and the affront it contained to Anne, in Mrs. Clay's being of so much use, while Anne could be of none, was a very sore aggravation.

Anne herself was become hardened to such affronts; but she felt the imprudence of the arrangement quite as keenly as Lady Russell. With a great deal of quiet observation, and a knowledge, which she often wished less, of her father's character, she was sensible that results the most serious to his family from the intimacy, were more than possible. She did not imagine that her father had at present an idea of the kind. Mrs. Clay had freckles, and a projecting tooth, and a clumsy wrist, which he was continually making severe remarks upon, in her absence; but she was young, and certainly altogether well-looking, and possessed, in an acute mind and assiduous pleasing manners, infinitely more dangerous attractions than any merely personal might have been. Anne was so impressed by the degree of their danger, that she could not excuse herself from trying to make it perceptible to her sister. She had little hope of success; but Elizabeth, who in the event of such a reverse would be so much more to be pitied than herself, should never, she thought, have reason to reproach her for giving no warning.

She spoke, and seemed only to offend. Elizabeth could not conceive how such an absurd suspicion should occur to her; and indignantly answered for each party's perfectly knowing their situation.

"Mrs. Clay," said she warmly, "never forgets who she is; and as I am rather better acquainted with her sentiments than you can be, I

---

2. Lady Russell's residence.

can assure you, that upon the subject of marriage they are particularly nice; and that she reprobates all inequality of condition and rank more strongly than most people. And as to my father, I really should not have thought that he, who has kept himself single so long for our sakes, need be suspected now. If Mrs. Clay were a very beautiful woman, I grant you, it might be wrong to have her so much with me; not that any thing in the world, I am sure, would induce my father to make a degrading match; but he might be rendered unhappy. But poor Mrs. Clay, who, with all her merits, can never have been reckoned tolerably pretty! I really think poor Mrs. Clay may be staying here in perfect safety. One would imagine you had never heard my father speak of her personal misfortunes, though I know you must fifty times. That tooth of her's! and those freckles! Freckles do not disgust me so very much as they do him: I have known a face not materially disfigured by a few, but he abominates them. You must have heard him notice Mrs. Clay's freckles."

"There is hardly any personal defect," replied Anne, "which an agreeable manner might not gradually reconcile one to."

"I think very differently," answered Elizabeth, shortly; "an agreeable manner may set off handsome features, but can never alter plain ones. However, at any rate, as I have a great deal more at stake on this point than any body else can have, I think it rather unnecessary in you to be advising me."

Anne had done—glad that it was over, and not absolutely hopeless of doing good. Elizabeth, though resenting the suspicion, might yet be made observant by it.

The last office of the four carriage-horses was to draw Sir Walter, Miss Elliot, and Mrs. Clay to Bath. The party drove off in very good spirits; Sir Walter prepared with condescending bows for all the afflicted tenantry and cottagers who might have had a hint to shew themselves: and Anne walked up at the same time, in a sort of desolate tranquillity, to the Lodge, where she was to spend the first week.

Her friend was not in better spirits than herself. Lady Russell felt this break-up of the family exceedingly. Their respectability was as dear to her as her own; and a daily intercourse had become precious by habit. It was painful to look upon their deserted grounds, and still worse to anticipate the new hands they were to fall into; and to escape the solitariness and the melancholy of so altered a village, and be out of the way when Admiral and Mrs. Croft first arrived, she had determined to make her own absence from home begin when she must give up Anne. Accordingly their removal was made together, and Anne was set down at Uppercross Cottage, in the first stage of Lady Russell's journey.

Uppercross was a moderate-sized village; which a few years back had been completely in the old English style; containing only two houses superior in appearance to those of the yeomen[3] and labourers,—the mansion of the 'squire, with its high walls, great gates, and old trees, substantial and unmodernized—and the compact, tight parsonage, enclosed in its own neat garden, with a vine and a pear-tree trained round its casements; but upon the marriage of the young 'squire, it had received the improvement of a farmhouse elevated into a cottage for his residence; and Uppercross Cottage, with its veranda, French windows, and other prettinesses, was quite as likely to catch the traveller's eye, as the more consistent and considerable aspect and premises of the Great House, about a quarter of a mile farther on.

Here Anne had often been staying. She knew the ways of Uppercross as well as those of Kellynch. The two families were so continually meeting, so much in the habit of running in and out of each other's house at all hours, that it was rather a surprise to her to find Mary alone; but being alone, her being unwell and out of spirits, was almost a matter of course. Though better endowed than the elder sister, Mary had not Anne's understanding or temper. While well, and happy, and properly attended to, she had great good humour and excellent spirits; but any indisposition sunk her completely; she had no resources for solitude; and inheriting a considerable share of the Elliot self-importance, was very prone to add to every other distress that of fancying herself neglected and ill-used. In person, she was inferior to both sisters, and had, even in her bloom, only reached the dignity of being "a fine girl." She was now lying on the faded sofa of the pretty little drawing-room, the once elegant furniture of which had been gradually growing shabby, under the influence of four summers and two children; and, on Anne's appearing, greeted her with,

"So, you are come at last! I began to think I should never see you. I am so ill I can hardly speak. I have not seen a creature the whole morning!"

"I am sorry to find you unwell," replied Anne. "You sent me such a good account of yourself on Thursday!"

"Yes, I made the best of it; I always do; but I was very far from well at the time; and I do not think I ever was so ill in my life as I have been all this morning—very unfit to be left alone, I am sure. Suppose I were to be seized of a sudden in some dreadful way, and not able to ring the bell! So, Lady Russell would not get out. I do not think she has been in this house three times this summer."

Anne said what was proper, and enquired after her husband. "Oh! Charles is out shooting. I have not seen him since seven o'clock. He would go, though I told him how ill I was. He said he should not

3. A class of farmers who own the land they cultivate; "gentlemen farmers."

stay out long; but he has never come back, and now it is almost one. I assure you, I have not seen a soul this whole long morning."

"You have had your little boys with you?"

"Yes, as long as I could bear their noise; but they are so unmanageable that they do me more harm than good. Little Charles does not mind a word I say, and Walter is growing quite as bad."

"Well, you will soon be better now," replied Anne, cheerfully. "You know I always cure you when I come. How are your neighbours at the Great House?"

"I can give you no account of them. I have not seen one of them to-day, except Mr. Musgrove, who just stopped and spoke through the window, but without getting off his horse; and though I told him how ill I was, not one of them have been near me. It did not happen to suit the Miss Musgroves, I suppose, and they never put themselves out of their way."

"You will see them yet, perhaps, before the morning[4] is gone. It is early."

"I never want them, I assure you. They talk and laugh a great deal too much for me. Oh! Anne, I am so very unwell! It was quite unkind of you not to come on Thursday."

"My dear Mary, recollect what a comfortable account you sent me of yourself! You wrote in the cheerfullest manner, and said you were perfectly well, and in no hurry for me; and that being the case, you must be aware that my wish would be to remain with Lady Russell to the last: and besides what I felt on her account, I have really been so busy, have had so much to do, that I could not very conveniently have left Kellynch sooner."

"Dear me! what can *you* possibly have to do?"

"A great many things, I assure you. More than I can recollect in a moment: but I can tell you some. I have been making a duplicate of the catalogue of my father's books and pictures. I have been several times in the garden with Mackenzie, trying to understand, and make him understand, which of Elizabeth's plants are for Lady Russell. I have had all my own little concerns to arrange—books and music to divide, and all my trunks to repack, from not having understood in time what was intended as to the waggons. And one thing I have had to do, Mary, of a more trying nature; going to almost every house in the parish, as a sort of take-leave. I was told that they wished it. But all these things took up a great deal of time."

"Oh! well;"—and after a moment's pause, "But you have never asked me one word about our dinner at the Pooles yesterday."

---

4. At this time a period extending from about 11 a.m., immediately after breakfast, to 3 p.m., roughly the time when young women would begin dressing for dinner.

"Did you go then? I have made no enquiries, because I concluded you must have been obliged to give up the party."

"Oh! yes, I went. I was very well yesterday; nothing at all the matter with me till this morning. It would have been strange if I had not gone."

"I am very glad you were well enough, and I hope you had a pleasant party."

"Nothing remarkable. One always knows beforehand what the dinner will be, and who will be there. And it is so very uncomfortable, not having a carriage of one's own. Mr. and Mrs. Musgrove took me, and we were so crowded! They are both so very large, and take up so much room! And Mr. Musgrove always sits forward. So, there was I, crowded into the back seat with Henrietta and Louisa. And I think it very likely that my illness to-day may be owing to it."

A little farther perseverance in patience, and forced cheerfulness on Anne's side, produced nearly a cure on Mary's. She could soon sit upright on the sofa, and began to hope she might be able to leave it by dinner-time. Then, forgetting to think of it, she was at the other end of the room, beautifying a nosegay;[5] then, she ate her cold meat; and then she was well enough to propose a little walk.

"Where shall we go?" said she, when they were ready. "I suppose you will not like to call at the Great House before they have been to see you?"

"I have not the smallest objection on that account," replied Anne. "I should never think of standing on such ceremony with people I know so well as Mrs. and the Miss Musgroves."

"Oh! but they ought to call upon you as soon as possible. They ought to feel what is due to you as *my* sister. However, we may as well go and sit with them a little while, and when we have got that over, we can enjoy our walk."

Anne had always thought such a style of intercourse highly imprudent; but she had ceased to endeavour to check it, from believing that, though there were on each side continual subjects of offence, neither family could now do without it. To the Great House accordingly they went, to sit the full half hour in the old-fashioned square parlour, with a small carpet and shining floor, to which the present daughters of the house were gradually giving the proper air of confusion by a grand piano forte and a harp, flower-stands and little tables placed in every direction. Oh! could the originals of the portraits against the wainscot, could the gentlemen in brown velvet and the ladies in blue satin have seen what was going on, have been conscious of such an overthrow of all order and neatness! The portraits themselves seemed to be staring in astonishment.

---

5. A small bouquet of sweet-smelling flowers or herbs.

The Musgroves, like their houses, were in a state of alteration, perhaps of improvement. The father and mother were in the old English style, and the young people in the new. Mr. and Mrs. Musgrove were a very good sort of people; friendly and hospitable, not much educated, and not at all elegant. Their children had more modern minds and manners. There was a numerous family; but the only two grown up, excepting Charles, were Henrietta and Louisa, young ladies of nineteen and twenty, who had brought from a school at Exeter all the usual stock of accomplishments, and were now, like thousands of other young ladies, living to be fashionable, happy, and merry. Their dress had every advantage, their faces were rather pretty, their spirits extremely good, their manners unembarrassed and pleasant; they were of consequence at home, and favourites abroad. Anne always contemplated them as some of the happiest creatures of her acquaintance; but still, saved as we all are by some comfortable feeling of superiority from wishing for the possibility of exchange, she would not have given up her own more elegant and cultivated mind for all their enjoyments; and envied them nothing but that seemingly perfect good understanding and agreement together, that good-humoured mutual affection, of which she had known so little herself with either of her sisters.

They were received with great cordiality. Nothing seemed amiss on the side of the Great House family, which was generally, as Anne very well knew, the least to blame. The half hour was chatted away pleasantly enough; and she was not at all surprised, at the end of it, to have their walking party joined by both the Miss Musgroves, at Mary's particular invitation.

Chapter VI

Anne had not wanted[6] this visit to Uppercross, to learn that a removal from one set of people to another, though at a distance of only three miles, will often include a total change of conversation, opinion, and idea. She had never been staying there before, without being struck by it, or without wishing that other Elliots could have her advantage in seeing how unknown, or unconsidered there, were the affairs which at Kellynch-hall were treated as of such general publicity and pervading interest; yet, with all this experience, she believed she must now submit to feel that another lesson, in the art of knowing our own nothingness beyond our own circle, was become necessary for her;—for certainly, coming as she did, with a heart full of the subject which had been completely occupying both houses in

6. Needed.

Kellynch for many weeks, she had expected rather more curiosity and sympathy than she found in the separate, but very similar remark of Mr. and Mrs. Musgrove—"So, Miss Anne, Sir Walter and your sister are gone; and what part of Bath do you think they will settle in?" and this, without much waiting for an answer;—or in the young ladies' addition of, "I hope *we* shall be in Bath in the winter; but remember, papa, if we do go, we must be in a good situation—none of your Queen-squares for us!" or in the anxious supplement from Mary, of "Upon my word, I shall be pretty well off, when you are all gone away to be happy at Bath!"

She could only resolve to avoid such self-delusion in future, and think with heightened gratitude of the extraordinary blessing of having one such truly sympathising friend as Lady Russell.

The Mr. Musgroves had their own game to guard, and to destroy; their own horses, dogs, and newspapers to engage them; and the females were fully occupied in all the other common subjects of house-keeping, neighbours, dress, dancing, and music. She acknowledged it to be very fitting, that every little social commonwealth should dictate its own matters of discourse; and hoped, ere long, to become a not unworthy member of the one she was now transplanted into.—With the prospect of spending at least two months at Uppercross, it was highly incumbent on her to clothe her imagination, her memory, and all her ideas in as much of Uppercross as possible.

She had no dread of these two months. Mary was not so repulsive[7] and unsisterly as Elizabeth, nor so inaccessible to all influence of hers; neither was there any thing among the other component parts of the cottage inimical to comfort.—She was always on friendly terms with her brother-in-law; and in the children, who loved her nearly as well, and respected her a great deal more than their mother, she had an object of interest, amusement, and wholesome exertion.

Charles Musgrove was civil and agreeable; in sense and temper he was undoubtedly superior to his wife; but not of powers, or conversation, or grace, to make the past, as they were connected together, at all a dangerous contemplation; though, at the same time, Anne could believe, with Lady Russell, that a more equal match might have greatly improved him; and that a woman of real understanding might have given more consequence to his character, and more usefulness, rationality, and elegance to his habits and pursuits. As it was, he did nothing with much zeal, but sport; and his time was otherwise trifled away, without benefit from books, or any thing else. He had very good spirits, which never seemed much affected by his wife's occasional lowness; bore with her unreasonableness sometimes to Anne's admiration; and, upon the whole, though there

---

7. Cold in manner.

was very often a little disagreement, (in which she had sometimes more share than she wished, being appealed to by both parties) they might pass for a happy couple. They were always perfectly agreed in the want of more money, and a strong inclination for a handsome present from his father; but here, as on most topics, he had the superiority, for while Mary thought it a great shame that such a present was not made, he always contended for his father's having many other uses for his money, and a right to spend it as he liked.

As to the management of their children, his theory was much better than his wife's, and his practice not so bad.—"I could manage them very well, if it were not for Mary's interference,"—was what Anne often heard him say; and had a good deal of faith in; but when listening in turn to Mary's reproach of "Charles spoils the children so that I cannot get them into any order,"—she never had the smallest temptation to say, "Very true."

One of the least agreeable circumstances of her residence there, was her being treated with too much confidence by all parties, and being too much in the secret of the complaints of each house. Known to have some influence with her sister, she was continually requested, or at least receiving hints to exert it, beyond what was practicable. "I wish you could persuade Mary not to be always fancying herself ill," was Charles's language; and, in an unhappy mood, thus spoke Mary;—"I do believe if Charles were to see me dying, he would not think there was any thing the matter with me. I am sure, Anne, if you would, you might persuade him that I really am very ill—a great deal worse than I ever own."[8]

Mary's declaration was, "I hate sending the children to the Great House, though their grandmamma is always wanting to see them, for she humours and indulges them to such a degree, and gives them so much trash and sweet things, that they are sure to come back sick and cross for the rest of the day."—And Mrs. Musgrove took the first opportunity of being alone with Anne, to say, "Oh! Miss Anne, I cannot help wishing Mrs. Charles had a little of your method with those children. They are quite different creatures with you! But to be sure, in general they are so spoilt! It is a pity you cannot put your sister in the way of managing them. They are as fine healthy children as ever were seen, poor little dears, without partiality; but Mrs. Charles knows no more how they should be treated!—Bless me, how troublesome they are sometimes!—I assure you, Miss Anne, it prevents my wishing to see them at our house so often as I otherwise should. I believe Mrs. Charles is not quite pleased with my not inviting them oftener; but you know it is very bad to have children with one, that one is obliged to be checking every moment; 'don't do this, and

8. Acknowledge.

don't do that;'—or that one can only keep in tolerable order by more cake than is good for them."

She had this communication, moreover, from Mary. "Mrs. Musgrove thinks all her servants so steady, that it would be high treason to call it in question; but I am sure, without exaggeration, that her upper house-maid and laundry-maid, instead of being in their business, are gadding about the village, all day long. I meet them wherever I go; and I declare, I never go twice into my nursery without seeing something of them. If Jemima were not the trustiest, steadiest creature in the world, it would be enough to spoil her; for she tells me, they are always tempting her to take a walk with them." And on Mrs. Musgrove's side, it was,—"I make a rule of never interfering in any of my daughter-in-law's concerns, for I know it would not do; but I shall tell *you*, Miss Anne, because you may be able to set things to rights, that I have no very good opinion of Mrs. Charles's nursery-maid: I hear strange stories of her; she is always upon the gad: and from my own knowledge, I can declare, she is such a fine-dressing lady, that she is enough to ruin any servants she comes near. Mrs. Charles quite swears by her, I know; but I just give you this hint, that you may be upon the watch; because, if you see any thing amiss, you need not be afraid of mentioning it."

Again; it was Mary's complaint that Mrs. Musgrove was very apt not to give her the precedence that was her due,[9] when they dined at the Great House with other families; and she did not see any reason why she was to be considered so much at home as to lose her place. And one day, when Anne was walking with only the Miss Musgroves, one of them, after talking of rank, people of rank, and jealousy of rank, said, "I have no scruple of observing to *you*, how nonsensical some persons are about their place, because, all the world knows how easy and indifferent you are about it: but I wish any body could give Mary a hint that it would be a great deal better if she were not so very tenacious; especially, if she would not be always putting herself forward to take place of mamma. Nobody doubts her right to have precedence of mamma, but it would be more becoming in her not to be always insisting on it. It is not that mamma cares about it the least in the world, but I know it is taken notice of by many persons."

How was Anne to set all these matters to rights? She could do little more than listen patiently, soften every grievance, and excuse each to the other; give them all hints of the forbearance necessary between such near neighbours, and make those hints broadest which were meant for her sister's benefit.

In all other respects, her visit began and proceeded very well. Her own spirits improved by change of place and subject, by being

9. As the daughter of a baronet, Mary has the superior claim in social situations.

removed three miles from Kellynch: Mary's ailments lessened by having a constant companion; and their daily intercourse with the other family, since there was neither superior affection, confidence, nor employment in the cottage, to be interrupted by it, was rather an advantage. It was certainly carried nearly as far as possible, for they met every morning, and hardly ever spent an evening asunder; but she believed they should not have done so well without the sight of Mr. and Mrs. Musgrove's respectable forms in the usual places, or without the talking, laughing, and singing of their daughters.

She played a great deal better than either of the Miss Musgroves; but having no voice, no knowledge of the harp, and no fond parents to sit by and fancy themselves delighted, her performance was little thought of, only out of civility, or to refresh the others, as she was well aware. She knew that when she played she was giving pleasure only to herself; but this was no new sensation: excepting one short period of her life, she had never, since the age of fourteen, never since the loss of her dear mother, known the happiness of being listened to, or encouraged by any just appreciation or real taste. In music she had been always used to feel alone in the world; and Mr. and Mrs. Musgrove's fond partiality for their own daughters' performance, and total indifference to any other person's, gave her much more pleasure for their sakes, than mortification for her own.

The party at the Great House was sometimes increased by other company. The neighbourhood was not large, but the Musgroves were visited by every body, and had more dinner parties, and more callers, more visitors by invitation and by chance, than any other family. They were more completely popular.

The girls were wild for dancing; and the evenings ended, occasionally, in an unpremeditated little ball. There was a family of cousins within a walk of Uppercross, in less affluent circumstances, who depended on the Musgroves for all their pleasures: they would come at any time, and help play at any thing, or dance any where; and Anne, very much preferring the office of musician to a more active post, played country dances to them by the hour together; a kindness which always recommended her musical powers to the notice of Mr. and Mrs. Musgrove more than any thing else, and often drew this compliment;—"Well done, Miss Anne! very well done indeed! Lord bless me! how those little fingers of yours fly about!"

So passed the first three weeks. Michaelmas came; and now Anne's heart must be in Kellynch again. A beloved home made over to others; all the precious rooms and furniture, groves, and prospects, beginning to own other eyes and other limbs! She could not think of much else on the 29th of September; and she had this sympathetic touch in the evening, from Mary, who, on having occasion to note down the day of the month, exclaimed, "Dear me! is not this the day the Crofts were to come to Kellynch? I am glad I did not think of it before. How low it makes me!"

The Crofts took possession with true naval alertness, and were to be visited. Mary deplored the necessity for herself. "Nobody knew how much she should suffer. She should put it off as long as she could." But was not easy till she had talked Charles into driving her over on an early day; and was in a very animated, comfortable state of imaginary agitation, when she came back. Anne had very sincerely rejoiced in there being no means of her going.[1] She wished, however, to see the Crofts, and was glad to be within when the visit was returned. They came; the master of the house was not at home, but the two sisters were together; and as it chanced that Mrs. Croft fell to the share of Anne, while the admiral sat by Mary, and made himself very agreeable by his good-humoured notice of her little boys, she was well able to watch for a likeness, and if it failed her in the features, to catch it in the voice, or the turn of sentiment and expression.

Mrs. Croft, though neither tall nor fat, had a squareness, upright-ness, and vigour of form, which gave importance to her person.[2] She had bright dark eyes, good teeth, and altogether an agreeable face; though her reddened and weather-beaten complexion, the conse-quence of her having been almost as much at sea as her husband, made her seem to have lived some years longer in the world than her real eight and thirty. Her manners were open, easy, and decided, like one who had no distrust of herself, and no doubts of what to do; without any approach to coarseness, however, or any want of good humour. Anne gave her credit, indeed, for feelings of great con-sideration towards herself, in all that related to Kellynch; and it pleased her: especially, as she had satisfied herself in the very first half minute, in the instant even of introduction, that there was not the smallest symptom of any knowledge or suspicion on Mrs. Croft's side, to give a bias of any sort. She was quite easy on that head, and consequently full of strength and courage, till for a moment electri-fied by Mrs. Croft's suddenly saying,—

"It was you, and not your sister, I find, that my brother had the pleasure of being acquainted with, when he was in this country."

Anne hoped she had outlived the age of blushing; but the age of emotion she certainly had not.

"Perhaps you may not have heard that he is married," added Mrs. Croft.

She could now answer as she ought; and was happy to feel, when Mrs. Croft's next words explained it to be Mr. Wentworth of whom she spoke, that she had said nothing which might not do for either brother.

1. Because Charles, as we learn later, drives a curricle, which holds only two people.
2. Physical appearance.

She immediately felt how reasonable it was, that Mrs. Croft should be thinking and speaking of Edward, and not of Frederick; and with shame at her own forgetfulness, applied herself to the knowledge of their former neighbour's present state, with proper interest.

The rest was all tranquillity; till just as they were moving, she heard the admiral say to Mary,

"We are expecting a brother of Mrs. Croft's here soon; I dare say you know him by name."

He was cut short by the eager attacks of the little boys, clinging to him like an old friend, and declaring he should not go; and being too much engrossed by proposals of carrying them away in his coat pocket, etc. to have another moment for finishing or recollecting what he had begun, Anne was left to persuade herself, as well as she could, that the same brother must still be in question. She could not, however, reach such a degree of certainty, as not to be anxious to hear whether any thing had been said on the subject at the other house, where the Crofts had previously been calling.

The folks of Great House were to spend the evening of this day at the Cottage; and it being now too late in the year for such visits to be made on foot, the coach was beginning to be listened for, when the youngest Miss Musgrove walked in. That she was coming to apologize, and that they should have to spend the evening by themselves, was the first black idea;[3] and Mary was quite ready to be affronted, when Louisa made all right by saying, that she only came on foot, to leave more room for the harp, which was bringing[4] in the carriage.

"And I will tell you our reason," she added, "and all about it. I am come on to give you notice, that papa and mamma are out of spirits this evening, especially mamma; she is thinking so much of poor Richard! And we agreed it would be best to have the harp, for it seems to amuse her more than the piano-forte. I will tell you why she is out of spirits. When the Crofts called this morning, (they called here afterwards, did not they?) they happened to say, that her brother, Captain Wentworth, is just returned to England, or paid off, or something, and is coming to see them almost directly; and most unluckily it came into mamma's head, when they were gone, that Wentworth, or something very like it, was the name of poor Richard's captain, at one time, I do not know when or where, but a great while before he died, poor fellow! And upon looking over his letters and things, she found it was so; and is perfectly sure that this must be the very man, and her head is quite full of it, and of poor Richard! So we must all be as merry as we can, that she may not be dwelling upon such gloomy things."

3. Phrase denoting a difficult or discerning topic.
4. Being brought.

The real circumstances of this pathetic piece of family history were, that the Musgroves had had the ill fortune of a very troublesome, hopeless son; and the good fortune to lose him before he reached his twentieth year; that he had been sent to sea, because he was stupid and unmanageable on shore; that he had been very little cared for at any time by his family, though quite as much as he deserved; seldom heard of, and scarcely at all regretted, when the intelligence[5] of his death abroad had worked its way to Uppercross, two years before.

He had, in fact, though his sisters were now doing all they could for him, by calling him "poor Richard," been nothing better than a thick-headed, unfeeling, unprofitable Dick Musgrove, who had never done any thing to entitle himself to more than the abbreviation of his name, living or dead.

He had been several years at sea, and had, in the course of those removals to which all midshipmen are liable, and especially such midshipmen as every captain wishes to get rid of, been six months on board Captain Frederick Wentworth's frigate,[6] the Laconia; and from the Laconia he had, under the influence of his captain, written the only two letters which his father and mother had ever received from him during the whole of his absence; that is to say, the only two disinterested letters; all the rest had been mere applications for money.

In each letter he had spoken well of his captain; but yet, so little were they in the habit of attending to such matters, so unobservant and incurious were they as to the names of men or ships, that it had made scarcely any impression at the time; and that Mrs. Musgrove should have been suddenly struck, this very day, with a recollection of the name of Wentworth, as connected with her son, seemed one of those extraordinary bursts of mind which do sometimes occur.

She had gone to her letters, and found it all as she supposed; and the reperusal of these letters, after so long an interval, her poor son gone for ever, and all the strength of his faults forgotten, had affected her spirits exceedingly, and thrown her into greater grief for him than she had known on first hearing of his death. Mr. Musgrove was, in a lesser degree, affected likewise; and when they reached the cottage, they were evidently in want, first, of being listened to anew on this subject, and afterwards, of all the relief which cheerful companions could give.

---

5. News.
6. The Royal Museums Greenwich describes frigates as the British Royal Navy's "glamour ships": "the fast scouts of the battle fleet, when not operating in an independent cruising role, searching out enemy merchant ships, privateers, or enemy fleets." Ships of the fifth rate, frigates had thirty-two to forty guns, tonnage from 700 to 1,450 tons, and crews of about 300 men. In the British Royal Navy, a fifth-rate ship was the second smallest class of warships in a hierarchical system of six ratings based on size and firepower.

To hear them talking so much of Captain Wentworth, repeating his name so often, puzzling over past years, and at last ascertaining that it *might*, that it probably *would*, turn out to be the very same Captain Wentworth whom they recollected meeting, once or twice, after their coming back from Clifton;—a very fine young man; but they could not say whether it was seven or eight years ago,—was a new sort of trial to Anne's nerves. She found, however, that it was one to which she must enure herself. Since he actually was expected in the country, she must teach herself to be insensible on such points. And not only did it appear that he was expected, and speedily, but the Musgroves, in their warm gratitude for the kindness he had shewn poor Dick, and very high respect for his character, stamped as it was by poor Dick's having been six months under his care, and mentioning him in strong, though not perfectly well spelt praise, as "a fine dashing felow, only two perticular about the schoolmaster,"[7] were bent on introducing themselves, and seeking his acquaintance, as soon as they could hear of his arrival.

The resolution of doing so helped to form the comfort of their evening.

Chapter VII

A very few days more, and Captain Wentworth was known to be at Kellynch, and Mr. Musgrove had called on him, and come back warm in his praise, and he was engaged with the Crofts to dine at Uppercross, by the end of another week. It had been a great disappointment to Mr. Musgrove, to find that no earlier day could be fixed, so impatient was he to shew his gratitude, by seeing Captain Wentworth under his own roof, and welcoming him to all that was strongest and best in his cellars.[8] But a week must pass; only a week, in Anne's reckoning, and then, she supposed, they must meet; and soon she began to wish that she could feel secure even for a week.

Captain Wentworth made a very early return to Mr. Musgrove's civility, and she was all but calling there in the same half hour!— She and Mary were actually setting forward for the great house, where, as she afterwards learnt, they must inevitably have found him, when they were stopped by the eldest boy's being at that moment brought home in consequence of a bad fall. The child's situation put the visit entirely aside, but she could not hear of her escape with indifference, even in the midst of the serious anxiety which they afterwards felt on his account.

7. Royal Navy ships all carried schoolmasters who instructed shipmen in a variety of topics, including navigation, gunnery, weather, mapping, and mathematics.
8. Wine cellars.

His collar-bone was found to be dislocated, and such injury received in the back, as roused the most alarming ideas. It was an afternoon of distress, and Anne had every thing to do at once—the apothecary[9] to send for—the father to have pursued and informed—the mother to support and keep from hysterics—the servants to control—the youngest child to banish, and the poor suffering one to attend and soothe;—besides sending, as soon as she recollected it, proper notice to the other house, which brought her an accession rather of frightened, enquiring companions, than of very useful assistants.

Her brother's[1] return was the first comfort; he could take best care of his wife, and the second blessing was the arrival of the apothecary. Till he came and had examined the child, their apprehensions were the worse for being vague;—they suspected great injury, but knew not where; but now the collar-bone was soon replaced, and though Mr. Robinson felt and felt, and rubbed, and looked grave, and spoke low words both to the father and the aunt, still they were all to hope the best, and to be able to part and eat their dinner in tolerable ease of mind; and then it was, just before they parted, that the two young aunts were able so far to digress from their nephew's state, as to give the information of Captain Wentworth's visit;—staying five minutes behind their father and mother, to endeavour to express how perfectly delighted they were with him, how much handsomer, how infinitely more agreeable they thought him than any individual among their male acquaintance, who had been at all a favourite before—how glad they had been to hear papa invite him to stay dinner—how sorry when he said it was quite out of his power—and how glad again, when he had promised in reply to papa and mamma's farther pressing invitations, to come and dine with them on the morrow, actually on the morrow!—And he had promised it in so pleasant a manner, as if he felt all the motive of their attention just as he ought!—And, in short, he had looked and said every thing with such exquisite grace, that they could assure them all, their heads were both turned by him!—And off they ran, quite as full of glee as of love, and apparently more full of Captain Wentworth than of little Charles.

The same story and the same raptures were repeated, when the two girls came with their father, through the gloom of the evening, to make enquiries; and Mr. Musgrove, no longer under the first uneasiness about his heir, could add his confirmation and praise, and hope there would be now no occasion for putting Captain Wentworth off, and only be sorry to think that the cottage party, probably, would not like to leave the little boy, to give him the meeting.—"Oh,

9. At this time a general medical practitioner.
1. Brother-in-law's. At this time in-laws were customarily referred to as if they were natural relatives.

no! as to leaving the little boy!"—both father and mother were in much too strong and recent alarm to bear the thought; and Anne, in the joy of the escape, could not help adding her warm protestations to theirs.

Charles Musgrove, indeed, afterwards shewed more of inclination; "the child was going on so well—and he wished so much to be introduced to Captain Wentworth, that, perhaps, he might join them in the evening; he would not dine from home, but he might walk in for half an hour." But in this he was eagerly opposed by his wife, with "Oh, no! indeed, Charles, I cannot bear to have you go away. Only think, if any thing should happen!"

The child had a good night, and was going on well the next day. It must be a work of time to ascertain that no injury had been done to the spine, but Mr. Robinson found nothing to increase alarm, and Charles Musgrove began consequently to feel no necessity for longer confinement. The child was to be kept in bed, and amused as quietly as possible; but what was there for a father to do? This was quite a female case, and it would be highly absurd in him, who could be of no use at home, to shut himself up. His father very much wished him to meet Captain Wentworth, and there being no sufficient reason against it, he ought to go; and it ended in his making a bold public declaration, when he came in from shooting, of his meaning to dress directly, and dine at the other house.

"Nothing can be going on better than the child," said he, "so I told my father just now that I would come, and he thought me quite right. Your sister being with you, my love, I have no scruple at all. You would not like to leave him yourself, but you see I can be of no use. Anne will send for me if any thing is the matter."

Husbands and wives generally understand when opposition will be vain. Mary knew, from Charles's manner of speaking, that he was quite determined on going, and that it would be of no use to teaze him. She said nothing, therefore, till he was out of the room, but as soon as there was only Anne to hear,

"So! You and I are to be left to shift by ourselves, with this poor sick child—and not a creature coming near us all the evening! I knew how it would be. This is always my luck! If there is any thing disagreeable going on, men are always sure to get out of it, and Charles is as bad as any of them. Very unfeeling! I must say it is very unfeeling of him, to be running away from his poor little boy; talks of his being going on so well! How does he know that he is going on well, or that there may not be a sudden change half an hour hence? I did not think Charles would have been so unfeeling. So, here he is to go away and enjoy himself, and because I am the poor mother, I am not to be allowed to stir;—and yet, I am sure, I am more unfit than any body else to be about the child. My being the mother is the very reason why my feelings should not be tried. I am not at all equal to it. You saw how hysterical I was yesterday."

"But that was only the effect of the suddenness of your alarm—of the shock. You will not be hysterical again. I dare say we shall have nothing to distress us. I perfectly understand Mr. Robinson's directions, and have no fears; and indeed, Mary, I cannot wonder at your husband. Nursing does not belong to a man, it is not his province. A sick child is always the mother's property, her own feelings generally make it so."

"I hope I am as fond of my child as any mother—but I do not know that I am of any more use in the sick-room than Charles, for I cannot be always scolding and teazing a poor child when it is ill; and you saw, this morning, that if I told him to keep quiet, he was sure to begin kicking about. I have not nerves for the sort of thing."

"But, could you be comfortable yourself, to be spending the whole evening away from the poor boy?"

"Yes; you see his papa can, and why should not I?—Jemima is so careful! And she could send us word every hour how he was. I really think Charles might as well have told his father we would all come. I am not more alarmed about little Charles now than he is. I was dreadfully alarmed yesterday, but the case is very different to-day."

"Well—if you do not think it too late to give notice for yourself, suppose you were to go, as well as your husband. Leave little Charles to my care. Mr. and Mrs. Musgrove cannot think it wrong, while I remain with him."

"Are you serious?" cried Mary, her eyes brightening. "Dear me! that's a very good thought, very good indeed. To be sure I may just as well go as not, for I am of no use at home—am I? and it only harasses me. You, who have not a mother's feelings, are a great deal the properest person. You can make little Charles do any thing; he always minds you at a word. It will be a great deal better than leaving him with only Jemima. Oh! I will certainly go; I am sure I ought if I can, quite as much as Charles, for they want me excessively[2] to be acquainted with Captain Wentworth, and I know you do not mind being left alone. An excellent thought of yours, indeed, Anne! I will go and tell Charles, and get ready directly. You can send for us, you know, at a moment's notice, if any thing is the matter; but I dare say there will be nothing to alarm you. I should not go, you may be sure, if I did not feel quite at ease about my dear child."

The next moment she was tapping at her husband's dressing-room door, and as Anne followed her up stairs, she was in time for the whole conversation, which began with Mary's saying, in a tone of great exultation,

2. According to Johnson's *Dictionary*, exceedingly, eminently, in a great degree.

"I mean to go with you, Charles, for I am of no more use at home than you are. If I were to shut myself up for ever with the child, I should not be able to persuade him to do any thing he did not like. Anne will stay; Anne undertakes to stay at home and take care of him. It is Anne's own proposal, and so I shall go with you, which will be a great deal better, for I have not dined at the other house since Tuesday."

"This is very kind of Anne," was her husband's answer, "and I should be very glad to have you go; but it seems rather hard that she should be left at home by herself, to nurse our sick child."

Anne was now at hand to take up her own cause, and the sincerity of her manner being soon sufficient to convince him, where conviction was at least very agreeable, he had no farther scruples as to her being left to dine alone, though he still wanted her to join them in the evening, when the child might be at rest for the night, and kindly urged her to let him come and fetch her; but she was quite unpersuadable; and this being the case, she had ere long the pleasure of seeing them set off together in high spirits. They were gone, she hoped, to be happy, however oddly constructed such happiness might seem; as for herself, she was left with as many sensations of comfort, as were, perhaps, ever likely to be hers. She knew herself to be of the first utility to the child; and what was it to her, if Frederick Wentworth were only half a mile distant, making himself agreeable to others!

She would have liked to know how he felt as to a meeting. Perhaps indifferent, if indifference could exist under such circumstances. He must be either indifferent or unwilling. Had he wished ever to see her again, he need not have waited till this time; he would have done what she could not but believe that in his place she should have done long ago, when events had been early giving him the independence which alone had been wanting.

Her brother and sister came back delighted with their new acquaintance, and their visit in general. There had been music, singing, talking, laughing, all that was most agreeable; charming manners in Captain Wentworth, no shyness or reserve; they seemed all to know each other perfectly, and he was coming the very next morning to shoot with Charles. He was to come to breakfast, but not at the Cottage, though that had been proposed at first; but then he had been pressed to come to the Great House instead, and he seemed afraid of being in Mrs. Charles Musgrove's way, on account of the child; and therefore, somehow, they hardly knew how, it, ended in Charles's being to meet him to breakfast at his father's.

Anne understood it. He wished to avoid seeing her. He had enquired after her, she found, slightly, as might suit a former slight acquaintance, seeming to acknowledge such as she had acknowledged, actuated, perhaps, by the same view of escaping introduction when they were to meet.

The morning hours of the Cottage were always later than those of the other house; and on the morrow the difference was so great, that Mary and Anne were not more than beginning breakfast when Charles came in to say that they were just setting off, that he was come for his dogs, that his sisters were following with Captain Wentworth, his sisters meaning to visit Mary and the child, and Captain Wentworth proposing also to wait on her for a few minutes, if not inconvenient; and though Charles had answered for the child's being in no such state as could make it inconvenient, Captain Wentworth would not be satisfied without his running on to give notice.

Mary, very much gratified by this attention, was delighted to receive him; while a thousand feelings rushed on Anne, of which this was the most consoling, that it would soon be over. And it was soon over. In two minutes after Charles's preparation, the others appeared; they were in the drawing-room. Her eye half met Captain Wentworth's; a bow, a curtsey passed; she heard his voice—he talked to Mary, said all that was right; said something to the Miss Musgroves, enough to mark an easy footing: the room seemed full—full of persons and voices—but a few minutes ended it. Charles shewed himself at the window, all was ready, their visitor had bowed and was gone; the Miss Musgroves were gone too, suddenly resolving to walk to the end of the village with the sportsmen: the room was cleared, and Anne might finish her breakfast as she could.

"It is over! it is over!" she repeated to herself again, and again, in nervous gratitude. "The worst is over!"

Mary talked, but she could not attend. She had seen him. They had met. They had been once more in the same room!

Soon, however, she began to reason with herself, and try to be feeling less. Eight years, almost eight years had passed, since all had been given up. How absurd to be resuming the agitation which such an interval had banished into distance and indistinctness! What might not eight years do? Events of every description, changes, alienations, removals,—all, all must be comprised in it; and oblivion of the past—how natural, how certain too! It included nearly a third part of her own life.

Alas! with all her reasonings, she found, that to retentive feelings eight years may be little more than nothing.

Now, how were his sentiments to be read? Was this like wishing to avoid her? And the next moment she was hating herself for the folly which asked the question.

On one other question, which perhaps her utmost wisdom might not have prevented, she was soon spared all suspense; for after the

Miss Musgroves had returned and finished their visit at the Cottage, she had this spontaneous information from Mary:

"Captain Wentworth is not very gallant by you, Anne, though he was so attentive to me. Henrietta asked him what he thought of you, when they went away; and he said, 'You were so altered he should not have known you again.'"

Mary had no feelings to make her respect her sister's in a common way; but she was perfectly unsuspicious of being inflicting any peculiar wound.

"Altered beyond his knowledge!" Anne fully submitted, in silent, deep mortification. Doubtless it was so; and she could take no revenge, for he was not altered, or not for the worse. She had already acknowledged it to herself, and she could not think differently, let him think of her as he would. No; the years which had destroyed her youth and bloom had only given him a more glowing, manly, open look, in no respect lessening his personal advantages. She had seen the same Frederick Wentworth.

"So altered that he should not have known her again!" These were words which could not but dwell with her. Yet she soon began to rejoice that she had heard them. They were of sobering tendency; they allayed agitation; they composed, and consequently must make her happier.

Frederick Wentworth had used such words, or something like them, but without an idea that they would be carried round to her. He had thought her wretchedly altered, and, in the first moment of appeal, had spoken as he felt. He had not forgiven Anne Elliot. She had used him ill; deserted and disappointed him; and worse, she had shewn a feebleness of character in doing so, which his own decided, confident temper could not endure. She had given him up to oblige others. It had been the effect of over-persuasion. It had been weakness and timidity.

He had been most warmly attached to her, and had never seen a woman since whom he thought her equal; but, except from some natural sensation of curiosity, he had no desire of meeting her again. Her power with him was gone for ever.

It was now his object to marry. He was rich, and being turned on shore, fully intended to settle as soon as he could be properly tempted; actually looking round, ready to fall in love with all the speed which a clear head and quick taste could allow. He had a heart for either of the Miss Musgroves, if they could catch it; a heart, in short, for any pleasing young woman who came in his way, excepting Anne Elliot. This was his only secret exception, when he said to his sister, in answer to her suppositions,

"Yes, here I am, Sophia, quite ready to make a foolish match. Any body between fifteen and thirty may have me for asking. A little beauty, and a few smiles, and a few compliments to the navy, and I am a lost man. Should not this be enough for a sailor, who has had no society among women to make him nice?"

He said it, she knew, to be contradicted. His bright, proud eye spoke the happy conviction that he was nice; and Anne Elliot was not out of his thoughts, when he more seriously described the woman he should wish to meet with. "A strong mind, with sweetness of manner," made the first and the last of the description.

"This is the woman I want," said he. "Something a little inferior I shall of course put up with, but it must not be much. If I am a fool, I shall be a fool indeed, for I have thought on the subject more than most men."

Chapter VIII

From this time Captain Wentworth and Anne Elliot were repeatedly in the same circle. They were soon dining in company together at Mr. Musgrove's, for the little boy's state could no longer supply his aunt with a pretence for absenting herself; and this was but the beginning of other dinings and other meetings.

Whether former feelings were to be renewed, must be brought to the proof; former times must undoubtedly be brought to the recollection of each; *they* could not but be reverted to; the year of their engagement could not but be named by him, in the little narratives or descriptions which conversation called forth. His profession qualified him, his disposition led him, to talk; and "*That* was in the year six;" "*That* happened before I went to sea in the year six," occurred in the course of the first evening they spent together: and though his voice did not falter, and though she had no reason to suppose his eye wandering towards her while he spoke, Anne felt the utter impossibility, from her knowledge of his mind, that he could be unvisited by remembrance any more than herself. There must be the same immediate association of thought, though she was very far from conceiving it to be of equal pain.

They had no conversation together, no intercourse but what the commonest civility required. Once so much to each other! Now nothing! There *had* been a time, when of all the large party now filling the drawing-room at Uppercross, they would have found it most difficult to cease to speak to one another. With the exception, perhaps, of Admiral and Mrs. Croft, who seemed particularly attached and happy, (Anne could allow no other exception even among the married couples) there could have been no two hearts so open, no tastes so similar, no feelings so in unison, no countenances so beloved. Now they were as strangers; nay, worse than strangers, for they could never become acquainted. It was a perpetual estrangement.

When he talked, she heard the same voice, and discerned the same mind. There was a very general ignorance of all naval matters throughout the party; and he was very much questioned, and especially by the two Miss Musgroves, who seemed hardly to have any eyes but for him, as to the manner of living on board, daily regulations, food, hours, etc.; and their surprise at his accounts, at learning the degree of accommodation and arrangement which was practicable, drew from him some pleasant ridicule, which reminded Anne of the early days when she too had been ignorant, and she too had been accused of supposing sailors to be living on board without any thing to eat, or any cook to dress it if there were, or any servant to wait, or any knife and fork to use.

From thus listening and thinking, she was roused by a whisper of Mrs. Musgrove's, who, overcome by fond regrets, could not help saying,

"Ah! Miss Anne, if it had pleased Heaven to spare my poor son, I dare say he would have been just such another by this time."

Anne suppressed a smile, and listened kindly, while Mrs. Musgrove relieved her heart a little more; and for a few minutes, therefore, could not keep pace with the conversation of the others.—When she could let her attention take its natural course again, she found the Miss Musgroves just fetching the navy-list,—(their own navy list, the first that had ever been at Uppercross); and sitting down together to pore over it, with the professed view of finding out the ships which Captain Wentworth had commanded.

"Your first was the Asp, I remember; we will look for the Asp."

"You will not find her there.—Quite worn out and broken up. I was the last man who commanded her.—Hardly fit for service then.—Reported fit for home service for a year or two,—and so I was sent off to the West Indies."

The girls looked all amazement.

"The admiralty," he continued, "entertain themselves now and then, with sending a few hundred men to sea, in a ship not fit to be employed. But they have a great many to provide for; and among the thousands that may just as well go to the bottom as not, it is impossible for them to distinguish the very set who may be least missed."

"Phoo! phoo!" cried the admiral, "what stuff these young fellows talk! Never was a better sloop than the Asp in her day.—For an old built sloop,[3] you would not see her equal. Lucky fellow to get her!—He

---

3. A small, fast ship with a single gun deck, built in Jamaica and Bermuda. Its speed and evasive capacities made the sloop appealing to smugglers and pirates, as well as for prize-taking.

knows there must have been twenty better men than himself applying for her at the same time. Lucky fellow to get any thing so soon,
with no more interest[4] than his."

"I felt my luck, admiral, I assure you;" replied Captain Wentworth,
seriously.—"I was as well satisfied with my appointment as you can
desire. It was a great object with me, at that time, to be at sea,—a
very great object. I wanted to be doing something."

"To be sure you did.—What should a young fellow, like you, do
ashore, for half a year together?—If a man has not a wife, he soon
wants to be afloat again."

"But, Captain Wentworth," cried Louisa, "how vexed you must
have been when you came to the Asp, to see what an old thing they
had given you."

"I knew pretty well what she was, before that day;" said he, smiling. "I had no more discoveries to make, than you would have as to
the fashion and strength of any old pelisse,[5] which you had seen lent
about among half your acquaintance, ever since you could remember, and which at last, on some very wet day, is lent to yourself.—Ah!
she was a dear old Asp to me. She did all that I wanted. I knew she
would.—I knew that we should either go to the bottom together, or
that she would be the making of me; and I never had two days of
foul weather all the time I was at sea in her; and after taking privateers enough to be very entertaining, I had the good luck, in my
passage home the next autumn, to fall in with the very French frigate[6] I wanted.—I brought her into Plymouth;[7] and here was another
instance of luck. We had not been six hours in the Sound, when a
gale came on, which lasted four days and nights, and which would
have done for poor old Asp, in half the time; our touch with the
Great Nation[8] not having much improved our condition. Four-and-
twenty hours later, and I should only have been a gallant Captain
Wentworth, in a small paragraph at one corner of the newspapers;
and being lost in only a sloop, nobody would have thought about me."

Anne's shudderings were to herself, alone: but the Miss Musgroves
could be as open as they were sincere, in their exclamations of pity
and horror.

"And so then, I suppose," said Mrs. Musgrove, in a low voice, as
if thinking aloud, "so then he went away to the Laconia, and there
he met with our poor boy.—Charles, my dear," (beckoning him to

---

4. Influence. Promotion was not guaranteed and remained heavily dependent on patronage and social connections as opposed to merit alone.
5. A long cloak.
6. Wentworth's successful capture of a larger frigate while commanding the *Asp* demonstrates his naval skill and bravery.
7. Major naval base. After his 1815 defeat at Waterloo, Napoleon Bonaparte was held
   prisoner in the Plymouth Sound aboard HMS *Bellerophon*.
8. France.

her), "do ask Captain Wentworth where it was he first met with your poor brother. I always forget."

"It was at Gibraltar,[9] mother, I know. Dick had been left ill at Gibraltar, with a recommendation from his former captain to Captain Wentworth."

"Oh!—but, Charles, tell Captain Wentworth, he need not be afraid of mentioning poor Dick before me, for it would be rather a pleasure to hear him talked of, by such a good friend."

Charles, being somewhat more mindful of the probabilities of the case, only nodded in reply, and walked away.

The girls were now hunting for the Laconia; and Captain Wentworth could not deny himself the pleasure of taking the precious volume into his own hands to save them the trouble, and once more read aloud the little statement of her name and rate,[1] and present non-commissioned class, observing over it, that she too had been one of the best friends man ever had.

"Ah! those were pleasant days when I had the Laconia! How fast I made money in her.—A friend of mine, and I, had such a lovely cruise together off the Western Islands.—Poor Harville, sister! You know how much he wanted money—worse than myself. He had a wife.—Excellent fellow! I shall never forget his happiness. He felt it all, so much for her sake.—I wished for him again the next summer, when I had still the same luck in the Mediterranean."

"And I am sure, Sir," said Mrs. Musgrove, "it was a lucky day for *us*, when you were put captain into that ship. *We* shall never forget what you did."

Her feelings made her speak low; and Captain Wentworth, hearing only in part, and probably not having Dick Musgrove at all near his thoughts, looked rather in suspense, and as if waiting for more.

"My brother," whispered one of the girls; "mamma is thinking of poor Richard."

"Poor dear fellow!" continued Mrs. Musgrove; "he was grown so steady, and such an excellent correspondent, while he was under your care! Ah! it would have been a happy thing, if he had never left you. I assure you, Captain Wentworth, we are very sorry he ever left you."

There was a momentary expression in Captain Wentworth's face at this speech, a certain glance of his bright eye, and curl of his handsome mouth, which convinced Anne, that instead of sharing in Mrs. Musgrove's kind wishes, as to her son, he had probably been at some pains to get rid of him; but it was too transient an indulgence of self-amusement to be detected by any who understood him less than

9. Key strategic British naval and supply base near the entrance of the Mediterranean Sea.
1. Naval classification based on size, speed, tonnage, and armament capabilities.

herself; in another moment he was perfectly collected and serious; and almost instantly afterwards coming up to the sofa, on which she and Mrs. Musgrove were sitting, took a place by the latter, and entered into conversation with her, in a low voice, about her son, doing it with so much sympathy and natural grace, as shewed the kindest consideration for all that was real and unabsurd in the parent's feelings.

They were actually on the same sofa, for Mrs. Musgrove had most readily made room for him;—they were divided only by Mrs. Musgrove. It was no insignificant barrier indeed. Mrs. Musgrove was of a comfortable substantial size, infinitely more fitted by nature to express good cheer and good humour, than tenderness and sentiment; and while the agitations of Anne's slender form, and pensive face, may be considered as very completely screened, Captain Wentworth should be allowed some credit for the self-command with which he attended to her large fat sighings over the destiny of a son, whom alive nobody had cared for.

Personal size and mental sorrow have certainly no necessary proportions. A large bulky figure has as good a right to be in deep affliction, as the most graceful set of limbs in the world. But, fair or not fair, there are unbecoming conjunctions, which reason will patronize in vain,—which taste cannot tolerate,—which ridicule will seize.

The admiral, after taking two or three refreshing turns about the room with his hands behind him, being called to order by his wife, now came up to Captain Wentworth, and without any observation of what he might be interrupting, thinking only of his own thoughts, began with,

"If you had been a week later at Lisbon, last spring, Frederick, you would have been asked to give a passage to Lady Mary Grierson and her daughters."

"Should I? I am glad I was not a week later then."

The admiral abused him for his want of gallantry. He defended himself; though professing that he would never willingly admit any ladies on board a ship of his, excepting for a ball, or a visit, which a few hours might comprehend.

"But, if I know myself," said he, "this is from no want of gallantry towards them. It is rather from feeling how impossible it is, with all one's efforts, and all one's sacrifices, to make the accommodations on board, such as women ought to have. There can be no want of gallantry, admiral, in rating the claims of women to every personal comfort *high*—and this is what I do. I hate to hear of women on board, or to see them on board; and no ship, under my command, shall ever convey a family of ladies any where, if I can help it."

This brought his sister upon him.

"Oh Frederick!—But I cannot believe it of you.—All idle refinement!—Women may be as comfortable on board, as in the best house in England. I believe I have lived as much on board as most women, and I know nothing superior to the accommodations of a man of war. I declare I have not a comfort or an indulgence about me, even at Kellynch-hall," (with a kind bow to Anne) "beyond what I always had in most of the ships I have lived in; and they have been five altogether."

"Nothing to the purpose," replied her brother. "You were living with your husband; and were the only woman on board."

"But you, yourself, brought Mrs. Harville, her sister, her cousin, and the three children, round from Portsmouth to Plymouth. Where was this superfine, extraordinary sort of gallantry of yours, then?"

"All merged in my friendship, Sophia. I would assist any brother officer's wife that I could, and I would bring any thing of Harville's from the world's end, if he wanted it. But do not imagine that I did not feel it an evil in itself."

"Depend upon it they were all perfectly comfortable."

"I might not like them the better for that, perhaps. Such a number of women and children have no *right* to be comfortable on board."

"My dear Frederick, you are talking quite idly. Pray, what would become of us poor sailors' wives, who often want to be conveyed to one port or another, after our husbands, if every body had your feelings?"

"My feelings, you see, did not prevent my taking Mrs. Harville, and all her family, to Plymouth."

"But I hate to hear you talking so, like a fine gentleman, and as if women were all fine ladies, instead of rational creatures. We none of us expect to be in smooth water all our days."

"Ah! my dear," said the admiral, "when he has got a wife, he will sing a different tune. When he is married, if we have the good luck to live to another war, we shall see him do as you and I, and a great many others, have done. We shall have him very thankful to any body that will bring him his wife."

"Ay, that we shall."

"Now I have done," cried Captain Wentworth—"When once married people begin to attack me with, 'Oh! you will think very differently, when you are married.' I can only say, 'No, I shall not;' and then they say again, 'Yes, you will,' and there is an end of it."

He got up and moved away.

"What a great traveller you must have been, ma'am!" said Mrs. Musgrove to Mrs. Croft.

"Pretty well, ma'am, in the fifteen years of my marriage; though many women have done more. I have crossed the Atlantic four times, and have been once to the East Indies, and back again; and only once, besides being in different places about home—Cork, and Lisbon, and Gibraltar. But I never went beyond the Streights—and never was in the West Indies. We do not call Bermuda or Bahama, you know, the West Indies."[2]

Mrs. Musgrove had not a word to say in dissent; she could not accuse herself of having ever called them any thing in the whole course of her life.

"And I do assure you, ma'am," pursued Mrs. Croft, "that nothing can exceed the accommodations of a man of war;[3] I speak, you know, of the higher rates. When you come to a frigate, of course, you are more confined—though any reasonable woman may be perfectly happy in one of them; and I can safely say, that the happiest part of my life has been spent on board a ship. While we were together, you know, there was nothing to be feared. Thank God! I have always been blessed with excellent health, and no climate disagrees with me. A little disordered always the first twenty-four hours of going to sea, but never knew what sickness was afterwards. The only time that I ever really suffered in body or mind, the only time that I ever fancied myself unwell, or had any ideas of danger, was the winter that I passed by myself at Deal, when the Admiral (*Captain* Croft then) was in the North Seas.[4] I lived in perpetual fright at that time, and had all manner of imaginary complaints from not knowing what to do with myself, or when I should hear from him next; but as long as we could be together, nothing ever ailed me, and I never met with the smallest inconvenience."

"Ay, to be sure.—Yes, indeed, oh yes, I am quite of your opinion, Mrs. Croft," was Mrs. Musgrove's hearty answer. "There is nothing so bad as a separation. I am quite of your opinion. *I* know what it is, for Mr. Musgrove always attends the assizes,[5] and I am so glad when they are over, and he is safe back again."

The evening ended with dancing. On its being proposed, Anne offered her services, as usual, and though her eyes would sometimes fill with tears as she sat at the instrument, she was extremely glad to be employed, and desired nothing in return but to be unobserved.

It was a merry, joyous party, and no one seemed in higher spirits than Captain Wentworth. She felt that he had every thing to elevate

2. The East Indies referred to India, Malaysia, and other lands near the Indian Ocean, the West Indies to lands between the Atlantic Ocean and the Caribbean Sea. As Bermuda and the Bahamas are located in the Atlantic, Mrs. Croft excludes them from the Caribbean West Indies. Cork was a major Irish naval port from 1797, and Portugal the base for the Mediterranean fleet. "The Streights" refers either to the Straits of Gibraltar or the Straits of Florida, located between the Atlantic and the Gulf of Mexico.
3. General term for a masted warship. A frigate was a midsized man-of-war, while a ship of the line was larger.
4. Connecting Britain, Norway, Denmark, Germany, the Netherlands, Belgium, and France, an area of the Atlantic Ocean controlled by the British navy.
5. Periodical sessions of the judges of superior courts, held in every county.

him, which general attention and deference, and especially the attention of all the young women could do. The Miss Hayters, the females of the family of cousins already mentioned, were apparently admitted to the honour of being in love with him; and as for Henrietta and Louisa, they both seemed so entirely occupied by him, that nothing but the continued appearance of the most perfect good-will between themselves, could have made it credible that they were not decided rivals. If he were a little spoilt by such universal, such eager admiration, who could wonder?

These were some of the thoughts which occupied Anne, while her fingers were mechanically at work, proceeding for half an hour together, equally without error, and without consciousness. *Once* she felt that he was looking at herself—observing her altered features, perhaps, trying to trace in them the ruins of the face which had once charmed him; and *once* she knew that he must have spoken of her;—she was hardly aware of it, till she heard the answer; but then she was sure of his having asked his partner whether Miss Elliot never danced? The answer was, "Oh! no, never; she has quite given up dancing. She had rather play. She is never tired of playing." Once, too, he spoke to her. She had left the instrument on the dancing being over, and he had sat down to try to make out an air which he wished to give the Miss Musgroves an idea of. Unintentionally she returned to that part of the room; he saw her, and, instantly rising, said, with studied politeness,

"I beg your pardon, madam, this is your seat;" and though she immediately drew back with a decided negative, he was not to be induced to sit down again.

Anne did not wish for more of such looks and speeches. His cold politeness, his ceremonious grace, were worse than any thing.

Chapter IX

Captain Wentworth was come to Kellynch as to a home, to stay as long as he liked, being as thoroughly the object of the Admiral's fraternal kindness as of his wife's. He had intended, on first arriving, to proceed very soon into Shropshire, and visit the brother settled in that county, but the attractions of Uppercross induced him to put this off. There was so much of friendliness, and of flattery, and of every thing most bewitching in his reception there; the old were so hospitable, the young so agreeable, that he could not but resolve to remain where he was, and take all the charms and perfections of Edward's wife upon credit a little longer.

It was soon Uppercross with him almost every day. The Musgroves could hardly be more ready to invite than he to come, particularly in the morning, when he had no companion at home, for the Admiral and Mrs. Croft were generally out of doors together, interesting themselves in their new possessions, their grass, and their sheep, and dawdling about in a way not endurable to a third person, or driving out in a gig,[6] lately added to their establishment.

Hitherto there had been but one opinion of Captain Wentworth, among the Musgroves and their dependencies. It was unvarying, warm admiration every where. But this intimate footing was not more than established, when a certain Charles Hayter returned among them, to be a good deal disturbed by it, and to think Captain Wentworth very much in the way.

Charles Hayter was the eldest of all the cousins, and a very amiable, pleasing young man, between whom and Henrietta there had been a considerable appearance of attachment previous to Captain Wentworth's introduction. He was in orders,[7] and having a curacy in the neighbourhood where residence was not required, lived at his father's house, only two miles from Uppercross. A short absence from home had left his fair one unguarded by his attentions at this critical period, and when he came back he had the pain of finding very altered manners, and of seeing Captain Wentworth.

Mrs. Musgrove and Mrs. Hayter were sisters. They had each had money, but their marriages had made a material difference in their degree of consequence. Mr. Hayter had some property of his own, but it was insignificant compared with Mr. Musgrove's; and while the Musgroves were in the first class of society in the country, the young Hayters would, from their parents' inferior, retired, and unpolished way of living, and their own defective education, have been hardly in any class at all, but for their connexion with Uppercross; this eldest son of course excepted, who had chosen to be a scholar and a gentleman,[8] and who was very superior in cultivation and manners to all the rest.

The two families had always been on excellent terms, there being no pride on one side, and no envy on the other, and only such a consciousness of superiority in the Miss Musgroves, as made them pleased to improve their cousins.—Charles's attentions to Henrietta had been observed by her father and mother without any disapprobation. "It would not be a great match for her; but if Henrietta liked him,—and Henrietta *did* seem to like him."

Henrietta fully thought so herself, before Captain Wentworth came; but from that time Cousin Charles had been very much forgotten.

6. A light, two-wheeled, one-horse carriage.
7. A clergyman in the Church of England. The curacy he holds makes him assistant or deputy to a rector or vicar.
8. I.e., to go to university—at the time, Oxford or Cambridge.

Which of the two sisters was preferred by Captain Wentworth was as yet quite doubtful, as far as Anne's observation reached. Henrietta was perhaps the prettiest, Louisa had the higher spirits; and she knew not *now*, whether the more gentle or the more lively character were most likely to attract him.

Mr. and Mrs. Musgrove, either from seeing little, or from an entire confidence in the discretion of both their daughters, and of all the young men who came near them, seemed to leave every thing to take its chance. There was not the smallest appearance of solicitude or remark about them, in the Mansion-house; but it was different at the Cottage: the young couple there were more disposed to speculate and wonder; and Captain Wentworth had not been above four or five times in the Miss Musgroves' company, and Charles Hayter had but just reappeared, when Anne had to listen to the opinions of her brother and sister, as to *which* was the one liked best. Charles gave it for Louisa, Mary for Henrietta, but quite agreeing that to have him marry either would be extremely delightful.

Charles "had never seen a pleasanter man in his life; and from what he had once heard Captain Wentworth himself say, was very sure that he had not made less than twenty thousand pounds[9] by the war. Here was a fortune at once; besides which, there would be the chance of what might be done in any future war; and he was sure Captain Wentworth was as likely a man to distinguish himself as any officer in the navy. Oh! it would be a capital match for either of his sisters."

"Upon my word it would," replied Mary. "Dear me! If he should rise to any very great honours! If he should ever be made a Baronet! 'Lady Wentworth' sounds very well. That would be a noble thing, indeed, for Henrietta! She would take place[1] of me then, and Henrietta would not dislike that. Sir Frederick and Lady Wentworth! It would be but a new creation, however, and I never think much of your new creations."

It suited Mary best to think Henrietta the one preferred, on the very account of Charles Hayter, whose pretensions she wished to see put an end to. She looked down very decidedly upon the Hayters, and thought it would be quite a misfortune to have the existing connection between the families renewed—very sad for herself and her children.

"You know," said she, "I cannot think him at all a fit match for Henrietta; and considering the alliances which the Musgroves have made, she has no right to throw herself away. I do not think any young woman has a right to make a choice that may be disagreeable

9. According to the National Archives currency converter, this sum translates into approximately £1,150,000 in today's currency.
1. Rank higher in order of precedence.

and inconvenient to the *principal* part of her family, and be giving bad connections to those who have not been used to them. And, pray, who is Charles Hayter? Nothing but a country curate. A most improper match for Miss Musgrove, of Uppercross."

Her husband, however, would not agree with her here; for besides having a regard for his cousin, Charles Hayter was an eldest son, and he saw things as an eldest son himself.

"Now you are talking nonsense, Mary," was therefore his answer. "It would not be a *great* match for Henrietta, but Charles has a very fair chance, through the Spicers, of getting something from the Bishop in the course of a year or two; and you will please to remember, that he is the eldest son; whenever my uncle dies, he steps into very pretty property. The estate at Winthrop is not less than two hundred and fifty acres, besides the farm near Taunton, which is some of the best land in the country. I grant you, that any of them but Charles would be a very shocking match for Henrietta, and indeed it could not be; he is the only one that could be possible; but he is a very good-natured, good sort of a fellow; and whenever Winthrop comes into his hands, he will make a different sort of place of it, and live in a very different sort of way; and with that property, he will never be a contemptible man. Good, freehold property.[2] No, no; Henrietta might do worse than marry Charles Hayter; and if she has him, and Louisa can get Captain Wentworth, I shall be very well satisfied."

"Charles may say what he pleases," cried Mary to Anne, as soon as he was out of the room, "but it would be shocking to have Henrietta marry Charles Hayter; a very bad thing for *her*, and still worse for *me*; and therefore it is very much to be wished that Captain Wentworth may soon put him quite out of her head, and I have very little doubt that he has. She took hardly any notice of Charles Hayter yesterday. I wish you had been there to see her behaviour. And as to Captain Wentworth's liking Louisa as well as Henrietta, it is nonsense to say so; for he certainly *does* like Henrietta a great deal the best. But Charles is so positive! I wish you had been with us yesterday, for then you might have decided between us; and I am sure you would have thought as I did, unless you had been determined to give it against me."

A dinner at Mr. Musgrove's had been the occasion, when all these things should have been seen by Anne; but she had staid at home, under the mixed plea of a head-ache of her own, and some return of indisposition in little Charles. She had thought only of avoiding Captain Wentworth; but an escape from being appealed to as umpire, was now added to the advantages of a quiet evening.

2. Property held for life.

As to Captain Wentworth's views, she deemed it of more consequence that he should know his own mind, early enough not to be endangering the happiness of either sister, or impeaching his own honour, than that he should prefer Henrietta to Louisa, or Louisa to Henrietta. Either of them would, in all probability, make him an affectionate, good-humoured wife. With regard to Charles Hayter, she had delicacy which must be pained by any lightness of conduct in a well-meaning young woman, and a heart to sympathize in any of the sufferings it occasioned; but if Henrietta found herself mistaken in the nature of her feelings, the alteration could not be understood too soon.

Charles Hayter had met with much to disquiet and mortify him in his cousin's behaviour. She had too old a regard for him to be so wholly estranged, as might in two meetings extinguish every past hope, and leave him nothing to do but to keep away from Uppercross; but there was such a change as became very alarming, when such a man as Captain Wentworth was to be regarded as the probable cause. He had been absent only two Sundays; and when they parted, had left her interested even to the height of his wishes, in his prospect of soon quitting his present curacy, and obtaining that of Uppercross instead. It had then seemed the object nearest her heart, that Dr. Shirley, the rector, who for more than forty years had been zealously discharging all the duties of his office, but was now growing too infirm for many of them, should be quite fixed on engaging a curate; should make his curacy quite as good as he could afford, and should give Charles Hayter the promise of it. The advantage of his having to come only to Uppercross, instead of going six miles another way; of his having, in every respect, a better curacy; of his belonging to their dear Dr. Shirley, and of dear, good Dr. Shirley's being relieved from the duty which he could no longer get through without most injurious fatigue, had been a great deal, even to Louisa, but had been almost every thing to Henrietta. When he came back, alas! the zeal of the business was gone by. Louisa could not listen at all to his account of a conversation which he had just held with Dr. Shirley: she was at [the] window, looking out for Captain Wentworth; and even Henrietta had at best only a divided attention to give, and seemed to have forgotten all the former doubt and solicitude of the negociation.

"Well, I am very glad indeed, but I always thought you would have it; I always thought you sure. It did not appear to me that—In short, you know, Dr. Shirley *must* have a curate, and you had secured his promise. Is he coming, Louisa?"

One morning, very soon after the dinner at the Musgroves, at which Anne had not been present, Captain Wentworth walked into the drawing-room at the Cottage, where were only herself and the little invalid Charles, who was lying on the sofa.

The surprise of finding himself almost alone with Anne Elliot, deprived his manners of their usual composure: he started, and could only say, "I thought the Miss Musgroves had been here—Mrs. Musgrove told me I should find them here," before he walked to the window to recollect himself, and feel how he ought to behave.

"They are up stairs with my sister—they will be down in a few moments, I dare say,"—had been Anne's reply, in all the confusion that was natural; and if the child had not called her to come and do something for him, she would have been out of the room the next moment, and released Captain Wentworth as well as herself.

He continued at the window; and after calmly and politely saying, "I hope the little boy is better," was silent.

She was obliged to kneel down by the sofa, and remain there to satisfy her patient; and thus they continued a few minutes, when, to her very great satisfaction, she heard some other person crossing the little vestibule. She hoped, on turning her head, to see the master of the house; but it proved to be one much less calculated for making matters easy—Charles Hayter, probably not at all better pleased by the sight of Captain Wentworth, than Captain Wentworth had been by the sight of Anne.

She only attempted to say, "How do you do? Will not you sit down? The others will be here presently."

Captain Wentworth, however, came from his window, apparently not ill-disposed for conversation; but Charles Hayter soon put an end to his attempts, by seating himself near the table, and taking up the newspaper; and Captain Wentworth returned to his window.

Another minute brought another addition. The younger boy, a remarkably stout,[3] forward child, of two years old, having got the door opened for him by some one without, made his determined appearance among them, and went straight to the sofa to see what was going on, and put in his claim to any thing good that might be giving away.

There being nothing to be eat, he could only have some play; and as his aunt would not let him teaze his sick brother, he began to fasten himself upon her, as she knelt, in such a way that, busy as she was about Charles, she could not shake him off. She spoke to him— ordered, intreated, and insisted in vain. Once she did contrive to push him away, but the boy had the greater pleasure in getting upon her back again directly.

"Walter," said she, "get down this moment. You are extremely troublesome. I am very angry with you."

"Walter," cried Charles Hayter, "why do you not do as you are bid? Do not you hear your aunt speak? Come to me, Walter, come to cousin Charles."

3. According to Johnson's *Dictionary*, strong, bold, firm, but also obstinate, pertinacious.

But not a bit did Walter stir.

In another moment, however, she found herself in the state of being released from him; some one was taking him from her, though he had bent down her head so much, that his little sturdy hands were unfastened from around her neck, and he was resolutely borne away, before she knew that Captain Wentworth had done it.

Her sensations on the discovery made her perfectly speechless. She could not even thank him. She could only hang over little Charles, with most disordered feelings. His kindness in stepping forward to her relief—the manner—the silence in which it had passed—the little particulars of the circumstance—with the conviction soon forced on her by the noise he was studiously making with the child, that he meant to avoid hearing her thanks, and rather sought to testify that her conversation was the last of his wants, produced such a confusion of varying, but very painful agitation, as she could not recover from, till enabled by the entrance of Mary and the Miss Musgroves to make over her little patient to their cares, and leave the room. She could not stay. It might have been an opportunity of watching the loves and jealousies of the four; they were now all together, but she could stay for none of it. It was evident that Charles Hayter was not well inclined towards Captain Wentworth. She had a strong impression of his having said, in a vext tone of voice, after Captain Wentworth's interference, "You ought to have minded *me*, Walter; I told you not to teaze your aunt;" and could comprehend his regretting that Captain Wentworth should do what he ought to have done himself. But neither Charles Hayter's feelings, nor any body's feelings, could interest her, till she had a little better arranged her own. She was ashamed of herself, quite ashamed of being so nervous, so overcome by such a trifle; but so it was; and it required a long application of solitude and reflection to recover her.

Chapter X

Other opportunities of making her observations could not fail to occur. Anne had soon been in company with all the four together often enough to have an opinion, though too wise to acknowledge as much at home, where she knew it would have satisfied neither husband nor wife; for while she considered Louisa to be rather the favourite, she could not but think, as far as she might dare to judge from memory and experience, that Captain Wentworth was not in love with either. They were more in love with him; yet there it was not love. It was a little fever of admiration; but it might, probably must, end in love with some. Charles Hayter seemed aware of being slighted, and yet Henrietta had sometimes the air of being divided between them. Anne longed for the power of representing to them all what they were about, and of pointing out some of the evils they were exposing themselves to. She did not attribute guile to any. It was the highest satisfaction to her, to believe Captain Wentworth not in the least aware of the pain he was occasioning. There was no triumph, no pitiful triumph in his manner. He had, probably, never heard, and never thought of any claims of Charles Hayter. He was only wrong in accepting the attentions—(for accepting must be the word) of two young women at once.

After a short struggle, however, Charles Hayter seemed to quit the field. Three days had passed without his coming once to Uppercross; a most decided change. He had even refused one regular invitation to dinner; and having been found on the occasion by Mr. Musgrove with some large books before him, Mr. and Mrs. Musgrove were sure all could not be right, and talked, with grave faces, of his studying himself to death. It was Mary's hope and belief, that he had received a positive dismissal from Henrietta, and her husband lived under the constant dependance of seeing him to-morrow. Anne could only feel that Charles Hayter was wise.

One morning, about this time, Charles Musgrove and Captain Wentworth being gone a shooting together, as the sisters in the cottage were sitting quietly at work, they were visited at the window by the sisters from the mansion-house.

It was a very fine November day, and the Miss Musgroves came through the little grounds, and stopped for no other purpose than to say, that they were going to take a *long* walk, and, therefore, concluded Mary could not like to go with them; and when Mary immediately replied, with some jealousy, at not being supposed a good walker, "Oh, yes, I should like to join you very much, I am very fond of a long walk," Anne felt persuaded, by the looks of the two girls, that it was precisely what they did not wish, and admired[4] again the sort of necessity which the family-habits seemed to produce, of every thing being to be communicated, and every thing being to be done together, however undesired and inconvenient. She tried to dissuade Mary from going, but in vain; and that being the case, thought it best to accept the Miss Musgroves' much more cordial invitation to herself to go likewise, as she might be useful in turning back with her sister, and lessening the interference in any plan of their own.

"I cannot imagine why they should suppose I should not like a long walk!" said Mary, as she went up stairs. "Every body is always supposing that I am not a good walker! And yet they would not have been pleased, if we had refused to join them. When people come in this manner on purpose to ask us, how can one say no?"

4. Wondered at.

Just as they were setting off, the gentlemen returned. They had taken out a young dog, who had spoilt their sport, and sent them back early. Their time and strength, and spirits, were, therefore, exactly ready for this walk, and they entered into it with pleasure. Could Anne have foreseen such a junction, she would have staid at home; but, from some feelings of interest and curiosity, she fancied now that it was too late to retract, and the whole six set forward together in the direction chosen by the Miss Musgroves, who evidently considered the walk as under their guidance.

Anne's object was, not to be in the way of any body, and where the narrow paths across the fields made many separations necessary, to keep with her brother and sister. Her *pleasure* in the walk must arise from the exercise and the day, from the view of the last smiles of the year upon the tawny leaves and withered hedges, and from repeating to herself some few of the thousand poetical descriptions extant of autumn, that season of peculiar and inexhaustible influence on the mind of taste and tenderness, that season which has drawn from every poet, worthy of being read, some attempt at description, or some lines of feeling. She occupied her mind as much as possible in such like musings and quotations; but it was not possible, that when within reach of Captain Wentworth's conversation with either of the Miss Musgroves, she should not try to hear it; yet she caught little very remarkable. It was mere lively chat,—such as any young persons, on an intimate footing, might fall into. He was more engaged with Louisa than with Henrietta. Louisa certainly put more forward for his notice than her sister. This distinction appeared to increase, and there was one speech of Louisa's which struck her. After one of the many praises of the day, which were continually bursting forth, Captain Wentworth added,

"What glorious weather for the Admiral and my sister! They meant to take a long drive this morning; perhaps we may hail them from some of these hills. They talked of coming into this side of the country. I wonder whereabouts they will upset to-day. Oh! it does happen very often, I assure you—but my sister makes nothing of it—she would as lieve[5] be tossed out as not."

"Ah! You make the most of it, I know," cried Louisa, "but if it were really so, I should do just the same in her place. If I loved a man, as she loves the Admiral, I would be always with him, nothing should ever separate us, and I would rather be overturned by him, than driven safely by anybody else."

It was spoken with enthusiasm.

"Had you?" cried he, catching the same tone; "I honour you!" And there was silence between them for a little while.

5. Willingly.

Anne could not immediately fall into a quotation again. The sweet scenes of autumn were for a while put by—unless some tender sonnet, fraught with the apt analogy of the declining year, with declining happiness, and the images of youth and hope, and spring, all gone together, blessed her memory. She roused herself to say, as they struck by order into another path, "Is not this one of the ways to Winthrop?" But nobody heard, or, at least, nobody answered her.

Winthrop, however, or its environs—for young men are, sometimes, to be met with, strolling about near home, was their destination; and after another half mile of gradual ascent through large enclosures, where the ploughs at work, and the fresh-made path spoke the farmer, counteracting the sweets of poetical despondence, and meaning to have spring again, they gained the summit of the most considerable hill, which parted Uppercross and Winthrop, and soon commanded a full view of the latter, at the foot of the hill on the other side.

Winthrop, without beauty and without dignity, was stretched before them; an indifferent house, standing low, and hemmed in by the barns and buildings of a farm-yard.

Mary exclaimed, "Bless me! here is Winthrop—I declare I had no idea!—well, now I think we had better turn back; I am excessively tired."

Henrietta, conscious[6] and ashamed, and seeing no cousin Charles walking along any path, or leaning against any gate, was ready to do as Mary wished; but "No," said Charles Musgrove, and "No, no," cried Louisa more eagerly, and taking her sister aside, seemed to be arguing the matter warmly.

Charles, in the meanwhile, was very decidedly declaring his resolution of calling on his aunt, now that he was so near; and very evidently, though more fearfully, trying to induce his wife to go too. But this was one of the points on which the lady shewed her strength, and when he recommended the advantage of resting herself a quarter of an hour at Winthrop, as she felt so tired, she resolutely answered, "Oh! no, indeed!—walking up that hill again would do her more harm than any sitting down could do her good;"—and, in short, her look and manner declared, that go she would not.

After a little succession of these sort of debates and consultations, it was settled between Charles and his two sisters, that he, and Henrietta, should just run down for a few minutes, to see their aunt and cousins, while the rest of the party waited for them at the top of the hill. Louisa seemed the principal arranger of the plan; and, as she went a little way with them, down the hill, still talking to

---

6. Embarrassed on the basis of secret awareness of something.

Henrietta, Mary took the opportunity of looking scornfully around her, and saying to Captain Wentworth,

"It is very unpleasant, having such connexions! But I assure you, I have never been in the house above twice in my life."

She received no other answer, than an artificial, assenting smile, followed by a contemptuous glance, as he turned away, which Anne perfectly knew the meaning of.

The brow of the hill, where they remained, was a cheerful spot; Louisa returned, and Mary finding a comfortable seat for herself, on the step of a stile,[7] was very well satisfied so long as the others all stood about her; but when Louisa drew Captain Wentworth away, to try for a gleaning of nuts in an adjoining hedge-row,[8] and they were gone by degrees quite out of sight and sound, Mary was happy no longer; she quarrelled with her own seat,—was sure Louisa had got a much better somewhere,—and nothing could prevent her from going to look for a better also. She turned through the same gate,—but could not see them.—Anne found a nice seat for her, on a dry sunny bank, under the hedge-row, in which she had no doubt of their still being—in some spot or other. Mary sat down for a moment, but it would not do; she was sure Louisa had found a better seat somewhere else, and she would go on, till she overtook her.

Anne, really tired herself, was glad to sit down; and she very soon heard Captain Wentworth and Louisa in the hedge-row, behind her, as if making their way back, along the rough, wild sort of channel, down the centre. They were speaking as they drew near. Louisa's voice was the first distinguished. She seemed to be in the middle of some eager speech. What Anne first heard was,

"And so, I made her go. I could not bear that she should be frightened from the visit by such nonsense. What!—would I be turned back from doing a thing that I had determined to do, and that I knew to be right, by the airs and interference of such a person?—or, of any person I may say. No,—I have no idea of being so easily persuaded. When I have made up my mind, I have made it. And Henrietta seemed entirely to have made up hers to call at Winthrop to-day—and yet, she was as near giving it up, out of nonsensical complaisance!"

"She would have turned back then, but for you?"

"She would indeed. I am almost ashamed to say it."

"Happy for her, to have such a mind as yours at hand!—After the hints you gave just now, which did but confirm my own observations, the last time I was in company with him, I need not affect to have no comprehension of what is going on. I see that more than a mere

---

7. A set of steps between enclosures.
8. Trees or bushes planted along edges of enclosures.

dutiful morning-visit to your aunt was in question;—and woe betide him, and her too, when it comes to things of consequence, when they are placed in circumstances, requiring fortitude and strength of mind, if she have not resolution enough to resist idle interference in such a trifle as this. Your sister is an amiable creature; but *yours* is the character of decision and firmness, I see. If you value her conduct or happiness, infuse as much of your own spirit into her, as you can. But this, no doubt, you have been always doing. It is the worst evil of too yielding and indecisive a character, that no influence over it can be depended on.—You are never sure of a good impression being durable. Every body may sway it; let those who would be happy be firm.—Here is a nut," said he, catching one down from an upper bough. "To exemplify,—a beautiful glossy nut, which, blessed with original strength, has outlived all the storms of autumn. Not a puncture, not a weak spot any where.—This nut," he continued, with playful solemnity,—"while so many of its brethren have fallen and been trodden under foot, is still in possession of all the happiness that a hazel-nut can be supposed capable of." Then, returning to his former earnest tone: "My first wish for all, whom I am interested in, is that they should be firm. If Louisa Musgrove would be beautiful and happy in her November of life, she will cherish all her present powers of mind."

He had done,—and was unanswered. It would have surprised Anne, if Louisa could have readily answered such a speech—words of such interest, spoken with such serious warmth!—she could imagine what Louisa was feeling. For herself—she feared to move, lest she should be seen. While she remained, a bush of low rambling holly protected her, and they were moving on. Before they were beyond her hearing, however, Louisa spoke again.

"Mary is good-natured enough in many respects," said she; "but she does sometimes provoke me excessively, by her nonsense and her pride; the Elliot pride. She has a great deal too much of the Elliot pride.—We do so wish that Charles had married Anne instead.—I suppose you know he wanted to marry Anne?"

After a moment's pause, Captain Wentworth said,

"Do you mean that she refused him?"

"Oh! yes, certainly."

"When did that happen?"

"I do not exactly know, for Henrietta and I were at school at the time; but I believe about a year before he married Mary. I wish she had accepted him. We should all have liked her a great deal better; and papa and mamma always think it was her great friend Lady Russell's doing, that she did not.—They think Charles might not be learned and bookish enough to please Lady Russell, and that therefore, she persuaded Anne to refuse him."

The sounds were retreating, and Anne distinguished no more. Her own emotions still kept her fixed. She had much to recover from, before she could move. The listener's proverbial fate was not absolutely hers; she had heard no evil of herself,—but she had heard a great deal of very painful import. She saw how her own character was considered by Captain Wentworth; and there had been just that degree of feeling and curiosity about her in his manner, which must give her extreme agitation.

As soon as she could, she went after Mary, and having found, and walked back with her to their former station, by the stile, felt some comfort in their whole party being immediately afterwards collected, and once more in motion together. Her spirits wanted the solitude and silence which only numbers could give.

Charles and Henrietta returned, bringing, as may be conjectured, Charles Hayter with them. The minutiæ of the business Anne could not attempt to understand; even Captain Wentworth did not seem admitted to perfect confidence here; but that there had been a withdrawing on the gentleman's side, and a relenting on the lady's, and that they were now very glad to be together again, did not admit a doubt. Henrietta looked a little ashamed, but very well pleased;—Charles Hayter exceedingly happy, and they were devoted to each other almost from the first instant of their all setting forward for Uppercross.

Every thing now marked out Louisa for Captain Wentworth; nothing could be plainer; and where many divisions were necessary, or even where they were not, they walked side by side, nearly as much as the other two. In a long strip of meadow-land, where there was ample space for all, they were thus divided—forming three distinct parties; and to that party of the three which boasted least animation, and least complaisance, Anne necessarily belonged. She joined Charles and Mary, and was tired enough to be very glad of Charles's other arm;—but Charles, though in very good humour with her, was out of temper with his wife. Mary had shewn herself disobliging to him, and was now to reap the consequence, which consequence was his dropping her arm almost every moment, to cut off the heads of some nettles in the hedge with his switch;[9] and when Mary began to complain of it, and lament her being ill-used, according to custom, in being on the hedge side, while Anne was never incommoded on the other, he dropped the arms of both to hunt after a weasel which he had a momentary glance of; and they could hardly get him along at all.

This long meadow bordered a lane, which their footpath, at the end of it, was to cross; and when the party had all reached the gate

9. A slender, tapering riding whip.

of exit, the carriage advancing in the same direction, which had been some time heard, was just coming up, and proved to be Admiral Croft's gig.—He and his wife had taken their intended drive, and were returning home. Upon hearing how long a walk the young people had engaged in, they kindly offered a seat to any lady who might be particularly tired; it would save her full a mile, and they were going through Uppercross. The invitation was general, and generally declined. The Miss Musgroves were not at all tired, and Mary was either offended, by not being asked before any of the others, or what Louisa called the Elliot pride could not endure to make a third in a one horse chaise.

The walking-party had crossed the lane, and were surmounting an opposite stile; and the admiral was putting his horse into motion again, when Captain Wentworth cleared the hedge in a moment to say something to his sister.—The something might be guessed by its effects.

"Miss Elliot, I am sure *you* are tired," cried Mrs. Croft. "Do let us have the pleasure of taking you home. Here is excellent room for three, I assure you. If we were all like you, I believe we might sit four.—You must, indeed, you must."

Anne was still in the lane; and though instinctively beginning to decline, she was not allowed to proceed. The admiral's kind urgency came in support of his wife's; they would not be refused; they compressed themselves into the smallest possible space to leave her a corner, and Captain Wentworth, without saying a word, turned to her, and quietly obliged her to be assisted into the carriage.

Yes,—he had done it. She was in the carriage, and felt that he had placed her there, that his will and his hands had done it, that she owed it to his perception of her fatigue, and his resolution to give her rest. She was very much affected by the view of his disposition towards her which all these things made apparent. This little circumstance seemed the completion of all that had gone before. She understood him. He could not forgive her,—but he could not be unfeeling. Though condemning her for the past, and considering it with high and unjust resentment, though perfectly careless of[1] her, and though becoming attached to another, still he could not see her suffer, without the desire of giving her relief. It was a remainder of former sentiment; it was an impulse of pure, though unacknowledged friendship; it was a proof of his own warm and amiable heart, which she could not contemplate without emotions so compounded of pleasure and pain, that she knew not which prevailed.

Her answers to the kindness and the remarks of her companions were at first unconsciously given. They had travelled half their way

1. Not caring for.

along the rough lane, before she was quite awake to what they said. She then found them talking of "Frederick."

"He certainly means to have one or other of those two girls, Sophy," said the admiral;—"but there is no saying which. He has been running after them, too, long enough, one would think, to make up his mind. Ay, this comes of the peace. If it were war, now, he would have settled it long ago.—We sailors, Miss Elliot, cannot afford to make long courtships in time of war. How many days was it, my dear, between the first time of my seeing you, and our sitting down together in our lodgings at North Yarmouth?"[2]

"We had better not talk about it, my dear," replied Mrs. Croft, pleasantly; "for if Miss Elliot were to hear how soon we came to an understanding, she would never be persuaded that we could be happy together. I had known you by character, however, long before."

"Well, and I had heard of you as a very pretty girl; and what were we to wait for besides?—I do not like having such things so long in hand. I wish Frederick would spread a little more canvas,[3] and bring us home one of these young ladies to Kellynch. Then, there would always be company for them.—And very nice young ladies they both are; I hardly know one from the other."

"Very good humoured, unaffected girls, indeed," said Mrs. Croft, in a tone of calmer praise, such as made Anne suspect that her keener powers might not consider either of them as quite worthy of her brother; "and a very respectable family. One could not be connected with better people.—My dear admiral, that post!—we shall certainly take that post."

But by coolly giving the reins a better direction herself, they happily passed the danger; and by once afterwards judiciously putting out her hand, they neither fell into a rut, nor ran foul of a dungcart;[4] and Anne, with some amusement at their style of driving, which she imagined no bad representation of the general guidance of their affairs, found herself safely deposited by them at the cottage.

Chapter XI

The time now approached for Lady Russell's return; the day was even fixed, and Anne, being engaged to join her as soon as she was resettled, was looking forward to an early removal to Kellynch, and beginning to think how her own comfort was likely to be affected by it.

It would place her in the same village with Captain Wentworth, within half a mile of him; they would have to frequent the same

2. Seaside town in Norfolk, and an important naval supply base.
3. Put up more or bigger sails, move faster.
4. For carting animal manure.

church, and there must be intercourse between the two families. This was against her; but, on the other hand, he spent so much of his time at Uppercross, that in removing thence she might be considered rather as leaving him behind, than as going towards him; and, upon the whole, she believed she must, on this interesting question, be the gainer, almost as certainly as in her change of domestic society, in leaving poor Mary for Lady Russell.

She wished it might be possible for her to avoid ever seeing Captain Wentworth at the hall;—those rooms had witnessed former meetings which would be brought too painfully before her; but she was yet more anxious for the possibility of Lady Russell and Captain Wentworth never meeting any where. They did not like each other, and no renewal of acquaintance now could do any good; and were Lady Russell to see them together, she might think that he had too much self-possession, and she too little.

These points formed her chief solicitude in anticipating her removal from Uppercross, where she felt she had been stationed quite long enough. Her usefulness to little Charles would always give some sweetness to the memory of her two months visit there, but he was gaining strength apace, and she had nothing else to stay for.

The conclusion of her visit, however, was diversified in a way which she had not at all imagined. Captain Wentworth, after being unseen and unheard of at Uppercross for two whole days, appeared again among them to justify himself by a relation of what had kept him away.

A letter from his friend, Captain Harville, having found him out at last, had brought intelligence of Captain Harville's being settled with his family at Lyme[5] for the winter; of their being, therefore, quite unknowingly, within twenty miles of each other. Captain Harville had never been in good health since a severe wound which he received two years before, and Captain Wentworth's anxiety to see him had determined him to go immediately to Lyme. He had been there for four-and-twenty hours. His acquittal was complete, his friendship warmly honoured, a lively interest excited for his friend, and his description of the fine country about Lyme so feelingly attended to by the party, that an earnest desire to see Lyme themselves, and a project for going thither was the consequence.

The young people were all wild to see Lyme. Captain Wentworth talked of going there again himself; it was only seventeen miles from Uppercross; though November, the weather was by no means bad; and, in short, Louisa, who was the most eager of the eager, having formed the resolution to go, and besides the pleasure of doing as she

5. Lyme Regis, the "Pearl of Dorset," known for its shipbuilding, busy port, and artificial harbor, the latter created by a stone breakwater known as the Cobb.

liked, being now armed with the idea of merit in maintaining her own way, bore down all the wishes of her father and mother for putting it off till summer; and to Lyme they were to go—Charles, Mary, Anne, Henrietta, Louisa, and Captain Wentworth.

The first heedless scheme had been to go in the morning and return at night, but to this Mr. Musgrove, for the sake of his horses, would not consent; and when it came to be rationally considered, a day in the middle of November would not leave much time for seeing a new place, after deducting seven hours, as the nature of the country required, for going and returning. They were consequently to stay the night there, and not to be expected back till the next day's dinner. This was felt to be a considerable amendment; and though they all met at the Great House at rather an early breakfast hour, and set off very punctually, it was so much past noon before the two carriages, Mr. Musgrove's coach containing the four ladies, and Charles's curricle,[6] in which he drove Captain Wentworth, were descending the long hill into Lyme, and entering upon the still steeper street of the town itself, that it was very evident they would not have more than time for looking about them, before the light and warmth of the day were gone.

After securing accommodations, and ordering a dinner at one of the inns, the next thing to be done was unquestionably to walk directly down to the sea. They were come too late in the year for any amusement or variety which Lyme, as a public place, might offer; the rooms[7] were shut up, the lodgers almost all gone, scarcely any family but of the residents left—and, as there is nothing to admire in the buildings themselves, the remarkable situation of the town, the principal street almost hurrying into the water, the walk to the Cobb, skirting round the pleasant little bay, which in the season is animated with bathing machines[8] and company, the Cobb itself, its old wonders and new improvements, with the very beautiful line of cliffs stretching out to the east of the town, are what the stranger's eye will seek; and a very strange stranger it must be, who does not see charms in the immediate environs of Lyme, to make him wish to know it better. The scenes in its neighbourhood, Charmouth, with its high grounds and extensive sweeps of country, and still more its sweet retired bay, backed by dark cliffs, where fragments of low rock among the sands make it the happiest spot for watching the

6. A small, two-wheeled carriage, drawn by two horses abreast. A curricle is more elegant than the gig the Crofts drive.
7. The public assembly rooms.
8. Essentially a cart with a roof and walls, bathing machines were popular in the 18th and 19th centuries, allowing users to wade in the ocean without being seen from the shore in their bathing costumes. Entering the machine in street clothes, the bather (usually a woman) would be wheeled into the sea, changing into her bathing costume inside and then walking down steps into the water, protected from view.

flow of the tide, for sitting in unwearied contemplation;—the woody varieties of the cheerful village of Up Lyme, and, above all, Pinny, with its green chasms between romantic rocks, where the scattered forest trees and orchards of luxuriant growth declare that many a generation must have passed away since the first partial falling of the cliff prepared the ground for such a state, where a scene so wonderful and so lovely is exhibited, as may more than equal any of the resembling scenes of the far-famed Isle of Wight: these places[9] must be visited, and visited again, to make the worth of Lyme understood.

The party from Uppercross passing down by the now deserted and melancholy looking rooms, and still descending, soon found themselves on the sea shore, and lingering only, as all must linger and gaze on a first return to the sea, who ever deserve to look on it at all, proceeded towards the Cobb, equally their object in itself and on Captain Wentworth's account; for in a small house, near the foot of an old pier of unknown date, were the Harvilles settled. Captain Wentworth turned in to call on his friend; the others walked on, and he was to join them on the Cobb.

They were by no means tired of wondering and admiring; and not even Louisa seemed to feel that they had parted with Captain Wentworth long, when they saw him coming after them, with three companions, all well known already by description to be Captain and Mrs. Harville, and a Captain Benwick, who was staying with them.

Captain Benwick had some time ago been first lieutenant of the Laconia; and the account which Captain Wentworth had given of him, on his return from Lyme before; his warm praise of him as an excellent young man and an officer, whom he had always valued highly, which must have stamped him well in the esteem of every listener, had been followed by a little history of his private life, which rendered him perfectly interesting in the eyes of all the ladies. He had been engaged to Captain Harville's sister, and was now mourning her loss. They had been a year or two waiting for fortune and promotion. Fortune came, his prize-money as lieutenant being great,—promotion, too, came at *last*; but Fanny Harville did not live to know it. She had died the preceding summer, while he was at sea. Captain Wentworth believed it impossible for man to be more attached to woman than poor Benwick had been to Fanny Harville, or to be more deeply afflicted under the dreadful change. He considered his disposition as of the sort which must suffer heavily, uniting very strong feelings with quiet, serious, and retiring manners,

9. Austen compares less celebrated local environs in and near Dorset (Charmouth, Up Lyme, and Pinney) with the renowned Isle of Wight, a fashionable destination located in the English Channel and the site where King Charles I was held captive for over a year before being executed in 1649.

and a decided taste for reading, and sedentary pursuits. To finish the interest of the story, the friendship between him and the Harvilles seemed, if possible, augmented by the event which closed all their views of alliance, and Captain Benwick was now living with them entirely. Captain Harville had taken his present house for half a year, his taste, and his health, and his fortune all directing him to a residence unexpensive, and by the sea; and the grandeur of the country, and the retirement of Lyme in the winter, appeared exactly adapted to Captain Benwick's state of mind. The sympathy and good-will excited towards Captain Benwick was very great.

"And yet," said Anne to herself, as they now moved forward to meet the party, "he has not, perhaps, a more sorrowing heart than I have. I cannot believe his prospects so blighted for ever. He is younger than I am; younger in feeling, if not in fact; younger as a man. He will rally again, and be happy with another."

They all met, and were introduced. Captain Harville was a tall, dark man, with a sensible, benevolent countenance; a little lame; and from strong features, and want of health, looking much older than Captain Wentworth. Captain Benwick looked and was the youngest of the three, and, compared with either of them, a little man. He had a pleasing face and a melancholy air, just as he ought to have, and drew back from conversation.

Captain Harville, though not equalling Captain Wentworth in manners, was a perfect gentleman, unaffected, warm, and obliging. Mrs. Harville, a degree less polished than her husband, seemed however to have the same good feelings; and nothing could be more pleasant than their desire of considering the whole party as friends of their own, because the friends of Captain Wentworth, or more kindly hospitable than their entreaties for their all promising to dine with them. The dinner, already ordered at the inn, was at last, though unwillingly, accepted as an excuse; but they seemed almost hurt that Captain Wentworth should have brought any such party to Lyme, without considering it as a thing of course that they should dine with them.

There was so much attachment to Captain Wentworth in all this, and such a bewitching charm in a degree of hospitality so uncommon, so unlike the usual style of give-and-take invitations, and dinners of formality and display, that Anne felt her spirits not likely to be benefited by an increasing acquaintance among his brother-officers. "These would have been all my friends," was her thought; and she had to struggle against a great tendency to lowness.[1]

On quitting the Cobb, they all went indoors with their new friends, and found rooms so small as none but those who invite from the heart could think capable of accommodating so many. Anne had a

1. Depression, lowness of spirits.

moment's astonishment on the subject herself; but it was soon lost in the pleasanter feelings which sprang from the sight of all the ingenious contrivances and nice arrangements of Captain Harville, to turn the actual space to the best possible account, to supply the deficiencies of lodging-house furniture, and defend the windows and doors against the winter storms to be expected. The varieties in the fitting-up of the rooms, where the common necessaries provided by the owner, in the common indifferent plight,[2] were contrasted with some few articles of a rare species of wood, excellently worked up, and with something curious and valuable from all the distant countries Captain Harville had visited, were more than amusing[3] to Anne: connected as it all was with his profession, the fruit of its labours, the effect of its influence on his habits, the picture of repose and domestic happiness it presented, made it to her a something more, or less, than gratification.

Captain Harville was no reader; but he had contrived excellent accommodations, and fashioned very pretty shelves, for a tolerable collection of well-bound volumes, the property of Captain Benwick. His lameness prevented him from taking much exercise; but a mind of usefulness and ingenuity seemed to furnish him with constant employment within. He drew, he varnished, he carpentered, he glued; he made toys for the children, he fashioned new netting-needles and pins[4] with improvements; and if every thing else was done, sat down to his large fishing-net at one corner of the room.

Anne thought she left great happiness behind her when they quitted the house; and Louisa, by whom she found herself walking, burst forth into raptures of admiration and delight on the character of the navy—their friendliness, their brotherliness, their openness, their uprightness; protesting that she was convinced of sailors having more worth and warmth than any other set of men in England; that they only knew how to live, and they only deserved to be respected and loved.

They went back to dress and dine; and so well had the scheme answered[5] already, that nothing was found amiss; though its being "so entirely out of the season," and the "no-thorough-fare of Lyme," and the "no expectation of company," had brought many apologies from the heads of the inn.

---

2. Austen contrasts the worn furnishings of rented lodgings, indiscriminately used by all previous tenants, with the carved wood and other personal items belonging to Harville and reflecting his naval experience and travels.
3. Interesting, entertaining.
4. Implements employed in the making of netting. While it was acceptable for men like Harville to occupy themselves at home with netting used for stowage aboard ships, the reference to needles and pins also implies female craftwork and apparel items such as the netted purses or reticules popular at the time.
5. Suited.

Anne found herself by this time growing so much more hardened to being in Captain Wentworth's company than she had at first imagined could ever be, that the sitting down to the same table with him now, and the interchange of the common civilities attending on it—(they never got beyond) was become a mere nothing.

The nights were too dark for the ladies to meet again till the morrow, but Captain Harville had promised them a visit in the evening; and he came, bringing his friend also, which was more than had been expected, it having been agreed that Captain Benwick had all the appearance of being oppressed by the presence of so many strangers. He ventured among them again, however, though his spirits certainly did not seem fit for the mirth of the party in general.

While Captains Wentworth and Harville led the talk on one side of the room, and, by recurring to former days, supplied anecdotes in abundance to occupy and entertain the others, it fell to Anne's lot to be placed rather apart with Captain Benwick; and a very good impulse of her nature obliged her to begin an acquaintance with him. He was shy, and disposed to abstraction; but the engaging mildness of her countenance, and gentleness of her manners, soon had their effect; and Anne was well repaid the first trouble of exertion. He was evidently a young man of considerable taste in reading, though principally in poetry; and besides the persuasion of having given him at least an evening's indulgence in the discussion of subjects, which his usual companions had probably no concern in, she had the hope of being of real use to him in some suggestions as to the duty and benefit of struggling against affliction, which had naturally grown out of their conversation. For, though shy, he did not seem reserved; it had rather the appearance of feelings glad to burst their usual restraints; and having talked of poetry, the richness of the present age, and gone through a brief comparison of opinion as to the first-rate poets, trying to ascertain whether *Marmion* or *The Lady of the Lake* were to be preferred, and how ranked the *Giaour* and *The Bride of Abydos*;[6] and moreover, how the *Giaour* was to be pronounced, he shewed himself so intimately acquainted with all the tenderest songs of the one poet, and all the impassioned descriptions of hopeless agony of the other; he repeated, with such tremulous feeling, the various lines which imaged a broken heart, or a mind destroyed by wretchedness, and looked so entirely as if he meant to be understood, that she ventured to hope he did not always read only poetry; and to say, that she thought it was the misfortune of poetry, to be seldom safely enjoyed by those who enjoyed it completely; and

6. Titles of Romantic poems by Sir Walter Scott (1771–1832) and George Gordon, Lord Byron (1788–1824). Benwick's interests reflect topical knowledge of recent debates as to which of these poems—and poets—of love, revenge, and heroism was superior.

that the strong feelings which alone could estimate it truly, were the very feelings which ought to taste it but sparingly.

His looks shewing him not pained, but pleased with this allusion to his situation, she was emboldened to go on; and feeling in herself the right of seniority of mind, she ventured to recommend a larger allowance of prose in his daily study; and on being requested to particularize, mentioned such works of our best moralists, such collections of the finest letters, such memoirs of characters of worth and suffering, as occurred to her at the moment as calculated to rouse and fortify the mind by the highest precepts, and the strongest examples of moral and religious endurances.

Captain Benwick listened attentively, and seemed grateful for the interest implied; and though with a shake of the head, and sighs which declared his little faith in the efficacy of any books on grief like his, noted down the names of those she recommended, and promised to procure and read them.

When the evening was over, Anne could not but be amused at the idea of her coming to Lyme, to preach patience and resignation to a young man whom she had never seen before; nor could she help fearing, on more serious reflection, that, like many other great moralists and preachers, she had been eloquent on a point in which her own conduct would ill bear examination.

Chapter XII

Anne and Henrietta, finding themselves the earliest of the party the next morning, agreed to stroll down to the sea before breakfast.— They went to the sands, to watch the flowing of the tide, which a fine south-easterly breeze was bringing in with all the grandeur which so flat a shore admitted. They praised the morning; gloried in the sea; sympathized in the delight of the fresh-feeling breeze— and were silent; till Henrietta suddenly began again, with—

"Oh! yes,—I am quite convinced that, with very few exceptions, the sea-air always does good. There can be no doubt of its having been of the greatest service to Dr. Shirley, after his illness, last spring twelve-month.[7] He declares himself, that coming to Lyme for a month, did him more good than all the medicine he took; and, that being by the sea, always makes him feel young again. Now, I cannot help thinking it a pity that he does not live entirely by the sea. I do think he had better leave Uppercross entirely, and fix[8] at Lyme.—Do not you, Anne?—Do not you agree with me, that it is the best thing

7. A year ago last spring.
8. Settle.

he could do, both for himself and Mrs. Shirley?—She has cousins here, you know, and many acquaintance, which would make it cheerful for her,—and I am sure she would be glad to get to a place where she could have medical attendance at hand, in case of his having another seizure. Indeed I think it quite melancholy to have such excellent people as Dr. and Mrs. Shirley, who have been doing good all their lives, wearing out their last days in a place like Uppercross, where, excepting our family, they seem shut out from all the world. I wish his friends would propose it to him. I really think they ought. And, as to procuring a dispensation,[9] there could be no difficulty at his time of life, and with his character. My only doubt is, whether any thing could persuade him to leave his parish. He is so very strict and scrupulous in his notions; over-scrupulous, I must say. Do not you think, Anne, it is being over-scrupulous? Do not you think it is quite a mistaken point of conscience, when a clergyman sacrifices his health for the sake of duties, which may be just as well performed by another person?—And at Lyme too,—only seventeen miles off,—he would be near enough to hear, if people thought there was any thing to complain of."

Anne smiled more than once to herself during this speech, and entered into the subject, as ready to do good by entering into the feelings of a young lady as of a young man,—though here it was good of a lower standard, for what could be offered but general acquiescence?—She said all that was reasonable and proper on the business; felt the claims of Dr. Shirley to repose, as she ought; saw how very desirable it was that he should have some active, respectable young man, as a resident curate, and was even courteous enough to hint at the advantage of such resident curate's being married.

"I wish," said Henrietta, very well pleased with her companion, "I wish Lady Russell lived at Uppercross, and were intimate with Dr. Shirley. I have always heard of Lady Russell, as a woman of the greatest influence with every body! I always look upon her as able to persuade a person to any thing! I am afraid of her, as I have told you before, quite afraid of her, because she is so very clever; but I respect her amazingly, and wish we had such a neighbour at Uppercross."

Anne was amused by Henrietta's manner of being grateful, and amused also, that the course of events and the new interests of Henrietta's views should have placed her friend at all in favour with any of the Musgrove family; she had only time, however, for a general answer, and a wish that such another woman were at Uppercross, before all subjects suddenly ceased, on seeing Louisa and Captain Wentworth coming towards them. They came also for a

---

9. Dr. Shirley would need special permission from the church to be an absentee vicar—to draw the income of his post while having Charles Hayter do the actual work.

stroll till breakfast was likely to be ready; but Louisa recollecting, immediately afterwards, that she had something to procure at a shop, invited them all to go back with her into the town. They were all at her disposal.

When they came to the steps, leading upwards from the beach, a gentleman at the same moment preparing to come down, politely drew back, and stopped to give them way. They ascended and passed him; and as they passed, Anne's face caught his eye, and he looked at her with a degree of earnest admiration, which she could not be insensible of. She was looking remarkably well; her very regular, very pretty features, having the bloom and freshness of youth restored by the fine wind which had been blowing on her complexion, and by the animation of eye which it had also produced. It was evident that the gentleman, (completely a gentleman in manner) admired her exceedingly. Captain Wentworth looked round at her instantly in a way which shewed his noticing of it. He gave her a momentary glance,—a glance of brightness, which seemed to say, "That man is struck with you,—and even I, at this moment, see something like Anne Elliot again."

After attending Louisa through her business, and loitering about a little longer, they returned to the inn; and Anne in passing after-wards quickly from her own chamber to their dining-room, had nearly run against the very same gentleman, as he came out of an adjoining apartment. She had before conjectured him to be a stranger like themselves, and determined that a well-looking groom, who was strolling about near the two inns as they came back, should be his servant. Both master and man being in mourning, assisted the idea. It was now proved that he belonged to the same inn as themselves; and this second meeting, short as it was, also proved again by the gentleman's looks, that he thought hers very lovely, and by the readiness and propriety of his apologies, that he was a man of exceedingly good manners. He seemed about thirty, and, though not handsome, had an agreeable person. Anne felt that she should like to know who he was.

They had nearly done breakfast, when the sound of a carriage, (almost the first they had heard since entering Lyme) drew half the party to the window. "It was a gentleman's carriage—a curricle—but only coming round from the stable-yard to the front door—Somebody must be going away.—It was driven by a servant in mourning."

The word curricle made Charles Musgrove jump up, that he might compare it with his own, the servant in mourning roused Anne's curiosity, and the whole six were collected to look, by the time the owner of the curricle was to be seen issuing from the door amidst the bows and civilities of the household, and taking his seat, to drive off.

"Ah!" cried Captain Wentworth, instantly, and with half a glance at Anne; "it is the very man we passed."

The Miss Musgroves agreed to it; and having all kindly watched him as far up the hill as they could, they returned to the breakfast-table. The waiter came into the room soon afterwards.

"Pray," said Captain Wentworth, immediately, "can you tell us the name of the gentleman who is just gone away?"

"Yes, Sir, a Mr. Elliot; a gentleman of large fortune,—came in last night from Sidmouth,—dare say you heard the carriage, Sir, while you were at dinner; and going on now for Crewkherne, in his way to Bath and London."

"Elliot!"—Many had looked on each other, and many had repeated the name, before all this had been got through, even by the smart rapidity of a waiter.

"Bless me!" cried Mary; "it must be our cousin;—it must be our Mr. Elliot, it must, indeed!—Charles, Anne, must not it? In mourning, you see, just as our Mr. Elliot must be. How very extraordinary! In the very same inn with us! Anne, must not it be our Mr. Elliot; my father's next heir? Pray Sir," (turning to the waiter), "did not you hear—did not his servant say whether he belonged to the Kellynch family?"

"No, ma'am,—he did not mention no particular family; but he said his master was a very rich gentleman, and would be a baronight some day."

"There! you see!" cried Mary, in an ecstacy, "Just as I said! Heir to Sir Walter Elliot!—I was sure that would come out, if it was so. Depend upon it, that is a circumstance which his servants take care to publish wherever he goes. But, Anne, only conceive how extraordinary! I wish I had looked at him more. I wish we had been aware in time, who it was, that he might have been introduced to us. What a pity that we should not have been introduced to each other!—Do you think he had the Elliot countenance? I hardly looked at him, I was looking at the horses; but I think he had something of the Elliot countenance. I wonder the arms[1] did not strike me! Oh!—the great-coat was hanging over the pannel, and hid the arms; so it did, otherwise, I am sure, I should have observed them, and the livery too; if the servant had not been in mourning, one should have known him by the livery."

"Putting all these very extraordinary circumstances together," said Captain Wentworth, "we must consider it to be the arrangement of Providence, that you should not be introduced to your cousin."

When she could command Mary's attention, Anne quietly tried to convince her that their father and Mr. Elliot had not, for many

---

1. Coat of arms (which would appear on the side of the carriage).

years, been on such terms as to make the power of attempting an introduction at all desirable.

At the same time, however, it was a secret gratification to herself to have seen her cousin, and to know that the future owner of Kellynch was undoubtedly a gentleman, and had an air of good sense. She would not, upon any account, mention her having met with him the second time; luckily Mary did not much attend to their having passed close by him in their early walk, but she would have felt quite ill-used by Anne's having actually run against him in the passage, and received his very polite excuses, while she had never been near him at all; no, that cousinly little interview must remain a perfect secret.

"Of course," said Mary, "you will mention our seeing Mr. Elliot, the next time you write to Bath. I think my father certainly ought to hear of it; do mention all about him."

Anne avoided a direct reply, but it was just the circumstance which she considered as not merely unnecessary to be communicated, but as what ought to be suppressed. The offence which had been given her father, many years back, she knew; Elizabeth's particular share in it she suspected; and that Mr. Elliot's idea always produced irritation in both, was beyond a doubt. Mary never wrote to Bath herself; all the toil of keeping up a slow and unsatisfactory correspondence with Elizabeth fell on Anne.

Breakfast had not been long over, when they were joined by Captain and Mrs. Harville, and Captain Benwick, with whom they had appointed to take their last walk about Lyme. They ought to be setting off for Uppercross by one, and in the meanwhile were to be all together, and out of doors as long as they could.

Anne found Captain Benwick getting near her, as soon as they were all fairly in the street. Their conversation, the preceding evening, did not disincline him to seek her again; and they walked together some time, talking as before of Mr. Scott and Lord Byron, and still as unable, as before, and as unable as any other two readers, to think exactly alike of the merits of either, till something occasioned an almost general change amongst their party, and instead of Captain Benwick, she had Captain Harville by her side.

"Miss Elliot," said he, speaking rather low, "you have done a good deed in making that poor fellow talk so much. I wish he could have such company oftener. It is bad for him, I know, to be shut up as he is; but what can we do? we cannot part."

"No," said Anne, "that I can easily believe to be impossible; but in time, perhaps—we know what time does in every case of affliction, and you must remember, Captain Harville, that your friend may yet be called a young mourner—Only last summer, I understand."

"Ay, true enough," (with a deep sigh) "only June."

"And not known to him, perhaps, so soon."

"Not till the first week in August, when he came home from the Cape,—just made into the Grappler.[2] I was at Plymouth, dreading to hear of him; he sent in letters, but the Grappler was under orders for Portsmouth. There the news must follow him, but who was to tell it? not I. I would as soon have been run up to the yard-arm.[3] Nobody could do it, but that good fellow, (pointing to Captain Wentworth.) The Laconia had come into Plymouth the week before; no danger of her being sent to sea again. He stood his chance for the rest—wrote up for leave of absence, but without waiting the return, travelled night and day till he got to Portsmouth, rowed off to the Grappler that instant, and never left the poor fellow for a week; that's what he did, and nobody else could have saved poor James. You may think, Miss Elliot, whether he is dear to us!"

Anne did think on the question with perfect decision, and said as much in reply as her own feelings could accomplish, or as his seemed able to bear, for he was too much affected to renew the subject— and when he spoke again, it was of something totally different.

Mrs. Harville's giving it as her opinion that her husband would have quite walking enough by the time he reached home, determined the direction of all the party in what was to be their last walk; they would accompany them to their door, and then return and set off themselves. By all their calculations there was just time for this; but as they drew near the Cobb, there was such a general wish to walk along it once more, all were so inclined, and Louisa soon grew so determined, that the difference of a quarter of an hour, it was found, would be no difference at all, so with all the kind leave-taking, and all the kind interchange of invitations and promises which may be imagined, they parted from Captain and Mrs. Harville at their own door, and still accompanied by Captain Benwick, who seemed to cling to them to the last, proceeded to make the proper adieus to the Cobb.

Anne found Captain Benwick again drawing near her. Lord Byron's "dark blue seas"[4] could not fail of being brought forward by their present view, and she gladly gave him all her attention as long as attention was possible. It was soon drawn per force another way.

---

2. Promoted into command of a new ship. The Cape of Good Hope changed hands several times during the Napoleonic period. Taken from France by the British in 1795, it was relinquished to the Dutch in 1802 with the Treaty of Amiens, then reoccupied by Britain in 1806 after the Battle of Blaauwberg. See Chapter XXIII, where Captain Harville shows Anne a small miniature painting of Benwick drawn by "a clever young German artist at the Cape" (166).
3. Hanged.
4. Lines recalling Byron's sea poems *Childe Harold's Pilgrimage* (1812) and *The Corsair* (1814). The latter poem (excerpted in this volume) opens: "O'er the glad waters of the dark blue sea, / Our thoughts as boundless, and our souls as free, / Far as the breeze can bear, the billows foam, / Survey our empire, and behold our home!" (*The Works of Lord Byron*, vol. 3, ed. Ernest Hartley Coleridge [London, 1900]).

There was too much wind to make the high part of the new Cobb[5] pleasant for the ladies, and they agreed to get down the steps to the lower, and all were contented to pass quietly and carefully down the steep flight, excepting Louisa; she must be jumped down them by Captain Wentworth. In all their walks, he had had to jump her from the stiles; the sensation was delightful to her. The hardness of the pavement for her feet, made him less willing upon the present occasion; he did it, however; she was safely down, and instantly, to shew her enjoyment, ran up the steps to be jumped down again. He advised her against it, thought the jar too great; but no, he reasoned and talked in vain; she smiled and said, "I am determined I will:" he put out his hands; she was too precipitate by half a second, she fell on the pavement on the Lower Cobb, and was taken up lifeless!

There was no wound, no blood, no visible bruise; but her eyes were closed, she breathed not, her face was like death.—The horror of that moment to all who stood around!

Captain Wentworth, who had caught her up, knelt with her in his arms, looking on her with a face as pallid as her own, in an agony of silence. "She is dead! she is dead!" screamed Mary, catching hold of her husband, and contributing with his own horror to make him immoveable; and in another moment, Henrietta, sinking under the conviction, lost her senses too, and would have fallen on the steps, but for Captain Benwick and Anne, who caught and supported her between them.

"Is there no one to help me?" were the first words which burst from Captain Wentworth, in a tone of despair, and as if all his own strength were gone.

"Go to him, go to him," cried Anne, "for heaven's sake go to him. I can support her myself. Leave me, and go to him. Rub her hands, rub her temples; here are salts,[6]—take them, take them."

Captain Benwick obeyed, and Charles at the same moment, disengaging himself from his wife, they were both with him; and Louisa was raised up and supported more firmly between them, and every thing was done that Anne had prompted, but in vain; while Captain Wentworth, staggering against the wall for his support, exclaimed in the bitterest agony,

"Oh God! her father and mother!"

"A surgeon!"[7] said Anne.

---

5. The Cobb's southern arm, added to the existing structure in the 1690s, was rebuilt in 1793 after being destroyed in a storm the previous year. The new Cobb may refer more generally to the upper level, as opposed to the original, lower level.
6. Smelling salts.
7. Lower in rank than the gentleman doctor (or "physician," the category that includes Dr. Shirley), surgeons trained as apprentices and generally did not have university training. Specializing in treating broken bones and wounds, they were commonly ex-soldiers making use of their prior experiences in battle.

He caught the word; it seemed to rouse him at once, and saying only "True, true, a surgeon this instant," was darting away, when Anne eagerly suggested,

"Captain Benwick, would not it be better for Captain Benwick? He knows where a surgeon is to be found."

Every one capable of thinking felt the advantage of the idea, and in a moment (it was all done in rapid moments) Captain Benwick had resigned the poor corpse-like figure entirely to the brother's care, and was off for the town with the utmost rapidity.

As to the wretched party left behind, it could scarcely be said which of the three, who were completely rational, was suffering most, Captain Wentworth, Anne, or Charles, who, really a very affectionate brother, hung over Louisa with sobs of grief, and could only turn his eyes from one sister, to see the other in a state as insensible, or to witness the hysterical agitations of his wife, calling on him for help which he could not give.

Anne, attending with all the strength and zeal, and thought, which instinct supplied, to Henrietta, still tried, at intervals, to suggest comfort to the others, tried to quiet Mary, to animate Charles, to assuage the feelings of Captain Wentworth. Both seemed to look to her for directions.

"Anne, Anne," cried Charles, "what is to be done next? What, in heaven's name, is to be done next?"

Captain Wentworth's eyes were also turned towards her.

"Had not she better be carried to the inn? Yes, I am sure, carry her gently to the inn."

"Yes, yes, to the inn," repeated Captain Wentworth, comparatively collected, and eager to be doing something. "I will carry her myself. Musgrove, take care of the others."

By this time the report of the accident had spread among the workmen and boatmen about the Cobb, and many were collected near them, to be useful if wanted, at any rate, to enjoy[8] the sight of a dead young lady, nay, two dead young ladies, for it proved twice as fine as the first report. To some of the best-looking of these good people Henrietta was consigned, for, though partially revived, she was quite helpless; and in this manner, Anne walking by her side, and Charles attending to his wife, they set forward, treading back with feelings unutterable, the ground which so lately, so very lately, and so light of heart, they had passed along.

They were not off the Cobb, before the Harvilles met them. Captain Benwick had been seen flying by their house, with a countenance

8. The *Oxford English Dictionary* notes that although the term usually indicates pleasure, it could also mean to have the use or benefit of. That the spectacle "proved twice as fine as the first report" suggests that, this being the off-season, the workmen are eager for distraction.

which shewed something to be wrong; and they had set off immediately, informed and directed, as they passed, towards the spot.
Shocked as Captain Harville was, he brought senses and nerves that
could be instantly useful; and a look between him and his wife
decided what was to be done. She must be taken to their house—all
must go to their house—and wait the surgeon's arrival there. They
would not listen to scruples: he was obeyed; they were all beneath his
roof; and while Louisa, under Mrs. Harville's direction, was conveyed
up stairs, and given possession of her own bed, assistance, cordials,
restoratives were supplied by her husband to all who needed them.

Louisa had once opened her eyes, but soon closed them again,
without apparent consciousness. This had been a proof of life, however, of service to her sister; and Henrietta, though perfectly incapable of being in the same room with Louisa, was kept, by the
agitation of hope and fear, from a return of her own insensibility.
Mary, too, was growing calmer.

The surgeon was with them almost before it had seemed possible. They were sick with horror while he examined; but he was not
hopeless. The head had received a severe contusion, but he had seen
greater injuries recovered from: he was by no means hopeless; he
spoke cheerfully.

That he did not regard it as a desperate case—that he did not say
a few hours must end it—was at first felt, beyond the hope of most;
and the ecstasy of such a reprieve, the rejoicing, deep and silent,
after a few fervent ejaculations of gratitude to Heaven had been
offered, may be conceived.

The tone, the look, with which "Thank God!" was uttered by Captain Wentworth, Anne was sure could never be forgotten by her;
nor the sight of him afterwards, as he sat near a table, leaning over
it with folded arms, and face concealed, as if overpowered by the
various feelings of his soul, and trying by prayer and reflection to
calm them.

Louisa's limbs had escaped. There was no injury but to the head.

It now became necessary for the party to consider what was best
to be done, as to their general situation. They were now able to speak
to each other, and consult. That Louisa must remain where she was,
however distressing to her friends to be involving the Harvilles in
such trouble, did not admit a doubt. Her removal was impossible.
The Harvilles silenced all scruples; and, as much as they could, all
gratitude. They had looked forward and arranged every thing, before
the others began to reflect. Captain Benwick must give up his room
to them, and get a bed elsewhere—and the whole was settled. They
were only concerned that the house could accommodate no more;
and yet perhaps by "putting the children away in the maids' room,
or swinging a cot somewhere," they could hardly bear to think of

not finding room for two or three besides, supposing they might wish to stay; though, with regard to any attendance on Miss Musgrove, there need not be the least uneasiness in leaving her to Mrs. Harville's care entirely. Mrs. Harville was a very experienced nurse; and her nursery-maid, who had lived with her long and gone about with her every where, was just such another. Between those two, she could want no possible attendance by day or night. And all this was said with a truth and sincerity of feeling irresistible.

Charles, Henrietta, and Captain Wentworth were the three in consultation, and for a little while it was only an interchange of perplexity and terror. "Uppercross,—the necessity of some one's going to Uppercross,—the news to be conveyed—how it could be broken to Mr. and Mrs. Musgrove—the lateness of the morning,—an hour already gone since they ought to have been off,—the impossibility of being in tolerable time. At first, they were capable of nothing more to the purpose than such exclamations; but, after a while, Captain Wentworth, exerting himself, said,

"We must be decided, and without the loss of another minute. Every minute is valuable. Some must resolve on being off for Uppercross instantly. Musgrove, either you or I must go."

Charles agreed; but declared his resolution of not going away. He would be as little incumbrance as possible to Captain and Mrs. Harville; but as to leaving his sister in such a state, he neither ought, nor would. So far it was decided; and Henrietta at first declared the same. She, however, was soon persuaded to think differently. The usefulness of her staying!—She, who had not been able to remain in Louisa's room, or to look at her, without sufferings which made her worse than helpless! She was forced to acknowledge that she could do no good; yet was still unwilling to be away, till touched by the thought of her father and mother, she gave it up; she consented, she was anxious to be at home.

The plan had reached this point, when Anne, coming quietly down from Louisa's room, could not but hear what followed, for the parlour door was open.

"Then it is settled, Musgrove," cried Captain Wentworth, "that you stay, and that I take care of your sister home. But as to the rest;—as to the others;—If one stays to assist Mrs. Harville, I think it need be only one.—Mrs. Charles Musgrove will, of course, wish to get back to her children; but, if Anne will stay, no one so proper, so capable as Anne!"

She paused a moment to recover from the emotion of hearing herself so spoken of. The other two warmly agreed to what he said, and she then appeared.

"You will stay, I am sure; you will stay and nurse her;" cried he, turning to her and speaking with a glow, and yet a gentleness, which seemed almost restoring the past.—She coloured deeply; and he rec-ollected himself, and moved away.—She expressed herself most will-ing, ready, happy to remain. "It was what she had been thinking of, and wishing to be allowed to do.—A bed on the floor in Louisa's room would be sufficient for her, if Mrs. Harville would but think so."

One thing more, and all seemed arranged. Though it was rather desirable that Mr. and Mrs. Musgrove should be previously alarmed by some share of delay; yet the time required by the Uppercross horses to take them back, would be a dreadful extension of suspense; and Captain Wentworth proposed, and Charles Musgrove agreed, that it would be much better for him to take a chaise from the inn, and leave Mr. Musgrove's carriage and horses to be sent home the next morning early, when there would be the farther advantage of sending an account of Louisa's night.

Captain Wentworth now hurried off to get every thing ready on his part, and to be soon followed by the two ladies. When the plan was made known to Mary, however, there was an end of all peace in it. She was so wretched, and so vehement, complained so much of injustice in being expected to go away, instead of Anne;—Anne, who was nothing to Louisa, while she was her sister, and had the best right to stay in Henrietta's stead! Why was not she to be as useful as Anne? And to go home without Charles, too—without her husband! No, it was too unkind! And, in short, she said more than her hus-band could long withstand; and as none of the others could oppose when he gave way, there was no help for it: the change of Mary for Anne was inevitable.

Anne had never submitted more reluctantly to the jealous and ill-judging claims of Mary; but so it must be, and they set off for the town, Charles taking care of his sister, and Captain Benwick attend-ing to her. She gave a moment's recollection, as they hurried along, to the little circumstances which the same spots had witnessed earlier in the morning. There she had listened to Henrietta's schemes for Dr. Shirley's leaving Uppercross; farther on, she had first seen Mr. Elliot; a moment seemed all that could now be given to any one but Louisa, or those who were wrapt up in her welfare.

Captain Benwick was most considerately attentive to her; and, united as they all seemed by the distress of the day, she felt an increasing degree of good-will towards him, and a pleasure even in thinking that it might, perhaps, be the occasion of continuing their acquaintance.

Captain Wentworth was on the watch for them, and a chaise and four in waiting, stationed for their convenience in the lowest part of the street; but his evident surprise and vexation, at the substitution of one sister for the other—the change of his countenance—the astonishment—the expressions begun and suppressed, with which

Charles was listened to, made but a mortifying reception of Anne; or must at least convince her that she was valued only as she could be useful to Louisa.

She endeavoured to be composed, and to be just. Without emulating the feelings of an Emma towards her Henry,[9] she would have attended on Louisa with a zeal above the common claims of regard, for his sake; and she hoped he would not long be so unjust as to suppose she would shrink unnecessarily from the office of a friend.

In the meanwhile she was in the carriage. He had handed them both in, and placed himself between them; and in this manner, under these circumstances full of astonishment and emotion to Anne, she quitted Lyme. How the long stage would pass; how it was to affect their manners; what was to be their sort of intercourse, she could not foresee. It was all quite natural, however. He was devoted to Henrietta; always turning towards her; and when he spoke at all, always with the view of supporting her hopes and raising her spirits. In general, his voice and manner were studiously calm. To spare Henrietta from agitation seemed the governing principle. Once only, when she had been grieving over the last ill-judged, ill-fated walk to the Cobb, bitterly lamenting that it ever had been thought of, he burst forth, as if wholly overcome—

"Don't talk of it, don't talk of it," he cried. "Oh God! that I had not given way to her at the fatal moment! Had I done as I ought! But so eager and so resolute! Dear, sweet Louisa!"

Anne wondered whether it ever occurred to him now, to question the justness of his own previous opinion as to the universal felicity and advantage of firmness of character; and whether it might not strike him, that, like all other qualities of the mind, it should have its proportions and limits. She thought it could scarcely escape him to feel, that a persuadable temper might sometimes be as much in favour of happiness, as a very resolute character.

They got on fast. Anne was astonished to recognise the same hills and the same objects so soon. Their actual speed, heightened by some dread of the conclusion, made the road appear but half as long as on the day before. It was growing quite dusk, however, before they were in the neighbourhood of Uppercross, and there had been total silence among them for some time, Henrietta leaning back in the

---

9. An allusion to *Henry and Emma, a Poem, upon the Model of the Nut-Brown Maid* (1709), by the English poet and diplomat Matthew Prior (1664–1721). Samuel Johnson's assessment deems the poem "a dull and tedious dialogue, which excites neither esteem for the man, nor tenderness for the woman. The example of Emma, who resolves to follow an outlawed murderer wherever fear and guilt shall drive him, deserves no imitation; and the experiment by which Henry tries the lady's constancy"—by deceiving her to test her faith—"is such as must end either in infamy to her, or in disappointment to himself" (*The Lives of the Poets*, in *The Works of Samuel Johnson*, vol. 8 [London, 1825], p. 16).

corner, with a shawl over her face, giving the hope of her having cried herself to sleep; when, as they were going up their last hill, Anne found herself all at once addressed by Captain Wentworth. In a low, cautious voice, he said,

"I have been considering what we had best do. She must not appear at first. She could not stand it. I have been thinking whether you had not better remain in the carriage with her, while I go in and break it to Mr. and Mrs. Musgrove. Do you think this a good plan?"

She did: he was satisfied, and said no more. But the remembrance of the appeal remained a pleasure to her—as a proof of friendship, and of deference for her judgment, a great pleasure; and when it became a sort of parting proof, its value did not lessen.

When the distressing communication at Uppercross was over, and he had seen the father and mother quite as composed as could be hoped, and the daughter all the better for being with them, he announced his intention of returning in the same carriage to Lyme; and when the horses were baited,[1] he was off.

Chapter XIII

The remainder of Anne's time at Uppercross, comprehending only two days, was spent entirely at the mansion-house, and she had the satisfaction of knowing herself extremely useful there, both as an immediate companion, and as assisting in all those arrangements for the future, which, in Mr. and Mrs. Musgrove's distressed state of spirits, would have been difficulties.

They had an early account from Lyme the next morning. Louisa was much the same. No symptoms worse than before had appeared. Charles came a few hours afterwards, to bring a later and more particular account. He was tolerably cheerful. A speedy cure must not be hoped, but every thing was going on as well as the nature of the case admitted. In speaking of the Harvilles, he seemed unable to satisfy his own sense of their kindness, especially of Mrs. Harville's exertions as a nurse. "She really left nothing for Mary to do. He and Mary had been persuaded to go early to their inn last night. Mary had been hysterical again this morning. When he came away, she was going to walk out with Captain Benwick, which, he hoped, would do her good. He almost wished she had been prevailed on to come home the day before; but the truth was, that Mrs. Harville left nothing for any body to do."

Charles was to return to Lyme the same afternoon, and his father had at first half a mind to go with him, but the ladies could not

1. Fed.

consent. It would be going only to multiply trouble to the others, and increase his own distress; and a much better scheme followed and was acted upon. A chaise was sent for from Crewkherne, and Charles conveyed back a far more useful person in the old nursery-maid of the family, one who having brought up all the children, and seen the very last, the lingering and long-petted master Harry, sent to school after his brothers, was now living in her deserted nursery to mend stockings, and dress all the blains[2] and bruises she could get near her, and who, consequently, was only too happy in being allowed to go and help nurse dear Miss Louisa. Vague wishes of getting Sarah thither, had occurred before to Mrs. Musgrove and Henrietta; but without Anne, it would hardly have been resolved on, and found practicable so soon.

They were indebted, the next day, to Charles Hayter for all the minute knowledge of Louisa, which it was so essential to obtain every twenty-four hours. He made it his business to go to Lyme, and his account was still encouraging. The intervals of sense and consciousness were believed to be stronger. Every report agreed in Captain Wentworth's appearing fixed in Lyme.

Anne was to leave them on the morrow, an event which they all dreaded. "What should they do without her? They were wretched comforters for one another!" And so much was said in this way, that Anne thought she could not do better than impart among them the general inclination to which she was privy, and persuade them all to go to Lyme at once. She had little difficulty; it was soon determined that they would go, go to-morrow, fix themselves at the inn, or get into lodgings, as it suited, and there remain till dear Louisa could be moved. They must be taking off some trouble from the good people she was with; they might at least relieve Mrs. Harville from the care of her own children; and in short they were so happy in the decision, that Anne was delighted with what she had done, and felt that she could not spend her last morning at Uppercross better than in assisting their preparations, and sending them off at an early hour, though her being left to the solitary range of the house was the consequence.

She was the last, excepting the little boys at the cottage, she was the very last, the only remaining one of all that had filled and animated both houses, of all that had given Uppercross its cheerful character. A few days had made a change indeed!

If Louisa recovered, it would all be well again. More than former happiness would be restored. There could not be a doubt, to her mind there was none, of what would follow her recovery. A few months hence, and the room now so deserted, occupied but by her silent,

2. Chilblains, inflammatory swellings produced by cold.

pensive self, might be filled again with all that was happy and gay,
all that was glowing and bright in prosperous love, all that was most
unlike Anne Elliot!

An hour's complete leisure for such reflections as these, on a dark
November day, a small[3] thick rain almost blotting out the very few
objects ever to be discerned from the windows, was enough to make
the sound of Lady Russell's carriage exceedingly welcome; and yet,
though desirous to be gone, she could not quit the mansion-house,
or look an adieu to the cottage, with its black, dripping, and comfort-
less veranda, or even notice through the misty glasses the last humble
tenements[4] of the village, without a saddened heart.—Scenes had
passed in Uppercross, which made it precious. It stood the record
of many sensations of pain, once severe, but now softened; and of
some instances of relenting feeling, some breathings of friendship
and reconciliation, which could never be looked for again, and
which could never cease to be dear. She left it all behind her; all but
the recollection that such things had been.

Anne had never entered Kellynch since her quitting Lady Russell's
house, in September. It had not been necessary, and the few occasions of its being possible for her to go to the hall she had contrived
to evade and escape from. Her first return, was to resume her place
in the modern and elegant apartments of the lodge, and to gladden
the eyes of its mistress.

There was some anxiety mixed with Lady Russell's joy in meeting
her. She knew who had been frequenting Uppercross. But happily,
either Anne was improved in plumpness and looks, or Lady Russell
fancied her so; and Anne, in receiving her compliments on the occasion, had the amusement of connecting them with the silent admiration of her cousin, and of hoping that she was to be blessed with
a second spring of youth and beauty.

When they came to converse, she was soon sensible of some
mental change. The subjects of which her heart had been full on
leaving Kellynch, and which she had felt slighted, and been compelled to smother among the Musgroves, were now become but of
secondary interest. She had lately lost sight even of her father and
sister and Bath. Their concerns had been sunk under those of Uppercross, and when Lady Russell reverted to their former hopes and
fears, and spoke her satisfaction in the house in Camden-place,
which had been taken, and her regret that Mrs. Clay should still be
with them, Anne would have been ashamed to have it known, how
much more she was thinking of Lyme, and Louisa Musgrove, and
all her acquaintance there; how much more interesting to her was

3. Gentle.
4. Houses.

the home and the friendship of the Harvilles and Captain Benwick, than her own father's house in Camden-place, or her own sister's intimacy with Mrs. Clay. She was actually forced to exert herself, to meet Lady Russell with any thing like the appearance of equal solicitude, on topics which had by nature the first claim on her.

There was a little awkwardness at first in their discourse on another subject. They must speak of the accident at Lyme. Lady Russell had not been arrived five minutes the day before, when a full account of the whole had burst on her; but still it must be talked of, she must make enquiries, she must regret the imprudence, lament the result, and Captain Wentworth's name must be mentioned by both. Anne was conscious of not doing it so well as Lady Russell. She could not speak the name, and look straight forward to Lady Russell's eye, till she had adopted the expedient of telling her briefly what she thought of the attachment between him and Louisa. When this was told, his name distressed her no longer.

Lady Russell had only to listen composedly, and wish them happy; but internally her heart revelled in angry pleasure, in pleased contempt, that the man who at twenty-three had seemed to understand somewhat of the value of an Anne Elliot, should, eight years afterwards, be charmed by a Louisa Musgrove.

The first three or four days passed most quietly, with no circumstance to mark them excepting the receipt of a note or two from Lyme, which found their way to Anne, she could not tell how, and brought a rather improving account of Louisa. At the end of that period, Lady Russell's politeness could repose no longer, and the fainter self-threatenings of the past, became in a decided tone, "I must call on Mrs. Croft; I really must call upon her soon. Anne, have you courage to go with me, and pay a visit in that house? It will be some trial to us both."

Anne did not shrink from it; on the contrary, she truly felt as she said, in observing,

"I think you are very likely to suffer the most of the two; your feelings are less reconciled to the change than mine. By remaining in the neighbourhood, I am become inured to it."

She could have said more on the subject; for she had in fact so high an opinion of the Crofts, and considered her father so very fortunate in his tenants, felt the parish to be so sure of a good example, and the poor of the best attention and relief, that however sorry and ashamed for the necessity of the removal, she could not but in conscience feel that they were gone who deserved not to stay, and that Kellynch-hall had passed into better hands than its owners'. These convictions must unquestionably have their own pain, and severe was its kind; but they precluded that pain which Lady Russell would suffer in entering the house again, and returning through the well-known apartments.

In such moments Anne had no power of saying to herself, "These rooms ought to belong only to us. Oh, how fallen in their destination! How unworthily occupied! An ancient family to be so driven away! Strangers filling their place!" No, except when she thought of her mother, and remembered where she had been used to sit and preside, she had no sigh of that description to heave.

Mrs. Croft always met her with a kindness which gave her the pleasure of fancying herself a favourite; and on the present occasion, receiving her in that house, there was particular attention.

The sad accident at Lyme was soon the prevailing topic; and on comparing their latest accounts of the invalid, it appeared that each lady dated her intelligence from the same hour of yester morn, that Captain Wentworth had been in Kellynch yesterday—(the first time since the accident) had brought Anne the last note, which she had not been able to trace the exact steps of, had staid a few hours and then returned again to Lyme—and without any present intention of quitting it any more.—He had enquired after her, she found, particularly;—had expressed his hope of Miss Elliot's not being the worse for her exertions, and had spoken of those exertions as great.—This was handsome,—and gave her more pleasure than almost any thing else could have done.

As to the sad catastrophe itself, it could be canvassed[5] only in one style by a couple of steady, sensible women, whose judgments had to work on ascertained events; and it was perfectly decided that it had been the consequence of much thoughtlessness and much imprudence; that its effects were most alarming, and that it was frightful to think, how long Miss Musgrove's recovery might yet be doubtful, and how liable she would still remain to suffer from the concussion hereafter!—The Admiral wound it all up summarily by exclaiming,

"Ay, a very bad business indeed.—A new sort of way this, for a young fellow to be making love, by breaking his mistress's head!—is not it, Miss Elliot?—This is breaking a head and giving a plaister truly!"[6]

Admiral Croft's manners were not quite of the tone to suit Lady Russell, but they delighted Anne. His goodness of heart and simplicity of character were irresistible.

"Now, this must be very bad for you," said he, suddenly rousing from a little reverie, "to be coming and finding us here.—I had not recollected it before, I declare,—but it must be very bad.—But now, do not stand upon ceremony.—Get up and go over all the rooms in the house if you like it."

"Another time, Sir, I thank you, not now."

5. Discussed, gone over.
6. "To break a man's head and give him a plaster" was a proverbial expression, meaning that someone both gives and remedies an injury.

"Well, whenever it suits you.—You can slip in from the shrubbery at any time. And there you will find we keep our umbrellas, hanging up by that door. A good place, is not it? But" (checking himself) "you will not think it a good place, for yours were always kept in the butler's room. Ay, so it always is, I believe. One man's ways may be as good as another's, but we all like our own best. And so you must judge for yourself, whether it would be better for you to go about the house or not."

Anne, finding she might decline it, did so, very gratefully.

"We have made very few changes either!" continued the Admiral, after thinking a moment. "Very few.—We told you about the laundry-door, at Uppercross. That has been a very great improvement. The wonder was, how any family upon earth could bear with the inconvenience of its opening as it did, so long!—You will tell Sir Walter what we have done, and that Mr. Shepherd thinks it the greatest improvement the house ever had. Indeed, I must do ourselves the justice to say, that the few alterations we have made have been all very much for the better. My wife should have the credit of them, however. I have done very little besides sending away some of the large looking-glasses from my dressing-room, which was your father's. A very good man, and very much the gentleman I am sure—but I should think, Miss Elliot" (looking with serious reflection) "I should think he must be rather a dressy man for his time of life.—Such a number of looking-glasses! oh Lord! there was no getting away from oneself. So I got Sophy to lend me a hand, and we soon shifted their quarters; and now I am quite snug, with my little shaving glass in one corner, and another great thing that I never go near."

Anne, amused in spite of herself, was rather distressed for an answer, and the Admiral, fearing he might not have been civil enough, took up the subject again, to say,

"The next time you write to your good father, Miss Elliot, pray give my compliments and Mrs. Croft's, and say that we are settled here quite to our liking, and have no fault at all to find with the place. The breakfast-room chimney smokes a little, I grant you, but it is only when the wind is due north and blows hard, which may not happen three times a winter. And take it altogether, now that we have been into most of the houses hereabouts and can judge, there is not one that we like better than this. Pray say so, with my compliments. He will be glad to hear it."

Lady Russell and Mrs. Croft were very well pleased with each other; but the acquaintance which this visit began, was fated not to proceed far at present; for when it was returned, the Crofts announced themselves to be going away for a few weeks, to visit their connexions[7] in the north of the county, and probably might not be at home again before Lady Russell would be removing to Bath.

So ended all danger to Anne of meeting Captain Wentworth at Kellynch-hall, or of seeing him in company with her friend. Every thing was safe enough, and she smiled over the many anxious feelings she had wasted on the subject.

Chapter XIV

Though Charles and Mary had remained at Lyme much longer after Mr. and Mrs. Musgrove's going, than Anne conceived they could have been at all wanted, they were yet the first of the family to be at home again, and as soon as possible after their return to Uppercross, they drove over to the lodge.—They had left Louisa beginning to sit up; but her head, though clear, was exceedingly weak, and her nerves susceptible to the highest extreme of tenderness; and though she might be pronounced to be altogether doing very well, it was still impossible to say when she might be able to bear the removal home; and her father and mother, who must return in time to receive their younger children for the Christmas holidays, had hardly a hope of being allowed to bring her with them.

They had been all in lodgings together. Mrs. Musgrove had got Mrs. Harville's children away as much as she could, every possible supply from Uppercross had been furnished, to lighten the inconvenience to the Harvilles, while the Harvilles had been wanting them to come to dinner every day; and in short, it seemed to have been only a struggle on each side as to which should be most disinterested and hospitable.

Mary had had her evils; but upon the whole, as was evident by her staying so long, she had found more to enjoy than to suffer.— Charles Hayter had been at Lyme oftener than suited her, and when they dined with the Harvilles there had been only a maidservant to wait, and at first, Mrs. Harville had always given Mrs. Musgrove precedence; but then, she had received so very handsome an apology from her on finding out whose daughter she was, and there had been so much going on every day, there had been so many walks between their lodgings and the Harvilles, and she had got books from the library and changed them so often, that the balance had certainly been much in favour of Lyme. She had been taken to Charmouth too, and she had bathed,[8] and she had gone to church, and there were a great many more people to look at in the church at

7. Relatives.
8. Mary has taken a sea bath (see n. 8, p. 69, on bathing machines).

Lyme than at Uppercross,—and all this, joined to the sense of being so very useful, had made really an agreeable fortnight.

Anne enquired after Captain Benwick. Mary's face was clouded directly. Charles laughed.

"Oh! Captain Benwick is very well, I believe, but he is a very odd young man. I do not know what he would be at. We asked him to come home with us for a day or two; Charles undertook to give him some shooting, and he seemed quite delighted, and for my part, I thought it was all settled; when behold! on Tuesday night, he made a very awkward sort of excuse; "he never shot" and he had "been quite misunderstood,"—and he had promised this and he had promised that, and the end of it was, I found, that he did not mean to come. I suppose he was afraid of finding it dull; but upon my word I should have thought we were lively enough at the Cottage for such a heart-broken man as Captain Benwick."

Charles laughed again and said, "Now Mary, you know very well how it really was.—It was all your doing," (turning to Anne.) "He fancied that if he went with us, he should find you close by; he fancied every body to be living in Uppercross; and when he discovered that Lady Russell lived three miles off, his heart failed him, and he had not courage to come. That is the fact, upon my honour. Mary knows it is."

But Mary did not give into it very graciously; whether from not considering Captain Benwick entitled by birth and situation to be in love with an Elliot, or from not wanting to believe Anne a greater attraction to Uppercross than herself, must be left to be guessed. Anne's good-will, however, was not to be lessened by what she heard. She boldly acknowledged herself flattered, and continued her enquiries.

"Oh! he talks of you," cried Charles, "in such terms,"—Mary interrupted him. "I declare, Charles, I never heard him mention Anne twice all the time I was there. I declare, Anne, he never talks of you at all."

"No," admitted Charles, "I do not know that he ever does, in a general way—but however, it is a very clear thing that he admires you exceedingly.—His head is full of some books that he is reading upon your recommendation, and he wants to talk to you about them; he has found out something or other in one of them which he thinks—Oh! I cannot pretend to remember it, but it was something very fine—I overheard him telling Henrietta all about it—and then 'Miss Elliot' was spoken of in the highest terms!—Now Mary, I declare it was so, I heard it myself, and you were in the other room.— 'Elegance, sweetness, beauty,' Oh! there was no end of Miss Elliot's charms."

"And I am sure," cried Mary warmly, "it was very little to his credit, if he did. Miss Harville only died last June. Such a heart is very little worth having; is it, Lady Russell? I am sure you will agree with me."

"I must see Captain Benwick before I decide," said Lady Russell, smiling.

"And that you are very likely to do very soon, I can tell you, ma'am," said Charles. "Though he had not nerves for coming away with us and setting off again afterwards to pay a formal visit here, he will make his way over to Kellynch one day by himself, you may depend on it. I told him the distance and the road, and I told him of the church's being so very well worth seeing, for as he has a taste for those sort of things, I thought that would be a good excuse, and he listened with all his understanding and soul; and I am sure from his manner that you will have him calling here soon. So, I give you notice, Lady Russell."

"Any acquaintance of Anne's will always be welcome to me," was Lady Russell's kind answer.

"Oh! as to being Anne's acquaintance," said Mary, "I think he is rather my acquaintance, for I have been seeing him every day this last fortnight."

"Well, as your joint acquaintance, then, I shall be very happy to see Captain Benwick."

"You will not find any thing very agreeable in him, I assure you, ma'am. He is one of the dullest young men that ever lived. He has walked with me, sometimes, from one end of the sands to the other, without saying a word. He is not at all a well-bred young man. I am sure you will not like him."

"There we differ, Mary," said Anne. "I think Lady Russell would like him. I think she would be so much pleased with his mind, that she would very soon see no deficiency in his manner."

"So do I, Anne," said Charles. "I am sure Lady Russell would like him. He is just Lady Russell's sort. Give him a book, and he will read all day long."

"Yes, that he will!" exclaimed Mary, tauntingly. "He will sit poring over his book, and not know when a person speaks to him, or when one drops one's scissors, or any thing that happens. Do you think Lady Russell would like that?"

Lady Russell could not help laughing. "Upon my word," said she, "I should not have supposed that my opinion of any one could have admitted of such difference of conjecture, steady and matter of fact as I may call myself. I have really a curiosity to see the person who can give occasion to such directly opposite notions. I wish he may be induced to call here. And when he does, Mary, you may depend upon hearing my opinion; but I am determined not to judge him before-hand."

"You will not like him, I will answer for it."

Lady Russell began talking of something else. Mary spoke with animation of their meeting with, or rather missing, Mr. Elliot so extraordinarily.

"He is a man," said Lady Russell, "whom I have no wish to see. His declining to be on cordial terms with the head of his family, has left a very strong impression in his disfavour with me."

This decision checked Mary's eagerness, and stopped her short in the midst of the Elliot countenance.

With regard to Captain Wentworth, though Anne hazarded no enquiries, there was voluntary communication sufficient. His spirits had been greatly recovering lately, as might be expected. As Louisa improved, he had improved; and he was now quite a different creature from what he had been the first week. He had not seen Louisa; and was so extremely fearful of any ill consequence to her from an interview, that he did not press for it at all; and, on the contrary, seemed to have a plan of going away for a week or ten days, till her head were stronger. He had talked of going down to Plymouth for a week, and wanted to persuade Captain Benwick to go with him; but, as Charles maintained to the last, Captain Benwick seemed much more disposed to ride over to Kellynch.

There can be no doubt that Lady Russell and Anne were both occasionally thinking of Captain Benwick, from this time. Lady Russell could not hear the door-bell without feeling that it might be his herald; nor could Anne return from any stroll of solitary indulgence in her father's grounds, or any visit of charity in the village, without wondering whether she might see him or hear of him. Captain Benwick came not, however. He was either less disposed for it than Charles had imagined, or he was too shy; and after giving him a week's indulgence, Lady Russell determined him to be unworthy of the interest which he had been beginning to excite.

The Musgroves came back to receive their happy boys and girls from school, bringing with them Mrs. Harville's little children, to improve the noise of Uppercross, and lessen that of Lyme. Henrietta remained with Louisa; but all the rest of the family were again in their usual quarters.

Lady Russell and Anne paid their compliments to them once, when Anne could not but feel that Uppercross was already quite alive again. Though neither Henrietta, nor Louisa, nor Charles Hayter, nor Captain Wentworth were there, the room presented as strong a contrast as could be wished, to the last state she had seen it in.

Immediately surrounding Mrs. Musgrove were the little Harvilles, whom she was sedulously guarding from the tyranny of the two children from the Cottage, expressly arrived to amuse them. On one side was a table, occupied by some chattering girls, cutting up silk and gold paper; and on the other were tressels and trays, bending

under the weight of brawn[9] and cold pies, where riotous boys were
holding high revel; the whole completed by a roaring Christmas fire,
which seemed determined to be heard, in spite of all the noise of
the others. Charles and Mary also came in, of course, during their
visit; and Mr. Musgrove made a point of paying his respects to Lady
Russell, and sat down close to her for ten minutes, talking with a
very raised voice, but, from the clamour of the children on his knees,
generally in vain. It was a fine family-piece.[1]

Anne, judging from her own temperament, would have deemed
such a domestic hurricane a bad restorative of the nerves, which
Louisa's illness must have so greatly shaken; but Mrs. Musgrove,
who got Anne near her on purpose to thank her most cordially, again
and again, for all her attentions to them, concluded a short recapit-
ulation of what she had suffered herself, by observing, with a happy
glance round the room, that after all she had gone through, nothing was so likely to do her good as a little quiet cheerfulness at home.

Louisa was now recovering apace. Her mother could even think
of her being able to join their party at home, before her brothers
and sisters went to school again. The Harvilles had promised to
come with her and stay at Uppercross, whenever she returned. Captain Wentworth was gone, for the present, to see his brother in
Shropshire.

"I hope I shall remember, in future," said Lady Russell, as soon
as they were reseated in the carriage, "not to call at Uppercross in
the Christmas holidays."

Every body has their taste in noises as well as in other matters;
and sounds are quite innoxious, or most distressing, by their sort
rather than their quantity. When Lady Russell, not long afterwards,
was entering Bath on a wet afternoon, and driving through the long
course of streets from the Old Bridge to Camden-place, amidst the
dash of other carriages, the heavy rumble of carts and drays, the
bawling of newsmen, muffin-men and milk-men, and the ceaseless
clink of pattens,[2] she made no complaint. No, these were noises
which belonged to the winter pleasures; her spirits rose under their
influence; and, like Mrs. Musgrove, she was feeling, though not saying, that, after being long in the country, nothing could be so good
for her as a little quiet cheerfulness.

Anne did not share these feelings. She persisted in a very determined, though very silent, disinclination for Bath; caught the first
dim view of the extensive buildings, smoking in rain, without any
wish of seeing them better; felt their progress through the streets to

9. Pork, especially pickled or potted pork. *Tressels*: trestles, supports for the trays that
   converted them to tables.
1. A painting representing a family.
2. Wooden clogs, worn to elevate feet above the mud of the street.

be, however disagreeable, yet too rapid; for who would be glad to see her when she arrived? And looked back, with fond regret, to the bustles of Uppercross and the seclusion of Kellynch.

Elizabeth's last letter had communicated a piece of news of some interest. Mr. Elliot was in Bath. He had called in Camden-place; had called a second time, a third; had been pointedly attentive: if Elizabeth and her father did not deceive themselves, had been taking as much pains to seek the acquaintance, and proclaim the value of the connection, as he had formerly taken pains to shew neglect. This was very wonderful,[3] if it were true; and Lady Russell was in a state of very agreeable curiosity and perplexity about Mr. Elliot, already recanting the sentiment she had so lately expressed to Mary, of his being "a man whom she had no wish to see." She had a great wish to see him. If he really sought to reconcile himself like a dutiful branch, he must be forgiven for having dismembered himself from the paternal tree.

Anne was not animated to an equal pitch by the circumstance; but she felt that she would rather see Mr. Elliot again than not, which was more than she could say for many other persons in Bath.

She was put down in Camden-place; and Lady Russell then drove to her own lodgings, in Rivers-street.

Chapter XV

Sir Walter had taken a very good house in Camden-place, a lofty, dignified situation, such as becomes a man of consequence; and both he and Elizabeth were settled there, much to their satisfaction.

Anne entered it with a sinking heart, anticipating an imprison-ment of many months, and anxiously saying to herself, "Oh! when shall I leave you again?" A degree of unexpected cordiality, however, in the welcome she received, did her good. Her father and sister were glad to see her, for the sake of shewing her the house and furniture, and met her with kindness. Her making a fourth, when they sat down to dinner, was noticed as an advantage.

Mrs. Clay was very pleasant, and very smiling; but her courtesies and smiles were more a matter of course. Anne had always felt that she would pretend what was proper on her arrival; but the complai-sance of the others was unlooked for. They were evidently in excel-lent spirits, and she was soon to listen to the causes. They had no inclination to listen to her. After laying out[4] for some compliments of being deeply regretted in their old neighbourhood, which Anne

3. Remarkable.
4. Angling for.

could not pay, they had only a few faint enquiries to make, before
the talk must be all their own. Uppercross excited no interest, Kellynch very little, it was all Bath.

They had the pleasure of assuring her that Bath more than
answered their expectations in every respect. Their house was
undoubtedly the best in Camden-place; their drawing-rooms had
many decided advantages over all the others which they had either
seen or heard of; and the superiority was not less in the style of the
fitting-up,[5] or the taste of the furniture. Their acquaintance was
exceedingly sought after. Every body was wanting to visit them. They
had drawn back from many introductions, and still were perpetually having cards[6] left by people of whom they knew nothing.

Here were funds of enjoyment! Could Anne wonder that her father
and sister were happy? She might not wonder, but she must sigh that
her father should feel no degradation in his change; should see nothing to regret in the duties and dignity of the resident landholder;
should find so much to be vain of in the littlenesses of a town; and
she must sigh, and smile, and wonder too, as Elizabeth threw open
the folding-doors, and walked with exultation from one drawing-
room to the other, boasting of their space, at the possibility of that
woman, who had been mistress of Kellynch-hall, finding extent to
be proud of between two walls, perhaps thirty feet asunder.

But this was not all which they had to make them happy. They
had Mr. Elliot, too. Anne had a great deal to hear of Mr. Elliot. He
was not only pardoned, they were delighted with him. He had been
in Bath about a fortnight; (he had passed through Bath in November, in his way to London, when the intelligence of Sir Walter's being
settled there had of course reached him, though only twenty-four
hours in the place, but he had not been able to avail himself of it):
but he had now been a fortnight in Bath, and his first object, on
arriving, had been to leave his card in Camden-place, following it
up by such assiduous endeavours to meet, and, when they did meet,
by such great openness of conduct, such readiness to apologize for
the past, such solicitude to be received as a relation again, that their
former good understanding was completely re-established.

They had not a fault to find in him. He had explained away all
the appearance of neglect on his own side. It had originated in misapprehension entirely. He had never had an idea of throwing himself off; he had feared that he was thrown off, but knew not why;
and delicacy had kept him silent. Upon the hint of having spoken

5. Decorating.
6. Small rectangular cards printed with one's name and handed to a butler or servant to
   announce one's arrival for a visit. Calling cards could be used either in place of a visit
   for a card owner who preferred not to appear in person, or for screening purposes, to
   refuse entry to a socially undesirable guest.

disrespectfully or carelessly of the family, and the family honours, he was quite indignant. He, who had ever boasted of being an Elliot, and whose feelings, as to connection, were only too strict to suit the unfeudal tone of the present day! He was astonished, indeed! But his character and general conduct must refute it. He could refer Sir Walter to all who knew him; and, certainly, the pains he had been taking on this, the first opportunity of reconciliation, to be restored to the footing of a relation and heir-presumptive, was a strong proof of his opinions on the subject.

The circumstances of his marriage too were found to admit of much extenuation. This was an article not to be entered on by himself; but a very intimate friend of his, a Colonel[7] Wallis, a highly respectable man, perfectly the gentleman, (and not an ill-looking man, Sir Walter added) who was living in very good style in Marl-borough Buildings, and had, at his own particular request, been admitted to their acquaintance through Mr. Elliot, had mentioned one or two things relative to the marriage, which made a material difference in the discredit of it.

Colonel Wallis had known Mr. Elliot long, had been well acquainted also with his wife, had perfectly understood the whole story. She was certainly not a woman of family, but well educated, accomplished, rich, and excessively in love with his friend. There had been the charm. She had sought him. Without that attraction, not all her money would have tempted Elliot, and Sir Walter was, moreover, assured of her having been a very fine[8] woman. Here was a great deal to soften the business. A very fine woman, with a large fortune, in love with him! Sir Walter seemed to admit it as complete apol-ogy, and though Elizabeth could not see the circumstance in quite so favourable a light, she allowed it be a great extenuation.

Mr. Elliot had called repeatedly, had dined with them once, evi-dently delighted by the distinction of being asked, for they gave no dinners in general; delighted, in short, by every proof of cousinly notice, and placing his whole happiness in being on intimate terms in Camden-place.

Anne listened, but without quite understanding it. Allowances, large allowances, she knew, must be made for the ideas of those who spoke. She heard it all under embellishment. All that sounded extrav-agant or irrational in the progress of the reconciliation might have no origin but in the language of the relators. Still, however, she had the sensation of there being something more than immediately appeared, in Mr. Elliot's wishing, after an interval of so many years,

7. The rank just below brigadier in the British military. Only ranks below colonel could be purchased.
8. Good-looking.

to be well received by them. In a worldly view, he had nothing to gain by being on terms with Sir Walter, nothing to risk by a state of variance. In all probability he was already the richer of the two, and the Kellynch estate would as surely be his hereafter as the title. A sensible man! and he had looked like a *very* sensible man, why should it be an object to him? She could only offer one solution; it was, perhaps, for Elizabeth's sake. There might really have been a liking formerly, though convenience and accident had drawn him a different way, and now that he could afford to please himself, he might mean to pay his addresses to her. Elizabeth was certainly very handsome, with well-bred, elegant manners, and her character might never have been penetrated by Mr. Elliot, knowing her but in public, and when very young himself. How her temper and understanding might bear the investigation of his present keener time of life was another concern, and rather a fearful one. Most earnestly did she wish that he might not be too nice,[9] or too observant, if Elizabeth were his object; and that Elizabeth was disposed to believe herself so, and that her friend Mrs. Clay was encouraging the idea, seemed apparent by a glance or two between them, while Mr. Elliot's frequent visits were talked of.

Anne mentioned the glimpses she had had of him at Lyme, but without being much attended to. "Oh! yes, perhaps, it had been Mr. Elliot. They did not know. It might be him, perhaps." They could not listen to her description of him. They were describing him themselves; Sir Walter especially. He did justice to his very gentleman-like appearance, his air of elegance and fashion, his good shaped face, his sensible eye, but, at the same time, "must lament his being very much under-hung,[1] a defect which time seemed to have increased; nor could he pretend to say that ten years had not altered almost every feature for the worse. Mr. Elliot appeared to think that he (Sir Walter) was looking exactly as he had done when they last parted;" but Sir Walter had "not been able to return the compliment entirely, which had embarrassed him. He did not mean to complain, however. Mr. Elliot was better to look at than most men, and he had no objection to being seen with him any where."

Mr. Elliot, and his friends in Marlborough Buildings, were talked of the whole evening. "Colonel Wallis had been so impatient to be introduced to them! and Mr. Elliot so anxious that he should!" And there was a Mrs. Wallis, at present only known to them by description, as she was in daily expectation of her confinement;[2] but Mr. Elliot spoke of her as "a most charming woman, quite worthy of being known in Camden-place," and as soon as she recovered, they were to be acquainted. Sir Walter thought much of Mrs. Wallis; she

9. Exacting, scrupulous.
1. Having a projecting lower jaw.
2. Lying-in for childbirth.

was said to be an excessively pretty woman, beautiful. "He longed to see her. He hoped she might make some amends for the many very plain faces he was continually passing in the streets. The worst of Bath was, the number of its plain women. He did not mean to say that there were no pretty women, but the number of the plain was out of all proportion. He had frequently observed, as he walked, that one handsome face would be followed by thirty, or five and thirty frights; and once, as he had stood in a shop in Bond-street, he had counted eighty-seven women go by, one after another, without there being a tolerable face among them. It had been a frosty morning, to be sure, a sharp frost, which hardly one woman in a thousand could stand the test of. But still, there certainly were a dreadful multitude of ugly women in Bath; and as for the men! they were infinitely worse. Such scare-crows as the streets were full of! It was evident how little the women were used to the sight of any thing tolerable, by the effect which a man of decent appearance produced. He had never walked any where arm in arm with Colonel Wallis, (who was a fine military figure, though sandy-haired) without observing that every woman's eye was upon him; every woman's eye was sure to be upon Colonel Wallis." Modest Sir Walter! He was not allowed to escape, however. His daughter and Mrs. Clay united in hinting that Colonel Wallis's companion might have as good a figure as Colonel Wallis, and certainly was not sandy-haired.

"How is Mary looking?" said Sir Walter, in the height of his good humour. "The last time I saw her, she had a red nose, but I hope that may not happen every day."

"Oh! no, that must have been quite accidental. In general she has been in very good health, and very good looks since Michaelmas."

"If I thought it would not tempt her to go out in sharp winds, and grow coarse, I would send her a new hat and pelisse."

Anne was considering whether she should venture to suggest that a gown, or a cap, would not be liable to any such misuse, when a knock at the door suspended every thing. "A knock at the door! and so late! It was ten o'clock. Could it be Mr. Elliot? They knew he was to dine in Lansdown Crescent.[3] It was possible that he might stop in his way home, to ask them how they did. They could think of no one else. Mrs. Clay decidedly thought it Mr. Elliot's knock." Mrs. Clay was right. With all the state which a butler and foot-boy could give, Mr. Elliot was ushered into the room.

It was the same, the very same man, with no difference but of dress. Anne drew a little back, while the others received his compliments, and her sister his apologies for calling at so unusual an hour,

---

3. A building in the Georgian style, designed by the English architect John Palmer (1738–1817) and newly built from 1789 to 1793.

but "he could not be so near without wishing to know that neither
she nor her friend had taken cold the day before, etc. etc." which was
all as politely done, and as politely taken as possible, but her part
must follow then. Sir Walter talked of his youngest daughter;
"Mr. Elliot must give him leave to present him to his youngest
daughter"—(there was no occasion for remembering Mary) and
Anne, smiling and blushing, very becomingly shewed to Mr. Elliot
the pretty features which he had by no means forgotten, and instantly
saw, with amusement at his little start of surprise, that he had not
been at all aware of who she was. He looked completely astonished,
but not more astonished than pleased; his eyes brightened, and with
the most perfect alacrity he welcomed the relationship, alluded to
the past, and entreated to be received as an acquaintance already. He
was quite as good-looking as he had appeared at Lyme, his countenance improved by speaking, and his manners were so exactly what
they ought to be, so polished, so easy, so particularly agreeable, that
she could compare them in excellence to only one person's manners.
They were not the same, but they were, perhaps, equally good.

He sat down with them, and improved their conversation very
much. There could be no doubt of his being a sensible man. Ten minutes were enough to certify that. His tone, his expressions, his choice
of subject, his knowing where to stop,—it was all the operation of a
sensible, discerning mind. As soon as he could, he began to talk to
her of Lyme, wanting to compare opinions respecting the place, but
especially wanting to speak of the circumstance of their happening to
be guests in the same inn at the same time, to give his own route,
understand something of hers, and regret that he should have lost
such an opportunity of paying his respects to her. She gave him a
short account of her party, and business at Lyme. His regret increased
as he listened. He had spent his whole solitary evening in the room
adjoining theirs; had heard voices—mirth continually; thought they
must be a most delightful set of people—longed to be with them; but
certainly without the smallest suspicion of his possessing the shadow
of a right to introduce himself. If he had but asked who the party
were! The name of Musgrove would have told him enough. "Well, it
would serve to cure him of an absurd practice of never asking a question at an inn, which he had adopted, when quite a young man, on
the principle of its being very ungenteel to be curious.[4]

"The notions of a young man of one or two and twenty," said he,
"as to what is necessary in manners to make him quite the thing,
are more absurd, I believe, than those of any other set of beings in

4. In his *Letters of Advice to His Son* (1774), Lord Chesterfield cautions: "frivolous curiosity about trifles, and a laborious attention to little objects, which neither require nor
deserve a moment's thought, lower a man; who from thence is thought (and not
unjustly) incapable of greater matters" (p. 83). As heir to the Kellynch estate, Mr. Elliot
ought not to consider courtesy toward family a trifling matter.

the world. The folly of the means they often employ is only to be equalled by the folly of what they have in view."

But he must not be addressing his reflections to Anne alone; he knew it; he was soon diffused again among the others, and it was only at intervals that he could return to Lyme.

His enquiries, however, produced at length an account of the scene she had been engaged in there, soon after his leaving the place. Having alluded to "an accident," he must hear the whole. When he questioned, Sir Walter and Elizabeth began to question also; but the difference in their manner of doing it could not be unfelt. She could only compare Mr. Elliot to Lady Russell, in the wish of really comprehending what had passed, and in the degree of concern for what she must have suffered in witnessing it.

He staid an hour with them. The elegant little clock on the mantlepiece had struck "eleven with its silver sounds,"[5] and the watchman was beginning to be heard at a distance telling the same tale, before Mr. Elliot or any of them seemed to feel that he had been there long.

Anne could not have supposed it possible that her first evening in Camden-place could have passed so well!

Chapter XVI

There was one point which Anne, on returning to her family, would have been more thankful to ascertain, even than Mr. Elliot's being in love with Elizabeth, which was, her father's not being in love with Mrs. Clay; and she was very far from easy about it, when she had been at home a few hours. On going down to breakfast the next morning, she found there had just been a decent pretence on the lady's side of meaning to leave them. She could imagine Mrs. Clay to have said, that "now Miss Anne was come, she could not suppose herself at all wanted;" for Elizabeth was replying, in a sort of whisper, "That must not be any reason, indeed. I assure you I feel it none. She is nothing to me, compared with you;" and she was in full time to hear her father say, "My dear Madam, this must not be. As yet, you have seen nothing of Bath. You have been here only to be useful. You must not run away from us now. You must stay to be acquainted with Mrs. Wallis, the beautiful Mrs. Wallis. To your fine mind, I well know the sight of beauty is a real gratification."

He spoke and looked so much in earnest, that Anne was not surprised to see Mrs. Clay stealing a glance at Elizabeth and herself. Her countenance, perhaps, might express some watchfulness; but

5. Perhaps an allusion to Alexander Pope's *The Rape of the Lock* (1714): "And the pressed watch returned a silver sound" (1.18).

the praise of the fine mind did not appear to excite a thought in her sister. The lady could not but yield to such joint entreaties, and promise to stay.

In the course of the same morning, Anne and her father chancing to be alone together, he began to compliment her on her improved looks; he thought her "less thin in her person, in her cheeks; her skin, her complexion, greatly improved—clearer, fresher. Had she been using any thing in particular?" "No, nothing." "Merely Gowland,"[6] he supposed. "No, nothing at all." "Ha! he was surprised at that;" and added, "Certainly you cannot do better than continue as you are; you cannot be better than well; or I should recommend Gowland, the constant use of Gowland, during the spring months. Mrs. Clay has been using it at my recommendation, and you see what it has done for her. You see how it has carried away her freckles."

If Elizabeth could but have heard this! Such personal praise might have struck her, especially as it did not appear to Anne that the freckles were at all lessened. But every thing must take its chance. The evil of the marriage would be much diminished, if Elizabeth were also to marry. As for herself, she might always command a home with Lady Russell.

Lady Russell's composed mind and polite manners were put to some trial on this point, in her intercourse in Camden-place. The sight of Mrs. Clay in such favour, and of Anne so overlooked, was a perpetual provocation to her there; and vexed her as much when she was away, as a person in Bath who drinks the water, gets all the new publications, and has a very large acquaintance, has time to be vexed.

As Mr. Elliot became known to her, she grew more charitable, or more indifferent, towards the others. His manners were an immediate recommendation; and on conversing with him she found the solid so fully supporting the superficial, that she was at first, as she told Anne, almost ready to exclaim, "Can this be Mr. Elliot?" and could not seriously picture to herself a more agreeable or estimable man. Every thing united in him; good understanding, correct opinions, knowledge of the world, and a warm heart. He had strong feelings of family-attachment and family-honour, without pride or weakness; he lived with the liberality of a man of fortune, without display; he judged for himself in every thing essential, without defying public opinion in any point of worldly decorum. He was steady, observant, moderate, candid; never run away with by spirits or by selfishness, which fancied itself strong feeling; and yet, with a sensibility to what was amiable and lovely, and a value for all the felicities of domestic life, which characters of fancied enthusiasm and

6. Gowland's Lotion, intended for the face, was supposed to remedy ailments of the skin. See p. x in the introduction.

violent agitation seldom really possess. She was sure that he had not been happy in marriage. Colonel Wallis said it, and Lady Russell saw it; but it had been no unhappiness to sour his mind, nor (she began pretty soon to suspect) to prevent his thinking of a second choice. Her satisfaction in Mr. Elliot outweighed all the plague of Mrs. Clay.

It was now some years since Anne had begun to learn that she and her excellent friend could sometimes think differently; and it did not surprise her, therefore, that Lady Russell should see nothing suspicious or inconsistent, nothing to require more motives than appeared, in Mr. Elliot's great desire of a reconciliation. In Lady Russell's view, it was perfectly natural that Mr. Elliot, at a mature time of life, should feel it a most desirable object, and what would very generally recommend him, among all sensible people, to be on good terms with the head of his family; the simplest process in the world of time upon a head naturally clear, and only erring in the heyday of youth. Anne presumed, however, still to smile about it; and at last to mention "Elizabeth." Lady Russell listened, and looked, and made only this cautious reply: "Elizabeth! Very well. Time will explain."

It was a reference to the future, which Anne, after a little observation, felt she must submit to. She could determine nothing at present. In that house Elizabeth must be first; and she was in the habit of such general observance as "Miss Elliot," that any particularity of attention seemed almost impossible. Mr. Elliot, too, it must be remembered, had not been a widower seven months. A little delay on his side might be very excusable. In fact, Anne could never see the crape[7] round his hat, without fearing that she was the inexcusable one, in attributing to him such imaginations; for though his marriage had not been very happy, still it had existed so many years that she could not comprehend a very rapid recovery from the awful[8] impression of its being dissolved.

However it might end, he was without any question their pleasantest acquaintance in Bath; she saw nobody equal to him; and it was a great indulgence now and then to talk to him about Lyme, which he seemed to have as lively a wish to see again, and to see more of, as herself. They went through the particulars of their first meeting a great many times. He gave her to understand that he had looked at her with some earnestness. She knew it well; and she remembered another person's look also.

They did not always think alike. His value for rank and connexion she perceived to be greater than hers. It was not merely complaisance, it must be a liking to the cause, which made him enter warmly into her father and sister's solicitudes on a subject which she

7. Crepe; a sign of mourning.
8. Great, substantial, but also disagreeable, objectionable.

thought unworthy to excite them. The Bath paper one morning announced the arrival of the Dowager Viscountess Dalrymple, and her daughter, the Honourable Miss Carteret;[9] and all the comfort of No. —, Camden-place, was swept away for many days; for the Dalrymples (in Anne's opinion, most unfortunately) were cousins of the Elliots; and the agony was, how to introduce themselves properly.

Anne had never seen her father and sister before in contact with nobility, and she must acknowledge herself disappointed. She had hoped better things from their high ideas of their own situation in life, and was reduced to form a wish which she had never foreseen—a wish that they had more pride; for "our cousins Lady Dalrymple and Miss Carteret;" "our cousins, the Dalrymples," sounded in her ears all day long.

Sir Walter had once been in company with the late Viscount, but had never seen any of the rest of the family, and the difficulties of the case arose from there having been a suspension of all intercourse by letters of ceremony, ever since the death of that said late Viscount, when, in consequence of a dangerous illness of Sir Walter's at the same time, there had been an unlucky omission at Kellynch. No letter of condolence had been sent to Ireland. The neglect had been visited on the head of the sinner, for when poor Lady Elliot died herself, no letter of condolence was received at Kellynch, and, consequently, there was but too much reason to apprehend that the Dalrymples considered the relationship as closed. How to have this anxious business set to rights, and be admitted as cousins again, was the question; and it was a question which, in a more rational manner, neither Lady Russell nor Mr. Elliot thought unimportant. "Family connexions were always worth preserving, good company always worth seeking; Lady Dalrymple had taken a house, for three months, in Laura-place, and would be living in style. She had been at Bath the year before, and Lady Russell had heard her spoken of as a charming woman. It was very desirable that the connexion should be renewed, if it could be done, without any compromise of propriety on the side of the Elliots."

Sir Walter, however, would choose his own means, and at last wrote a very fine letter of ample explanation, regret and entreaty, to his right honourable cousin. Neither Lady Russell nor Mr. Elliot could admire the letter; but it did all that was wanted, in bringing three lines of scrawl from the Dowager Viscountess. "She was very

---

9. A widow with noble rank, Lady Dalrymple may have reminded Austen's readers of Grace Dalrymple Elliott (ca. 1754–1823), famed Scottish courtesan and spy, whose *Journal of My Life During the French Revolution* (posthumously published in 1859) detailed her experiences transporting correspondence on behalf of the French Royalists and surviving the Terror. The name Cartaret has ties to royalism, baronetcy, and the navy in the figure of Vice Admiral Sir George Cartaret, 1st Baronet (ca. 1610–1680).

much honoured, and should be happy in their acquaintance." The toils of the business were over, the sweets began. They visited in Laura-place, they had the cards of Dowager Viscountess Dalrymple, and the Hon. Miss Carteret, to be arranged wherever they might be most visible; and "Our cousins in Laura-place,"—"Our cousins, Lady Dalrymple and Miss Carteret," were talked of to every body.

Anne was ashamed. Had Lady Dalrymple and her daughter even been very agreeable, she would still have been ashamed of the agitation they created, but they were nothing. There was no superiority of manner, accomplishment, or understanding. Lady Dalrymple had acquired the name of "a charming woman," because she had a smile and a civil answer for every body. Miss Carteret, with still less to say, was so plain and so awkward, that she would never have been tolerated in Camden-place but for her birth.

Lady Russell confessed that she had expected something better; but yet "it was an acquaintance worth having," and when Anne ventured to speak her opinion of them to Mr. Elliot, he agreed to their being nothing in themselves, but still maintained that as a family connexion, as good company, as those who would collect good company around them, they had their value. Anne smiled and said,

"My idea of good company, Mr. Elliot, is the company of clever, well-informed people, who have a great deal of conversation; that is what I call good company."

"You are mistaken," said he gently, "that is not good company, that is the best. Good company requires only birth, education and manners, and with regard to education is not very nice. Birth and good manners are essential; but a little learning is by no means a dangerous thing in good company, on the contrary, it will do very well. My cousin, Anne, shakes her head. She is not satisfied. She is fastidious. My dear cousin, (sitting down by her) you have a better right to be fastidious than almost any other woman I know; but will it answer?[1] Will it make you happy? Will it not be wiser to accept the society of these good ladies in Laura-place, and enjoy all the advantages of the connexion as far as possible? You may depend upon it, that they will move in the first set in Bath this winter, and as rank is rank, your being known to be related to them will have its use in fixing your family (our family let me say) in that degree of consideration which we must all wish for."

"Yes," sighed Anne, "we shall, indeed, be known to be related to them!"—then recollecting herself, and not wishing to be answered, she added, "I certainly do think there has been by far too much trouble taken to procure the acquaintance. I suppose (smiling) I have more pride than any of you; but I confess it does vex me, that we

---

1. Suffice, serve the purpose.

should be so solicitous to have the relationship acknowledged, which we may be very sure is a matter of perfect indifference to them."

"Pardon me, my dear cousin, you are unjust to your own claims. In London, perhaps, in your present quiet style of living, it might be as you say; but in Bath, Sir Walter Elliot and his family will always be worth knowing, always acceptable as acquaintance."

"Well," said Anne, "I certainly am proud, too proud to enjoy a welcome which depends so entirely upon place."

"I love your indignation," said he; "it is very natural. But here you are in Bath, and the object is to be established here with all the credit and dignity which ought to belong to Sir Walter Elliot. You talk of being proud, I am called proud I know, and I shall not wish to believe myself otherwise, for our pride, if investigated, would have the same object, I have no doubt, though the kind may seem a little different. In one point, I am sure, my dear cousin, (he continued, speaking lower, though there was no one else in the room) in one point, I am sure, we must feel alike. We must feel that every addition to your father's society, among his equals or superiors, may be of use in diverting his thoughts from those who are beneath him."

He looked, as he spoke, to the seat which Mrs. Clay had been lately occupying, a sufficient explanation of what he particularly meant; and though Anne could not believe in their having the same sort of pride, she was pleased with him for not liking Mrs. Clay; and her conscience admitted that his wishing to promote her father's getting great acquaintance, was more than excusable in the view of defeating her.

Chapter XVII

While Sir Walter and Elizabeth were assiduously pushing their good fortune in Laura-place, Anne was renewing an acquaintance of a very different description.

She had called on her former governess, and had heard from her of there being an old school-fellow in Bath, who had the two strong claims on her attention, of past kindness and present suffering. Miss Hamilton, now Mrs. Smith, had shewn her kindness in one of those periods of her life when it had been most valuable. Anne had gone unhappy to school, grieving for the loss of a mother whom she had dearly loved, feeling her separation from home, and suffering as a girl of fourteen, of strong sensibility and not high spirits, must suffer at such a time; and Miss Hamilton, three years older than herself, but still from her want of near relations and a settled home, remaining another year at school, had been useful and good to her in a way which had considerably lessened her misery, and could never be remembered with indifference.

Miss Hamilton had left school, had married not long afterwards, was said to have married a man of fortune, and this was all that Anne had known of her, till now that their governess's account brought her situation forward in a more decided but very different form.

She was a widow, and poor. Her husband had been extravagant; and at his death, about two years before, had left his affairs dreadfully involved. She had had difficulties of every sort to contend with, and in addition to these distresses, had been afflicted with a severe rheumatic fever, which finally settling in her legs, had made her for the present a cripple. She had come to Bath on that account, and was now in lodgings near the hotbaths, living in a very humble way, unable even to afford herself the comfort of a servant, and of course almost excluded from society.

Their mutual friend answered for the satisfaction which a visit from Miss Elliot would give Mrs. Smith, and Anne therefore lost no time in going. She mentioned nothing of what she had heard, or what she intended, at home. It would excite no proper interest there. She only consulted Lady Russell, who entered thoroughly into her sentiments, and was most happy to convey her as near to Mrs. Smith's lodgings in Westgate-buildings, as Anne chose to be taken.

The visit was paid, their acquaintance re-established, their interest in each other more than re-kindled. The first ten minutes had its awkwardness and its emotion. Twelve years were gone since they had parted, and each presented a somewhat different person from what the other had imagined. Twelve years had changed Anne from the blooming, silent, unformed girl of fifteen, to the elegant little woman of seven and twenty, with every beauty excepting bloom, and with manners as consciously right as they were invariably gentle; and twelve years had transformed the fine-looking, well-grown Miss Hamilton, in all the glow of health and confidence of superiority, into a poor, infirm, helpless widow, receiving the visit of her former protegeé as a favour; but all that was uncomfortable in the meeting had soon passed away, and left only the interesting charm of remembering former partialities and talking over old times.

Anne found in Mrs. Smith the good sense and agreeable manners which she had almost ventured to depend on, and a disposition to converse and be cheerful beyond her expectation. Neither the dissipations of the past—and she had lived very much in the world, nor the restrictions of the present; neither sickness nor sorrow seemed to have closed her heart or ruined her spirits.

In the course of a second visit she talked with great openness, and Anne's astonishment increased. She could scarcely imagine a more cheerless situation in itself than Mrs. Smith's. She had been very fond of her husband,—she had buried him. She had been used to affluence,—it was gone. She had no child to connect her with life and happiness again, no relations to assist in the arrangement of perplexed affairs, no health to make all the rest supportable. Her accommodations were limited to a noisy parlour, and a dark bedroom behind, with no possibility of moving from one to the other without assistance, which there was only one servant in the house to afford, and she never quitted the house but to be conveyed into the warm bath.[2]—Yet, in spite of all this, Anne had reason to believe that she had moments only of languor and depression, to hours of occupation and enjoyment. How could it be?—She watched—observed—reflected—and finally determined that this was not a case of fortitude or of resignation only.—A submissive spirit might be patient, a strong understanding would supply resolution, but here was something more; here was that elasticity of mind, that disposition to be comforted, that power of turning readily from evil to good, and of finding employment which carried her out of herself, which was from Nature alone. It was the choicest gift of Heaven; and Anne viewed her friend as one of those instances in which, by a merciful appointment, it seems designed to counterbalance almost every other want.

There had been a time, Mrs. Smith told her, when her spirits had nearly failed. She could not call herself an invalid now, compared with her state on first reaching Bath. Then, she had indeed been a pitiable object—for she had caught cold on the journey, and had hardly taken possession of her lodgings, before she was again confined to her bed, and suffering under severe and constant pain; and all this among strangers—with the absolute necessity of having a regular nurse, and finances at that moment particularly unfit to meet any extraordinary expense. She had weathered it however, and could truly say that it had done her good. It had increased her comforts by making her feel herself to be in good hands. She had seen too much of the world, to expect sudden or disinterested attachment any where, but her illness had proved to her that her landlady had a character[3] to preserve, and would not use her ill; and she had been particularly fortunate in her nurse, as a sister of her landlady, a nurse by profession, and who had always a home in that house when unemployed, chanced to be at liberty just in time to attend her.—"And she," said Mrs. Smith, "besides nursing me most admirably, has really proved an invaluable acquaintance.—As soon as I could use

2. Mrs. Smith's rheumatism has brought her to Bath in the hopes that the medicinal qualities believed present in the mineral springs will have a healing effect.
3. Reputation.

my hands, she taught me to knit, which has been a great amusement; and she put me in the way of making these little thread-cases, pin-cushions and card-racks,[4] which you always find me so busy about, and which supply me with the means of doing a little good to one or two very poor families in this neighbourhood. She has a large acquaintance, of course professionally, among those who can afford to buy, and she disposes of my merchandize. She always takes the right time for applying. Every body's heart is open, you know, when they have recently escaped from severe pain, or are recovering the blessing of health, and nurse Rooke thoroughly understands when to speak. She is a shrewd, intelligent, sensible woman. Hers is a line for seeing human nature; and she has a fund of good sense and observation which, as a companion, make her infinitely superior to thousands of those who having only received "the best education in the world," know nothing worth attending to. Call it gossip if you will; but when nurse Rooke has half an hour's leisure to bestow on me, she is sure to have something to relate that is entertaining and profitable, something that makes one know one's species better. One likes to hear what is going on, to be *au fait*[5] as to the newest modes of being trifling and silly. To me, who live so much alone, her conversation I assure you is a treat."

Anne, far from wishing to cavil at the pleasure, replied, "I can easily believe it. Women of that class have great opportunities, and if they are intelligent may be well worth listening to. Such varieties of human nature as they are in the habit of witnessing! And it is not merely in its follies, that they are well read; for they see it occasionally under every circumstance that can be most interesting or affecting. What instances must pass before them of ardent, disinterested, self-denying attachment, of heroism, fortitude, patience, resignation—of all the conflicts and all the sacrifices that ennoble us most. A sick chamber may often furnish the worth of volumes."

"Yes," said Mrs. Smith more doubtingly, "sometimes it may, though I fear its lessons are not often in the elevated style you describe. Here and there, human nature may be great in times of trial, but generally speaking it is its weakness and not its strength that appears in a sick chamber; it is selfishness and impatience rather than generosity and fortitude, that one hears of. There is so little real friendship in the world!—and unfortunately" (speaking low and tremulously) "there are so many who forget to think seriously till it is almost too late."

---

4. Mrs. Smith engages in the conventional female handicrafts of the gentlewoman. Using the sales of these items to do "a little good to one or two very poor families in this neighbourhood" allows her to maintain her status despite her reduced circumstances.
5. Aware, in the know.

Anne saw the misery of such feelings. The husband had not been what he ought, and the wife had been led among that part of mankind which made her think worse of the world, than she hoped it deserved. It was but a passing emotion however with Mrs. Smith, she shook it off, and soon added in a different tone,

"I do not suppose the situation my friend Mrs. Rooke is in at present, will furnish much either to interest or edify me.—She is only nursing Mrs. Wallis of Marlborough-buildings—a mere pretty, silly, expensive, fashionable woman, I believe—and of course will have nothing to report but of lace and finery.—I mean to make my profit of Mrs. Wallis, however. She has plenty of money, and I intend she shall buy all the high-priced things I have in hand now."

Anne had called several times on her friend, before the existence of such a person was known in Camden-place. At last, it became necessary to speak of her.—Sir Walter, Elizabeth and Mrs. Clay returned one morning from Laura-place, with a sudden invitation from Lady Dalrymple for the same evening, and Anne was already engaged, to spend that evening in Westgate-buildings. She was not sorry for the excuse. They were only asked, she was sure, because Lady Dalrymple being kept at home by a bad cold, was glad to make use of the relationship which had been so pressed on her,—and she declined on her own account with great alacrity—"She was engaged to spend the evening with an old schoolfellow." They were not much interested in any thing relative to Anne, but still there were questions enough asked, to make it understood what this old schoolfellow was; and Elizabeth was disdainful, and Sir Walter severe.

"Westgate-buildings!" said he; "and who is Miss Anne Elliot to be visiting in Westgate-buildings?—A Mrs. Smith. A widow Mrs. Smith,—and who was her husband? One of the five thousand Mr. Smiths[6] whose names are to be met with every where. And what is her attraction? That she is old and sickly.—Upon my word, Miss Anne Elliot, you have the most extraordinary taste! Every thing that revolts other people, low company, paltry rooms, foul air, disgusting associations are inviting to you. But surely, you may put off this old lady till to-morrow. She is not so near her end, I presume, but that she may hope to see another day. What is her age? Forty?"

"No, Sir, she is not one and thirty; but I do not think I can put off my engagement, because it is the only evening for some time which will at once suit her and myself.—She goes into the warm bath tomorrow, and for the rest of the week you know we are engaged."

"But what does Lady Russell think of this acquaintance?" asked Elizabeth.

---

6. "Smith" implies metalworking, blacksmithing, and similar forms of dirty, menial labor, to which association Sir Walter objects.

"She sees nothing to blame in it," replied Anne; "on the contrary, she approves it; and has generally taken me, when I have called on Mrs. Smith."

"Westgate-buildings must have been rather surprised by the appearance of a carriage drawn up near its pavement!" observed Sir Walter.—"Sir Henry Russell's widow, indeed, has no honours[7] to distinguish her arms; but still, it is a handsome equipage, and no doubt is well known to convey a Miss Elliot.—A widow Mrs. Smith, lodging in Westgate-buildings!—A poor widow, barely able to live, between thirty and forty—a mere Mrs. Smith, an every day Mrs. Smith, of all people and all names in the world, to be the chosen friend of Miss Anne Elliot, and to be preferred by her, to her own family connections among the nobility of England and Ireland! Mrs. Smith, such a name!"

Mrs. Clay, who had been present while all this passed, now thought it advisable to leave the room, and Anne could have said much and did long to say a little, in defence of *her* friend's not very dissimilar claims to theirs, but her sense of personal respect to her father prevented her. She made no reply. She left it to himself to recollect, that Mrs. Smith was not the only widow in Bath between thirty and forty, with little to live on, and no sirname[8] of dignity.

Anne kept her appointment; the others kept theirs, and of course she heard the next morning that they had had a delightful evening.—She had been the only one of the set absent; for Sir Walter and Elizabeth had not only been quite at her ladyship's service themselves, but had actually been happy to be employed by her in collecting others, and had been at the trouble of inviting both Lady Russell and Mr. Elliot; and Mr. Elliot had made a point of leaving Colonel Wallis early, and Lady Russell had fresh arranged all her evening engagements in order to wait on her. Anne had the whole history of all that such an evening could supply, from Lady Russell. To her, its greatest interest must be, in having been very much talked of between her friend and Mr. Elliot, in having been wished for, regretted, and at the same time honoured for staying away in such a cause.—Her kind, compassionate visits to this old schoolfellow, sick and reduced, seemed to have quite delighted Mr. Elliot. He thought her a most extraordinary young woman; in her temper, manners, mind, a model of female excellence. He could meet even Lady Russell in a discussion of her merits; and Anne could not be given to understand so much by her friend, could not know herself to be so highly rated by a sensible man, without many of those agreeable sensations which her friend meant to create.

7. Emblems of special achievement added to a coat of arms.
8. Surname, family name.

Lady Russell was now perfectly decided in her opinion of Mr. Elliot. She was as much convinced of his meaning to gain Anne in time, as of his deserving her; and was beginning to calculate the number of weeks which would free him from all the remaining restraints of widowhood, and leave him at liberty to exert his most open powers of pleasing. She would not speak to Anne with half the certainty she felt on the subject, she would venture on little more than hints of what might be hereafter, of a possible attachment on his side, of the desirableness of the alliance, supposing such attachment to be real, and returned. Anne heard her, and made no violent exclamations. She only smiled, blushed, and gently shook her head.

"I am no match-maker, as you well know," said Lady Russell, "being much too well aware of the uncertainty of all human events and calculations. I only mean that if Mr. Elliot should some time hence pay his addresses to you, and if you should be disposed to accept him, I think there would be every possibility of your being happy together. A most suitable connection every body must consider it—but I think it might be a very happy one."

"Mr. Elliot is an exceedingly agreeable man, and in many respects I think highly of him," said Anne; "but we should not suit."

Lady Russell let this pass, and only said in rejoinder, "I own that to be able to regard you as the future mistress of Kellynch, the future Lady Elliot—to look forward and see you occupying your dear mother's place, succeeding to all her rights, and all her popularity, as well as to all her virtues, would be the highest possible gratification to me.—You are your mother's self in countenance and disposition; and if I might be allowed to fancy you such as she was, in situation, and name, and home, presiding and blessing in the same spot, and only superior to her in being more highly valued! My dearest Anne, it would give me more delight than is often felt at my time of life!"

Anne was obliged to turn away, to rise, to walk to a distant table, and, leaning there in pretended employment, try to subdue the feelings this picture excited. For a few moments her imagination and her heart were bewitched. The idea of becoming what her mother had been; of having the precious name of "Lady Elliot" first revived in herself; of being restored to Kellynch, calling it her home again, her home for ever, was a charm which she could not immediately resist. Lady Russell said not another word, willing to leave the matter to its own operation; and believing that, could Mr. Elliot at that moment with propriety have spoken for himself!—She believed, in short, what Anne did not believe. The same image of Mr. Elliot speaking for himself, brought Anne to composure again. The charm of Kellynch and of "Lady Elliot" all faded away. She never could accept him. And it was not only that her feelings were still adverse to any man save one; her judgment, on a serious consideration of the possibilities of such a case, was against Mr. Elliot.

Though they had now been acquainted a month, she could not be satisfied that she really knew his character. That he was a sensible man, an agreeable man,—that he talked well, professed good opinions, seemed to judge properly and as a man of principle,—this was all clear enough. He certainly knew what was right, nor could she fix on any one article of moral duty evidently transgressed; but yet she would have been afraid to answer for his conduct. She distrusted the past, if not the present. The names which occasionally dropt of former associates, the allusions to former practices and pursuits, suggested suspicions not favourable of what he had been. She saw that there had been bad habits; that Sunday-travelling[9] had been a common thing; that there had been a period of his life (and probably not a short one) when he had been, at least, careless on all serious matters; and, though he might now think very differently, who could answer for the true sentiments of a clever, cautious man, grown old enough to appreciate a fair character?[1] How could it ever be ascertained that his mind was truly cleansed?

Mr. Elliot was rational, discreet, polished,—but he was not open. There was never any burst of feeling, any warmth of indignation or delight, at the evil or good of others. This, to Anne, was a decided imperfection. Her early impressions were incurable. She prized the frank, the open-hearted, the eager character beyond all others. Warmth and enthusiasm did captivate her still. She felt that she could so much more depend upon the sincerity of those who sometimes looked or said a careless or a hasty thing, than of those whose presence of mind never varied, whose tongue never slipped.

Mr. Elliot was too generally agreeable. Various as were the tempers in her father's house, he pleased them all. He endured too well,—stood too well with everybody. He had spoken to her with some degree of openness of Mrs. Clay; had appeared completely to see what Mrs. Clay was about, and to hold her in contempt; and yet Mrs. Clay found him as agreeable as anybody.

Lady Russell saw either less or more than her young friend, for she saw nothing to excite distrust. She could not imagine a man more exactly what he ought to be than Mr. Elliot; nor did she ever enjoy a sweeter feeling than the hope of seeing him receive the hand of her beloved Anne in Kellynch church, in the course of the following autumn.

9. Traveling on Sunday was disapproved of by some members of many Protestant denominations.
1. Reputation.

Chapter XVIII

It was the beginning of February; and Anne, having been a month in Bath, was growing very eager for news from Uppercross and Lyme. She wanted to hear much more than Mary communicated. It was three weeks since she had heard at all. She only knew that Henrietta was at home again; and that Louisa, though considered to be recovering fast, was still at Lyme; and she was thinking of them all very intently one evening, when a thicker letter than usual from Mary was delivered to her, and, to quicken the pleasure and surprise, with Admiral and Mrs. Croft's compliments.

The Crofts must be in Bath! A circumstance to interest her. They were people whom her heart turned to very naturally.

"What is this?" cried Sir Walter. "The Crofts arrived in Bath? The Crofts who rent Kellynch? What have they brought you?"

"A letter from Uppercross Cottage, Sir."

"Oh! those letters are convenient passports. They secure an introduction. I should have visited Admiral Croft, however, at any rate. I know what is due to my tenant."

Anne could listen no longer; she could not even have told how the poor Admiral's complexion escaped; her letter engrossed her. It had been begun several days back.

> February 1st, ——.
>
> MY DEAR ANNE,
>
> I make no apology for my silence, because I know how little people think of letters in such a place as Bath. You must be a great deal too happy to care for Uppercross, which, as you well know, affords little to write about. We have had a very dull Christmas; Mr. and Mrs. Musgrove have not had one dinner-party all the holidays. I do not reckon the Hayters as any body. The holidays, however, are over at last: I believe no children ever had such long ones. I am sure I had not. The house was cleared yesterday, except of the little Harvilles; but you will be surprised to hear that they have never gone home. Mrs. Harville must be an odd mother to part with them so long. I do not understand it. They are not at all nice children, in my opinion; but Mrs. Musgrove seems to like them quite as well, if not better, than her grand-children. What dreadful weather we have had! It may not be felt in Bath, with your nice pavements; but in the country it is of some consequence. I have not had a creature call on me since the second week in January, except Charles Hayter, who has been calling much oftener than was welcome. Between ourselves, I think it a great pity Henrietta did not remain at Lyme as long as Louisa; it would have kept

her a little out of his way. The carriage is gone to-day, to bring
Louisa and the Harvilles to-morrow. We are not asked to dine
with them, however, till the day after, Mrs. Musgrove is so
afraid of her being fatigued by the journey, which is not very
likely, considering the care that will be taken of her; and it
would be much more convenient to me to dine there tomorrow. I am glad you find Mr. Elliot so agreeable, and wish I
could be acquainted with him too; but I have my usual luck, I
am always out of the way when any thing desirable is going on;
always the last of my family to be noticed. What an immense
time Mrs. Clay has been staying with Elizabeth! Does she
never mean to go away? But perhaps if she were to leave the
room vacant we might not be invited. Let me know what you
think of this. I do not expect my children to be asked, you
know. I can leave them at the Great House very well, for a
month or six weeks. I have this moment heard that the Crofts
are going to Bath almost immediately; they think the admiral
gouty.[2] Charles heard it quite by chance: they have not had the
civility to give me any notice, or offer to take any thing. I do
not think they improve at all as neighbours. We see nothing
of them, and this is really an instance of gross inattention.
Charles joins me in love, and every thing proper.

Yours affectionately,
MARY M———.

I am sorry to say that I am very far from well; and Jemima has
just told me that the butcher says there is a bad sore-throat very
much about. I dare say I shall catch it; and my sore-throats, you
know, are always worse than anybody's."

So ended the first part, which had been afterwards put into an
envelop, containing nearly as much more.

"I kept my letter open, that I might send you word how Louisa
bore her journey, and now I am extremely glad I did, having a
great deal to add. In the first place, I had a note from Mrs. Croft
yesterday, offering to convey any thing to you; a very kind,
friendly note indeed, addressed to me, just as it ought; I shall
therefore be able to make my letter as long as I like. The admiral
does not seem very ill, and I sincerely hope Bath will do him all
the good he wants. I shall be truly glad to have them back again.
Our neighbourhood cannot spare such a pleasant family. But
now for Louisa. I have something to communicate that will
astonish you not a little. She and the Harvilles came on Tuesday
very safely, and in the evening we went to ask her how she did,

---

2. Gout causes inflammation of the smaller joints, particularly the big toe. In Austen's
time, gout implied excess and swollenness, as from the overconsumption of alcohol and
rich foods, as well as a dyspeptic disposition.

when we were rather surprised not to find Captain Benwick of the party, for he had been invited as well as the Harvilles; and what do you think was the reason? Neither more nor less than his being in love with Louisa, and not choosing to venture to Uppercross till he had had an answer from Mr. Musgrove; for it was all settled between him and her before she came away, and he had written to her father by Captain Harville. True, upon my honour. Are not you astonished? I shall be surprised at least if you ever received a hint of it, for I never did. Mrs. Musgrove protests solemnly that she knew nothing of the matter. We are all very well pleased, however; for though it is not equal to her marrying Captain Wentworth, it is infinitely better than Charles Hayter; and Mr. Musgrove has written his consent, and Captain Benwick is expected to-day. Mrs. Harville says her husband feels a good deal on his poor sister's account; but, however, Louisa is a great favourite with both. Indeed Mrs. Harville and I quite agree that we love her the better for having nursed her. Charles wonders what Captain Wentworth will say; but if you remember, I never thought him attached to Louisa; I never could see any thing of it. And this is the end, you see, of Captain Benwick's being supposed to be an admirer of yours. How Charles could take such a thing into his head was always incomprehensible to me. I hope he will be more agreeable now. Certainly not a great match for Louisa Musgrove; but a million times better than marrying among the Hayters."

Mary need not have feared her sister's being in any degree prepared for the news. She had never in her life been more astonished. Captain Benwick and Louisa Musgrove! It was almost too wonderful for belief; and it was with the greatest effort that she could remain in the room, preserve an air of calmness, and answer the common questions of the moment. Happily for her, they were not many. Sir Walter wanted to know whether the Crofts travelled with four horses, and whether they were likely to be situated in such a part of Bath as it might suit Miss Elliot and himself to visit in; but had little curiosity beyond.

"How is Mary?" said Elizabeth; and without waiting for an answer, "And pray what brings the Crofts to Bath?"

"They come on the Admiral's account. He is thought to be gouty."

"Gout and decrepitude!" said Sir Walter. "Poor old gentleman."

"Have they any acquaintance here?" asked Elizabeth.

"I do not know; but I can hardly suppose that, at Admiral Croft's time of life, and in his profession, he should not have many acquaintance in such a place as this."

"I suspect," said Sir Walter coolly, "that Admiral Croft will be best known in Bath as the renter of Kellynch-hall. Elizabeth, may we venture to present him and his wife in Laura-place?"

"Oh! no, I think not. Situated as we are with Lady Dalrymple, cousins, we ought to be very careful not to embarrass her with acquaintance she might not approve. If we were not related, it would not signify; but as cousins, she would feel scrupulous as to any proposal of ours. We had better leave the Crofts to find their own level. There are several odd-looking men walking about here, who, I am told, are sailors. The Crofts will associate with them!"

This was Sir Walter and Elizabeth's share of interest in the letter; when Mrs. Clay had paid her tribute of more decent attention, in an enquiry after Mrs. Charles Musgrove, and her fine little boys, Anne was at liberty.

In her own room she tried to comprehend it. Well might Charles wonder how Captain Wentworth would feel! Perhaps he had quitted the field, had given Louisa up, had ceased to love, had found he did not love her. She could not endure the idea of treachery or levity, or any thing akin to ill-usage between him and his friend. She could not endure that such a friendship as theirs should be severed unfairly.

Captain Benwick and Louisa Musgrove! The high-spirited, joyous, talking Louisa Musgrove, and the dejected, thinking, feeling, reading Captain Benwick, seemed each of them every thing that would not suit the other. Their minds most dissimilar! Where could have been the attraction? The answer soon presented itself. It had been in situation. They had been thrown together several weeks; they had been living in the same small family party; since Henrietta's coming away, they must have been depending almost entirely on each other, and Louisa, just recovering from illness, had been in an interesting state, and Captain Benwick was not inconsolable. That was a point which Anne had not been able to avoid suspecting before; and instead of drawing the same conclusion as Mary, from the present course of events, they served only to confirm the idea of his having felt some dawning of tenderness toward herself. She did not mean, however, to derive much more from it to gratify her vanity, than Mary might have allowed. She was persuaded that any tolerably pleasing young woman who had listened and seemed to feel for him, would have received the same compliment. He had an affectionate heart. He must love somebody.

She saw no reason against their being happy. Louisa had fine naval fervour to begin with, and they would soon grow more alike. He would gain cheerfulness, and she would learn to be an enthusiast for Scott and Lord Byron; nay, that was probably learnt already; of course they had fallen in love over poetry. The idea of Louisa Musgrove turned into a person of literary taste, and sentimental reflection, was amusing, but she had no doubt of its being so. The day at Lyme, the fall from the Cobb, might influence her health, her nerves, her courage, her character to the end of her life, as thoroughly as it appeared to have influenced her fate.

The conclusion of the whole was, that if the woman who had been sensible of Captain Wentworth's merits could be allowed to prefer another man, there was nothing in the engagement to excite lasting wonder; and if Captain Wentworth lost no friend by it, certainly nothing to be regretted. No, it was not regret which made Anne's heart beat in spite of herself, and brought the colour into her cheeks when she thought of Captain Wentworth unshackled and free. She had some feelings which she was ashamed to investigate. They were too much like joy, senseless joy!

She longed to see the Crofts, but when the meeting took place, it was evident that no rumour of the news had yet reached them. The visit of ceremony was paid and returned, and Louisa Musgrove was mentioned, and Captain Benwick too, without even half a smile.

The Crofts had placed themselves in lodgings in Gay-street, perfectly to Sir Walter's satisfaction. He was not at all ashamed of the acquaintance, and did, in fact, think and talk a great deal more about the Admiral, than the Admiral ever thought or talked about him.

The Crofts knew quite as many people in Bath as they wished for, and considered their intercourse with the Elliots as a mere matter of form, and not in the least likely to afford them any pleasure. They brought with them their country habit of being almost always together. He was ordered to walk, to keep off the gout, and Mrs. Croft seemed to go shares with him in every thing, and to walk for her life, to do him good. Anne saw them wherever she went. Lady Russell took her out in her carriage almost every morning, and she never failed to think of them, and never failed to see them. Knowing their feelings as she did, it was a most attractive picture of happiness to her. She always watched them as long as she could; delighted to fancy she understood what they might be talking of, as they walked along in happy independence, or equally delighted to see the Admiral's hearty shake of the hand when he encountered an old friend, and observe their eagerness of conversation when occasionally forming into a little knot of the navy, Mrs. Croft looking as intelligent and keen as any of the officers around her.

Anne was too much engaged with Lady Russell to be often walking herself, but it so happened that one morning, about a week or ten days after the Crofts' arrival, it suited her best to leave her friend, or her friend's carriage, in the lower part of the town, and return alone to Camden-place; and in walking up Milsom-street, she had the good fortune to meet with the Admiral. He was standing by himself, at a print-shop window, with his hands behind him, in earnest contemplation of some print, and she not only might have passed him unseen, but was obliged to touch as well as address him before she could catch his notice. When he did perceive and acknowledge her, however, it was done with all his usual frankness and good humour. "Ha! is it you? Thank you, thank you. This is treating me like a friend. Here I am, you see, staring at a picture. I can never get by this shop without stopping. But what a thing here is, by way of a boat. Do look at it. Did you ever see the like? What queer fellows your fine painters must be, to think that any body would venture their lives in such a shapeless old cockleshell as that. And yet, here are two gentlemen stuck up in it mightily at their ease, and looking about them at the rocks and mountains, as if they were not to be upset the next moment, which they certainly must be. I wonder where that boat was built!" (laughing heartily) "I would not venture over a horsepond in it. Well," (turning away) "now, where are you bound? Can I go any where for you, or with you? Can I be of any use?"

"None, I thank you, unless you will give me the pleasure of your company the little way our road lies together. I am going home."

"That I will, with all my heart, and farther too. Yes, yes, we will have a snug walk together; and I have something to tell you as we go along. There, take my arm; that's right; I do not feel comfortable if I have not a woman there. Lord! what a boat it is!" taking a last look at the picture, as they began to be in motion.

"Did you say that you had something to tell me, sir?"

"Yes, I have. Presently. But here comes a friend, Captain Brigden; I shall only say, 'How d'ye do,' as we pass, however. I shall not stop. 'How d'ye do.' Brigden stares to see anybody with me but my wife. She, poor soul, is tied by the leg. She has a blister on one of her heels, as large as a three shilling piece.[3] If you look across the street, you will see Admiral Brand coming down and his brother. Shabby fellows, both of them! I am glad they are not on this side of the way. Sophy cannot bear them. They played me a pitiful trick once—got away some of my best men.[4] I will tell you the whole story another time. There comes old Sir Archibald Drew and his grandson. Look, he sees us; he kisses his hand to you; he takes you for my wife. Ah! the peace has come too soon for that younker.[5] Poor old Sir Archibald! How do you like Bath, Miss Elliot? It suits us very well. We are always meeting with some old friend or other; the streets full of them every morning; sure to have plenty of chat; and then we get away from them all, and shut ourselves into our lodgings, and draw in our chairs, and are as snug as if we were at Kellynch, ay, or as we used to be even at North Yarmouth and Deal. We do not like our

3. From 1811 to 1816, the Bank of England issued unofficial, lightweight three-shilling tokens in response to rising silver prices "so great," according to the *Gentleman's Magazine*, "that the dollars or tokens issued by the Bank sell for more bullion than they are current as coin" (W. J. Davis, *The Nineteenth Century Token Coinage of Great Britain, Ireland, the Channel Islands, and the Isle of Man* [London, 1904], p. xxvii).
4. Their "trick" reflects the competitive nature of hiring and maintaining naval crews during the Napoleonic period.
5. Youngster. The grandson is presumably in the navy.

lodgings here the worse, I can tell you, for putting us in mind of those we first had at North Yarmouth. The wind blows through one of the cupboards just in the same way."

When they were got a little farther, Anne ventured to press again for what he had to communicate. She had hoped, when clear of Milsom-street, to have her curiosity gratified; but she was still obliged to wait, for the Admiral had made up his mind not to begin, till they had gained the greater space and quiet of Belmont, and as she was not really Mrs. Croft, she must let him have his own way. As soon as they were fairly ascending Belmont, he began,

"Well, now you shall hear something that will surprise you. But first of all, you must tell me the name of the young lady I am going to talk about. That young lady, you know, that we have all been so concerned for. The Miss Musgrove, that all this has been happening to. Her christian name—I always forget her christian name."

Anne had been ashamed to appear to comprehend so soon as she really did; but now she could safely suggest the name of "Louisa."

"Ay, ay, Miss Louisa Musgrove, that is the name. I wish young ladies had not such a number of fine christian names. I should never be out, if they were all Sophys, or something of that sort. Well, this Miss Louisa, we all thought, you know, was to marry Frederick. He was courting her week after week. The only wonder was, what they could be waiting for, till the business at Lyme came; then, indeed, it was clear enough that they must wait till her brain was set to right. But even then, there was something odd in their way of going on. Instead of staying at Lyme, he went off to Plymouth, and then he went off to see Edward. When we came back from Minehead, he was gone down to Edward's, and there he has been ever since. We have seen nothing of him since November. Even Sophy could not understand it. But now, the matter has taken the strangest turn of all; for this young lady, this same Miss Musgrove, instead of being to marry Frederick, is to marry James Benwick. You know James Benwick."

"A little. I am a little acquainted with Captain Benwick."

"Well, she is to marry him. Nay, most likely they are married already, for I do not know what they should wait for."

"I thought Captain Benwick a very pleasing young man," said Anne, "and I understand that he bears an excellent character."

"Oh! yes, yes, there is not a word to be said against James Benwick. He is only a commander, it is true, made last summer, and these are bad times for getting on,[6] but he has not another fault that I know of. An excellent, good-hearted fellow, I assure you, a very

6. Ironic, since during a time of peace Benwick does not have the lucrative opportunities for prize-taking that were available during wartime.

active, zealous officer too, which is more than you would think for, perhaps, for that soft sort of manner does not do him justice."

"Indeed you are mistaken there, sir. I should never augur want of spirit from Captain Benwick's manners. I thought them particularly pleasing, and I will answer for it they would generally please."

"Well, well, ladies are the best judges; but James Benwick is rather too piano[7] for me, and though very likely it is all our partiality, Sophy and I cannot help thinking Frederick's manners better than his. There is something about Frederick more to our taste."

Anne was caught. She had only meant to oppose the too-common idea of spirit and gentleness being incompatible with each other, not at all to represent Captain Benwick's manners as the very best that could possibly be, and, after a little hesitation, she was beginning to say, "I was not entering into any comparison of the two friends," but the Admiral interrupted her with,

"And the thing is certainly true. It is not a mere bit of gossip. We have it from Frederick himself. His sister had a letter from him yesterday, in which he tells us of it, and he had just had it in a letter from Harville, written upon the spot, from Uppercross. I fancy they are all at Uppercross."

This was an opportunity which Anne could not resist; she said, therefore, "I hope, Admiral, I hope there is nothing in the style of Captain Wentworth's letter to make you and Mrs. Croft particularly uneasy. It did certainly seem, last autumn, as if there were an attachment between him and Louisa Musgrove; but I hope it may be understood to have worn out on each side equally, and without violence. I hope his letter does not breathe the spirit of an ill-used man."

"Not at all, not at all; there is not an oath or a murmur from beginning to end."

Anne looked down to hide her smile.

"No, no; Frederick is not a man to whine and complain; he has too much spirit for that. If the girl likes another man better, it is very fit she should have him."

"Certainly. But what I mean is, that I hope there is nothing in Captain Wentworth's manner of writing to make you suppose he thinks himself ill-used by his friend, which might appear, you know, without its being absolutely said. I should be very sorry that such a friendship as has subsisted between him and Captain Benwick should be destroyed, or even wounded, by a circumstance of this sort."

"Yes, yes, I understand you. But there is nothing at all of that nature in the letter. He does not give the least fling at Benwick; does not so much as say, 'I wonder at it, I have a reason of my own for wondering at it.' No, you would not guess, from his way of writing, that he had

7. Quiet (Italian).

ever thought of this Miss (what's her name?) for himself. He very handsomely hopes they will be happy together, and there is nothing very unforgiving in that, I think."

Anne did not receive the perfect conviction which the Admiral meant to convey, but it would have been useless to press the enquiry farther. She, therefore, satisfied herself with common-place remarks, or quiet attention, and the Admiral had it all his own way.

"Poor Frederick!" said he at last. "Now he must begin all over again with somebody else. I think we must get him to Bath. Sophy must write, and beg him to come to Bath. Here are pretty girls enough, I am sure. It would be of no use to go to Uppercross again, for that other Miss Musgrove, I find, is bespoke by her cousin, the young parson. Do not you think, Miss Elliot, we had better try to get him to Bath?"

Chapter XIX

While Admiral Croft was taking this walk with Anne, and expressing his wish of getting Captain Wentworth to Bath, Captain Wentworth was already on his way thither. Before Mrs. Croft had written, he was arrived; and the very next time Anne walked out, she saw him.

Mr. Elliot was attending his two cousins and Mrs. Clay. They were in Milsom-street. It began to rain, not much, but enough to make shelter desirable for women, and quite enough to make it very desirable for Miss Elliot to have the advantage of being conveyed home in Lady Dalrymple's carriage, which was seen waiting at a little distance; she, Anne, and Mrs. Clay, therefore, turned into Molland's,[8] while Mr. Elliot stepped to Lady Dalrymple, to request her assistance. He soon joined them again, successful, of course; Lady Dalrymple would be most happy to take them home, and would call for them in a few minutes.

Her ladyship's carriage was a barouche,[9] and did not hold more than four with any comfort. Miss Carteret was with her mother; consequently it was not reasonable to expect accommodation for all the three Camden-place ladies. There could be no doubt as to Miss Elliot. Whoever suffered inconvenience, she must suffer none, but it occupied a little time to settle the point of civility between the other two. The rain was a mere trifle, and Anne was most sincere in preferring a walk with Mr. Elliot. But the rain was also a mere trifle to Mrs. Clay; she would hardly allow it even to drop at all, and her boots were so thick! much thicker than Miss Anne's; and, in short, her

8. A confectionery.
9. A carriage with seats for two couples to sit facing each other.

civility rendered her quite as anxious to be left to walk with Mr. Elliot, as Anne could be, and it was discussed between them with a generosity so polite and so determined, that the others were obliged to settle it for them; Miss Elliot maintaining that Mrs. Clay had a little cold already, and Mr. Elliot deciding on appeal, that his cousin Anne's boots were rather the thickest.

It was fixed accordingly that Mrs. Clay should be of the party in the carriage; and they had just reached this point when Anne, as she sat near the window, descried, most decidedly and distinctly, Captain Wentworth walking down the street.

Her start was perceptible only to herself; but she instantly felt that she was the greatest simpleton in the world, the most unaccountable and absurd! For a few minutes she saw nothing before her. It was all confusion. She was lost; and when she had scolded back her senses, she found the others still waiting for the carriage, and Mr. Elliot (always obliging) just setting off for Union-street on a commission of Mrs. Clay's.

She now felt a great inclination to go to the outer door; she wanted to see if it rained. Why was she to suspect herself of another motive? Captain Wentworth must be out of sight. She left her seat, she would go, one half of her should not be always so much wiser than the other half, or always suspecting the other of being worse than it was. She would see if it rained. She was sent back, however, in a moment by the entrance of Captain Wentworth himself, among a party of gentlemen and ladies, evidently his acquaintance, and whom he must have joined a little below Milsom-street. He was more obviously struck and confused by the sight of her, than she had ever observed before; he looked quite red. For the first time, since their renewed acquaintance, she felt that she was betraying the least sensibility of the two. She had the advantage of him, in the preparation of the last few moments. All the overpowering, blinding, bewildering, first effects of strong surprise were over with her. Still, however, she had enough to feel! It was agitation, pain, pleasure, a something between delight and misery.

He spoke to her, and then turned away. The character of his manner was embarrassment. She could not have called it either cold or friendly, or any thing so certainly as embarrassed.

After a short interval, however, he came towards her and spoke again. Mutual enquiries on common subjects passed; neither of them, probably, much the wiser for what they heard, and Anne continuing fully sensible of his being less at ease than formerly. They had, by dint of being so very much together, got to speak to each other with a considerable portion of apparent indifference and calmness; but he could not do it now. Time had changed him, or Louisa had changed him. There was consciousness of some sort or other.

He looked very well, not as if he had been suffering in health or spirits, and he talked of Uppercross, of the Musgroves, nay, even of Louisa, and had even a momentary look of his own arch significance as he named her; but yet it was Captain Wentworth not comfortable, not easy, not able to feign that he was.

It did not surprise, but it grieved Anne to observe that Elizabeth would not know him.[1] She saw that he saw Elizabeth, that Elizabeth saw him, that there was complete internal recognition on each side; she was convinced that he was ready to be acknowledged as an acquaintance, expecting it, and she had the pain of seeing her sister turn away with unalterable coldness.

Lady Dalrymple's carriage, for which Miss Elliot was growing very impatient, now drew up; the servant came in to announce it. It was beginning to rain again, and altogether there was a delay, and a bustle, and a talking, which must make all the little crowd in the shop understand that Lady Dalrymple was calling to convey Miss Elliot. At last Miss Elliot and her friend, unattended but by the servant, (for there was no cousin returned) were walking off; and Captain Wentworth, watching them, turned again to Anne, and by manner, rather than words, was offering his services to her.

"I am much obliged to you," was her answer, "but I am not going with them. The carriage would not accommodate so many. I walk. I prefer walking."

"But it rains."

"Oh! very little. Nothing that I regard."

After a moment's pause he said, "Though I came only yesterday, I have equipped myself properly for Bath already, you see," (pointing to a new umbrella) "I wish you would make use of it, if you are determined to walk; though, I think, it would be more prudent to let me get you a chair."[2]

She was very much obliged to him, but declined it all, repeating her conviction, that the rain would come to nothing at present, and adding, "I am only waiting for Mr. Elliot. He will be here in a moment, I am sure."

She had hardly spoken the words, when Mr. Elliot walked in. Captain Wentworth recollected him perfectly. There was no difference between him and the man who had stood on the steps at Lyme, admiring Anne as she passed, except in the air and look and manner of the privileged relation and friend. He came in with eagerness, appeared to see and think only of her, apologised for his stay, was

---

1. Would give no sign of recognition.
2. A sedan chair, a conveyance containing a single seat inside a cabin with a detachable roof, mounted on two poles and carried by two men, which allowed passengers to keep their shoes clean. In Bath, sedan chairs were plentiful as they were used to transport invalids between their lodgings and the baths.

grieved to have kept her waiting, and anxious to get her away with-out further loss of time, and before the rain increased; and in another moment they walked off together, her arm under his, a gentle and embarrassed glance, and a "good morning to you," being all that she had time for, as she passed away.

As soon as they were out of sight, the ladies of Captain Went-worth's party began talking of them.

"Mr. Elliot does not dislike his cousin, I fancy?"

"Oh! no, that is clear enough. One can guess what will happen there. He is always with them; half lives in the family, I believe. What a very good-looking man!"

"Yes, and Miss Atkinson, who dined with him once at the Wallises, says he is the most agreeable man she ever was in company with."

"She is pretty, I think; Anne Elliot; very pretty, when one comes to look at her. It is not the fashion to say so, but I confess I admire her more than her sister."

"Oh! so do I."

"And so do I. No comparison. But the men are all wild after Miss Elliot. Anne is too delicate for them."

Anne would have been particularly obliged to her cousin, if he would have walked by her side all the way to Camden-place, without saying a word. She had never found it so difficult to listen to him, though nothing could exceed his solicitude and care, and though his subjects were principally such as were wont to be always inter-esting—praise, warm, just, and discriminating, of Lady Russell, and insinuations highly rational against Mrs. Clay. But just now she could think only of Captain Wentworth. She could not understand his present feelings, whether he were really suffering much from dis-appointment or not; and till that point were settled, she could not be quite herself.

She hoped to be wise and reasonable in time; but alas! alas! she must confess to herself that she was not wise yet.

Another circumstance very essential for her to know, was how long he meant to be in Bath; he had not mentioned it, or she could not recollect it. He might be only passing through. But it was more prob-able that he should be come to stay. In that case, so liable as every body was to meet every body in Bath, Lady Russell would in all like-lihood see him somewhere.—Would she recollect him? How would it all be?

She had already been obliged to tell Lady Russell that Louisa Mus-grove was to marry Captain Benwick. It had cost her something to encounter Lady Russell's surprise; and now, if she were by any chance to be thrown into company with Captain Wentworth, her imperfect knowledge of the matter might add another shade of prej-udice against him.

The following morning Anne was out with her friend, and for the first hour, in an incessant and fearful sort of watch for him in vain; but at last, in returning down Pulteney-street, she distinguished him on the right hand pavement at such a distance as to have him in view the greater part of the street. There were many other men about him, many groups walking the same way, but there was no mistaking him. She looked instinctively at Lady Russell; but not from any mad idea of her recognising him so soon as she did herself. No, it was not to be supposed that Lady Russell would perceive him till they were nearly opposite. She looked at her however, from time to time, anxiously; and when the moment approached which must point him out, though not daring to look again (for her own countenance she knew was unfit to be seen), she was yet perfectly conscious of Lady Russell's eyes being turned exactly in the direction for him, of her being in short intently observing him. She could thoroughly comprehend the sort of fascination he must possess over Lady Russell's mind, the difficulty it must be for her to withdraw her eyes, the astonishment she must be feeling that eight or nine years should have passed over him, and in foreign climes and in active service too, without robbing him of one personal grace!

At last, Lady Russell drew back her head.—"Now, how would she speak of him?"

"You will wonder," said she, "what has been fixing my eye so long; but I was looking after some window-curtains, which Lady Alicia and Mrs. Frankland were telling me of last night. They described the drawing-room window-curtains of one of the houses on this side of the way, and this part of the street, as being the handsomest and best hung of any in Bath, but could not recollect the exact number, and I have been trying to find out which it could be; but I confess I can see no curtains hereabouts that answer their description."

Anne sighed and blushed and smiled, in pity and disdain, either at her friend or herself.—The part which provoked her most, was that in all this waste of foresight and caution, she should have lost the right moment for seeing whether he saw them.

A day or two passed without producing any thing.—The theatre or the rooms, where he was most likely to be, were not fashionable enough for the Elliots, whose evening amusements were solely in the elegant stupidity of private parties, in which they were getting more and more engaged; and Anne, wearied of such a state of stagnation, sick of knowing nothing, and fancying herself stronger because her strength was not tried, was quite impatient for the concert evening. It was a concert for the benefit of a person patronised by Lady Dalrymple. Of course they must attend. It was really expected to be a good one, and Captain Wentworth was very fond of music. If she could only have a few minutes conversation with him again, she fancied she should be satisfied; and as to the power of addressing him she felt all over courage if the opportunity occurred. Elizabeth had turned from him, Lady Russell overlooked him; her nerves were strengthened by these circumstances; she felt that she owed him attention.

She had once partly promised Mrs. Smith to spend the evening with her; but in a short hurried call she excused herself and put it off, with the more decided promise of a longer visit on the morrow. Mrs. Smith gave a most good-humoured acquiescence.

"By all means," said she; "only tell me all about it, when you do come. Who is your party?"

Anne named them all. Mrs. Smith made no reply; but when she was leaving her, said, and with an expression half serious, half arch, "Well, I heartily wish your concert may answer; and do not fail me to-morrow if you can come; for I begin to have a foreboding that I may have many more visits from you."

Anne was startled and confused, but after standing in a moment's suspense, was obliged, and not sorry to be obliged, to hurry away.

Chapter XX

Sir Walter, his two daughters, and Mrs. Clay, were the earliest of all their party, at the rooms in the evening; and as Lady Dalrymple must be waited for, they took their station by one of the fires in the octagon room.[3] But hardly were they so settled, when the door opened again, and Captain Wentworth walked in alone. Anne was the nearest to him, and making yet a little advance, she instantly spoke. He was preparing only to bow and pass on, but her gentle "How do you do?" brought him out of the straight line to stand near her, and make enquiries in return, in spite of the formidable father and sister in the back ground. Their being in the back ground was a support to Anne; she knew nothing of their looks, and felt equal to everything which she believed right to be done.

While they were speaking, a whispering between her father and Elizabeth caught her ear. She could not distinguish, but she must guess the subject; and on Captain Wentworth's making a distant bow, she comprehended that her father had judged so well as to give him that simple acknowledgment of acquaintance, and she was just in time by a side glance to see a slight curtsey from Elizabeth herself. This, though late and reluctant and ungracious, was yet better than nothing, and her spirits improved.

3. Assembly room built by the English architect John Wood the Younger (1728–1782), with a U-shaped design. Opening in 1771, it was at the time a fashionable gathering place. Wood was responsible for building or refurbishing many important structures in 18th-century Bath, including the Royal Crescent.

After talking however of the weather and Bath and the concert, their conversation began to flag, and so little was said at last, that she was expecting him to go every moment; but he did not; he seemed in no hurry to leave her; and presently with renewed spirit, with a little smile, a little glow, he said,

"I have hardly seen you since our day at Lyme. I am afraid you must have suffered from the shock, and the more from its not over-powering you at the time."

She assured him that she had not.

"It was a frightful hour," said he, "a frightful day!" and he passed his hand across his eyes, as if the remembrance were still too pain-ful; but in a moment half smiling again, added, "The day has pro-duced some effects however—has had some consequences which must be considered as the very reverse of frightful.—When you had the presence of mind to suggest that Benwick would be the proper-est person to fetch a surgeon, you could have little idea of his being eventually one of those most concerned in her recovery."

"Certainly I could have none. But it appears—I should hope it would be a very happy match. There are on both sides good princi-ples and good temper."

"Yes," said he, looking not exactly forward—"but there I think ends the resemblance. With all my soul I wish them happy, and rejoice over every circumstance in favour of it. They have no diffi-culties to contend with at home, no opposition, no caprice, no delays.—The Musgroves are behaving like themselves, most honour-ably and kindly, only anxious with true parental hearts to promote their daughter's comfort. All this is much, very much in favour of their happiness; more than perhaps—"

He stopped. A sudden recollection seemed to occur, and to give him some taste of that emotion which was reddening Anne's cheeks and fixing her eyes on the ground.—After clearing his throat, how-ever, he proceeded thus,

"I confess that I do think there is a disparity, too great a disparity, and in a point no less essential than mind.—I regard Louisa Musgrove as a very amiable, sweet-tempered girl, and not deficient in under-standing; but Benwick is something more. He is a clever man, a read-ing man—and I confess that I do consider his attaching himself to her, with some surprise. Had it been the effect of gratitude, had he learnt to love her, because he believed her to be preferring him, it would have been another thing. But I have no reason to suppose it so. It seems, on the contrary, to have been a perfectly spontaneous, untaught feeling on his side, and this surprises me. A man like him, in his situation! With a heart pierced, wounded, almost broken! Fanny Harville was a very superior creature; and his attachment to her was indeed attachment. A man does not recover from such a devotion of the heart to such a woman!—He ought not—he does not."

Either from the consciousness, however, that his friend had recovered, or from some other consciousness, he went no farther; and Anne, who, in spite of the agitated voice in which the latter part had been uttered, and in spite of all the various noises of the room, the almost ceaseless slam of the door, and ceaseless buzz of persons walking through, had distinguished every word, was struck, gratified, confused, and beginning to breathe very quick, and feel an hundred things in a moment. It was impossible for her to enter on such a subject; and yet, after a pause, feeling the necessity of speaking, and having not the smallest wish for a total change, she only deviated so far as to say,

"You were a good while at Lyme, I think?"

"About a fortnight. I could not leave it till Louisa's doing well was quite ascertained. I had been too deeply concerned in the mischief to be soon at peace. It had been my doing—solely mine. She would not have been obstinate if I had not been weak. The country round Lyme is very fine. I walked and rode a great deal; and the more I saw, the more I found to admire."

"I should very much like to see Lyme again," said Anne.

"Indeed! I should not have supposed that you could have found any thing in Lyme to inspire such a feeling. The horror and distress you were involved in—the stretch of mind, the wear of spirits!—I should have thought your last impressions of Lyme must have been strong disgust."

"The last few hours were certainly very painful," replied Anne: "but when pain is over, the remembrance of it often becomes a pleasure. One does not love a place the less for having suffered in it, unless it has been all suffering, nothing but suffering—which was by no means the case at Lyme. We were only in anxiety and distress during the last two hours; and, previously, there had been a great deal of enjoyment. So much novelty and beauty! I have travelled so little, that every fresh place would be interesting to me—but there is real beauty at Lyme: and in short" (with a faint blush at some recollections) "altogether my impressions of the place are very agreeable."

As she ceased, the entrance door opened again, and the very party appeared for whom they were waiting. "Lady Dalrymple, Lady Dalrymple," was the rejoicing sound; and with all the eagerness compatible with anxious elegance, Sir Walter and his two ladies stepped forward to meet her. Lady Dalrymple and Miss Carteret, escorted by Mr. Elliot and Colonel Wallis, who had happened to arrive nearly at the same instant, advanced into the room. The others joined them, and it was a group in which Anne found herself also necessarily included. She was divided from Captain Wentworth. Their interest-ing, almost too interesting conversation must be broken up for a time; but slight was the penance compared with the happiness which brought it on! She had learnt, in the last ten minutes, more of his feelings towards Louisa, more of all his feelings, than she dared to think of! and she gave herself up to the demands of the party, to the needful civilities of the moment, with exquisite, though agitated sen-sations. She was in good humour with all. She had received ideas which disposed her to be courteous and kind to all, and to pity every one, as being less happy than herself.

The delightful emotions were a little subdued, when, on stepping back from the group, to be joined again by Captain Wentworth, she saw that he was gone. She was just in time to see him turn into the concert room. He was gone—he had disappeared: she felt a moment's regret. But "they should meet again. He would look for her—he would find her out long before the evening were over—and at present, perhaps, it was as well to be asunder. She was in need of a little interval for recollection."

Upon Lady Russell's appearance soon afterwards, the whole party was collected, and all that remained, was to marshal themselves, and proceed into the concert room; and be of all the consequence in their power, draw as many eyes, excite as many whispers, and disturb as many people as they could.

Very, very happy were both Elizabeth and Anne Elliot as they walked in. Elizabeth, arm in arm with Miss Carteret, and looking on the broad back of the dowager Viscountess Dalrymple before her, had nothing to wish for which did not seem within her reach; and Anne——but it would be an insult to the nature of Anne's felicity, to draw any comparison between it and her sister's; the origin of one all selfish vanity, of the other all generous attachment.

Anne saw nothing, thought nothing of the brilliancy of the room. Her happiness was from within. Her eyes were bright, and her cheeks glowed,—but she knew nothing about it. She was thinking only of the last half hour, and as they passed to their seats, her mind took a hasty range over it. His choice of subjects, his expressions, and still more his manner and look, had been such as she could see in only one light. His opinion of Louisa Musgrove's inferiority, an opinion which he had seemed solicitous to give, his wonder at Captain Ben-wick, his feelings as to a first, strong attachment,—sentences begun which he could not finish—his half averted eyes, and more than half expressive glance,—all, all declared that he had a heart returning to her at least; that anger, resentment, avoidance, were no more; and that they were succeeded, not merely by friendship and regard, but by the tenderness of the past; yes, some share of the tenderness of the past. She could not contemplate the change as implying less.—He must love her.

These were thoughts, with their attendant visions, which occupied and flurried her too much to leave her any power of observation; and she passed along the room without having a glimpse of him, without even trying to discern him. When their places were determined on, and they were all properly arranged, she looked round to see if he should happen to be in the same part of the room, but he was not, her eye could not reach him; and the concert being just opening, she must consent for a time to be happy in an humbler way.

The party was divided, and disposed of on two contiguous benches: Anne was among those on the foremost, and Mr. Elliot had manœuvred so well, with the assistance of his friend Colonel Wallis, as to have a seat by her. Miss Elliot, surrounded by her cousins, and the principal object of Colonel Wallis's gallantry, was quite contented.

Anne's mind was in a most favourable state for the entertainment of the evening: it was just occupation enough: she had feelings for the tender, spirits for the gay, attention for the scientific, and patience for the wearisome; and had never liked a concert better, at least during the first act. Towards the close of it, in the interval[4] succeeding an Italian song, she explained the words of the song to Mr. Elliot.— They had a concert bill between them.

"This," said she, "is nearly the sense, or rather the meaning of the words, for certainly the sense of an Italian love-song must not be talked of,—but it is as nearly the meaning as I can give; for I do not pretend to understand the language. I am a very poor Italian scholar."

"Yes, yes, I see you are. I see you know nothing of the matter. You have only knowledge enough of the language, to translate at sight these inverted, transposed, curtailed Italian lines, into clear, comprehensible, elegant English. You need not say anything more of your ignorance.—Here is complete proof."

"I will not oppose such kind politeness; but I should be sorry to be examined by a real proficient."

"I have not had the pleasure of visiting in Camden-place so long," replied he, "without knowing something of Miss Anne Elliot; and I do regard her as one who is too modest, for the world in general to be aware of half her accomplishments, and too highly accomplished for modesty to be natural in any other woman."

"For shame! for shame!—this is too much of flattery. I forget what we are to have next," turning to the bill.

"Perhaps," said Mr. Elliot, speaking low, "I have had a longer acquaintance with your character than you are aware of."

4. Intermission.

"Indeed!—How so? You can have been acquainted with it only since I came to Bath, excepting as you might hear me previously spoken of in my own family."

"I knew you by report long before you came to Bath. I had heard you described by those who knew you intimately. I have been acquainted with you by character many years. Your person, your disposition, accomplishments, manner—they were all described, they were all present to me."

Mr. Elliot was not disappointed in the interest he hoped to raise. No one can withstand the charm of such a mystery. To have been described long ago to a recent acquaintance, by nameless people, is irresistible; and Anne was all curiosity. She wondered, and questioned him eagerly—but in vain. He delighted in being asked, but he would not tell.

"No, no—some time or other perhaps, but not now. He would mention no names now; but such, he could assure her, had been the fact. He had many years ago received such a description of Miss Anne Elliot, as had inspired him with the highest idea of her merit, and excited the warmest curiosity to know her."

Anne could think of no one so likely to have spoken with partiality of her many years ago, as the Mr. Wentworth, of Monkford, Captain Wentworth's brother. He might have been in Mr. Elliot's company, but she had not courage to ask the question.

"The name of Anne Elliot," said he, "has long had an interesting sound to me. Very long has it possessed a charm over my fancy; and, if I dared, I would breathe my wishes that the name might never change."[5]

Such she believed were his words; but scarcely had she received their sound, than her attention was caught by other sounds immediately behind her, which rendered every thing else trivial. Her father and Lady Dalrymple were speaking.

"A well-looking man," said Sir Walter, "a very well-looking man."

"A very fine young man indeed!" said Lady Dalrymple. "More air than one often sees in Bath.—Irish, I dare say."[6]

"No, I just know his name. A bowing acquaintance. Wentworth—Captain Wentworth of the navy. His sister married my tenant in Somersetshire,—the Croft, who rents Kellynch."

Before Sir Walter had reached this point, Anne's eyes had caught the right direction, and distinguished Captain Wentworth, standing among a cluster of men at a little distance. As her eyes fell on him, his seemed to be withdrawn from her. It had that appearance. It seemed as if she had been one moment too late; and as long as

5. An implicit proposal of marriage, since a union of Anne with her cousin Elliot would leave her surname unchanged.
6. Reflecting a disagreement about the derivation, Scotch or Irish, of the name Wentworth.

she dared observe, he did not look again: but the performance was re-commencing, and she was forced to seem to restore her attention to the orchestra, and look straight forward.

When she could give another glance, he had moved away. He could not have come nearer to her if he would; she was so surrounded and shut in: but she would rather have caught his eye.

Mr. Elliot's speech too distressed her. She had no longer any inclination to talk to him. She wished him not so near her.

The first act was over. Now she hoped for some beneficial change; and, after a period of nothing-saying amongst the party, some of them did decide on going in quest of tea. Anne was one of the few who did not choose to move. She remained in her seat, and so did Lady Russell; but she had the pleasure of getting rid of Mr. Elliot; and she did not mean, whatever she might feel on Lady Russell's account, to shrink from conversation with Captain Wentworth, if he gave her the opportunity. She was persuaded by Lady Russell's countenance that she had seen him.

He did not come however. Anne sometimes fancied she discerned him at a distance, but he never came. The anxious interval wore away unproductively. The others returned, the room filled again, benches were reclaimed and re-possessed, and another hour of pleasure or of penance was to be set out, another hour of music was to give delight or the gapes,[7] as real or affected taste for it prevailed. To Anne, it chiefly wore the prospect of an hour of agitation. She could not quit that room in peace without seeing Captain Wentworth once more, without the interchange of one friendly look.

In re-settling themselves, there were now many changes, the result of which was favourable for her. Colonel Wallis declined sitting down again, and Mr. Elliot was invited by Elizabeth and Miss Carteret, in a manner not to be refused, to sit between them; and by some other removals, and a little scheming of her own, Anne was enabled to place herself much nearer the end of the bench than she had been before, much more within reach of a passer-by. She could not do so, without comparing herself with Miss Larolles, the inimitable Miss Larolles,[8]—but still she did it, and not with much happier effect; though by what seemed prosperity in the shape of an early abdication in her next neighbours, she found herself at the very end of the bench before the concert closed.

Such was her situation, with a vacant space at hand, when Captain Wentworth was again in sight. She saw him not far off. He saw her too; yet he looked grave, and seemed irresolute, and only by very slow degrees came at last near enough to speak to her. She felt that

7. Yawns.
8. A minor character in Frances Burney's *Cecilia* (1782) who chooses her seat at public events so as to be in a good position for talking to choice persons.

something must be the matter. The change was indubitable. The difference between his present air and what it had been in the octagon room was strikingly great.—Why was it? She thought of her father— of Lady Russell. Could there have been any unpleasant glances? He began by speaking of the concert, gravely; more like the Captain Wentworth of Uppercross; owned himself disappointed, had expected better singing; and, in short, must confess that he should not be sorry when it was over. Anne replied, and spoke in defence of the performance so well, and yet in allowance for his feelings, so pleasantly, that his countenance improved, and he replied again with almost a smile. They talked for a few minutes more; the improvement held; he even looked down towards the bench, as if he saw a place on it well worth occupying; when, at that moment, a touch on her shoulder obliged Anne to turn round.—It came from Mr. Elliot. He begged her pardon, but she must be applied to, to explain Italian again. Miss Carteret was very anxious to have a general idea of what was next to be sung. Anne could not refuse; but never had she sacrificed to politeness with a more suffering spirit.

A few minutes, though as few as possible, were inevitably consumed; and when her own mistress again, when able to turn and look as she had done before, she found herself accosted by Captain Wentworth, in a reserved yet hurried sort of farewell. "He must wish her good night. He was going—he should get home as fast as he could."

"Is not this song worth staying for?" said Anne, suddenly struck by an idea which made her yet more anxious to be encouraging.

"No!" he replied impressively, "there is nothing worth my staying for;" and he was gone directly.

Jealousy of Mr. Elliot! It was the only intelligible motive. Captain Wentworth jealous of her affection! Could she have believed it a week ago—three hours ago! For a moment the gratification was exquisite. But alas! there were very different thoughts to succeed. How was such jealousy to be quieted? How was the truth to reach him? How, in all the peculiar disadvantages of their respective situations, would he ever learn her real sentiments? It was misery to think of Mr. Elliot's attentions.—Their evil was incalculable.

Chapter XXI

Anne recollected with pleasure the next morning her promise of going to Mrs. Smith; meaning that it should engage her from home at the time when Mr. Elliot would be most likely to call; for to avoid Mr. Elliot was almost a first object.

She felt a great deal of good will towards him. In spite of the mischief of his attentions, she owed him gratitude and regard, perhaps compassion. She could not help thinking much of the extraordinary circumstances attending their acquaintance; of the right which he seemed to have to interest her, by every thing in situation, by his own sentiments, by his early prepossession. It was altogether very extraordinary.—Flattering, but painful. There was much to regret. How she might have felt, had there been no Captain Wentworth in the case, was not worth enquiry; for there was a Captain Wentworth: and be the conclusion of the present suspense good or bad, her affection would be his for ever. Their union, she believed, could not divide her more from other men, than their final separation.

Prettier musings of high-wrought love and eternal constancy, could never have passed along the streets of Bath, than Anne was sporting with from Camden-place to Westgate-buildings. It was almost enough to spread purification and perfume all the way.

She was sure of a pleasant reception; and her friend seemed this morning particularly obliged to her for coming, seemed hardly to have expected her, though it had been an appointment.

An account of the concert was immediately claimed; and Anne's recollections of the concert were quite happy enough to animate her features, and make her rejoice to talk of it. All that she could tell, she told most gladly; but the all was little for one who had been there, and unsatisfactory for such an enquirer as Mrs. Smith, who had already heard, through the short cut of a laundress and a waiter, rather more of the general success and produce of the evening than Anne could relate; and who now asked in vain for several particulars of the company. Every body of any consequence or notoriety in Bath was well known by name to Mrs. Smith.

"The little Durands were there, I conclude," said she, "with their mouths open to catch the music; like unfledged sparrows ready to be fed. They never miss a concert."

"Yes. I did not see them myself, but I heard Mr. Elliot say they were in the room."

"The Ibbotsons—were they there? and the two new beauties, with the tall Irish officer, who is talked of for one of them."

"I do not know.—I do not think they were."

"Old Lady Mary Maclean? I need not ask after her. She never misses, I know; and you must have seen her. She must have been in your own circle, for as you went with Lady Dalrymple, you were in the seats of grandeur; round the orchestra, of course."

"No, that was what I dreaded. It would have been very unpleasant to me in every respect. But happily Lady Dalrymple always chooses to be farther off; and we were exceedingly well placed—that is for hearing; I must not say for seeing, because I appear to have seen very little."

"Oh! you saw enough for your own amusement.—I can understand. There is a sort of domestic enjoyment to be known even in a crowd, and this you had. You were a large party in yourselves, and you wanted nothing beyond."

"But I ought to have looked about me more," said Anne, conscious while she spoke, that there had in fact been no want of looking about; that the object only had been deficient.

"No, no—you were better employed. You need not tell me that you had a pleasant evening. I see it in your eye. I perfectly see how the hours passed—that you had always something agreeable to listen to. In the intervals of the concert, it was conversation."

Anne half smiled and said, "Do you see that in my eye?"

"Yes, I do. Your countenance perfectly informs me that you were in company last night with the person, whom you think the most agreeable in the world, the person who interests you at this present time, more than all the rest of the world put together."

A blush overspread Anne's cheeks. She could say nothing.

"And such being the case," continued Mrs. Smith, after a short pause, "I hope you believe that I do know how to value your kindness in coming to me this morning. It is really very good of you to come and sit with me, when you must have so many pleasanter demands upon your time."

Anne heard nothing of this. She was still in the astonishment and confusion excited by her friend's penetration, unable to imagine how any report of Captain Wentworth could have reached her. After another short silence—

"Pray," said Mrs. Smith, "is Mr. Elliot aware of your acquaintance with me? Does he know that I am in Bath?"

"Mr. Elliot!" repeated Anne, looking up surprised. A moment's reflection shewed her the mistake she had been under. She caught it instantaneously; and, recovering courage with the feeling of safety, soon added, more composedly, "are you acquainted with Mr. Elliot?"

"I have been a good deal acquainted with him," replied Mrs. Smith, gravely, "but it seems worn out now. It is a great while since we met."

"I was not at all aware of this. You never mentioned it before. Had I known it, I would have had the pleasure of talking to him about you."

"To confess the truth," said Mrs. Smith, assuming her usual air of cheerfulness, "that is exactly the pleasure I want you to have. I want you to talk about me to Mr. Elliot. I want your interest with him. He can be of essential service to me; and if you would have the goodness, my dear Miss Elliot, to make it an object to yourself, of course it is done."

"I should be extremely happy—I hope you cannot doubt my willingness to be of even the slightest use to you," replied Anne; "but I suspect that you are considering me as having a higher claim on Mr. Elliot—a greater right to influence him, than is really the case. I am sure you have, somehow or other, imbibed such a notion. You must consider me only as Mr. Elliot's relation. If in that light, if there is any thing which you suppose his cousin might fairly ask of him, I beg you would not hesitate to employ me."

Mrs. Smith gave her a penetrating glance, and then, smiling, said,

"I have been a little premature, I perceive. I beg your pardon. I ought to have waited for official information. But now, my dear Miss Elliot, as an old friend, do give me a hint as to when I may speak. Next week? To be sure by next week I may be allowed to think it all settled, and build my own selfish schemes on Mr. Elliot's good fortune."

"No," replied Anne, "nor next week, nor next, nor next. I assure you that nothing of the sort you are thinking of will be settled any week. I am not going to marry Mr. Elliot. I should like to know why you imagine I am."

Mrs. Smith looked at her again, looked earnestly, smiled, shook her head, and exclaimed,

"Now, how I do wish I understood you! How I do wish I knew what you were at! I have a great idea that you do not design to be cruel, when the right moment comes. Till it does come, you know, we women never mean to have any body. It is a thing of course among us, that every man is refused—till he offers. But why should you be cruel? Let me plead for my—present friend I cannot call him—but for my former friend. Where can you look for a more suitable match? Where could you expect a more gentlemanlike, agreeable man? Let me recommend Mr. Elliot. I am sure you hear nothing but good of him from Colonel Wallis; and who can know him better than Colonel Wallis?"

"My dear Mrs. Smith, Mr. Elliot's wife has not been dead much above half a year. He ought not to be supposed to be paying his addresses to any one."

"Oh! if these are your only objections," cried Mrs. Smith, archly, "Mr. Elliot is safe, and I shall give myself no more trouble about him. Do not forget me when you are married, that's all. Let him know me to be a friend of yours, and then he will think little of the trouble required, which it is very natural for him now, with so many affairs and engagements of his own, to avoid and get rid of as he can—very natural, perhaps. Ninety-nine out of a hundred would do the same. Of course, he cannot be aware of the importance to me. Well, my dear Miss Elliot, I hope and trust you will be very happy. Mr. Elliot has sense to understand the value of such a woman. Your peace will not be shipwrecked as mine has been. You are safe in all worldly matters, and safe in his character. He will not be led astray, he will not be misled by others to his ruin."

"No," said Anne, "I can readily believe all that of my cousin. He seems to have a calm, decided temper, not at all open to dangerous impressions. I consider him with great respect. I have no reason, from any thing that has fallen within my observation, to do otherwise. But I have not known him long; and he is not a man, I think, to be known intimately soon. Will not this manner of speaking of him, Mrs. Smith, convince you that he is nothing to me? Surely, this must be calm enough. And, upon my word, he is nothing to me. Should he ever propose to me (which I have very little reason to imagine he has any thought of doing), I shall not accept him. I assure you I shall not. I assure you Mr. Elliot had not the share which you have been supposing, in whatever pleasure the concert of last night might afford:—not Mr. Elliot; it is not Mr. Elliot that—"

She stopped, regretting with a deep blush that she had implied so much; but less would hardly have been sufficient. Mrs. Smith would hardly have believed so soon in Mr. Elliot's failure, but from the perception of there being a somebody else. As it was, she instantly submitted, and with all the semblance of seeing nothing beyond; and Anne, eager to escape farther notice, was impatient to know why Mrs. Smith should have fancied she was to marry Mr. Elliot, where she could have received the idea, or from whom she could have heard it.

"Do tell me how it first came into your head."

"It first came into my head," replied Mrs. Smith, "upon finding how much you were together, and feeling it to be the most probable thing in the world to be wished for by everybody belonging to either of you; and you may depend upon it that all your acquaintance have disposed of you in the same way. But I never heard it spoken of till two days ago."

"And has it indeed been spoken of?"

"Did you observe the woman who opened the door to you, when you called yesterday?"

"No. Was not it Mrs. Speed, as usual, or the maid? I observed no one in particular."

"It was my friend, Mrs. Rooke—Nurse Rooke, who, by the by, had a great curiosity to see you, and was delighted to be in the way to let you in. She came away from Marlborough-buildings only on Sunday; and she it was who told me you were to marry Mr. Elliot. She had had it from Mrs. Wallis herself, which did not seem bad authority. She sat an hour with me on Monday evening, and gave me the whole history."

"The whole history!" repeated Anne, laughing. "She could not make a very long history, I think, of one such little article of unfounded news."

Mrs. Smith said nothing.

"But," continued Anne, presently, "though there is no truth in my having this claim on Mr. Elliot, I should be extremely happy to be of use to you, in any way that I could. Shall I mention to him your being in Bath? Shall I take any message?"

"No, I thank you: no, certainly not. In the warmth of the moment, and under a mistaken impression, I might, perhaps, have endeavoured to interest you in some circumstances. But not now: no, I thank you, I have nothing to trouble you with."

"I think you spoke of having known Mr. Elliot many years?"

"I did."

"Not before he married, I suppose?"

"Yes; he was not married when I knew him first."

"And—were you much acquainted?"

"Intimately."

"Indeed! Then do tell me what he was at that time of life. I have a great curiosity to know what Mr. Elliot was as a very young man. Was he at all such as he appears now?"

"I have not seen Mr. Elliot these three years," was Mrs. Smith's answer, given so gravely that it was impossible to pursue the subject farther; and Anne felt that she had gained nothing but an increase of curiosity. They were both silent—Mrs. Smith very thoughtful. At last,

"I beg your pardon, my dear Miss Elliot," she cried, in her natural tone of cordiality, "I beg your pardon for the short answers I have been giving you, but I have been uncertain what I ought to do. I have been doubting and considering as to what I ought to tell you. There were many things to be taken into the account. One hates to be officious, to be giving bad impressions, making mischief. Even the smooth surface of family-union seems worth preserving, though there may be nothing durable beneath. However, I have determined; I think I am right; I think you ought to be made acquainted with Mr. Elliot's real character. Though I fully believe that, at present, you have not the smallest intention of accepting him, there is no saying what may happen. You might, some time or other, be differently affected towards him. Hear the truth, therefore, now, while you are unprejudiced. Mr. Elliot is a man without heart or conscience; a designing, wary, cold-blooded being, who thinks only of himself; who, for his own interest or ease, would be guilty of any cruelty, or any treachery, that could be perpetrated without risk of his general character. He has no feeling for others. Those whom he has been the chief cause of leading into ruin, he can neglect and desert without the smallest compunction. He is totally beyond the reach of any sentiment of justice or compassion. Oh! he is black at heart, hollow and black!"

Anne's astonished air, and exclamation of wonder, made her pause, and in a calmer manner she added,

"My expressions startle you. You must allow for an injured, angry woman. But I will try to command myself. I will not abuse him. I will only tell you what I have found him. Facts shall speak. He was the intimate friend of my dear husband, who trusted and loved him, and thought him as good as himself. The intimacy had been formed before our marriage. I found them most intimate friends; and I, too, became excessively pleased with Mr. Elliot, and entertained the highest opinion of him. At nineteen, you know, one does not think very seriously, but Mr. Elliot appeared to me quite as good as others, and much more agreeable than most others, and we were almost always together. We were principally in town, living in very good style. He was then the inferior in circumstances, he was then the poor one; he had chambers in the Temple,[9] and it was as much as he could do to support the appearance of a gentleman. He had always a home with us whenever he chose it; he was always welcome; he was like a brother. My poor Charles, who had the finest, most generous spirit in the world, would have divided his last farthing with him; and I know that his purse was open to him; I know that he often assisted him."

"This must have been about that very period of Mr. Elliot's life," said Anne, "which has always excited my particular curiosity. It must have been about the same time that he became known to my father and sister. I never knew him myself, I only heard of him, but there was a something in his conduct then with regard to my father and sister, and afterwards in the circumstances of his marriage, which I never could quite reconcile with present times. It seemed to announce a different sort of man."

"I know it all, I know it all," cried Mrs. Smith. "He had been introduced to Sir Walter and your sister before I was acquainted with him, but I heard him speak of them for ever. I know he was invited and encouraged, and I know he did not choose to go. I can satisfy you, perhaps, on points which you would little expect; and as to his marriage, I knew all about it at the time. I was privy to all the fors and againsts, I was the friend to whom he confided his hopes and plans, and though I did not know his wife previously, (her inferior situation in society, indeed, rendered that impossible) yet I knew her all her life afterwards, or, at least, till within the last two years of her life, and can answer any question you wish to put."

"Nay," said Anne, "I have no particular enquiry to make about her. I have always understood they were not a happy couple. But I should like to know why, at that time of his life, he should slight my father's acquaintance as he did. My father was certainly disposed to take very kind and proper notice of him. Why did Mr. Elliot draw back?"

9. The Inns of Court, in London, where lawyers lived and studied.

"Mr. Elliot," replied Mrs. Smith, "at that period of his life, had one object in view—to make his fortune, and by a rather quicker process than the law. He was determined to make it by marriage. He was determined, at least, not to mar it by an imprudent marriage; and I know it was his belief, (whether justly or not, of course I cannot decide) that your father and sister, in their civilities and invitations, were designing a match between the heir and the young lady; and it was impossible that such a match should have answered his ideas of wealth and independance. That was his motive for drawing back, I can assure you. He told me the whole story. He had no concealments with me. It was curious, that having just left you behind me in Bath, my first and principal acquaintance on marrying, should be your cousin; and that, through him, I should be continually hearing of your father and sister. He described one Miss Elliot, and I thought very affectionately of the other."

"Perhaps," cried Anne, struck by a sudden idea, "you sometimes spoke of me to Mr. Elliot?"

"To be sure I did, very often. I used to boast of my own Anne Elliot, and vouch for your being a very different creature from—"

She checked herself just in time.

"This accounts for something which Mr. Elliot said last night," cried Anne. "This explains it. I found he had been used to hear of me. I could not comprehend how. What wild imaginations one forms, where dear self is concerned! How sure to be mistaken! But I beg your pardon; I have interrupted you. Mr. Elliot married, then, completely for money? The circumstance, probably, which first opened your eyes to his character."

Mrs. Smith hesitated a little here. "Oh! those things are too common. When one lives in the world, a man or woman's marrying for money is too common to strike one as it ought. I was very young, and associated only with the young, and we were a thoughtless, gay set, without any strict rules of conduct. We lived for enjoyment. I think differently now; time and sickness, and sorrow, have given me other notions; but, at that period, I must own I saw nothing reprehensible in what Mr. Elliot was doing. 'To do the best for himself,' passed as a duty."

"But was not she a very low woman?"

"Yes; which I objected to, but he would not regard. Money, money, was all that he wanted. Her father was a grazier,[1] her grandfather had been a butcher, but that was all nothing. She was a fine woman, had had a decent education, was brought forward by some cousins, thrown by chance into Mr. Elliot's company, and fell in love with him; and not a difficulty or a scruple was there on his side, with

1. One who feeds cattle for market; a lower-class occupation.

respect to her birth. All his caution was spent in being secured[2] of the real amount of her fortune, before he committed himself. Depend upon it, whatever esteem Mr. Elliot may have for his own situation in life now, as a young man he had not the smallest value for it. His chance of the Kellynch estate was something, but all the honour of the family he held as cheap as dirt. I have often heard him declare, that if baronetcies were saleable, any body should have his for fifty pounds, arms and motto, name and livery included; but I will not pretend to repeat half that I used to hear him say on that subject. It would not be fair. And yet you ought to have proof; for what is all this but assertion? and you shall have proof."

"Indeed, my dear Mrs. Smith, I want none," cried Anne. "You have asserted nothing contradictory to what Mr. Elliot appeared to be some years ago. This is all in confirmation, rather, of what we used to hear and believe. I am more curious to know why he should be so different now?"

"But for my satisfaction; if you will have the goodness to ring for Mary—stay, I am sure you will have the still greater goodness of going yourself into my bed-room, and bringing me the small inlaid box which you will find on the upper shelf of the closet."

Anne, seeing her friend to be earnestly bent on it, did as she was desired. The box was brought and placed before her, and Mrs. Smith, sighing over it as she unlocked it, said,

"This is full of papers belonging to him, to my husband, a small portion only of what I had to look over when I lost him. The letter I am looking for, was one written by Mr. Elliot to him before our marriage, and happened to be saved; why, one can hardly imagine. But he was careless and immethodical, like other men, about those things; and when I came to examine his papers, I found it with others still more trivial from different people scattered here and there, while many letters and memorandums of real importance had been destroyed. Here it is. I would not burn it, because being even then very little satisfied with Mr. Elliot, I was determined to preserve every document of former intimacy. I have now another motive for being glad that I can produce it."

This was the letter, directed to "Charles Smith, Esq. Tunbridge Wells," and dated from London, as far back as July, 1803.

Dear Smith,
I have received yours. Your kindness almost overpowers me. I wish nature had made such hearts as yours more common, but I have lived three and twenty years in the world, and have seen none like it. At present, believe me, I have no need of your services, being in cash again. Give me joy: I have got rid of Sir

2. Assured.

Walter and Miss. They are gone back to Kellynch, and almost made me swear to visit them this summer, but my first visit to Kellynch will be with a surveyor, to tell me how to bring it with best advantage to the hammer.[3] The baronet, nevertheless, is not unlikely to marry again; he is quite fool enough. If he does, however, they will leave me in peace, which may be a decent equivalent for the reversion.[4] He is worse than last year.

I wish I had any name but Elliot. I am sick of it. The name of Walter I can drop, thank God! and I desire you will never insult me with my second W. again, meaning, for the rest of my life, to be only yours truly,

WM. ELLIOT.

Such a letter could not be read without putting Anne in a glow; and Mrs. Smith, observing the high colour in her face, said,

"The language, I know, is highly disrespectful. Though I have forgot the exact terms, I have a perfect impression of the general meaning. But it shews you the man. Mark his professions to my poor husband. Can any thing be stronger?"

Anne could not immediately get over the shock and mortification of finding such words applied to her father. She was obliged to recollect that her seeing the letter was a violation of the laws of honour, that no one ought to be judged or to be known by such testimonies, that no private correspondence could bear the eye of others, before she could recover calmness enough to return the letter which she had been meditating over, and say,

"Thank you. This is full proof undoubtedly, proof of every thing you were saying. But why be acquainted with us now?"

"I can explain this too," cried Mrs. Smith, smiling.

"Can you really?"

"Yes. I have shewn you Mr. Elliot, as he was a dozen years ago, and I will shew him as he is now. I cannot produce written proof again, but I can give as authentic oral testimony as you can desire, of what he is now wanting, and what he is now doing. He is no hypocrite now. He truly wants to marry you. His present attentions to your family are very sincere, quite from the heart. I will give you my authority; his friend Colonel Wallis."

"Colonel Wallis! are you acquainted with him?"

"No. It does not come to me in quite so direct a line as that; it takes a bend or two, but nothing of consequence. The stream is as good as at first; the little rubbish it collects in the turnings, is easily moved away. Mr. Elliot talks unreservedly to Colonel Wallis of his views on you—which said Colonel Wallis I imagine to be in himself

---

3. To be auctioned.
4. The passing of the estate to Mr. Elliot if Sir Walter dies without male heirs.

a sensible, careful, discerning sort of character; but Colonel Wallis has a very pretty silly wife, to whom he tells things which he had better not, and he repeats it all to her. She, in the overflowing spirits of her recovery, repeats it all to her nurse; and the nurse, knowing my acquaintance with you, very naturally brings it all to me. On Monday evening my good friend Mrs. Rooke let me thus much into the secrets of Marlborough-buildings. When I talked of a whole history therefore, you see, I was not romancing so much as you supposed."

"My dear Mrs. Smith, your authority is deficient. This will not do. Mr. Elliot's having any views on me will not in the least account for the efforts he made towards a reconciliation with my father. That was all prior to my coming to Bath. I found them on the most friendly terms when I arrived."

"I know you did; I know it all perfectly, but"—

"Indeed, Mrs. Smith, we must not expect to get real information in such a line. Facts or opinions which are to pass through the hands of so many, to be misconceived by folly in one, and ignorance in another, can hardly have much truth left."

"Only give me a hearing. You will soon be able to judge of the general credit due, by listening to some particulars which you can yourself immediately contradict or confirm. Nobody supposes that you were his first inducement. He had seen you indeed, before he came to Bath and admired you, but without knowing it to be you. So says my historian at least. Is this true? Did he see you last summer or autumn, 'somewhere down in the west,' to use her own words, without knowing it to be you?"

"He certainly did. So far it is very true. At Lyme; I happened to be at Lyme."

"Well," continued Mrs. Smith triumphantly, "grant my friend the credit due to the establishment of the first point asserted. He saw you then at Lyme, and liked you so well as to be exceedingly pleased to meet with you again in Camden-place, as Miss Anne Elliot, and from that moment, I have no doubt, had a double motive in his visits there. But there was another, and an earlier; which I will now explain. If there is any thing in my story which you know to be either false or improbable, stop me. My account states, that your sister's friend, the lady now staying with you, whom I have heard you mention, came to Bath with Miss Elliot and Sir Walter as long ago as September, (in short when they first came themselves) and has been staying there ever since; that she is a clever, insinuating, handsome woman, poor and plausible, and altogether such in situation and manner, as to give a general idea among Sir Walter's acquaintance, of her meaning to be Lady Elliot, and as general a surprise that Miss Elliot should be apparently blind to the danger."

Here Mrs. Smith paused a moment; but Anne had not a word to say, and she continued,

"This was the light in which it appeared to those who knew the family, long before your return to it; and Colonel Wallis had his eye upon your father enough to be sensible of it, though he did not then visit in Camden-place; but his regard for Mr. Elliot gave him an interest in watching all that was going on there, and when Mr. Elliot came to Bath for a day or two, as he happened to do a little before Christmas, Colonel Wallis made him acquainted with the appearance of things, and the reports beginning to prevail.—Now you are to understand that time had worked a very material change in Mr. Elliot's opinions as to the value of a baronetcy. Upon all points of blood and connexion, he is a completely altered man. Having long had as much money as he could spend, nothing to wish for on the side of avarice or indulgence, he has been gradually learning to pin his happiness upon the consequence he is heir to. I thought it coming on, before our acquaintance ceased, but it is now a confirmed feeling. He cannot bear the idea of not being Sir William. You may guess therefore that the news he heard from his friend, could not be very agreeable,[5] and you may guess what it produced; the resolution of coming back to Bath as soon as possible, and of fixing himself here for a time, with the view of renewing his former acquaintance and recovering such a footing in the family, as might give him the means of ascertaining the degree of his danger, and of circumventing the lady if he found it material. This was agreed upon between the two friends, as the only thing to be done; and Colonel Wallis was to assist in every way that he could. He was to be introduced, and Mrs. Wallis was to be introduced, and every body was to be introduced. Mr. Elliot came back accordingly; and on application was forgiven, as you know, and re-admitted into the family; and there it was his constant object, and his only object (till your arrival added another motive) to watch Sir Walter and Mrs. Clay. He omitted no opportunity of being with them, threw himself in their way, called at all hours—but I need not be particular on this subject. You can imagine what an artful man would do; and with this guide, perhaps, may recollect what you have seen him do."

"Yes," said Anne, "you tell me nothing which does not accord with what I have known, or could imagine. There is always something offensive in the details of cunning. The manœuvres of selfishness and duplicity must ever be revolting, but I have heard nothing which really surprises me. I know those who would be shocked by such a representation of Mr. Elliot, who would have difficulty in believing

5. Because if Sir Walter marries again, his wife may bear a son, who would inherit his title and estate.

it; but I have never been satisfied. I have always wanted some other motive for his conduct than appeared.—I should like to know his present opinion, as to the probability of the event he has been in dread of; whether he considers the danger to be lessening or not."

"Lessening, I understand," replied Mrs. Smith. "He thinks Mrs. Clay afraid of him, aware that he sees through her, and not daring to proceed as she might do in his absence. But since he must be absent some time or other, I do not perceive how he can ever be secure, while she holds her present influence. Mrs. Wallis has an amusing idea, as nurse tells me, that it is to be put into the marriage articles when you and Mr. Elliot marry, that your father is not to marry Mrs. Clay. A scheme, worthy of Mrs. Wallis's understanding, by all accounts; but my sensible nurse Rooke sees the absurdity of it.—'Why, to be sure, ma'am,' said she, 'it would not prevent his marrying any body else.' And indeed, to own the truth, I do not think nurse in her heart is a very strenuous opposer of Sir Walter's making a second match. She must be allowed to be a favourer of matrimony you know, and (since self will intrude) who can say that she may not have some flying visions of attending the next Lady Elliot, through Mrs. Wallis's recommendation?"

"I am very glad to know all this," said Anne, after a little thoughtfulness. "It will be more painful to me in some respects to be in company with him, but I shall know better what to do. My line of conduct will be more direct. Mr. Elliot is evidently a disingenuous, artificial, worldly man, who has never had any better principle to guide him than selfishness."

But Mr. Elliot was not yet done with. Mrs. Smith had been carried away from her first direction, and Anne had forgotten, in the interest of her own family concerns, how much had been originally implied against him; but her attention was now called to the explanation of those first hints, and she listened to a recital which, if it did not perfectly justify the unqualified bitterness of Mrs. Smith, proved him to have been very unfeeling in his conduct towards her, very deficient both in justice and compassion.

She learned that (the intimacy between them continuing unimpaired by Mr. Elliot's marriage) they had been as before always together, and Mr. Elliot had led his friend into expenses much beyond his fortune. Mrs. Smith did not want to take blame to herself, and was most tender of throwing any on her husband; but Anne could collect that their income had never been equal to their style of living, and that from the first, there had been a great deal of general and joint extravagance. From his wife's account of him, she could discern Mr. Smith to have been a man of warm feelings, easy temper, careless habits, and not strong understanding, much more amiable than his friend, and very unlike him—led by him, and probably despised by him. Mr. Elliot, raised by his marriage to great affluence, and disposed to every gratification of pleasure and vanity which could be commanded without involving himself, (for with all his self-indulgence he had become a prudent man) and beginning to be rich, just as his friend ought to have found himself to be poor, seemed to have had no concern at all for that friend's probable finances, but, on the contrary, had been prompting and encouraging expenses, which could end only in ruin. And the Smiths accordingly had been ruined.

The husband had died just in time to be spared the full knowledge of it. They had previously known embarrassments enough to try the friendship of their friends, and to prove that Mr. Elliot's had better not be tried; but it was not till his death that the wretched state of his affairs was fully known. With a confidence in Mr. Elliot's regard, more creditable to his feelings than his judgment, Mr. Smith had appointed him the executor of his will; but Mr. Elliot would not act, and the difficulties and distresses which this refusal had heaped on her, in addition to the inevitable sufferings of her situation, had been such as could not be related without anguish of spirit, or listened to without corresponding indignation.

Anne was shewn some letters of his on the occasion, answers to urgent applications from Mrs. Smith, which all breathed the same stern resolution of not engaging in a fruitless trouble, and, under a cold civility, the same hard-hearted indifference to any of the evils it might bring on her. It was a dreadful picture of ingratitude and inhumanity; and Anne felt at some moments, that no flagrant open crime could have been worse. She had a great deal to listen to; all the particulars of past sad scenes, all the minutiæ of distress upon distress, which in former conversations had been merely hinted at, were dwelt on now with a natural indulgence. Anne could perfectly comprehend the exquisite relief, and was only the more inclined to wonder at the composure of her friend's usual state of mind.

There was one circumstance in the history of her grievances of particular irritation. She had good reason to believe that some property of her husband in the West Indies, which had been for many years under a sort of sequestration for the payment of its own incumbrances,[6] might be recoverable by proper measures; and this property, though not large, would be enough to make her comparatively rich. But there was nobody to stir in it. Mr. Elliot would do nothing, and she could do nothing herself, equally disabled from personal exertion by her state of bodily weakness, and from

6. The income of the estate has been assigned, presumably by legal action, to pay legal claims against the owner. This property, likely a sugar plantation reliant on the labor of enslaved persons, is referenced again in the book's penultimate paragraph (see Chapter XXIV, p. 179).

employing others by her want of money. She had no natural con-nexions[7] to assist her even with their counsel, and she could not afford to purchase the assistance of the law. This was a cruel aggravation of actually streightened[8] means. To feel that she ought to be in better circumstances, that a little trouble in the right place might do it, and to fear that delay might be even weakening her claims, was hard to bear!

It was on this point that she had hoped to engage Anne's good offices with Mr. Elliot. She had previously, in the anticipation of their marriage, been very apprehensive of losing her friend by it; but on being assured that he could have made no attempt of that nature, since he did not even know her to be in Bath, it immediately occurred, that something might be done in her favour by the influence of the woman he loved, and she had been hastily preparing to interest Anne's feelings, as far as the observances due to Mr. Elliot's charac-ter[9] would allow, when Anne's refutation of the supposed engagement changed the face of every thing, and while it took from her the new-formed hope of succeeding in the object of her first anxiety, left her at least the comfort of telling the whole story her own way.

After listening to this full description of Mr. Elliot, Anne could not but express some surprise at Mrs. Smith's having spoken of him so favourably in the beginning of their conversation. "She had seemed to recommend and praise him!"

"My dear," was Mrs. Smith's reply, "there was nothing else to be done. I considered your marrying him as certain, though he might not yet have made the offer, and I could no more speak the truth of him, than if he had been your husband. My heart bled for you, as I talked of happiness. And yet, he is sensible, he is agreeable, and with such a woman as you, it was not absolutely hopeless. He was very unkind to his first wife. They were wretched together. But she was too ignorant and giddy for respect, and he had never loved her. I was willing to hope that you must fare better."

Anne could just acknowledge within herself such a possibility of having been induced to marry him, as made her shudder at the idea of the misery which must have followed. It was just possible that she might have been persuaded by Lady Russell! And under such a sup-position, which would have been most miserable, when time had dis-closed all, too late?

It was very desirable that Lady Russell should be no longer deceived; and one of the concluding arrangements of this important

7. Relatives.
8. Straitened, reduced.
9. Reputation. Mrs. Smith has extended the conventional good wishes for Anne's prospec-tive marriage to a man generally considered an upstanding and prosperous person.

conference, which carried them through the greater part of the morning, was, that Anne had full liberty to communicate to her friend every thing relative to Mrs. Smith, in which his conduct was involved.

Chapter XXII

Anne went home to think over all that she had heard. In one point, her feelings were relieved by this knowledge of Mr. Elliot. There was no longer any thing of tenderness due to him. He stood, as opposed to Captain Wentworth, in all his own unwelcome obtrusiveness; and the evil of his attentions last night, the irremediable mischief he might have done, was considered with sensations unqualified, unperplexed.—Pity for him was all over. But this was the only point of relief. In every other respect, in looking around her, or penetrating forward, she saw more to distrust and to apprehend. She was concerned for the disappointment and pain Lady Russell would be feeling, for the mortifications which must be hanging over her father and sister, and had all the distress of foreseeing many evils, without knowing how to avert any one of them.—She was most thankful for her own knowledge of him. She had never considered herself as entitled to reward for not slighting an old friend like Mrs. Smith, but here was a reward indeed springing from it!—Mrs. Smith had been able to tell her what no one else could have done. Could the knowledge have been extended through her family!—But this was a vain idea. She must talk to Lady Russell, tell her, consult with her, and having done her best, wait the event[1] with as much composure as possible; and after all, her greatest want of composure would be in that quarter of the mind which could not be opened to Lady Russell, in that flow of anxieties and fears which must be all to herself.

She found, on reaching home, that she had, as she intended, escaped seeing Mr. Elliot; that he had called and paid them a long morning visit; but hardly had she congratulated herself, and felt safe till to-morrow, when she heard that he was coming again in the evening.

"I had not the smallest intention of asking him," said Elizabeth, with affected carelessness, "but he gave so many hints; so Mrs. Clay says, at least."

"Indeed I do say it. I never saw any body in my life spell[2] harder for an invitation. Poor man! I was really in pain for him; for your hard-hearted sister, Miss Anne, seems bent on cruelty."

1. Outcome.
2. Suggest a desire.

"Oh!" cried Elizabeth, "I have been rather too much used to the game to be soon overcome by a gentleman's hints. However, when I found how excessively he was regretting that he should miss my father this morning, I gave way immediately, for I would never really omit an opportunity of bringing him and Sir Walter together. They appear to so much advantage in company with each other! Each behaving so pleasantly! Mr. Elliot looking up with so much respect!"

"Quite delightful!" cried Mrs. Clay, not daring, however, to turn her eyes towards Anne. "Exactly like father and son! Dear Miss Elliot, may I not say father and son?"

"Oh! I lay no embargo on any body's words. If you will have such ideas! But, upon my word, I am scarcely sensible of his attentions being beyond those of other men."

"My dear Miss Elliot!" exclaimed Mrs. Clay, lifting up her hands and eyes, and sinking all the rest of her astonishment in a convenient silence.

"Well, my dear Penelope, you need not be so alarmed about him. I did invite him, you know. I sent him away with smiles. When I found he was really going to his friends at Thornberry-park for the whole day tomorrow, I had compassion on him."

Anne admired the good acting of the friend, in being able to shew such pleasure as she did, in the expectation, and in the actual arrival of the very person whose presence must really be interfering with her prime object. It was impossible but that Mrs. Clay must hate the sight of Mr. Elliot; and yet she could assume a most obliging, placid look, and appear quite satisfied with the curtailed license of devoting herself only half as much to Sir Walter as she would have done otherwise.

To Anne herself it was most distressing to see Mr. Elliot enter the room; and quite painful to have him approach and speak to her. She had been used before to feel that he could not be always quite sincere, but now she saw insincerity in every thing. His attentive deference to her father, contrasted with his former language, was odious; and when she thought of his cruel conduct towards Mrs. Smith, she could hardly bear the sight of his present smiles and mildness, or the sound of his artificial good sentiments. She meant to avoid any such alteration of manners as might provoke a remonstrance on his side. It was a great object with her to escape all enquiry or eclat;[3] but it was her intention to be as decidedly cool to him as might be compatible with their relationship, and to retrace, as quietly as she could, the few steps of unnecessary intimacy she had been gradually led along. She was accordingly more guarded, and more cool, than she had been the night before.

3. Notoriety, conspicuousness (French).

He wanted to animate her curiosity again as to how and where he could have heard her formerly praised; wanted very much to be gratified by more solicitation; but the charm was broken: he found that the heat and animation of a public room were necessary to kindle his modest cousin's vanity; he found, at least, that it was not to be done now, by any of those attempts which he could hazard among the too-commanding claims of the others. He little surmised that it was a subject acting now exactly against his interest, bringing immediately into her thoughts all those parts of his conduct which were least excusable.

She had some satisfaction in finding that he was really going out of Bath the next morning, going early, and that he would be gone the greater part of two days. He was invited again to Camden-place the very evening of his return; but from Thursday to Saturday evening his absence was certain. It was bad enough that a Mrs. Clay should be always before her; but that a deeper hypocrite should be added to their party, seemed the destruction of every thing like peace and comfort. It was so humiliating to reflect on the constant deception practised on her father and Elizabeth; to consider the various sources of mortification preparing for them! Mrs. Clay's selfishness was not so complicate nor so revolting as his; and Anne would have compounded for the marriage at once, with all its evils, to be clear of Mr. Elliot's subtleties, in endeavouring to prevent it.

On Friday morning she meant to go very early to Lady Russell, and accomplish the necessary communication; and she would have gone directly after breakfast but that Mrs. Clay was also going out on some obliging purpose of saving her sister trouble, which determined her to wait till she might be safe from such a companion. She saw Mrs. Clay fairly off, therefore, before she began to talk of spending the morning in Rivers-street.

"Very well," said Elizabeth, "I have nothing to send but my love. Oh! you may as well take back that tiresome book she would lend me, and pretend I have read it through. I really cannot be plaguing myself for ever with all the new poems and states of the nation that come out. Lady Russell quite bores one with her new publications. You need not tell her so, but I thought her dress hideous the other night. I used to think she had some taste in dress, but I was ashamed of her at the concert. Something so formal and *arrangé*[4] in her air! and she sits so upright! My best love, of course."

"And mine," added Sir Walter. "Kindest regards. And you may say, that I mean to call upon her soon. Make a civil message. But I shall only leave my card.[5] Morning visits are never fair by women at her

4. Artificial, both designed and designing (French).
5. See n. 6, p. 98. Sir Walter will leave his card, in token of having called, but will not ask to see Lady Russell.

time of life, who make themselves up so little. If she would only wear rouge, she would not be afraid of being seen; but last time I called, I observed the blinds were let down immediately."

While her father spoke, there was a knock at the door. Who could it be? Anne, remembering the preconcerted visits, at all hours, of Mr. Elliot, would have expected him, but for his known engagement seven miles off. After the usual period of suspense, the usual sounds of approach were heard, and "Mr. and Mrs. Charles Musgrove" were ushered into the room.

Surprise was the strongest emotion raised by their appearance; but Anne was really glad to see them; and the others were not so sorry but that they could put on a decent air of welcome; and as soon as it became clear that these, their nearest relations, were not arrived with any views of accommodation in that house, Sir Walter and Elizabeth were able to rise in cordiality, and do the honours of it very well. They were come to Bath for a few days with Mrs. Musgrove, and were at the White Hart.[6] So much was pretty soon understood; but till Sir Walter and Elizabeth were walking Mary into the other drawing-room, and regaling themselves with her admiration, Anne could not draw upon Charles's brain for a regular history of their coming, or an explanation of some smiling hints of particular business, which had been ostentatiously dropped by Mary, as well as of some apparent confusion as to whom their party consisted of.

She then found that it consisted of Mrs. Musgrove, Henrietta, and Captain Harville, beside their two selves. He gave her a very plain, intelligible account of the whole; a narration in which she saw a great deal of most characteristic proceeding. The scheme had received its first impulse by Captain Harville's wanting to come to Bath on business. He had begun to talk of it a week ago; and by way of doing something, as shooting was over, Charles had proposed coming with him, and Mrs. Harville had seemed to like the idea of it very much, as an advantage to her husband; but Mary could not bear to be left, and had made herself so unhappy about it that, for a day or two, every thing seemed to be in suspense, or at an end. But then, it had been taken up by his father and mother. His mother had some old friends in Bath, whom she wanted to see; it was thought a good opportunity for Henrietta to come and buy wedding-clothes for herself and her sister; and, in short, it ended in being his mother's party, that every thing might be comfortable and easy to Captain Harville; and he and Mary were included in it, by way of general convenience. They had arrived late the night before. Mrs. Harville, her children, and Captain Benwick, remained with Mr. Musgrove and Louisa at Uppercross.

6. Bath's oldest recorded inn, dating to at least 1503.

Anne's only surprise was, that affairs should be in forwardness enough for Henrietta's wedding-clothes to be talked of: she had imagined such difficulties of fortune to exist there as must prevent the marriage from being near at hand; but she learned from Charles that, very recently, (since Mary's last letter to herself) Charles Hayter had been applied to by a friend to hold a living for a youth who could not possibly claim it under many years;[7] and that, on the strength of this present income, with almost a certainty of something more permanent long before the term in question, the two families had consented to the young people's wishes, and that their marriage was likely to take place in a few months, quite as soon as Louisa's. "And a very good living it was," Charles added, "only five-and-twenty miles from Uppercross, and in a very fine country—fine part of Dorsetshire. In the centre of some of the best preserves[8] in the kingdom, surrounded by three great proprietors, each more careful and jealous than the other; and to two of the three, at least, Charles Hayter might get a special recommendation. Not that he will value it as he ought," he observed, "Charles is too cool about sporting. That's the worst of him."

"I am extremely glad, indeed," cried Anne, "particularly glad that this should happen: and that of two sisters, who both deserve equally well, and who have always been such good friends, the pleasant prospects of one should not be dimming those of the other—that they should be so equal in their prosperity and comfort. I hope your father and mother are quite happy with regard to both."

"Oh! yes. My father would be as well pleased if the gentlemen were richer, but he has no other fault to find. Money, you know, coming down with money[9]—two daughters at once—it cannot be a very agreeable operation, and it streightens him as to many things. However, I do not mean to say they have not a right to it. It is very fit they should have daughters' shares; and I am sure he has always been a very kind, liberal father to me. Mary does not above half like Henrietta's match. She never did, you know. But she does not do him justice, nor think enough about Winthrop. I cannot make her attend to the value of the property. It is a very fair match, as times go; and I have liked Charles Hayter all my life, and I shall not leave off now."

"Such excellent parents as Mr. and Mrs. Musgrove," exclaimed Anne, "should be happy in their children's marriages. They do every thing to confer happiness, I am sure. What a blessing to young people

7. Charles, as a young clergyman, has been asked to serve as temporary pastor for a congregation that has been promised to someone still too young to be ordained. Many pastoral positions in England at this time were assigned by large landowners as a matter of patronage.
8. Game preserves, where animals were nurtured for the purpose of hunting them.
9. For dowries.

to be in such hands! Your father and mother seem so totally free from all those ambitious feelings which have led to so much misconduct and misery, both in young and old! I hope you think Louisa perfectly recovered now?"

He answered rather hesitatingly, "Yes, I believe I do—very much recovered; but she is altered: there is no running or jumping about, no laughing or dancing; it is quite different. If one happens only to shut the door a little hard, she starts and wriggles like a young dab chick[1] in the water; and Benwick sits at her elbow, reading verses, or whispering to her, all day long."

Anne could not help laughing. "That cannot be much to your taste, I know," said she; "but I do believe him to be an excellent young man."

"To be sure he is. Nobody doubts it; and I hope you do not think I am so illiberal as to want every man to have the same objects and pleasures as myself. I have a great value for Benwick; and when one can but get him to talk, he has plenty to say. His reading has done him no harm, for he has fought as well as read. He is a brave fellow. I got more acquainted with him last Monday than ever I did before. We had a famous set-to[2] at rat-hunting all the morning, in my father's great barns; and he played his part so well, that I have liked him the better ever since."

Here they were interrupted by the absolute necessity of Charles's following the others to admire mirrors and china; but Anne had heard enough to understand the present state of Uppercross, and rejoice in its happiness; and though she sighed as she rejoiced, her sigh had none of the ill-will of envy in it. She would certainly have risen to their blessings if she could, but she did not want to lessen theirs.

The visit passed off altogether in high good humour. Mary was in excellent spirits, enjoying the gaiety and the change; and so well satisfied with the journey in her mother-in-law's carriage with four horses, and with her own complete independence of Camden-place, that she was exactly in a temper to admire every thing as she ought, and enter most readily into all the superiorities of the house, as they were detailed to her. She had no demands on her father or sister, and her consequence was just enough increased by their handsome drawing-rooms.

Elizabeth was, for a short time, suffering a good deal. She felt that Mrs. Musgrove and all her party ought to be asked to dine with them, but she could not bear to have the difference of style, the reduction of servants, which a dinner must betray, witnessed by those who had been always so inferior to the Elliots of Kellynch. It was a struggle between propriety and vanity; but vanity

1. A small waterbird.
2. A "go at" or round.

got the better, and then Elizabeth was happy again. These were her internal persuasions.—"Old fashioned notions—country hospitality—we do not profess to give dinners—few people in Bath do—Lady Alicia never does; did not even ask her own sister's family, though they were here a month: and I dare say it would be very inconvenient to Mrs. Musgrove—put her quite out of her way. I am sure she would rather not come—she cannot feel easy with us. I will ask them all for an evening; that will be much better—that will be a novelty and a treat. They have not seen two such drawing rooms before. They will be delighted to come to-morrow evening. It shall be a regular party—small, but most elegant." And this satisfied Elizabeth: and when the invitation was given to the two present, and promised for the absent, Mary was as completely satisfied. She was particularly asked to meet Mr. Elliot, and be introduced to Lady Dalrymple and Miss Carteret, who were fortunately already engaged to come; and she could not have received a more gratifying attention. Miss Elliot was to have the honour of calling on Mrs. Musgrove in the course of the morning, and Anne walked off with Charles and Mary, to go and see her and Henrietta directly.

Her plan of sitting with Lady Russell must give way for the present. They all three called in Rivers-street for a couple of minutes; but Anne convinced herself that a day's delay of the intended communication could be of no consequence, and hastened forward to the White Hart, to see again the friends and companions of the last autumn, with an eagerness of good will which many associations contributed to form.

They found Mrs. Musgrove and her daughter within, and by themselves, and Anne had the kindest welcome from each. Henrietta was exactly in that state of recently-improved views, of fresh-formed happiness, which made her full of regard and interest for every body she had ever liked before at all; and Mrs. Musgrove's real affection had been won by her usefulness when they were in distress. It was a heartiness, and a warmth, and a sincerity which Anne delighted in the more, from the sad want of such blessings at home. She was intreated to give them as much of her time as possible, invited for every day and all day long, or rather claimed as a part of the family; and in return, she naturally fell into all her wonted ways of attention and assistance, and on Charles's leaving them together, was listening to Mrs. Musgrove's history of Louisa, and to Henrietta's of herself, giving opinions on business, and recommendations to shops; with intervals of every help which Mary required, from altering her ribbon to settling her accounts, from finding her keys, and assorting her trinkets, to trying to convince her that she was not ill used by any body; which Mary, well amused as she generally was in her station at a window overlooking the entrance to the pump-room,[3] could not but have her moments of imagining.

A morning of thorough confusion was to be expected. A large party in an hotel ensured a quick-changing, unsettled scene. One five minutes brought a note, the next a parcel, and Anne had not been there half an hour, when their dining-room, spacious as it was, seemed more than half filled: a party of steady old friends were seated round Mrs. Musgrove, and Charles came back with Captains Harville and Wentworth. The appearance of the latter could not be more than the surprise of the moment. It was impossible for her to have forgotten to feel, that this arrival of their common friends must be soon bringing them together again. Their last meeting had been most important in opening his feelings; she had derived from it a delightful conviction; but she feared from his looks, that the same unfortunate persuasion, which had hastened him away from the concert room, still governed. He did not seem to want to be near enough for conversation.

She tried to be calm, and leave things to take their course; and tried to dwell much on this argument of rational dependance— "Surely, if there be constant attachment on each side, our hearts must understand each other ere long. We are not boy and girl, to be captiously irritable, misled by every moment's inadvertence, and wantonly playing with our own happiness." And yet, a few minutes afterwards, she felt as if their being in company with each other, under their present circumstances, could only be exposing them to inadvertencies and misconstructions of the most mischievous kind.

"Anne," cried Mary, still at her window, "there is Mrs. Clay, I am sure, standing under the colonnade, and a gentleman with her. I saw them turn the corner from Bath-street just now. They seem deep in talk. Who is it?—Come, and tell me. Good heavens! I recollect.—It is Mr. Elliot himself."

"No," cried Anne quickly, "it cannot be Mr. Elliot, I assure you. He was to leave Bath at nine this morning, and does not come back till to-morrow."

As she spoke, she felt that Captain Wentworth was looking at her; the consciousness of which vexed and embarrassed her, and made her regret that she had said so much, simple as it was.

Mary, resenting that she should be supposed not to know her own cousin, began talking very warmly about the family features, and protesting still more positively that it was Mr. Elliot, calling again upon Anne to come and look herself; but Anne did not mean to stir, and tried to be cool and unconcerned. Her distress returned,

3. A central room in the public baths, where people assembled for social as well as medical reasons.

however, on perceiving smiles and intelligent glances pass between two or three of the lady visitors, as if they believed themselves quite in the secret. It was evident that the report concerning her had spread; and a short pause succeeded, which seemed to ensure that it would now spread farther.

"Do come, Anne," cried Mary, "come and look yourself. You will be too late, if you do not make haste. They are parting, they are shaking hands. He is turning away. Not know Mr. Elliot, indeed!—You seem to have forgot all about Lyme."

To pacify Mary, and perhaps screen her own embarrassment, Anne did move quietly to the window. She was just in time to ascertain that it really was Mr. Elliot (which she had never believed), before he disappeared on one side, as Mrs. Clay walked quickly off on the other; and checking the surprise which she could not but feel at such an appearance of friendly conference between two persons of totally opposite interests, she calmly said, "Yes, it is Mr. Elliot certainly. He has changed his hour of going, I suppose, that is all—or I may be mistaken; I might not attend;" and walked back to her chair, recomposed, and with the comfortable hope of having acquitted herself well.

The visitors took their leave; and Charles, having civilly seen them off, and then made a face at them, and abused them for coming, began with—

"Well, mother, I have done something for you that you will like. I have been to the theatre, and secured a box[4] for to-morrow night. A'n't I a good boy? I know you love a play; and there is room for us all. It holds nine. I have engaged Captain Wentworth. Anne will not be sorry to join us, I am sure. We all like a play. Have not I done well, mother?"

Mrs. Musgrove was good humouredly beginning to express her perfect readiness for the play, if Henrietta and all the others liked it, when Mary eagerly interrupted her by exclaiming,

"Good heavens, Charles! how can you think of such a thing? Take a box for to-morrow night! Have you forgot that we are engaged to Camden-place to-morrow night? and that we were most particularly asked on purpose to meet Lady Dalrymple and her daughter, and Mr. Elliot—all the principal family connexions—on purpose to be introduced to them? How can you be so forgetful?"

"Phoo! phoo!" replied Charles, "what's an evening party? Never worth remembering. Your father might have asked us to dinner, I think, if he had wanted to see us. You may do as you like, but I shall go to the play."

---

4. Private rented seats in the playhouse. Seated in boxes, the fashionable set was an attraction, as occupants wanted as much to be seen as to watch the performance.

"Oh! Charles, I declare it will be too abominable if you do! when you promised to go."

"No, I did not promise. I only smirked and bowed, and said the word 'happy.' There was no promise."

"But you must go, Charles. It would be unpardonable to fail. We were asked on purpose to be introduced. There was always such a great connexion between the Dalrymples and ourselves. Nothing ever happened on either side that was not announced immediately. We are quite near relations, you know: and Mr. Elliot too, whom you ought so particularly to be acquainted with! Every attention is due to Mr. Elliot. Consider, my father's heir—the future representative of the family."

"Don't talk to me about heirs and representatives," cried Charles. "I am not one of those who neglect the reigning power to bow to the rising sun. If I would not go for the sake of your father, I should think it scandalous to go for the sake of his heir. What is Mr. Elliot to me?"

The careless expression was life to Anne, who saw that Captain Wentworth was all attention, looking and listening with his whole soul; and that the last words brought his enquiring eyes from Charles to herself.

Charles and Mary still talked on in the same style; he, half serious and half jesting, maintaining the scheme for the play; and she, invariably serious, most warmly opposing it, and not omitting to make it known, that however determined to go to Camden-place herself, she should not think herself very well used, if they went to the play without her. Mrs. Musgrove interposed.

"We had better put it off. Charles, you had much better go back, and change the box for Tuesday. It would be a pity to be divided, and we should be losing Miss Anne too, if there is a party at her father's; and I am sure neither Henrietta nor I should care at all for the play, if Miss Anne could not be with us."

Anne felt truly obliged to her for such kindness; and quite as much so, moreover, for the opportunity it gave her of decidedly saying—

"If it depended only on my inclination, ma'am, the party at home (excepting on Mary's account) would not be the smallest impediment. I have no pleasure in the sort of meeting, and should be too happy to change it for a play, and with you. But, it had better not be attempted, perhaps."

She had spoken it; but she trembled when it was done, conscious that her words were listened to, and daring not even to try to observe their effect.

It was soon generally agreed that Tuesday should be the day, Charles only reserving the advantage of still teasing his wife, by persisting that he would go to the play to-morrow, if nobody else would.

Captain Wentworth left his seat, and walked to the fire-place; probably for the sake of walking away from it soon afterwards, and taking a station, with less barefaced design, by Anne.

"You have not been long enough in Bath," said he, "to enjoy the evening parties of the place."

"Oh! no. The usual character of them has nothing for me. I am no card-player."

"You were not formerly, I know. You did not use to like cards; but time makes many changes."

"I am not yet so much changed," cried Anne, and stopped, fearing she hardly knew what misconstruction. After waiting a few moments he said—and as if it were the result of immediate feeling—"It is a period, indeed! Eight years and a half is a period!"[5]

Whether he would have proceeded farther was left to Anne's imagination to ponder over in a calmer hour; for while still hearing the sounds he had uttered, she was startled to other subjects by Henrietta, eager to make use of the present leisure for getting out, and calling on her companions to lose no time, lest somebody else should come in.

They were obliged to move. Anne talked of being perfectly ready, and tried to look it; but she felt that could Henrietta have known the regret and reluctance of her heart in quitting that chair, in preparing to quit the room, she would have found, in all her own sensations for her cousin, in the very security of his affection, wherewith to pity her.

Their preparations, however, were stopped short. Alarming sounds were heard; other visitors approached, and the door was thrown open for Sir Walter and Miss Elliot, whose entrance seemed to give a general chill. Anne felt an instant oppression, and, wherever she looked, saw symptoms of the same. The comfort, the freedom, the gaiety of the room was over, hushed into cold composure, determined silence, or insipid talk, to meet the heartless elegance of her father and sister. How mortifying to feel that it was so!

Her jealous[6] eye was satisfied in one particular. Captain Wentworth was acknowledged again by each, by Elizabeth more graciously than before. She even addressed him once, and looked at him more than once. Elizabeth was, in fact, revolving a great measure. The sequel explained it. After the waste of a few minutes in saying the proper nothings, she began to give the invitation which was to comprise all the remaining dues of the Musgroves. "To-morrow

---

5. According to Johnson's *Dictionary*, a stated number of years; a round of time, at the end of which the things comprised within the calculation shall return to the state in which they were at beginning.
6. Watchful.

evening, to meet a few friends, no formal party." It was all said very
gracefully, and the cards with which she had provided herself, the
"Miss Elliot at home," were laid on the table, with a courteous, comprehensive smile to all; and one smile and one card more decidedly
for Captain Wentworth. The truth was, that Elizabeth had been long
enough in Bath, to understand the importance of a man of such an
air and appearance as his. The past was nothing. The present was
that Captain Wentworth would move about well in her drawing-
room. The card was pointedly given, and Sir Walter and Elizabeth
arose and disappeared.

The interruption had been short, though severe; and ease and animation returned to most of those they left, as the door shut them
out, but not to Anne. She could think only of the invitation she had
with such astonishment witnessed; and of the manner in which it
had been received, a manner of doubtful meaning, of surprise rather
than gratification, of polite acknowledgment rather than acceptance.
She knew him; she saw disdain in his eye, and could not venture to
believe that he had determined to accept such an offering, as atone-
ment for all the insolence of the past. Her spirits sank. He held the
card in his hand after they were gone, as if deeply considering it.

"Only think of Elizabeth's including every body!" whispered Mary
very audibly. "I do not wonder Captain Wentworth is delighted! You
see he cannot put the card out of his hand."

Anne caught his eye, saw his cheeks glow, and his mouth form
itself into a momentary expression of contempt, and turned away,
that she might neither see nor hear more to vex her.

The party separated. The gentlemen had their own pursuits, the
ladies proceeded on their own business, and they met no more while
Anne belonged to them. She was earnestly begged to return and
dine, and give them all the rest of the day; but her spirits had been
so long exerted, that at present she felt unequal to more, and fit only
for home, where she might be sure of being as silent as she chose.

Promising to be with them the whole of the following morning,
therefore, she closed the fatigues of the present, by a toilsome walk
to Camden-place, there to spend the evening chiefly in listening to
the busy arrangements of Elizabeth and Mrs. Clay for the morrow's
party, the frequent enumeration of the persons invited, and the continually improving detail of all the embellishments which were to
make it the most completely elegant of its kind in Bath, while harass-
ing herself in secret with the never-ending question, of whether
Captain Wentworth would come or not? They were reckoning him
as certain, but, with her, it was a gnawing solicitude never appeased
for five minutes together. She generally thought he would come,
because she generally thought he ought; but it was a case which she

could not so shape into any positive act of duty or discretion, as inevitably to defy the suggestions of very opposite feelings.

She only roused herself from the broodings of this restless agitation, to let Mrs. Clay know that she had been seen with Mr. Elliot three hours after his being supposed to be out of Bath; for having watched in vain for some intimation of the interview from the lady herself, she determined to mention it; and it seemed to her that there was guilt in Mrs. Clay's face as she listened. It was transient, cleared away in an instant, but Anne could imagine she read there the consciousness of having, by some complication of mutual trick, or some overbearing authority of his, been obliged to attend (perhaps for half an hour) to his lectures and restrictions on her designs on Sir Walter. She exclaimed, however, with a very tolerable imitation of nature,

"Oh dear! very true. Only think, Miss Elliot, to my great surprise I met with Mr. Elliot in Bath-street! I was never more astonished. He turned back and walked with me to the Pump-yard. He had been prevented setting off for Thornberry, but I really forget by what—for I was in a hurry, and could not much attend, and I can only answer for his being determined not to be delayed in his return. He wanted to know how early he might be admitted tomorrow. He was full of 'to-morrow;' and it is very evident that I have been full of it too ever since I entered the house, and learnt the extension of your plan, and all that had happened, or my seeing him could never have gone so entirely out of my head."

Chapter XXIII

One day only had passed since Anne's conversation with Mrs. Smith; but a keener interest had succeeded, and she was now so little touched by Mr. Elliot's conduct, except by its effects in one quarter, that it became a matter of course the next morning, still to defer her explanatory visit in Rivers-street. She had promised to be with the Musgroves from breakfast to dinner. Her faith was plighted, and Mr. Elliot's character, like the Sultaness Scheherazade's head,[7] must live another day.

She could not keep her appointment punctually, however; the weather was unfavourable, and she had grieved over the rain on her friends' account, and felt it very much on her own, before she was

7. Scheherazade, in the *Arabian Nights' Entertainment*, saved herself from beheading, night after night, by enthralling the sultan with her storytelling. The tales were based on the twelve-volume French translation by orientalist and archaeologist Antoine Galland (1646–1715) of the *Alf Layla wa-Layla*, a collection of Middle Eastern tales of disputed origin; their widespread popularity across Europe is linked to the rise of Romanticism.

able to attempt the walk. When she reached the White Hart, and made her way to the proper apartment, she found herself neither arriving quite in time, nor the first to arrive. The party before her were Mrs. Musgrove, talking to Mrs. Croft, and Captain Harville to Captain Wentworth, and she immediately heard that Mary and Henrietta, too impatient to wait, had gone out the moment it had cleared, but would be back again soon, and that the strictest injunctions had been left with Mrs. Musgrove, to keep her there till they returned. She had only to submit, sit down, be outwardly composed, and feel herself plunged at once in all the agitations which she had merely laid her account of[8] tasting a little before the morning closed. There was no delay, no waste of time. She was deep in the happiness of such misery, or the misery of such happiness, instantly. Two minutes after her entering the room, Captain Wentworth said,

"We will write the letter we were talking of, Harville, now, if you will give me materials."

Materials were all at hand, on a separate table; he went to it, and nearly turning his back on them all, was engrossed by writing.

Mrs. Musgrove was giving Mrs. Croft the history of her eldest daughter's engagement, and just in that inconvenient tone of voice which was perfectly audible while it pretended to be a whisper. Anne felt that she did not belong to the conversation, and yet, as Captain Harville seemed thoughtful and not disposed to talk, she could not avoid hearing many undesirable particulars, such as "how Mr. Musgrove and my brother Hayter had met again and again to talk it over; what my brother Hayter had said one day, and what Mr. Musgrove had proposed the next, and what had occurred to my sister Hayter, and what the young people had wished, and what I said at first I never could consent to, but was afterwards persuaded to think might do very well," and a great deal in the same style of openhearted communication—Minutiæ which, even with every advantage of taste and delicacy which good Mrs. Musgrove could not give, could be properly interesting only to the principals. Mrs. Croft was attending with great good humour, and whenever she spoke at all, it was very sensibly. Anne hoped the gentlemen might each be too much self-occupied to hear.

"And so, ma'am, all these things considered," said Mrs. Musgrove in her powerful whisper, "though we could have wished it different, yet altogether we did not think it fair to stand out any longer; for Charles Hayter was quite wild about it, and Henrietta was pretty near as bad; and so we thought they had better marry at once, and make the best of it, as many others have done before them. At any rate, said I, it will be better than a long engagement."

8. Reckoned on, anticipated.

"That is precisely what I was going to observe," cried Mrs. Croft. "I would rather have young people settle on a small income at once, and have to struggle with a few difficulties together, than be involved in a long engagement. I always think that no mutual—"

"Oh! dear Mrs. Croft," cried Mrs. Musgrove, unable to let her finish her speech, "there is nothing I so abominate for young people as a long engagement. It is what I always protested against for my children. It is all very well, I used to say, for young people to be engaged, if there is a certainty of their being able to marry in six months, or even in twelve, but a long engagement!"

"Yes, dear ma'am," said Mrs. Croft, "or an uncertain engagement; an engagement which may be long. To begin without knowing that at such a time there will be the means of marrying, I hold to be very unsafe and unwise, and what, I think, all parents should prevent as far as they can."

Anne found an unexpected interest here. She felt its application to herself, felt it in a nervous thrill all over her, and at the same moment that her eyes instinctively glanced towards the distant table, Captain Wentworth's pen ceased to move, his head was raised, pausing, listening, and he turned round the next instant to give a look—one quick, conscious look at her.

The two ladies continued to talk, to re-urge the same admitted truths, and enforce them with such examples of the ill effect of a contrary practice, as had fallen within their observation, but Anne heard nothing distinctly; it was only a buzz of words in her ear, her mind was in confusion.

Captain Harville, who had in truth been hearing none of it, now left his seat, and moved to a window; and Anne seeming to watch him, though it was from thorough absence of mind, became gradually sensible that he was inviting her to join him where he stood. He looked at her with a smile, and a little motion of the head, which expressed, "Come to me, I have something to say;" and the unaffected, easy kindness of manner which denoted the feelings of an older acquaintance than he really was, strongly enforced the invitation. She roused herself and went to him. The window at which he stood, was at the other end of the room from where the two ladies were sitting, and though nearer to Captain Wentworth's table, not very near. As she joined him, Captain Harville's countenance reassumed the serious, thoughtful expression which seemed its natural character.

"Look here," said he, unfolding a parcel in his hand, and displaying a small miniature painting, "do you know who that is?"

"Certainly, Captain Benwick."

"Yes, and you may guess who it is for. But (in a deep tone) it was not done for her. Miss Elliot, do you remember our walking together at Lyme, and grieving for him? I little thought then—but no matter. This was drawn at the Cape. He met with a clever young German artist at the Cape, and in compliance with a promise to my poor sister, sat to him, and was bringing it home for her. And I have now the charge of getting it properly set for another! It was a commission to me! But who else was there to employ? I hope I can allow for him. I am not sorry, indeed, to make it over to another. He undertakes it—(looking towards Captain Wentworth) he is writing about it now." And with a quivering lip he wound up the whole by adding, "Poor Fanny! she would not have forgotten him so soon!"

"No," replied Anne, in a low feeling voice. "That, I can easily believe."

"It was not in her nature. She doated on him."

"It would not be the nature of any woman who truly loved."

Captain Harville smiled, as much as to say, "Do you claim that for your sex?" and she answered the question, smiling also, "Yes. We certainly do not forget you, so soon as you forget us. It is, perhaps, our fate rather than our merit. We cannot help ourselves. We live at home, quiet, confined, and our feelings prey upon us. You are forced on exertion. You have always a profession, pursuits, business of some sort or other, to take you back into the world immediately, and continual occupation and change soon weaken impressions."

"Granting your assertion that the world does all this so soon for men, (which, however, I do not think I shall grant) it does not apply to Benwick. He has not been forced upon any exertion. The peace turned him on shore at the very moment, and he has been living with us, in our little family-circle, ever since."

"True," said Anne, "very true; I did not recollect; but what shall we say now, Captain Harville? If the change be not from outward circumstances, it must be from within; it must be nature, man's nature, which has done the business for Captain Benwick."

"No, no, it is not man's nature. I will not allow it to be more man's nature than woman's to be inconstant and forget those they do love, or have loved. I believe the reverse. I believe in a true analogy between our bodily frames and our mental; and that as our bodies are the strongest, so are our feelings; capable of bearing most rough usage, and riding out the heaviest weather."

"Your feelings may be the strongest," replied Anne, "but the same spirit of analogy will authorise me to assert that ours are the most tender. Man is more robust than woman, but he is not longer-lived; which exactly explains my view of the nature of their attachments. Nay, it would be too hard upon you, if it were otherwise. You have difficulties, and privations, and dangers enough to struggle with. You are always labouring and toiling, exposed to every risk and hardship. Your home, country, friends, all quitted. Neither time, nor health, nor life, to be called your own. It would be too hard indeed" (with a faltering voice) "if woman's feelings were to be added to all this."

"We shall never agree upon this question"—Captain Harville was beginning to say, when a slight noise called their attention to Captain Wentworth's hitherto perfectly quiet division of the room. It was nothing more than that his pen had fallen down, but Anne was startled at finding him nearer than she had supposed, and half inclined to suspect that the pen had only fallen, because he had been occupied by them, striving to catch sounds, which yet she did not think he could have caught.

"Have you finished your letter?" said Captain Harville.

"Not quite, a few lines more. I shall have done in five minutes."

"There is no hurry on my side. I am only ready whenever you are.—I am in very good anchorage here," (smiling at Anne) "well supplied, and want for nothing.—No hurry for a signal at all.—Well, Miss Elliot," (lowering his voice) "as I was saying, we shall never agree I suppose upon this point. No man and woman would, probably. But let me observe that all histories are against you, all stories, prose and verse. If I had such a memory as Benwick, I could bring you fifty quotations in a moment on my side the argument, and I do not think I ever opened a book in my life which had not something to say upon woman's inconstancy. Songs and proverbs, all talk of woman's fickleness. But perhaps you will say, these were all written by men."

"Perhaps I shall.—Yes, yes, if you please, no reference to examples in books. Men have had every advantage of us in telling their own story. Education has been theirs in so much higher a degree; the pen has been in their hands. I will not allow books to prove any thing."

"But how shall we prove any thing?"

"We never shall. We never can expect to prove any thing upon such a point. It is a difference of opinion which does not admit of proof. We each begin probably with a little bias towards our own sex, and upon that bias build every circumstance in favour of it which has occurred within our own circle; many of which circumstances (perhaps those very cases which strike us the most) may be precisely such as cannot be brought forward without betraying a confidence, or in some respect saying what should not be said."

"Ah!" cried Captain Harville, in a tone of strong feeling, "if I could but make you comprehend what a man suffers when he takes a last look at his wife and children, and watches the boat that he has sent them off in, as long as it is in sight, and then turns away and says, 'God knows whether we ever meet again!' And then, if I could convey to you the glow of his soul when he does see them again; when, coming back after a twelvemonth's absence perhaps, and obliged to put into another port, he calculates how soon it be possible to get them there, pretending to deceive himself, and saying, 'They cannot

be here till such a day,' but all the while hoping for them twelve hours
sooner, and seeing them arrive at last, as if Heaven had given them
wings, by many hours sooner still! If I could explain to you all this,
and all that a man can bear and do, and glories to do for the sake of
these treasures of his existence! I speak, you know, only of such men
as have hearts!" pressing his own with emotion.

"Oh!" cried Anne eagerly, "I hope I do justice to all that is felt by
you, and by those who resemble you. God forbid that I should under-
value the warm and faithful feelings of any of my fellow-creatures.
I should deserve utter contempt if I dared to suppose that true
attachment and constancy were known only by woman. No, I believe
you capable of every thing great and good in your married lives. I
believe you equal to every important exertion, and to every domestic forbearance, so long as—if I may be allowed the expression, so
long as you have an object. I mean, while the woman you love lives,
and lives for you. All the privilege I claim for my own sex (it is not a
very enviable one, you need not covet it) is that of loving longest,
when existence or when hope is gone."

She could not immediately have uttered another sentence; her
heart was too full, her breath too much oppressed.

"You are a good soul," cried Captain Harville, putting his hand
on her arm quite affectionately. "There is no quarrelling with you.—
And when I think of Benwick, my tongue is tied."

Their attention was called towards the others.—Mrs. Croft was
taking leave.

"Here, Frederick, you and I part company, I believe," said she. "I
am going home, and you have an engagement with your friend.—
To-night we may have the pleasure of all meeting again, at your
party," (turning to Anne.) "We had your sister's card yesterday, and
I understood Frederick had a card too, though I did not see it—and
you are disengaged, Frederick, are you not, as well as ourselves?"

Captain Wentworth was folding up a letter in great haste, and
either could not or would not answer fully.

"Yes," said he, "very true; here we separate, but Harville and I shall
soon be after you, that is, Harville, if you are ready, I am in half a
minute. I know you will not be sorry to be off. I shall be at your
service in half a minute."

Mrs. Croft left them, and Captain Wentworth, having sealed his
letter with great rapidity, was indeed ready, and had even a hurried,
agitated air, which shewed impatience to be gone. Anne knew not
how to understand it. She had the kindest "Good morning, God bless
you," from Captain Harville, but from him not a word, nor a look.
He had passed out of the room without a look!

She had only time, however, to move closer to the table where
he had been writing, when footsteps were heard returning; the

door opened; it was himself. He begged their pardon, but he had forgotten his gloves, and instantly crossing the room to the writing table, and standing with his back towards Mrs. Musgrove, he drew out a letter from under the scattered paper, placed it before Anne with eyes of glowing entreaty fixed on her for a moment, and hastily collecting his gloves, was again out of the room, almost before Mrs. Musgrove was aware of his being in it—the work of an instant!

The revolution which one instant had made in Anne, was almost beyond expression. The letter, with a direction hardly legible, to "Miss A. E—." was evidently the one which he had been folding so hastily. While supposed to be writing only to Captain Benwick, he had been also addressing her! On the contents of that letter depended all which this world could do for her! Any thing was possible, any thing might be defied rather than suspense. Mrs. Musgrove had little arrangements of her own at her own table; to their protection she must trust, and sinking into the chair which he had occupied, succeeding to the very spot where he had leaned and written, her eyes devoured the following words:

> I can listen no longer in silence. I must speak to you by such means as are within my reach. You pierce my soul. I am half agony, half hope. Tell me not that I am too late, that such precious feelings are gone for ever. I offer myself to you again with a heart even more your own, than when you almost broke it eight years and a half ago. Dare not say that man forgets sooner than woman, that his love has an earlier death. I have loved none but you. Unjust I may have been, weak and resentful I have been, but never inconstant. You alone have brought me to Bath. For you alone I think and plan.—Have you not seen this? Can you fail to have understood my wishes?—I had not[9] waited even these ten days, could I have read your feelings, as I think you must have penetrated mine. I can hardly write. I am every instant hearing something which overpowers me. You sink your voice, but I can distinguish the tones of that voice, when they would be lost on others.—Too good, too excellent creature! You do us justice indeed. You do believe that there is true attachment and constancy among men. Believe it to be most fervent, most undeviating in
>
> F. W.
>
> I must go, uncertain of my fate; but I shall return hither, or follow your party, as soon as possible. A word, a look will be enough to decide whether I enter your father's house this evening, or never.

9. Would not have.

Such a letter was not to be soon recovered from. Half an hour's solitude and reflection might have tranquillized her; but the ten minutes only, which now passed before she was interrupted, with all the restraints of her situation, could do nothing towards tranquillity. Every moment rather brought fresh agitation. It was an overpowering happiness. And before she was beyond the first stage of full sensation, Charles, Mary, and Henrietta all came in.

The absolute necessity of seeming like herself produced then an immediate struggle; but after a while she could do no more. She began not to understand a word they said, and was obliged to plead indisposition and excuse herself. They could then see that she looked very ill—were shocked and concerned—and would not stir without her for the world. This was dreadful! Would they only have gone away, and left her in the quiet possession of that room, it would have been her cure; but to have them all standing or waiting around her was distracting, and, in desperation, she said she would go home.

"By all means, my dear," cried Mrs. Musgrove, "go home directly and take care of yourself, that you may be fit for the evening. I wish Sarah was here to doctor you, but I am no doctor myself. Charles, ring and order a chair. She must not walk."

But the chair would never do. Worse than all! To lose the possibility of speaking two words to Captain Wentworth in the course of her quiet, solitary progress up the town (and she felt almost certain of meeting him) could not be borne. The chair was earnestly protested against; and Mrs. Musgrove, who thought only of one sort of illness, having assured herself, with some anxiety, that there had been no fall in the case; that Anne had not, at any time lately, slipped down, and got a blow on her head; that she was perfectly convinced of having had no fall, could part with her cheerfully, and depend on finding her better at night.

Anxious to omit no possible precaution, Anne struggled, and said,

"I am afraid, ma'am, that it is not perfectly understood. Pray be so good as to mention to the other gentlemen that we hope to see your whole party this evening. I am afraid there has been some mistake; and I wish you particularly to assure Captain Harville, and Captain Wentworth, that we hope to see them both."

"Oh! my dear, it is quite understood, I give you my word. Captain Harville has no thought but of going."

"Do you think so? But I am afraid; and I should be so very sorry! Will you promise me to mention it, when you see them again? You will see them both again this morning, I dare say. Do promise me."

"To be sure I will, if you wish it. Charles, if you see Captain Harville any where, remember to give Miss Anne's message. But indeed, my dear, you need not be uneasy. Captain Harville holds himself quite engaged, I'll answer for it; and Captain Wentworth the same, I dare say."

Anne could do no more; but her heart prophesied some mischance, to damp the perfection of her felicity. It could not be very lasting, however. Even if he did not come to Camden-place himself, it would be in her power to send an intelligible sentence by Captain Harville.

Another momentary vexation occurred. Charles, in his real concern and good-nature, would go home with her; there was no preventing him. This was almost cruel! But she could not be long ungrateful; he was sacrificing an engagement at a gunsmith's to be of use to her; and she set off with him, with no feeling but gratitude apparent.

They were in Union-street, when a quicker step behind, a something of familiar sound, gave her two moments preparation for the sight of Captain Wentworth. He joined them; but, as if irresolute whether to join or to pass on, said nothing—only looked. Anne could command herself enough to receive that look, and not repulsively. The cheeks which had been pale now glowed, and the movements which had hesitated were decided. He walked by her side. Presently, struck by a sudden thought, Charles said,

"Captain Wentworth, which way are you going? only to Gay-street, or farther up the town?"

"I hardly know," replied Captain Wentworth, surprised.

"Are you going as high as Belmont? Are you going near Camden-place? Because if you are, I shall have no scruple in asking you to take my place, and give Anne your arm to her father's door. She is rather done for this morning, and must not go so far without help. And I ought to be at that fellow's in the market-place. He promised me the sight of a capital gun he is just going to send off; said he would keep it unpacked to the last possible moment, that I might see it; and if I do not turn back now, I have no chance. By his description, a good deal like the second-sized double-barrel of mine, which you shot with one day, round Winthrop."

There could not be an objection. There could be only a most proper alacrity, a most obliging compliance for public view; and smiles reined in and spirits dancing in private rapture. In half a minute, Charles was at the bottom of Union-street again, and the other two proceeding together; and soon words enough had passed between them to decide their direction towards the comparatively quiet and retired gravel-walk, where the power of conversation would make the present hour a blessing indeed; and prepare for it all the immortality which the happiest recollections of their own future lives could bestow. There they exchanged again those feelings and those promises which had once before seemed to secure every thing, but which had been followed by so many, many years of division and estrangement. There they returned again into the past, more exquisitely happy, perhaps, in their re-union, than when it had been first projected; more tender, more tried, more fixed in a knowledge of each other's character, truth, and attachment; more equal to act, more justified in acting. And there, as they slowly paced the gradual ascent, heedless of every group around them, seeing neither sauntering politicians, bustling house-keepers, flirting girls, nor nurserymaids and children, they could indulge in those retrospections and acknowledgments, and especially in those explanations of what had directly preceded the present moment, which were so poignant and so ceaseless in interest. All the little variations of the last week were gone through; and of yesterday and to-day there could scarcely be an end.

She had not mistaken him. Jealousy of Mr. Elliot had been the retarding weight, the doubt, the torment. That had begun to operate in the very hour of first meeting her in Bath; that had returned, after a short suspension, to ruin the concert; and that had influenced him in every thing he had said and done, or omitted to say and do, in the last four-and-twenty hours. It had been gradually yielding to the better hopes which her looks, or words, or actions occasionally encouraged; it had been vanquished at last by those sentiments and those tones which had reached him while she talked with Captain Harville; and under the irresistible governance of which he had seized a sheet of paper, and poured out his feelings.

Of what he had then written, nothing was to be retracted or qualified. He persisted in having loved none but her. She had never been supplanted. He never even believed himself to see her equal. Thus much indeed he was obliged to acknowledge—that he had been constant unconsciously, nay unintentionally; that he had meant to forget her, and believed it to be done. He had imagined himself indifferent, when he had only been angry; and he had been unjust to her merits, because he had been a sufferer from them. Her character was now fixed on his mind as perfection itself, maintaining the loveliest medium of fortitude and gentleness; but he was obliged to acknowledge that only at Uppercross had he learnt to do her justice, and only at Lyme had he begun to understand himself.

At Lyme, he had received lessons of more than one sort. The passing admiration of Mr. Elliot had at least roused him, and the scenes on the Cobb, and at Captain Harville's, had fixed her superiority.

In his preceding attempts to attach himself to Louisa Musgrove (the attempts of angry pride), he protested that he had for ever felt it to be impossible; that he had not cared, could not care for Louisa; though, till that day, till the leisure for reflection which followed it, he had not understood the perfect excellence of the mind with which

Louisa's could so ill bear a comparison; or the perfect, unrivalled hold it possessed over his own. There, he had learnt to distinguish between the steadiness of principle and the obstinacy of self-will, between the darings of heedlessness and the resolution of a collected mind. There, he had seen every thing to exalt in his estimation the woman he had lost, and there begun to deplore the pride, the folly, the madness of resentment, which had kept him from trying to regain her when thrown in his way.

From that period his penance had become severe. He had no sooner been free from the horror and remorse attending the first few days of Louisa's accident, no sooner begun to feel himself alive again, than he had begun to feel himself, though alive, not at liberty.

"I found," said he, "that I was considered by Harville an engaged man! That neither Harville nor his wife entertained a doubt of our mutual attachment. I was startled and shocked. To a degree, I could contradict this instantly; but, when I began to reflect that others might have felt the same—her own family, nay, perhaps herself, I was no longer at my own disposal. I was hers in honour if she wished it. I had been unguarded. I had not thought seriously on this subject before. I had not considered that my excessive intimacy must have its danger of ill consequence in many ways: and that I had no right to be trying whether I could attach myself to either of the girls, at the risk of raising even an unpleasant report, were there no other ill effects. I had been grossly wrong, and must abide the consequences."

He found too late, in short, that he had entangled himself; and that precisely as he became fully satisfied of his not caring for Louisa at all, he must regard himself as bound to her, if her sentiments for him were what the Harvilles supposed. It determined him to leave Lyme, and await her complete recovery elsewhere. He would gladly weaken, by any fair means, whatever feelings or speculations concerning him might exist; and he went, therefore, to his brother's, meaning after a while to return to Kellynch, and act as circumstances might require.

"I was six weeks with Edward," said he, "and saw him happy. I could have no other pleasure. I deserved none. He enquired after you very particularly; asked even if you were personally altered, little suspecting that to my eye you could never alter."

Anne smiled, and let it pass. It was too pleasing a blunder for a reproach. It is something for a woman to be assured, in her eight-and-twentieth year, that she has not lost one charm of earlier youth: but the value of such homage was inexpressibly increased to Anne, by comparing it with former words, and feeling it to be the result, not the cause of a revival of his warm attachment.

He had remained in Shropshire, lamenting the blindness of his own pride, and the blunders of his own calculations, till at once released from Louisa by the astonishing and felicitous intelligence of her engagement with Benwick.

"Here," said he, "ended the worst of my state; for now I could at least put myself in the way of happiness, I could exert myself, I could do something. But to be waiting so long in inaction, and waiting only for evil, had been dreadful. Within the first five minutes I said, 'I will be at Bath on Wednesday,' and I was. Was it unpardonable to think it worth my while to come? and to arrive with some degree of hope? You were single. It was possible that you might retain the feelings of the past, as I did; and one encouragement happened to be mine. I could never doubt that you would be loved and sought by others, but I knew to a certainty that you had refused one man at least, of better pretensions than myself: and I could not help often saying, Was this for me?"

Their first meeting in Milsom-street afforded much to be said, but the concert still more. That evening seemed to be made up of exquisite moments. The moment of her stepping forward in the octagon-room to speak to him, the moment of Mr. Elliot's appearing and tearing her away, and one or two subsequent moments, marked by returning hope or increasing despondence, were dwelt on with energy.

"To see you," cried he, "in the midst of those who could not be my well-wishers, to see your cousin close by you, conversing and smiling, and feel all the horrible eligibilities and proprieties of the match! To consider it as the certain wish of every being who could hope to influence you! Even, if your own feelings were reluctant or indifferent, to consider what powerful supports would be his! Was it not enough to make the fool of me which I appeared? How could I look on without agony? Was not the very sight of the friend who sat behind you, was not the recollection of what had been, the knowledge of her influence, the indelible, immoveable impression of what persuasion had once done—was it not all against me?"

"You should have distinguished," replied Anne. "You should not have suspected me now; the case so different, and my age so different. If I was wrong in yielding to persuasion once, remember that it was to persuasion exerted on the side of safety, not of risk. When I yielded, I thought it was to duty; but no duty could be called in aid here. In marrying a man indifferent to me, all risk would have been incurred, and all duty violated."

"Perhaps I ought to have reasoned thus," he replied, "but I could not. I could not derive benefit from the late knowledge I had acquired of your character. I could not bring it into play: it was overwhelmed, buried, lost in those earlier feelings which I had been smarting under year after year. I could think of you only as one who had yielded, who had given me up, who had been influenced by any one rather than by me. I saw you with the very person who had guided you in that year of misery. I had no reason to believe her of less authority now.—The force of habit was to be added."

"I should have thought," said Anne, "that my manner to yourself might have spared you much or all of this."

"No, no! your manner might be only the ease which your engagement to another man would give. I left you in this belief; and yet—I was determined to see you again. My spirits rallied with the morning, and I felt that I had still a motive for remaining here."

At last Anne was at home again, and happier than any one in that house could have conceived. All the surprise and suspense, and every other painful part of the morning dissipated by this conversation, she reentered the house so happy as to be obliged to find an alloy in some momentary apprehensions of its being impossible to last. An interval of meditation, serious and grateful, was the best corrective of every thing dangerous in such high-wrought felicity; and she went to her room, and grew steadfast and fearless in the thankfulness of her enjoyment.

The evening came, the drawing-rooms were lighted up, the company assembled. It was but a card-party, it was but a mixture of those who had never met before, and those who met too often—a commonplace business, too numerous for intimacy, too small for variety; but Anne had never found an evening shorter. Glowing and lovely in sensibility and happiness, and more generally admired than she thought about or cared for, she had cheerful or forbearing feelings for every creature around her. Mr. Elliot was there; she avoided, but she could pity him. The Wallises; she had amusement in understanding them. Lady Dalrymple and Miss Carteret; they would soon be innoxious cousins to her. She cared not for Mrs. Clay, and had nothing to blush for in the public manners of her father and sister. With the Musgroves, there was the happy chat of perfect ease; with Captain Harville, the kind-hearted intercourse of brother and sister; with Lady Russell, attempts at conversation, which a delicious consciousness cut short; with Admiral and Mrs. Croft, every thing of peculiar cordiality and fervent interest, which the same consciousness sought to conceal;—and with Captain Wentworth, some moments of communication continually occurring, and always the hope of more, and always the knowledge of his being there!

It was in one of these short meetings, each apparently occupied in admiring a fine display of green-house plants, that she said—

"I have been thinking over the past, and trying impartially to judge of the right and wrong, I mean with regard to myself; and I must believe that I was right, much as I suffered from it, that I was perfectly right in being guided by the friend whom you will love better than you do now. To me, she was in the place of a parent. Do not mistake me, however. I am not saying that she did not err in her advice. It was, perhaps, one of those cases in which advice is good or bad only as the event decides; and for myself, I certainly never should, in any circumstance of tolerable similarity, give such advice. But I mean, that I was right in submitting to her, and that if I had done otherwise, I should have suffered more in continuing the engagement than I did even in giving it up, because I should have suffered in my conscience. I have now, as far as such a sentiment is allowable in human nature, nothing to reproach myself with; and if I mistake not, a strong sense of duty is no bad part of a woman's portion."

He looked at her, looked at Lady Russell, and looking again at her, replied, as if in cool deliberation,

"Not yet. But there are hopes of her being forgiven in time. I trust to being in charity with her soon. But I too have been thinking over the past, and a question has suggested itself, whether there may not have been one person more my enemy even than that lady? My own self. Tell me if, when I returned to England in the year eight, with a few thousand pounds, and was posted into the Laconia, if I had then written to you, would you have answered my letter? would you, in short, have renewed the engagement then?"

"Would I!" was all her answer; but the accent was decisive enough.

"Good God!" he cried, "you would! It is not that I did not think of it, or desire it, as what could alone crown all my other success. But I was proud, too proud to ask again. I did not understand you. I shut my eyes, and would not understand you, or do you justice. This is a recollection which ought to make me forgive every one sooner than myself. Six years of separation and suffering might have been spared. It is a sort of pain, too, which is new to me. I have been used to the gratification of believing myself to earn every blessing that I enjoyed. I have valued myself on honourable toils and just rewards. Like other great men under reverses," he added with a smile, "I must endeavour to subdue my mind to my fortune. I must learn to brook being happier than I deserve."

Chapter XXIV

Who can be in doubt of what followed? When any two young people take it into their heads to marry, they are pretty sure by perseverance to carry their point, be they ever so poor, or ever so imprudent, or ever so little likely to be necessary to each other's ultimate comfort. This may be bad morality to conclude with, but I believe it to be truth; and if such parties succeed, how should a Captain Wentworth and an Anne Elliot, with the advantage of maturity of mind, consciousness of right, and one independent fortune between them, fail of bearing down every opposition? They might in fact have borne down a great deal more than they met with, for there was little to distress them beyond the want of graciousness and warmth.—Sir Walter made no objection, and Elizabeth did nothing worse than look cold and unconcerned. Captain Wentworth, with five-and-twenty thousand pounds,[1] and as high in his profession as merit and activity could place him,[2] was no longer nobody. He was now esteemed quite worthy to address the daughter of a foolish, spend-thrift baronet, who had not had principle or sense enough to maintain himself in the situation in which Providence had placed him, and who could give his daughter at present but a small part of the share of ten thousand pounds which must be hers hereafter.

Sir Walter indeed, though he had no affection for Anne, and no vanity flattered, to make him really happy on the occasion, was very far from thinking it a bad match for her. On the contrary, when he saw more of Captain Wentworth, saw him repeatedly by daylight and eyed him well, he was very much struck by his personal claims, and felt that his superiority of appearance might be not unfairly balanced against her superiority of rank; and all this, assisted by his well-sounding name, enabled Sir Walter at last to prepare his pen with a very good grace for the insertion of the marriage in the volume of honour.

The only one among them, whose opposition of feeling could excite any serious anxiety, was Lady Russell. Anne knew that Lady Russell must be suffering some pain in understanding and relinquishing Mr. Elliot, and be making some struggles to become truly acquainted with, and do justice to Captain Wentworth. This however was what Lady Russell had now to do. She must learn to feel that she had been mistaken with regard to both; that she had been unfairly influenced by appearances in each; that because Captain Wentworth's manners had not suited her own ideas, she had been too quick in suspecting them to indicate a character of dangerous impetuosity; and that because Mr. Elliot's manners had precisely pleased her in their propriety and correctness, their general politeness and suavity, she had been too quick in receiving them as the certain result of the most correct opinions and well regulated mind. There was nothing less for Lady Russell to do, than to admit that she had been pretty completely wrong, and to take up a new set of opinions and of hopes.

1. Wentworth's prize-money has made him very rich. Compare the £30,000 to which Emma Woodhouse is entitled through inheritance in Austen's *Emma*.
2. Wentworth cannot achieve a higher rank through his efforts but must wait for a vacancy into which he might be promoted.

There is a quickness of perception in some, a nicety in the discernment of character, a natural penetration, in short, which no experience in others can equal, and Lady Russell had been less gifted in
this part of understanding than her young friend. But she was a very
good woman, and if her second object was to be sensible and well-
judging, her first was to see Anne happy. She loved Anne better than
she loved her own abilities; and when the awkwardness of the beginning was over, found little hardship in attaching herself as a mother
to the man who was securing the happiness of her other child.

Of all the family, Mary was probably the one most immediately
gratified by the circumstance. It was creditable to have a sister married, and she might flatter herself with having been greatly instrumental to the connexion, by keeping Anne with her in the autumn;
and as her own sister must be better than her husband's sisters, it
was very agreeable that Captain Wentworth should be a richer man
than either Captain Benwick or Charles Hayter.—She had something to suffer perhaps when they came into contact again, in seeing Anne restored to the rights of seniority, and the mistress of a
very pretty landaulette;[3] but she had a future to look forward to, of
powerful consolation. Anne had no Uppercross-hall before her, no
landed estate, no headship of a family; and if they could but keep
Captain Wentworth from being made a baronet, she would not
change situations with Anne.

It would be well for the eldest sister if she were equally satisfied
with her situation, for a change is not very probable there. She had
soon the mortification of seeing Mr. Elliot withdraw; and no one of
proper condition has since presented himself to raise even the
unfounded hopes which sunk with him.

The news of his cousin Anne's engagement burst on Mr. Elliot
most unexpectedly. It deranged his best plan of domestic happiness,
his best hope of keeping Sir Walter single by the watchfulness which
a son-in-law's rights would have given. But, though discomfited and
disappointed, he could still do something for his own interest and
his own enjoyment. He soon quitted Bath; and on Mrs. Clay's quitting it likewise soon afterwards, and being next heard of as established under his protection in London,[4] it was evident how double a
game he had been playing, and how determined he was to save himself from being cut out by one artful woman, at least.

Mrs. Clay's affections had overpowered her interest, and she had
sacrificed, for the young man's sake, the possibility of scheming longer for Sir Walter. She has abilities, however, as well as affections;
and it is now a doubtful point whether his cunning, or hers, may

3. A small carriage.
4. I.e., as his mistress.

finally carry the day; whether, after preventing her from being the wife of Sir Walter, he may not be wheedled and caressed at last into making her the wife of Sir William.

It cannot be doubted that Sir Walter and Elizabeth were shocked and mortified by the loss of their companion, and the discovery of their deception in her. They had their great cousins, to be sure, to resort to for comfort; but they must long feel that to flatter and follow others, without being flattered and followed in turn, is but a state of half enjoyment.

Anne, satisfied at a very early period of Lady Russell's meaning to love Captain Wentworth as she ought, had no other alloy to the happiness of her prospects than what arose from the consciousness of having no relations to bestow on him which a man of sense could value. There she felt her own inferiority keenly. The disproportion in their fortune was nothing; it did not give her a moment's regret; but to have no family to receive and estimate him properly; nothing of respectability, of harmony, of good-will to offer in return for all the worth and all the prompt welcome which met her in his brothers and sisters, was a source of as lively pain as her mind could well be sensible of, under circumstances of otherwise strong felicity. She had but two friends in the world to add to his list, Lady Russell and Mrs. Smith. To those, however, he was very well disposed to attach himself. Lady Russell, in spite of all her former transgressions, he could now value from his heart. While he was not obliged to say that he believed her to have been right in originally dividing them, he was ready to say almost every thing else in her favour; and as for Mrs. Smith, she had claims of various kinds to recommend her quickly and permanently.

Her recent good offices by Anne had been enough in themselves; and their marriage, instead of depriving her of one friend, secured her two. She was their earliest visitor in their settled life; and Captain Wentworth, by putting her in the way of recovering her husband's property in the West Indies; by writing for her, acting for her, and seeing her through all the petty difficulties of the case, with the activity and exertion of a fearless man and a determined friend, fully requited the services which she had rendered, or ever meant to render, to his wife.

Mrs. Smith's enjoyments were not spoiled by this improvement of income, with some improvement of health, and the acquisition of such friends to be often with, for her cheerfulness and mental alacrity did not fail her; and while these prime supplies of good remained, she might have bid defiance even to greater accessions of worldly prosperity. She might have been absolutely rich and perfectly healthy, and yet be happy. Her spring of felicity was in the glow of her spirits, as her friend Anne's was in the warmth of her heart. Anne was tenderness itself, and she had the full worth of it in Captain Wentworth's affection. His profession was all that could ever make her friends wish that tenderness less; the dread of a future war all that could dim her sunshine. She gloried in being a sailor's wife, but she must pay the tax of quick alarm for belonging to that profession which is, if possible, more distinguished in its domestic virtues than in its national importance.

THE END

The Original Ending of *Persuasion*[†]

[The two chapters printed here comprise Austen's original ending to *Persuasion*. They were replaced by the final two chapters of the present text.]

CHAPTER 10

July 8.

With all this knowledge of Mr E—and this authority to impart it, Anne left Westgate Buildgs—her mind deeply busy in revolving what she had heard, feeling, thinking, recalling and forseeing everything; shocked at Mr Elliot—sighing over future Kellynch, and pained for Lady Russell, whose confidence in him had been entire.—The Embarrassment which must be felt from this hour in his presence!—How to behave to him?—how to get rid of him?—what to do by any of the Party at home?—where to be blind? where to be active?—It was altogether a confusion of Images and Doubts—a perplexity, an agitation which she could not see the end of—and she was in Gay St and still so much engrossed, that she started on being addressed by Adml Croft, as if he were a person unlikely to be met there. It was within a few steps of his own door.—"You are going to call upon my wife, said he, she will be very glad to see you."—Anne denied it "No—she really had not time, she was in her way home"—but while she spoke, the Adml had stepped back and knocked at the door, calling out, "Yes, yes, do go in; she is all alone. go in and rest yourself."—Anne felt so little disposed at this time to be in company of any sort, that it vexed her to be thus constrained—but she was obliged to stop. "Since you are so very kind, said she, I will just ask Mrs Croft how she does, but I really cannot stay 5 minutes.—You are sure she is quite alone."—The possibility of Capt. W. had occurred—and most fearfully anxious was she to be assured—either that he was within

---

† From *Jane Austen's Autograph*, ed. R. W. Chapman (Oxford: Clarendon Press, 1926).

or that he was not; *which*, might have been a question.—"Oh! yes, quite alone—Nobody but her Mantuamaker[1] with her, and they have been shut up together this half hour, so it must be over soon."—"Her Mantua maker!—then I am sure my calling now, would be most inconvenient.—Indeed you must allow me to leave my Card and be so good as to explain it afterwards to Mrs C." "No, no, not at all, not at all. She will be very happy to see you. Mind—I will not swear that she has not something particular to say to you—but *that* will all come out in the right place. I give no hints.—Why, Miss Elliot, we begin to hear strange things of you—(smiling in her face)—But you have not much the Look of it—as Grave as a little Judge."—Anne blushed.—"Aye, aye, that will do. Now, it is right. I *thought* we were not mistaken." She was left to guess at the direction of his Suspicions;—the first wild idea had been of some disclosure from his Br in law—but she was ashamed the next moment—and felt how far more probable that he should be meaning Mr E.—The door was opened—and the Man evidently beginning to *deny* his Mistress, when the sight of his Master stopped him. The Adml enjoyed the joke exceedingly. Anne thought his triumph over Stephen rather too long. At last however, he was able to invite her upstairs, and stepping before her said—"I will just go up with you myself and shew you in—. I cannot stay, because I must go to the P. Office,[2] but if you will only sit down for 5 minutes I am sure Sophy will come—and you will find nobody to disturb you—there is nobody but Frederick here—" opening the door as he spoke.—Such a person to be passed over as a Nobody to *her*!—After being allowed to feel quite secure—indifferent—at her ease, to have it burst on her that she was to be the next moment in the same room with him!—No time for recollection!—for planning behaviour, or regulating manners!—There was time only to turn pale, before she had passed through the door, and met the astonished eyes of Capt. W—. who was sitting by the fire pretending to read and prepared for no greater surprise than the Admiral's hasty return.—Equally unexpected was the meeting, on each side. There was nothing to be done however, but to stifle feelings and be quietly polite;—and the Admiral was too much on the alert, to leave any troublesome pause.—He repeated again what he had said before about his wife and everybody—insisted on Anne's sitting down and being perfectly comfortable, was sorry he must leave her himself, but was sure Mrs Croft would

---

1. Dressmaker. A mantua was a kind of loose gown, fashionable during this period.
2. In 1782, the British postal system (or Royal Mail) was reformed by John Palmer, a theater owner in Bath who persuaded government authorities to apply his method for transporting actors speedily in coaches to the transportation of mail. For his ingenuity Palmer was made Comptroller of the Post Office in 1785. Distance traveled, number of sheets, and weight were factors in assessing postage costs, usually paid by the recipient rather than the sender.

be down very soon, and would go upstairs and give her notice directly.—Anne *was* sitting down, but now she arose again—to entreat him not to interrupt Mrs C—and re-urge the wish of going away and calling another time.—But the Adml would not hear of it;—and if she did not return to the charge with unconquerable Perseverance, or did not with a more passive Determination walk quietly out of the room—(as certainly she might have done) may she not be pardoned?—If she *had* no horror of a few minutes Tête-à-Tête[3] with Capt. W—, may she not be pardoned for not wishing to give him the idea that she *had*?—She reseated herself, and the Adml took leave; but on reaching the door, said, "Frederick, a word with *you*, if you please."—Capt. W—went to him; and instantly, before they were well out of the room, the Adml continued—"As I am going to leave you together, it is but fair I should give you something to talk of—and so, if you please—" Here the door was very firmly closed; she could guess by which of the two; and she lost entirely what immediately followed; but it was impossible for her not to distinguish parts of the rest, for the Adml on the strength of the Door's being shut was speaking without any management of voice, tho' she could hear his companion trying to check him.—She could not doubt their being speaking of her. She heard her own name and *Kellynch* repeatedly—she was very much distressed. She knew not what to do, or what to expect—and among other agonies felt the possibility of Capt. W—'s not returning into the room at all, which after *her* consenting to stay would have been—too bad for Language.—They seemed to be talking of the Admls Lease of Kellynch. She heard him say something of "the Lease being signed or not signed"—*that* was not likely to be a very agitating subject—but then followed "I hate to be at an uncertainty—I must know at once—Sophy thinks the same." Then, in a lower tone, Capt. W—seemed remonstrating—wanting to be excused—wanting to put something off. "Phoo, Phoo—answered the Admiral now is the Time. If *you* will not speak, I will stop and speak myself."—"Very well Sir, very well Sir, followed with some impatience from his companion, opening the door as he spoke.—"You will then—you promise you will?" replied the Admiral, in all the power of his natural voice, unbroken even by one thin door.—"Yes—Sir—Yes." And the Adml was hastily left, the door was closed, and the moment arrived in which Anne was alone with Capt. W—. She could not attempt to see how he looked; but he walked immediately to a window, as if irresolute and embarrassed;—and for about the space of 5 seconds, she repented what she had done—censured it as unwise, blushed over it as indelicate.—She longed to be able to speak of the weather or the Concert—but could

3. "Face-to-face," a private conversation between two people (French).

only compass[4] the releif of taking a Newspaper in her hand.—The distressing pause was soon over however; he turned round in half a minute, and coming towards the Table where she sat, said, in a voice of effort and constraint—"You must have heard too much already Madam to be in any doubt of my having promised Adml Croft to speak to you on some particular subject—and this conviction determines me to do it—however repugnant to my—to all my sense of propriety, to be taking so great a liberty.—You will acquit me of Impertinence I trust, by considering me as speaking only for another, and speaking by Necessity;—and the Adml is a Man who can never be thought Impertinent by one who knows him as you do—. His Intentions are always the kindest and the Best;—and you will perceive that he is actuated by none other, in the application which I am now with—with very peculiar feelings—obliged to make."—He stopped—but merely to recover breath;—not seeming to expect any answer.—Anne listened, as if her Life depended on the issue of his Speech.—He proceeded, with a forced alacrity.— "The Adml, Madam, was this morning confidently informed that you were—upon my word I am quite at a loss, ashamed—(breathing and speaking quick)—the awkwardness of *giving* Information of this sort to one of the Parties—You can be at no loss to understand me—It was very confidently said that Mr Elliot—that everything was settled in the family for an Union between Mr Elliot—and yourself. It was added that you were to live at Kellynch—that Kellynch was to be given up. This, the Admiral knew could not be correct—But it occurred to him that it might be the *wish* of the Parties—And my commission from him Madam, is to say, that if the Family wish is such, his Lease of Kellynch shall be cancel'd, and he and my sister will provide themselves with another home, without imagining themselves to be doing anything which under similar circumstances wd not be done for *them*.—This is all Madam.—A very few words in reply from you will be sufficient.—That *I* should be the person commissioned on this subject is extraordinary!—and beleive me Madam, it is no less painful.—A very few words however will put an end to the awkwardness and distress we may *both* be feeling." Anne spoke a word or two, but they were unintelligible— And before she could command herself, he added,—"If you only tell me that the Adml may address a Line to Sir Walter, it will be enough. Pronounce only the words, *he may*.—I shall immediately follow him with your message.—" This was spoken, as with a fortitude which seemed to meet the message.—"No Sir—said Anne— There is no message.—You are misin—the Adml is misinformed.—I do justice to the kindness of his Intentions, but he is quite mistaken.

4. Attain, procure.

There is no Truth in any such report."—He was a moment silent.—She turned her eyes towards him for the first time since his re-entering the room. His colour was varying—and he was looking at her with all the Power and Keenness, which she believed no other eyes than his, possessed. "*No* Truth in any such report!—he repeated.—No Truth in any *part* of it?"—"None."—He had been standing by a chair—enjoying the releif of leaning on it—or of playing with it;—he now sat down—drew it a little nearer to her—and looked, with an expression which had something more than penetration in it, something softer;—Her Countenance did not discourage.—It was a silent, but a very powerful Dialogue;—on his side, Supplication, on her's[5] acceptance.—Still, a little nearer—and a hand taken and pressed—and "Anne, my own dear Anne!"—bursting forth in the fullness of exquisite feeling—and all Suspense and Indecision were over.—They were re-united. They were restored to all that had been lost. They were carried back to the past, with only an increase of attachment and confidence, and only such a flutter of present Delight as made them little fit for the interruption of Mrs Croft, when she joined them not long afterwards.—*She* probably, in the observations of the next ten minutes, saw something to suspect—and tho' it was hardly possible for a woman of her description to wish the Mantuamaker had imprisoned her longer, she might be very likely wishing for some excuse to run about the house, some storm to break the windows above, or a summons to the Admiral's Shoemaker below.—Fortune favoured them all however in another way—in a gentle, steady rain—just happily set in as the Admiral returned and Anne rose to go.—She was earnestly invited to stay dinner;—a note was dispatched to Camden Place—and she staid;—staid till 10 at night. And during that time, the Husband and wife, either by the wife's contrivance, or by simply going on in their usual way, were frequently out of the room together—gone up stairs to hear a noise, or down stairs to settle their accounts, or upon the Landing place to trim the Lamp.[6]—And these precious moments were turned to so good an account that all the most anxious feelings of the past were gone through.—Before they parted at night, Anne had the felicity of being assured in the first place that—(so far from being altered for the worse!)—she had *gained* inexpressibly in personal Loveliness; and that as to Character—her's was now fixed on his Mind as Perfection itself—maintaining the just Medium of Fortitude and Gentleness;—that he had never ceased to love and

---

5. Hers. See also "it's" for "its" on the following page, and "Husbands'" for "husband's" on p. 188. Austen's preference for the "ei" spelling of words such as "yeilding" and "beleif" reflects a widespread practice of private or irregular spelling in letters.
6. Trim the wick of the oil lamp. Wicks required trimming to reduce smoke and increase brilliancy.

prefer her, though it had been only at Uppercross that he had learn't to do her Justice—and only at Lyme that he had begun to understand his own sensations;—that at Lyme he had received Lessons of more than one kind;—the passing admiration of Mr Elliot had at least *roused* him, and the scenes on the Cobb and at Capt. Harville's had fixed her superiority.—In his preceding *attempts* to attach himself to Louisa Musgrove, (the attempts of Anger and Pique)—he protested that he had continually felt the impossibility of really caring for Louisa, though till *that day*, till the leisure for reflection which followed it, he had not understood the perfect excellence of the Mind, with which Louisa's could so ill bear a comparison, or the perfect, the unrivalled hold it possessed over his own.—There he had learnt to distinguish between the steadiness of Principle and the Obstinacy of Self-will, between the Darings of Heedlessness, and the Resolution of a collected Mind—there he had seen everything to exalt in his estimation the Woman he had lost, and there begun to deplore the pride, the folly, the madness of resentment which had kept him from trying to regain her, when thrown in his way. From that period to the present had his penance been the most severe.—He had no sooner been free from the horror and remorse attending the first few days of Louisa's accident, no sooner begun to feel himself alive again, than he had begun to feel himself though alive, not at liberty.—He found that he was considered by his friend Harville, as an engaged Man. The Harvilles entertained not a doubt of a mutual attachment between him and Louisa—and though this to a *degree*, was contradicted instantly—it yet made him feel that perhaps by *her* family, by everybody, by *herself* even, the same idea might be held— and that he was not *free* in honour—though, if such were to be the conclusion, too free alas! in Heart.—He had never thought justly on this subject before—he had not sufficiently considered that his excessive Intimacy at Uppercross must have it's danger of ill consequence in many ways, and that while trying whether he *could* attach himself to either of the Girls, he might be exciting unpleasant reports, if not, raising unrequited regard!—He found, too late, that he had entangled himself—and that precisely as he became thoroughly satisfied of his not *caring* for Louisa at all, he must regard himself as bound to her, if her feelings for him, were what the Harvilles supposed.—It determined him to leave Lyme—and await her perfect recovery elsewhere. He would gladly weaken, by any *fair* means, whatever sentiments or speculations concerning him might exist; and he went therefore into Shropshire meaning after a while, to return to the Crofts at Kellynch, and act as he found requisite.—He had remained in Shropshire, lamenting the Blindness of his own Pride, and the Blunders of his own Calculations, till at once released from Louisa by the astonishing felicity of her engagement with Benwicke. Bath, Bath—had instantly followed, in *Thought*; and not long after, in *fact*. To Bath, to arrive with Hope, to be torn by Jealousy at the first sight of Mr E—, to experience all the changes of each at the Concert, to be miserable by this morning's circumstantial report, to be now, more happy than Language could express, or any heart but his own be capable of.

He was very eager and very delightful in the description of what he had felt at the Concert.—The Evening seemed to have been made up of exquisite moments;—the moment of her stepping forward in the Octagon Room to speak to him—the moment of Mr E's appearing and tearing her away, and one or two subsequent moments, marked by returning hope, or increasing Despondence, were all dwelt on with energy. "To see you, cried he, in the midst of those who could not be *my* well-wishers, to see your Cousin close by you—conversing and smiling—and feel all the horrible Eligibilities and Proprieties of the Match!—to consider it as the certain wish of every being who could hope to influence you—even, if your own feelings were reluctant, or indifferent—to consider what powerful supports would be his!—Was not it enough to make the fool of me, which my behaviour expressed?—How could I look on without agony?—Was not the very sight of the *Friend* who sat behind you?—was not the recollection of what *had* been—the knowledge of her Influence—the indelible, immoveable Impression of what *Persuasion* had *once* done, was not it all against me?"—

"You should have distinguished—replied Anne—You should not have suspected me *now*;—The case so different, and my age so different!—If I *was* wrong, in yeilding to Persuasion once, remember that it was to Persuasion exerted on the side of Safety, not of Risk. When I yeilded, I thought it was to *Duty*.—But no *Duty* could be called in aid here.—In marrying a Man indifferent to me, all Risk would have been incurred, and all Duty violated."—"Perhaps I ought to have reasoned thus, he replied, but I could not.—I could not derive benefit from the later knowledge of your Character which I had acquired, I could not bring it into play, it was overwhelmed, buried, lost in those earlier feelings, which I had been smarting under Year after Year.—I could think of you only as one who *had* yeilded, who *had* given me up, who *had* been influenced by any one rather than by *me*—I saw you with the very Person who had guided you in that year of Misery—I had no reason to think her of less authority now;—the force of Habit was to be added."—"I should have thought, said Anne, that my Manner to yourself, might have spared you much, or all of this."—"No—No—Your manner might be only the ease, which your engagement to another Man would give.—I left you with this beleif.—And yet—I was determined to see you again.—My spirits rallied with the morning, and I felt that I had still a motive for remaining here.—The Admirals news indeed, was a revulsion. Since that moment, I have been decided what to do—and had it been confirmed, this would have been my *last day* in Bath."

There was time for all this to pass—with such Interruptions only as enhanced the charm of the communication—and Bath could scarcely contain any other two Beings at once so rationally and so rapturously happy as during that eveng occupied the Sopha of Mrs Croft's Drawing room in Gay St.

Capt. W.—had taken care to meet the Adml as he returned into the house, to satisfy him as to Mr E—and Kellynch;—and the delicacy of the Admiral's good nature kept him from saying another word on the subject to Anne.—He was quite concerned lest he might have been giving her pain by touching a tender part. Who could say?—She might be liking her Cousin, better than he liked her.— And indeed, upon recollection, if they had been to marry at all why should they have waited so long?—

When the Eveng closed, it is probable that the Adml received some new Ideas from his Wife;—whose particularly friendly manner in parting with her, gave Anne the gratifying persuasion of her seeing and approving.

It had been such a day to Anne!—the hours which had passed since her leaving Camden Place, had done so much!—She was almost bewildered, almost too happy in looking back.—It was necessary to sit up half the Night and lie awake the remainder to comprehend with composure her present state, and pay for the overplus of Bliss, by Headake and Fatigue.—

CHAPTER II

Who can be in doubt of what followed?—When any two Young People take it into their heads to marry, they are pretty sure by perseverance to carry their point—be they ever so poor, or ever so imprudent, or ever so little likely to be necessary to each other's ultimate comfort. This may be bad Morality to conclude with, but I beleive it to be Truth—and if such parties succeed, how should a Capt. W—and an Anne E—, with the advantage of maturity of Mind, consciousness of Right, and one Independant Fortune between them, fail of bearing down every opposition? They might in fact, have born down a great deal more than they met with, for there was little to distress them beyond the want of Graciousness and Warmth. Sir W. made no objection, and Elizth did nothing worse than look cold and unconcerned.—Capt. W—with £25,000[7]—and as high in his Profession as Merit & Activity could place him, was

7. According to the National Archives currency converter, approximately £1,436,000 in today's currency.

no longer nobody. He was now esteemed quite worthy to address the Daughter of a foolish spendthrift Baronet, who had not had Principle or sense enough to maintain himself in the Situation in which Providence had placed him, and who could give his Daughter but a small part of the share of ten Thousand pounds which must be her's hereafter.—Sir Walter indeed tho' he had no affection for his Daughter and no vanity flattered to make him really happy on the occasion, was very far from thinking it a bad match for her.—On the contrary when he saw more of Capt. W.—and eyed him well, he was very much struck by his personal claims and felt that *his* superiority of appearance might be not unfairly balanced against *her* superiority of Rank;—and all this, together with his well-sounding name, enabled Sir W. at last to prepare his pen with a very good grace for the insertion of the Marriage in the volume of Honour.— The only person among them whose opposition of feelings could excite any serious anxiety, was Lady Russel.—Anne knew that Lady R—must be suffering some pain in understanding and relinquishing Mr E—and be making some struggles to become truly acquainted with and do justice to Capt. W.—This however, was what Lady R—had now to do. She must learn to feel that she had been mistaken with regard to both—that she had been unfairly influenced by appearances in each—that, because Capt. W.'s manners had not suited her own ideas, she had been too quick in suspecting them to indicate a Character of dangerous Impetuosity, and that because Mr Elliot's manners had precisely pleased her in their propriety and correctness, their general politeness and suavity, she had been too quick in receiving them as the certain result of the most correct opinions and well regulated Mind.—There was nothing less for Lady R. to do than to admit that she had been pretty completely wrong, and to take up a new set of opinions and hopes.—There *is* a quickness of perception in some, a nicety in the discernment of character—a natural Penetration in short which no Experience in others can equal—and Lady R. had been less gifted in this part of Understanding than her young friend;—but she was a very good Woman; and if her second object was to be sensible and well judging, her first was to see Anne happy. She loved Anne better than she loved her own abilities—and when the awkwardness of the Beginning was over, found little hardship in attaching herself as a Mother to the Man who was securing the happiness of her Child. Of all the family, Mary was probably the one most immediately gratified by the circumstance. It was creditable to have a Sister married, and she might flatter herself that she had been greatly instrumental to the connection, by having Anne staying with her in the Autumn; and as her own Sister must be better than her Husbands Sisters, it was very agreable that Captn W—should be a richer Man than either Capt. B.

or Charles Hayter.—She had something to suffer perhaps when they came into contact again, in seeing Anne restored to the rights of Seniority and the Mistress of a very pretty Landaulet—but *she* had a *future* to look forward to, of powerful consolation—Anne had no Uppercross Hall before her, no Landed Estate, no Headship of a family, and if they could but keep Capt. W—from being made a Baronet, she would not change situations with Anne.—It would be well for the *Eldest* Sister if she were equally satisfied with *her* situation, for a change is not very probable there.—She had soon the mortification of seeing Mr E. withdraw, and no one of proper condition has since presented himself to raise even the unfounded hopes which sunk with *him*. The news of his Cousin Anne's engagement burst on Mr Elliot most unexpectedly. It deranged his best plan of domestic Happiness, his best hopes of keeping Sir Walter single by the watchfulness which a son in law's rights would have given—But tho' discomfited and disappointed, he could still do something for his own interest and his own enjoyment. He soon quitted Bath and on Mrs Clay's quitting it likewise soon afterwards and being next heard of, as established under his Protection in London, it was evident how double a Game he had been playing, and how determined he was to save himself from being cut out by *one* artful woman at least.—Mrs Clay's affections had overpowered her Interest, and she had sacrificed for the Young Man's sake, the possibility of scheming longer for Sir Walter;—she has Abilities however as well as Affections, and it is now a doubtful point whether his cunning or hers may finally carry the day, whether, after preventing her from being the wife of Sir Walter, he may not be wheedled and caressed at last into making her the wife of Sir William.—

It cannot be doubted that Sir Walter and Eliz: were shocked and mortified by the loss of their companion and the discovery of their deception in her. They had their great cousins to be sure, to resort to for comfort—but they must long feel that to flatter and follow others, without being flattered and followed themselves is but a state of half enjoyment.

Anne, satisfied at a very early period, of Lady Russel's *meaning* to love Capt. W—as she ought, had no other alloy to the happiness of her prospects, than what arose from the consciousness of having no relations to bestow on him which a Man of Sense could value.— There, she felt her own Inferiority keenly.—The disproportion in their fortunes was nothing;—it did not give her a moment's regret;— but to have no Family to receive and estimate him properly, nothing of respectability, of Harmony, of Goodwill to offer in return for all the Worth and all the prompt welcome which met her in his Brothers and Sisters, was a source of as lively pain, as her Mind could well be sensible of, under circumstances of otherwise strong felicity.—She had but two friends in the World, to add to his List, Lady R. and Mrs Smith.—To those however, he was very well-disposed to attach himself. Lady R—inspite of all her former transgressions, he could now value from his heart;—while he was not obliged to say that he beleived her to have been right in originally dividing them, he was ready to say almost anything else in her favour;—and as for Mrs Smith, she had claims of various kinds to recommend her quickly and permanently.—Her recent good offices by Anne had been enough in themselves—and their marriage, instead of depriving her of one friend secured her two. She was one of their first visitors in their settled Life—and Capt. Wentworth, by putting her in the way of recovering her Husband's property in the W. Indies, by writing for her, and acting for her, and seeing her through all the petty Difficulties of the case, with the activity and exertion of a fearless Man, and a determined friend, fully requited the services she had rendered, or had ever meant to render, to his Wife. Mrs Smith's enjoyments were not *spoiled* by this improvement of Income, with some improvement of health, and the acquisition of such friends to be often with, for her chearfulness and mental Activity did not fail her, and while those prime supplies of Good remained, she might have bid defiance even to greater accessions of worldly Prosperity. She might have been absolutely rich and perfectly healthy, and yet be happy.—*Her* spring of Felicity was in the glow of her Spirits—as her friend Anne's was in the warmth of her Heart.—Anne was Tenderness itself;—and she had the full worth of it in Captn Wentworth's affection. His Profession was all that could ever make her friends wish *that* Tenderness less; the dread of a future War, all that could dim her Sunshine.—She gloried in being a Sailor's wife, but she must pay the tax of quick alarm, for belonging to that Profession which is—if possible—more distinguished in it's Domestic Virtues, than in it's National Importance.—

FINIS

July 18.—1816.

BACKGROUNDS AND CONTEXTS

STEEL'S

ORIGINAL AND CORRECT

List of the Royal Navy,

HIRED ARMED-VESSELS, GUN-BOATS, &c.

Packets, Excise and Revenue Cutters, &c.

WITH THEIR

COMMANDERS AND STATIONS:

TO WHICH ARE ADDED THE FOLLOWING LISTS, &c.

CORRECTED TO DECEMBER, 1802.

Continued Monthly, Price Eight-Pence on common, or One Shilling on fine, Paper.

Steel's Original and Correct List of the Royal Navy . . . Corrected to December, 1802 (London: Printed for David Steel by C. and W. Galabin, 1802).

By Authority.

THE

NAVY LIST,

CORRECTED TO

THE END OF DECEMBER, 1814.

CONTENTS.

PUBLISHED BY JOHN MURRAY,

BOOKSELLER OF THE ADMIRALTY AND BOARD OF LONGITUDE,

No. 50, ALBEMARLE-STREET.

The Navy List, Corrected to the end of December, 1814 (London: John Murray, 1814).

JANE AUSTEN

Selected Letters†

To Cassandra Austen   23 Tues. August 1796.¹

Cork Street² Tuesday morning

My dear Cassandra

Here I am once more in this Scene of Dissipation & vice, and I begin already to find my Morals corrupted.—We reached Staines yesterday I do not [know *omitted*] when, without suffering so much from the Heat as I had hoped to do. We set off again this morning at seven o'clock, & had a very pleasant Drive, as the morning was cloudy & perfectly cool—I came all the way in the Chaise from Hertford Bridge.—

Edward & Frank are both gone out to seek their fortunes; the latter is to return soon & help us seek ours. The former we shall never see again.³ We are to be at Astley's⁴ to night, which I am glad of. Edward has heard from Henry this morning. He has not been at the Races, at all, unless his driving Miss Pearson over to Rowling one day can be so called. We shall find him there on Thursday.

I hope you are all alive after our melancholy parting Yesterday, and that you pursued your intended avocation with Success.—

God Bless You—I must leave off, for we are going out. Yrs very affec:ᵗᵉˡʸ

J: Austen

Every Body's Love

---

† From *Jane Austen's Letters*, 3rd ed., ed. Deirdre Le Faye (Oxford & New York: Oxford University Press, 1995). All letters in this section are reprinted with permission. This edition © Deirde Le Faye 1995. Reproduced with permission of the licensor through PLSclear. Unless otherwise indicated, notes are by Le Faye. Some of Le Faye's notes have been omitted. Although the use of nonstandard punctuation and spelling was common at the time, Austen's novels were polished and regularized by her editor, William Gifford, an employee of the publisher John Murray. Gifford was responsible for introducing semicolons to Austen's published prose, whereas the manuscripts display frequent and haphazard use of dashes [*Editor's note*].

1. [From *Letters*, pp. 5 and 355.] The date "Aug. 1796" has been added by another hand in the top left corner of the first page; the full date can be ascertained by the reference given below to the Canterbury races. See Notes and Queries from *Jane Austen's Letters*, 232, no. 4 (December 1987): 478–81.
2. The young Austens had probably stayed overnight with Mr. Benjamin Langlois—see Deidre Le Faye, William Austen-Leigh, and Richard Arthur, *Jane Austen: A Family Record* (London, 1989).
3. Jane Austen's brothers, Edward Austen (later Knight) (1767–1852) and Francis (Frank) Austen (1774–1865), the latter nicknamed "Fly." In December 1798, Austen updates Cassandra about Frank's situation: "Frank writes in good spirits, but says that our correspondence cannot be so easily carried on in future as it has been, as the communication between Cadiz and Lisbon is less frequent than formerly. You and my mother, therefore, must not alarm yourselves at the long intervals that may divide his letters" (*Letters*, p. 23). Le Faye notes that "mother" ought to read "brother." Later that month Austen reports, "Frank is made.—He was yesterday raised to the Rank of Commander, & appointed to the Petterel Sloop, now at Gibraltar" (*Letters*, p. 23). At his death Frank was Admiral of the Fleet, the highest rank for a British naval officer [*Editor's note*].
4. Astley's Amphitheatre, near Westminster Bridge; an equestrian circus, originally opened by Philip Astley (1742–1814) in 1770. See Jane Austen, *Emma*, ed. R. W. Chapman, chaps. 18 and 19 (December 1815) (Oxford, 1966).

* * *

To Cassandra Austen   Weds. 21–Thurs. 22 January 1801[5]

Expect a most agreeable letter, for not being overburdened with subject—(having nothing at all to say)—I shall have no check to my Genius from beginning to end.—Well, & so, Frank's letter has made you very happy, but you are afraid he would not have patience to stay for the Haarlem, which you wish him to have done as being safer than the Merchantman.[6]—Poor fellow! to wait from the middle of November to the end of December, & perhaps even longer! it must be sad work!—especially in a place where the ink is so abominably pale. What a surprise to him it must have been on the 20th of Oct:r to be visited, collar'd & thrust out of the Petterell by Capt:n Inglis.[7]—He kindly passes over the poignancy of his feelings in quitting his Ship, his Officers, & his Men.—What a pity it is that he should not be in England at the time of this promotion, because he certainly would have had an appointment![8]—so everybody says, & therefore it must be right for me to say it too.—Had he been really here, the certainty of the appointment, I dare say, would not have been half so great—but as it could not be brought to the proof, his absence will be always a lucky source of regret.—If it be true, Mr Valentine may afford himself a fine Valentine's knot, & Charles may perhaps become 1st of the Endymion—tho' I suppose Capt: Durham is too likely to bring a villain with him under that denomination.[9] * * * I dined at

5. From *Letters*, pp. 74–75, 77 [*Editor's note*].
6. "Haarlem" refers to a Dutch ship of the line captured by the British navy in October 1797 at the Battle of Camperdown. It was considered safer to travel on a warship than on a merchant ship.
7. Captain Charles Inglis had been involved in capturing the *Guillaume Tell* off the coast of Malta in the Mediterranean Sea on March 31, 1800. The *Guillaume Tell* was one of two ships of the line that had survived a 1798 attack by the British fleet, led by Rear Admiral Nelson, on the French fleet anchored at Alexandria, Egypt. When the ship was captured in 1800, its crew was suffering from starvation. Inglis succeeded Frank Austen, who had taken command of HMS *Peterel*, a sixteen-gun warship, in February 1799. Frank's account of the capture of *La Ligurienne* was written on the *Peterel* in March 1800, appearing in the *London Gazette* in May and reprinted in the *Naval Chronicle*'s "Letters on Service" section in July. In 1804, the *Peterel* was deployed to the West Indies, specifically Jamaica and Barbados. For a detailed account of the naval careers of Austen's brothers and the seamen of *Persuasion*, see Hazel Jones, "She Had Only Navy-Lists and Newspapers for Her Authority," *Persuasions* 39.1 (2018) [*Editor's note*].
8. Refers to assignment to a new ship [*Editor's note*].
9. Charles John Austen (1779–1852), Jane Austen's youngest brother. Charles served on the *Endymion* and was later promoted to commander, taking charge of HMS *Indian*, a sloop built in Bermuda. In 1826 he became second in command of HMS *Aurora* at Jamaica Station and was likely involved in intercepting slave ships bound for America. He served in the Royal Navy for nearly sixty years and was promoted to rear admiral in 1846. On Charles's involvement with Betsy Austin and Hannah Lewis, "successful freewomen of mixed race who ran competing lodging and entertainment establishments in Barbados," see Ruth Knezevich and Devoney Looser, "Jane Austen's Afterlife, West Indian Madams, and the Literary Porter Family: Two New Letters from Charles Austen," *Modern Philology*, 112.3 (2015): 554–68, at 558 [*Editor's note*].

Deane[1] yesterday, as I told you I should;—& met the two Mr Holders.—We played at Vingt-un, which as Fulwar was unsuccessful,
gave him an opportunity of exposing himself as usual.[2] * * *

Miss Austen
Godmersham Park
Faversham
Kent

* * *

To Cassandra Austen   Tues. 26-Weds. 27 May, 1801[3]

My dear Cassandra

For your letter from Kintbury & for all the compliments on my
writing which it contained, I now return you my best thanks. * * * The
Endymion came into Portsmouth on Sunday, & I have sent Charles
a short letter by this day's post.—My adventures since I wrote to
you three days ago have been such as the time would easily contain;
I walked yesterday morning with Mrs Chamberlayne to Lyncombe &
Widcombe, and in the evening I drank tea with the Holders.[4]—
Mrs. Chamberlayne's pace was not quite so magnificent on this second trial as in the first; it was nothing more than I could keep up
with, without effort; & for many, many Yards together on a raised
narrow footpath I led the way.—The Walk was very beautiful as my
companion agreed, whenever I made the observation—And so ends
our friendship, for the Chamberlaynes leave Bath in a day or two.
* * * Frank writes me word that he *is* to be in London tomorrow;
some money Negociation from which he hopes to derive advantage,
hastens him from Kent, & will detain him a few days behind my
father in Town.—I have seen the Miss Mapletons this morning;
Marianne was buried yesterday, and I called without expecting to
be let in, to enquire after them all.—On the servant's invitation however I sent in my name, & Jane & Christiana who were walking in
the Garden came to me immediately, and I sat with them about ten
minutes.—They looked pale & dejected, but were more composed

1. According to Austen's nephew, James Edward Austen-Leigh, the house at Deane
   belonged to the Harwoods, "an old family with some racy peculiarities of character,"
   from whom the English novelist and author Henry Fielding (1707–1754) supposedly
   "took the idea of his Squire Western" in *Tom Jones* (1749). In *Recollections of the Early
   Days of the Vine Hunt* (Spottiswoode & Co., 1865), p. 65 [*Editor's note*].
2. Fowle family tradition recalls that Fulwar F. was irascible, especially where losing a
   game was concerned. [Fulwar Craven Fowle was the husband of Elizabeth (Eliza)
   Lloyd, a close friend of Jane and Cassandra. His brother Thomas (Tom) was engaged to
   Cassandra but died of yellow fever in San Domingo (now Haiti) in 1797 while serving
   as naval chaplain. Elizabeth's sister Mary married Jane's brother James, and her sister
   Martha married Austen's brother Frank —*Editor.*]
3. *Letters*, pp. 89–91, 379 [*Editor's note*].
4. For information on the families, friends, and acquaintances named in Austen's letters,
   see Le Faye's extensive notes and appendices [*Editor's note*].

than I had thought probable.—When I mentioned your coming here on Monday, they said that they should be very glad to see you.—We drink tea to night with Mrs Lysons;—Now this, says my Master[5] will be mighty dull.—On friday we are to have another party, & a sett of new people to you.—The Bradshaws & Greaves's, all belonging to one another, and I hope the Pickfords.—Mrs Evelyn called very civilly on sunday, to tell us that Mr Evelyn had seen Mr Philips the proprietor of No. 12 G. P. B.[6] and that Mr Philips was very willing to raise the kitchen floor;—but all this I fear is fruitless—tho' the water may be kept out of sight, it cannot be sent away, nor the ill effects of its' nearness be excluded.—I have nothing more to say on the subject of Houses;—except that we were mistaken as to the aspect of the one in Seymour Street, which instead of being due West is Northwest.—I assure you inspite of what I might chuse to insinuate in a former letter, that I have seen very little of Mr Evelyn since my coming here; I met him this morning for only the 4th time, & as to my anecdote about Sidney Gardens,[7] I made the most of the Story because it came in to advantage, but in fact he only asked me whether I were to be at Sidney Gardens in the evening or not.—There is now something like an engagement between us & the Phaeton,[8] which to confess my frailty I have a great desire to go out in;—whether it will come to anything must remain with him.—I really beleive he is very harmless; people do not seem afraid of him here, and he gets Groundsel for his birds & all that.—My Aunt will never be easy till she visits them;—she has been repeatedly trying to fancy a necessity for it now on our accounts, but she meets with no encouragement.—She ought to be particularly scrupulous in such matters, & she says so herself—but nevertheless————Well—I am come home from Mrs Lysons as yellow as I went;—You cannot like your yellow gown half so well as I do, nor a quarter neither. Mr Rice & Lucy are to be married, one on the 9th & the other on the 10th of July.—Y^rs affec:^ly J. A.

[*Continued on page, upside down between the lines.*] Wednesday.—I am just returned from my Airing in the very bewitching Phaeton & four, for which I was prepared by a note from Mr E. soon after breakfast: We went to the top of Kingsdown—& had a very pleasant drive: One pleasure succeeds another rapidly—On my

5. This suggests a quotation from Mrs. Piozzi * * * but it does not seem to be in her Johnsonian writings. [The reference is to *Anecdotes of the Late Samuel Johnson* (1786) by Welsh diarist and author Hester Thrale (Hester Lynch Piozzi) (1741–1821), based on her diaries, *Thraliana*, first published in 1942 —*Editor*.]
6. Green Park Buildings, one of the Austen family's Bath residences.
7. Jane Austen lived at No. 4 Sydney Place in Bath from 1801 to 1804. In *Persuasion*, Anne Elliot reflects on her "very determined, though very silent disinclination for Bath" as arising from circumstance, as she had visited soon after her mother's death and again after separating from Captain Wentworth; see p. 96 in this volume [*Editor's note*].
8. A sporty two-horse carriage on large wheels.

return I found your letter & a letter from Charles on the table. The contents of yours I suppose I need not repeat to you; to thank you for it will be enough.—I give Charles great credit for remembering my Uncle's direction, & he seems rather surprised at it himself.—He has received 30£ for his share of the privateer & expects 10£ more— but of what avail is it to take prizes if he lays out the produce in presents to his Sisters. He has been buying Gold chains & Topaze Crosses[9] for us;—he must be well scolded.—The Endymion has already received orders for taking Troops to Egypt—which I should not like at all if I did not trust to Charles' being removed from her somehow or other before she sails. He knows nothing of his own destination he says,—but desires me to write directly as the Endymion will probably sail in 3 or 4 days.[1]—He will receive my yesterday's letter to day, and I shall write again by this post to thank & reproach him.—We shall be unbearably fine.—I have made an engagement for you for Thursday the 4th of June; if my Mother & Aunt should not go to the fireworks,[2] which I dare say they will not, I have promised to join Mr Evelyn & Miss Wood—Miss Wood has lived with them you know ever "since my Son died—"

I will engage Mrs Mussell as you desire. She made my dark gown very well & may therefore be trusted I hope with Yours—but she does not always succeed with lighter Colours.—My white one I was obliged to alter a good deal.—Unless anything particular occurs, I shall not write again.

Miss Austen
The Rev:d F. C. Fowle's
Kintbury
Newbury

ANNA LAETITIA BARBAULD

Anna Laetitia Barbauld (Aikin) (1743–1825), the daughter of a Presbyterian Dissenting minister, published several collections of poetry, including *Poems* (1773), *Devotional Pieces* (1775), and *Hymns in Prose for Children* (1781), as well as the fifty-volume *The British Novelists* (1810). Barbauld wrote *Sins of Government, Sins of the Nation* (1793) in response to England's declaration of war against France.

---

9. These two crosses accompanied letter 38 in its later wanderings, and were also purchased by Mr. C. B. Hogan and presented by him to the JAMT in 1974 ° ° °. [*JAMT* refers to the Jane Austen Memorial Trust —*Editor*.]
1. HMS *Endymion* was a fast-sailing frigate used for capturing enemy ships, taking several before, during, and after Charles's time on board. Kindred estimates that his share of the prize-money would have been £4,000. Sheila Johnson Kindred, *Jane Austen's Transatlantic Sister: The Life and Letters of Fanny Palmer Austen* (McGill-Queen's UP, 2017) [*Editor's note*].
2. The usual celebrations for the king's birthday.

From Corsica[†]

—————— *A manly race*
Of unsubmitting spirit, wise and brave;
Who still thro' bleeding ages struggled hard
To hold a generous undiminish'd state;
Too much in vain!

Thomson.[1]

HAIL generous CORSICA! unconquer'd isle![2]
The fort of freedom; that amidst the waves
Stands like a rock of adamant, and dares
The wildest fury of the beating storm.

And are there yet, in this late sickly age   5
(Unkindly to the tow'ring growths of virtue)
Such bold exalted spirits? Men whose deeds,
To the bright annals of old GREECE oppos'd,
Would throw in shades her yet unrival'd name,
And dim the lustre of her fairest page!   10
And glows the flame of LIBERTY so strong
In this lone speck of earth! this spot obscure,
Shaggy with woods, and crusted o'er with rock,
By slaves surrounded and by slaves oppress'd!
What then should BRITONS feel? should they not catch   15
The warm contagion of heroic ardour,
And kindle at a fire so like their own?

Such were the working thoughts which swell'd the breast
Of generous BOSWEL;[3] when with nobler aim
And views beyond the narrow beaten track   20
By trivial fancy trod, he turn'd his course
From polish'd Gallia's soft delicious vales,
From the grey reliques of imperial Rome,
From her long galleries of laurel'd stone,
Her chisel'd heroes, and her marble gods,   25

---

† From *Poems* (London: Joseph Johnson, 1773), pp. 1–7, 12. [Written in the year 1769
—*Barbauld*.]
1. Lines from "August," from the four-part poem *The Seasons* (1730) by Scottish poet
James Thomson (1834–1882).
2. The fourth largest island in the Mediterranean and the birthplace of Napoleon Bonaparte, Corsica was governed by the Republic of Genoa from 1284 until 1755, when it
was ceded to France to pay off debts incurred in suppressing Corsican independence.
British liberal support for Corsican sovereignty grew after France reclaimed the island
after fifteen years of independence.
3. James Boswell (1740–1795), Scottish author and biographer, sought to support Corsican independence with the publication of *An Account of Corsica, the Journal of a Tour
to that Island, and Memoirs of Pascal Paoli* (1768) and *British Essays in Favour of the
Brave Corsicans* (1768).

(Whose dumb majestic pomp yet awes the world,)
To animated forms of patriot zeal;
Warm in the living majesty of virtue;
Elate with fearless spirit; firm; resolv'd;
By fortune unsubdu'd; unaw'd by power.   30

      How raptur'd fancy burns, while warm in thought
I trace the pictur'd landscape; while I kiss
With pilgram lips devout, the sacred soil
Stain'd with the blood of heroes. CYRNUS,[4] hail!
Hail to thy rocky, deep indented shores,   35
And pointed cliffs, which hear the chafing deep
Incessant foaming round their shaggy sides.
Hail to thy winding bays, thy shelt'ring ports
And ample harbours, which inviting stretch
Their hospitable arms to every sail: 40
Thy numerous streams, that bursting from the cliffs
Down the steep channel'd rock impetuous pour
With grateful murmur: on the fearful edge
Of the rude precipice, thy hamlets brown
And straw-roof'd cots, which from the level vale   45
Scarce seen, amongst the craggy hanging cliffs
Seem like an eagle's nest aerial built.
Thy swelling mountains, brown with solemn shade
Of various trees, that wave their giant arms
O'er the rough sons of freedom; lofty pines,   50
And hardy fir, and ilex ever green,
And spreading chesnut, with each humbler plant,
And shrub of fragrant leaf, that clothes their sides
With living verdure; whence the clust'ring bee
Extracts her golden dews: the shining box,   55
And sweet-leav'd myrtle, aromatic thyme,
The prickly juniper, and the green leaf
Which feeds the spinning worm; while glowing bright
Beneath the various foliage, wildly spreads
The arbutus, and rears his scarlet fruit   60
Luxuriant, mantling o'er the craggy steeps;
And thy own native laurel crowns the scene.
Hail to thy savage forests, awful, deep:
Thy tangled thickets, and thy crowded woods,
The haunt of herds untam'd; which sullen bound   65
From rock to rock with fierce unsocial air,
And wilder gaze, as conscious of the power
That loves to reign amid the lonely scenes
Of unbroke nature: precipices huge,

4. An alternative name for Corsica.

And tumbling torrents; trackless desarts, plains   70
Fenc'd in with guardian rocks, whose quarries teem
With shining steel, that to the cultur'd fields
And sunny hills which wave with bearded grain
Defends their homely produce. LIBERTY,
The mountain Goddess, loves to range at large   75
Amid such scenes, and on the iron soil
Prints her majestic step. For these she scorns
The green enamel'd vales, the velvet lap
Of smooth savannahs, where the pillow'd head
Of luxury reposes; balmy gales,   80
And bowers that breathe of bliss. For these, when first
This isle emerging like a beauteous gem
From the dark bosom of the Tyrrhene main
Rear'd its fair front, she mark'd it for her own,
And with her spirit warm'd. Her genuine sons,   85
A broken remnant, from the generous stock
Of ancient Greece, from Sparta's sad remains,
True to their high descent, preserv'd unquench'd
The sacred fire thro' many a barbarous age:
Whom, nor the iron rod of cruel Carthage,   90
Nor the dread sceptre of imperial Rome,
Nor bloody Goth, nor grisly Saracen,
Nor the long galling yoke of proud Liguria,
Could crush into subjection. Still unquell'd
They rose superior, bursting from their chains,   95
And claim'd man's dearest birthright, LIBERTY.
And long, thro' many a hard unequal strife
Maintain'd the glorious conflict; long withstood
With single arm, the whole collected force
Of haughty Genoa, and ambitious Gaul.   100
And shall withstand it, trust the faithful Muse!
It is not in the force of mortal arm,
Scarcely in fate, to bind the struggling soul
That gall'd by wanton power, indignant swells
Against oppression; breathing great revenge,   105
Careless of life, determin'd to be free.
And fav'ring heaven approves * * *

                         *   *   *

       So vainly wish'd, so fondly hop'd the Muse:
Too fondly hop'd. The iron fates prevail,   185
And CYRNUS is no more. Her generous sons,
Less vanquish'd than o'erwhelm'd, by numbers crush'd,
Admir'd, unaided fell. So strives the moon
In dubious battle with the gathering clouds,
And strikes a splendour thro' them; till at length   190

Storms roll'd on storms involve the face of heaven
And quench her struggling fires. Forgive the zeal
That, too presumptuous, whisper'd better things
And read the book of destiny amiss.
Not with the purple colouring of success   195
Is virtue best adorn'd: th' attempt is praise.
There yet remains a freedom, nobler far
Than kings or senates can destroy or give;
Beyond the proud oppressor's cruel grasp
Seated secure; uninjur'd; undestroy'd;   200
Worthy of Gods: The freedom of the mind.

Epistle to William Wilberforce, Esq.
on the Rejection of the Bill for Abolishing
the Slave Trade[†]

Cease, Wilberforce, to urge thy generous aim!
Thy Country knows the sin, and stands the shame!
The Preacher, Poet, Senator in vain
Has rattled in her sight the Negro's chain;
With his deep groans assail'd her startled ear,   5
And rent the veil that hid his constant tear;
Forc'd her averted eyes his stripes to scan,
Beneath the bloody scourge laid bare the man,
Claimed Pity's tear, urged Conscience' strong controul,
And flash'd conviction on her shrinking soul.   10
The Muse, too soon awaked, with ready tongue
At Mercy's shrine applausive peans rung;
And Freedom's eager sons, in vain foretold
A new Astrean[1] reign, an age of gold:
She knows and she persists—Still Afric bleeds,   15
Uncheck'd, the human traffic still proceeds;
She stamps her infamy to future time,
And on her harden'd forehead seals the crime.

---

† From *Poems* (London: Joseph Johnson, 1773), pp. 116–20. William Wilberforce (1759–1833), English politician and prominent abolitionist who lobbied against slavery throughout his life, dying days after the passage of the Slavery Abolition Act of 1833, which abolished legal enslavement in most of the British Empire.

1. Meaning "of the stars." Astraea is a Greek goddess of justice whose promised return to the human world, bringing about a new Golden Age, is referenced in numerous literary works, including John Milton's *Paradise Lost* (1667). Important to female poets and playwrights, Astraea was the pseudonym of English playwright and poet Aphra Behn (1640–1689), one of the first female authors to earn a living from writing. Astraea also figures prominently in English satirical novelist and playwright Delarivier Manley's (1663–1724) dystopian political satire *The New Atalantis* (1709), a roman à clef treating themes of political disenfranchisement, for which she was arrested for libel.

In vain, to thy white standard gathering round,
Wit, Worth, and Parts and Eloquence are found: 20
In vain, to push to birth thy great design,
Contending chiefs, and hostile virtues join;
All, from conflicting ranks, of power possest
To rouse, to melt, or to inform the breast.
Where seasoned tools of Avarice prevail,   25
A Nation's eloquence, combined, must fail:
Each flimsy sophistry by turns they try;
The plausive argument, the daring lye,
The artful gloss, that moral sense confounds,
Th' acknowledged thirst of gain that honour wounds: 30
Bane of ingenuous minds, th' unfeeling sneer,
Which, sudden, turns to stone the falling tear:
They search assiduous, with inverted skill,
For forms of wrong, and precedents of ill;
With impious mockery wrest the sacred page,   35
And glean up crimes from each remoter age:
Wrung Nature's tortures, shuddering, while you tell,
From scoffing fiends bursts forth the laugh of hell;
In Britain's senate, Misery's pangs give birth
To jests unseemly, and to horrid mirth——   40
Forbear!—thy virtues but provoke our doom,
And swell th' account of vengeance yet to come;
For, not unmarked in Heaven's impartial plan,
Shall man, proud worm, contemn his fellow-man?
And injur'd Afric, by herself redrest,   45
Darts her own serpents at her Tyrant's breast.
Each vice, to minds deprav'd by bondage known,
With sure contagion fastens on his own;
In sickly languors melts his nerveless frame,
And blows to rage impetuous Passion's flame: 50
Fermenting swift, the fiery venom gains
The milky innocence of infant veins;
There swells the stubborn will, damps learning's fire,
The whirlwind wakes of uncontroul'd desire,
Sears the young heart to images of woe,   55
And blasts the buds of Virtue as they blow.

Lo! where reclin'd, pale Beauty courts the breeze,
Diffus'd on sofas of voluptuous ease;
With anxious awe, her menial train around,
Catch her faint whispers of half-utter'd sound;   60
See her, in monstrous fellowship, unite
At once the Scythian, and the Sybarite;[2]

2. In the poetic tradition, meaning both warlike and sensuously self-indulgent.

Blending repugnant vices, misally'd,
Which *frugal* nature purpos'd to divide;
See her, with indolence to fierceness join'd,   65
Of body delicate, infirm of mind,
With languid tones imperious mandates urge;
With arm recumbent wield the household scourge;
And with unruffled mien, and placid sounds,
Contriving torture, and inflicting wounds.   70

    Nor, in their palmy walks and spicy groves,
The form benign of rural Pleasure roves;
No milk-maid's song, or hum of village talk,
Sooths the lone poet in his evening walk:
No willing arm the flail unweary'd plies,   75
Where the mix'd sounds of cheerful labour rise;
No blooming maids, and frolic swains are seen
To pay gay homage to their harvest queen:
No heart-expanding scenes their eyes must prove
Of thriving industry, and faithful love: 80
But shrieks and yells disturb the balmy air,
Dumb sullen looks of woe announce despair,
And angry eyes thro' dusky features glare.
Far from the sounding lash the Muses fly,
And sensual riot drowns each finer joy.   85

    Nor less from the gay East, on essenc'd wings,
Breathing unnam'd perfumes, Contagion springs;
The soft luxurious plague alike pervades
The marble palaces, and rural shades;
Hence throng'd Augusta[3] builds her rosy bowers,   90
And decks in summer wreaths her smoky towers;
And hence, in summer bow'rs, Art's costly hand
Pours courtly splendours o'er the dazzled land:
The manners melt—One undistinguish'd blaze
O'erwhelms the sober pomp of elder days;   95
Corruption follows with gigantic stride,
And scarce vouchsafes his shameless front to hide:
The spreading leprosy taints ev'ry part,
Infects each limb, and sickens at the heart.
Simplicity! most dear of rural maids,   100
Weeping resigns her violated shades:
Stern Independence from his glebe retires,
And anxious Freedom eyes her drooping fires;
By foreign wealth are British morals chang'd,
And Afric's sons, and India's, smile aveng'd.   105

3. An ancient Roman honorific, used poetically to designate greatness.

———

For you, whose temper'd ardour long has borne
Untir'd the labour, and unmov'd the scorn;
In Virtue's fast be inscrib'd your fame,
And utter'd your's with Howard's honour'd name,[4]
Friends of the friendless—Hail, ye generous band!   110
Whose efforts yet arrest Heav'n's lifted hand,
Around whose steady brows, in union bright,
The civic wreath, and Christian's palm unite:
Your merit stands, no greater and no less,
Without, or with the varnish of success;   115
But seek no more to break a Nation's fall,
For ye have sav'd yourselves—and that is all.
Succeeding times your struggles, and their fate,
With mingled shame and triumph shall relate,
While faithful History, in her various page,   120
Marking the features of this motley age,
To shed a glory, and to fix a stain,
Tells how you strove, and that you strove in vain.

———

Barbauld's "On the Origin and Progress of Novel-Writing" has been
hailed as producing the first British novel canon, one that importantly
included women. In discussing eight women novelists, Barbauld praises
Charlotte Smith (1749–1806) for "that descriptive talent which forms a
striking feature of her genius," though judging her poetry superior. Of
Frances (Fanny) Burney (1752–1840) she writes, "scarcely any name, if
any, stands higher in the list of novel-writers than hers," adding: "it is
evident that the author draws from life, and exhibits not only the passions of human nature, but the manners of the age and the affectation
of the day." She concludes the volume with a detailed discussion of Ann
Radcliffe (1764–1823), whose gothic novel *Mysteries of Udolpho* (1794)
figures prominently in Austen's *Northanger Abbey* (1817).

From On the Origin and Progress of Novel-Writing[†]

A Collection of Novels has a better chance of giving pleasure than
of commanding respect. Books of this description are condemned
by the grave, and despised by the fastidious; but their leaves are seldom found unopened, and they occupy the parlour and the dressing-
room while productions of higher name are often gathering dust
upon the shelf. It might not perhaps be difficult to show that this
species of composition is entitled to a higher rank than has been

———

4. John Howard (1726–1790), English prison reformer commemorated by a statue at
St. Paul's Square, Bedford.
† From *The British Novelists; with an Essay; and Prefaces, Biographical and Critical* (Lon-
don: F. C. and J. Rivington, 1810), vol. 1, pp. 1–3, 46–51, 53–54.

generally assigned it. Fictitious adventures, in one form or other, have made a part of the polite literature of every age and nation. These have been grafted upon the actions of their heroes; they have been interwoven with their mythology; they have been moulded upon the manners of the age,—and, in return, have influenced the manners of the succeeding generation by the sentiments they have infused and the sensibilities they have excited.

Adorned with the embellishments of Poetry, they produce the epic; more concentrated in the story, and exchanging narrative for action, they become dramatic. When allied with some great moral end, as in the *Telemaque* of Fenelon, and Marmontel's *Belisaire*, they may be termed didactic. They are often made the vehicles of satire, as in Swift's *Gulliver's Travels*, and the *Candide* and *Babouc* of Voltaire.[1] They take a tincture from the learning and politics of the times, and are made use of successfully to attack or recommend the prevailing systems of the day. When the range of this kind of writing is so extensive, and its effect so great, it seems evident that it ought to hold a respectable place among the productions of genius; nor is it easy to say, why the poet, who deals in one kind of fiction, should have so high a place allotted him in the temple of fame; and the romance-writer so low a one as in the general estimation he is confined to. To measure the dignity of a writer by the pleasure he affords his readers is not perhaps using an accurate criterion; but the invention of a story, the choice of proper incidents, the ordonnance of the plan, occasional beauties of description, and above all, the power exercised over the reader's heart by filling it with the successive emotions of love, pity, joy, anguish, transport, or indignation, together with the grave impressive moral resulting from the whole, imply talents of the highest order, and ought to be appreciated accordingly. A good novel is an epic in prose, with more of character and less (indeed in modern novels nothing) of the supernatural machinery.

* * *

* * * For my own part, I scruple not to confess that, when I take up a novel, my end and object is entertainment; and as I suspect that to be the case with most readers, I hesitate not to say that entertainment is their legitimate end and object. To read the productions of wit and genius is a very high pleasure to all persons of taste, and

1. Françoise Fénelon (1651–1715), *Les aventures de Télémaque, fils d'Ulysse* (1699); Jean-François Marmontel (1723–1799), *Bélisaire* (1767); Jonathan Swift (1667–1745), *Gulliver's Travels* (1726); Voltaire (François-Marie d'Arouet, 1694–1778), *Candide* (1759) and *Vision de Babouc; or, The World as It Goes* (1748). As Claudia L. Johnson argues, Barbauld's "diverse, politically self-conscious, and progressive canon always lay[s] bare the work of social dissent and the political associations and interests" of the authors she includes. In "'Let me make the novels of a country': Barbauld's *The British Novelists* (1810/1820)," *NOVEL: A Forum on Fiction* 34.2 (2001): 163–79, at 170.

the avidity with which they are read by all such shows sufficiently that they are calculated to answer this end. Reading is the cheapest of pleasures: it is a domestic pleasure. Dramatic exhibitions give a more poignant delight, but they are seldom enjoyed in perfection, and never without expense and trouble. Poetry requires in the reader a certain elevation of mind and a practised ear. It is seldom relished unless a taste be formed for it pretty early. But the humble novel is always ready to enliven the gloom of solitude, to soothe the languor of debility and disease, to win the attention from pain or vexatious occurrences, to take man from himself, (at many seasons the worst company he can be in,) and, while the moving picture of life passes before him, to make him forget the subject of his own complaints. It is pleasant to the mind to sport in the boundless regions of possibility; to find relief from the sameness of every-day occurrences by expatiating amidst brighter skies and fairer fields; to exhibit love that is always happy, valour that is always successful; to feed the appetite for wonder by a quick succession of marvellous events; and to distribute, like a ruling providence, rewards and punishments which fall just where they ought to fall.

It is sufficient therefore as an end, that these writings add to the innocent pleasures of life; and if they do no harm, the entertainment they give is a sufficient good. We cut down the tree that bears no fruit, but we ask nothing of a flower beyond its scent and its colour. The unpardonable sin in a novel is dullness: however grave or wise it may be, if its author possesses no powers of amusing, he has no business to write novels; he should employ his pen in some more serious part of literature.

But it is not necessary to rest the credit of these works on amusement alone, since it is certain they have had a very strong effect in infusing principles and moral feelings. It is impossible to deny that the most glowing and impressive sentiments of virtue are to be found in many of these compositions, and have been deeply imbibed by their youthful readers. They awaken a sense of finer feelings than the commerce of ordinary life inspires. Many a young woman has caught from such works as *Clarissa* or *Cecilia*, ideas of delicacy and refinement which were not, perhaps, to be gained in any society she could have access to.[2] Many a maxim of prudence is laid up in the memory from these stores, ready to operate when occasion offers.

The passion of love, the most seductive of all the passions, they certainly paint too high, and represent its influence beyond what it will be found to be in real life; but if they soften the heart they also refine it. They mix with the natural passions of our nature all that

2. *Clarissa; or, the History of a Young Lady* (1748) by Samuel Richardson (1689–1761) and *Cecilia; or, Memoirs of an Heiress* (1782) by Frances Burney. The equivalence Barbauld draws between these two novels and novelists is notable.

is tender in virtuous affection; all that is estimable in high principle and unshaken constancy; all that grace, delicacy, and sentiment can bestow of touching and attractive. Benevolence and sensibility to distress are almost always insisted on in modern works of this kind; and perhaps it is not too much to say, that much of the softness of our present manners, much of that tincture of humanity so conspicuous amidst all our vices, is owing to the bias given by our dramatic writings and fictitious stories. A high regard to female honour, generosity, and a spirit of self-sacrifice, are strongly inculcated. It costs nothing, it is true, to an author to make his hero generous, and very often he is extravagantly so; still, sentiments of this kind serve in some measure to counteract the spirit of the world, where selfish considerations have always more than their due weight. * * *

But not only those splendid sentiments with which, when properly presented, our feelings readily take part, and kindle as we read; the more severe and homely virtues of prudence and oeconomy have been enforced in the writings of a Burney and an Edgeworth.[3] Writers of their good sense have observed, that while these compositions cherished even a romantic degree of sensibility, the duties that have less brilliancy to recommend them were neglected. * * * When works of fancy are thus made subservient to the improvement of the rising generation, they certainly stand on a higher ground than mere entertainment, and we revere while we admire.

Some knowledge of the world is also gained by these writings, imperfect indeed, but attained with more ease, and attended with less danger, than by mixing in real life. If the stage is a mirror of life, so is the novel, and perhaps a more accurate one, as less is sacrificed to effect and representation. There are many descriptions of characters in the busy world, which a young woman in the retired scenes of life hardly meets with at all, and many whom it is safer to read of than to meet; and to either sex it must be desirable that the first impressions of fraud, selfishness, profligacy and perfidy should be connected, as in good novels they always will be, with infamy and ruin. At any rate, it is safer to meet with a bad character in the pages of a fictitious story, than in the polluted walks of life; but an author solicitous for the morals of his readers will be sparing in the introduction of such characters. * * *

* * *

Love is a passion particularly exaggerated in novels. It forms the chief interest of, by far, the greater part of them. In order to increase this interest, a false idea is given of the importance of the passion. It

3. Maria Edgeworth (1768–1849), Irish novelist who, like Barbauld, also wrote literature for children.

occupies the serious hours of life; events all hinge upon it; every thing gives way to its influence, and no length of time wears it out. When a young lady, having imbibed these notions, comes into the world, she finds that this formidable passion acts a very subordinate part on the great theatre of the world; that its vivid sensations are mostly limited to a very early period; and that it is by no means, as the poet sings,

> "All the colour of remaining life."[4]

* * * Least of all will a course of novels prepare a young lady for the neglect and tedium of life which she is perhaps doomed to encounter. If the novels she reads are virtuous, she has learned how to arm herself with proper reserve against the ardour of her lover; she has been instructed how to behave with the utmost propriety when run away with, like Miss Byron, or locked up by a cruel parent, like Clarissa; but she is not prepared for indifference and neglect.[5] Though young and beautiful, she may see her youth and beauty pass away without conquests, and the monotony of her life will be apt to appear more insipid when contrasted with scenes of perpetual courtship and passion.

* * *

CHARLOTTE DACRE

Charlotte Dacre (1771/72–1825) was an English poet and novelist, author of the gothic novel *Zofloya, or the Moor* (1806). Her two-volume *Hours of Solitude*, published in 1805, included graveyard poems from *Trifles of Helicon* (1798), written with her sister Sophia.

L'Absence[†]

Hast thou not seen the blooming rose
Turn to the God of day?
Her fragrant treasures all disclose,
Enchanted by his ray?

Hast thou not seen the sun decline!   5
Her bloomy beauty fade;

---

4. From *Solomon on the Vanity of the World* (1718), a poem in three books by Matthew Prior (1664–1721). The passage reads: "Love— / Love? why 'tis Joy or Sorrow, Peace or Strife: / 'Tis all the Colour of remaining Life" (lines 233–35).
5. Heroines in Richardson novels. Miss Harriet Byron appears in *The History of Charles Grandison* (1753).
† From *Hours of Solitude*, vol. 2 (London: D. N. Shury, 1805), pp. 68–69.

And joyless of his warmth divine,
Soon perish in the shade?

How say'st thou, love? thy bosom glows,
Bereft of *thee*, I fade; 10
My vanish'd sun—thy drooping rose
Will perish in the shade.

Thou art my sun—thou art my dew,
Spirit by which I live!
Come swift then, and a life renew, 15
To which thou *soul* cans't give!

We Can Love but Once†

TRUANT! You love me not—the reason this,
You told me that you lov'd a maid before;
And tho', perchance, you many more may kiss,
True love, felt *once*, can never be felt *more*.
Then ask not me to credit what you swore, 5
Nor e'er believe that I can give you bliss;
Go, go to her who taught you how to love—
Repeat to *her* your vows, and not to me;
For sooth I think, who can inconstant prove
To his *first* love, will ever faithless be. 10
In gaining wayward hearts no pride I see,
Nor have I pride in kindling in the breast
That *meteor* flame, call'd passion—no not I;
The *heart* I aim at, and of that possess'd,
Make it my castle, and all arts defy, 15
For that once fill'd—no longer roves the eye.

Peace‡1

RETURN, sweet Peace, and shed thy glories round,
And spread thy fair wings o'er a troubled isle;
No more let carnage stain the fruitful ground,

---

† From *Hours of Solitude*, vol. 2 (London: D. N. Shury, 1805), p. 81.
‡ From *Hours of Solitude*, vol. 2 (London: D. N. Shury, 1805), pp. 118–19.
1. This poem and its companion, "War," appear in an appendix. The volume also contains the poem "The Warrior," whose epigraph dedicates it to "a Young Gentleman, who, entering under the banners of Mars, signalized himself in the service of his country," concluding, "the authoress of these pages addressed to him the subsequent Ode in the year 1802, since which he unfortunately fell a martyr to his too enthusiastic courage and thirst for distinction, in the memorable engagement in Egypt, which proved the awful mausoleum of so many heroes" (p. 75).

And blood the works of Heaven's hand defile.
Shall Discord drive thee, mild-ey'd nymph, away?   5
A Faction strike thee with its ruthless hand?
Shall Havoc mock thee on the crimson'd way,
Confusion reign, and Ruin grinning stand?
Shall Famine point its all-consuming sword?
And Misery reach the sunny cottage door?   10
Shall naught remain to deck the frugal board,
Or bless the humble offspring of the poor?
Must the sad widow weep her loss in vain?
The little orphan vainly ask for bread?
Yet still shall strife and sanction'd murder reign,   15
And scalding tears be still unheeded shed?

JOHN BICKNELL AND THOMAS DAY

John Bicknell (1746–1787) and Thomas Day (1748–1789) were prominent English writers and abolitionists. The first edition of the poem,
published in 1773, was titled *The Dying Negro, a poetical epistle, supposed to be written by a black, (who lately shot himself on board a vessel
in the river Thames;) to his intended wife*. In the second, expanded and
revised edition (1774), Day added the dedication to Jean-Jacques Rousseau (1712–1778), Genevan philosopher who condemned the abstract
concept of slavery in *The Social Contract; or, the Principles of Political
Right* (1762). The poem's footnotes contain references to works depict-
ing European travel to West Africa, including *A New Voyage to Guinea*
(1774) by William Smith, an English surveyor working for the Royal
African Company, and *Description of the Coasts of North and South
Guinea* (1732), a largely plagiarized work by Jean Barbot, a French
Huguenot employed by the Compagnie du Sénégal.

From The Dying Negro†

Advertisement

THE *following* POEM *was occasioned by a fact which had recently
happened at the time of its first publication in 1773.*[1] *A Negro, belonging*

---

† From *The Dying Negro: a Poem*, 3rd ed. (London: W. Flexney, 1775), pp. ii, v–vii, 1–3,
   4–6, 7–8, 21–22. Unless otherwise indicated, notes are by the editor of this Norton
   Critical Edition.
1. The poem's subject concerns a story reportedly published in May 1773—in the *Morning
   Chronicle and London Advertiser, the General Evening Post*, and *Lloyd's Evening Post*—
   concerning the suicide of a West Indian man refused the right to marry a white British
   woman and facing reenslavement. In January of that year, enslaved persons held aboard
   the *New Britannia* blew up the ship on the Gambian River, killing everyone on board in
   a mass suicide. The legal argument the poem makes involves the 1772 case *Somerset v.
   Stewart*, brought by the English abolitionist Granville Sharpe (1735–1813). Its outcome

to the Captain of a West-Indiaman, having agreed to marry a white woman, his fellow-servant, in order to effect his purpose, had left his master's house, and procured himself to be baptized; but being detected and taken, he was sent on board the Captain's vessel then lying in the River; where, finding no chance of escaping, and preferring death to another voyage to America, he took an opportunity of shooting himself. As soon as his determination is fixed, he is supposed to write this Epistle to his intended Wife.

Dedication

* * * Happy should I esteem myself could these feeble efforts once more awaken that irresistible eloquence [of Jean-Jacques Rousseau], which was never prostituted to falsehood, or denied to truth; those talents of reasoning and investigation, which can never fail to convince the mind, that it is not debased by voluntary and incorrigible error; and that virtuous enthusiasm, which seems inspired by Heaven itself for the instruction of its creatures. How should I rejoice to see a cause like this rescued from my weak pen; to see the rights of humanity vindicated by him, who most intimately feels their force, and is most capable of expressing what he feels; to see that insolence, that successful avarice confounded, which, under the mask of commerce, has already ravaged the two extremities of the globe!— Astonish and instruct posterity by the dreadful spectacle of human crimes; and while you represent in one quarter of the world a band of insatiable wretches, spreading unprovoked desolation over its most beautiful regions; massacring the Bramin in the midst of his uncontaminated feasts, and staining with blood the purest altars of the Deity; let the other exhibit a race of Christian merchants, daily trafficking for hecatombs of their fellow-creatures in a lot; exhausting Africa to supply with slaves the countries they have depopulated in America;[2] and annually reducing millions to a state of misery still more dreadful than death itself.—Should there be room for scenes less striking, though equally instructive and important, let your enchanting pencil exhibit a nation renowned for arts and arms; let the surrounding ocean be covered with her fleets; and let her boast an inflexible sternness, and an unconquerable valour. Paint a savage and gloomy liberty exulting amidst the shock of foreign invasions and domestic tumults: let her wield a bloody ax, and trample alike on the mitre and the diadem: let superstition and civil war conspire to exalt her, until she has triumphed over opposition, and erected a

---

became known as the Mansfield Decision, which upheld the use of habeus corpus in making illegal the capture and forced transportation of fugitive enslaved persons.

2. In the single island of Jamaica above 60,000 of the natives are computed to have been cruelly exterminated by the first European settlers there [*Bicknell and Day's note*].

temple, whose foundations appear durable, as the world itself. Beneath a milder sky let peace introduce the genius and arts which adorned the states of Athens and of Rome, without insuring their duration: let gentler manners, and a less ferocious dignity succeed; let philosophy and science glory in a race of illustrious disciples, whose labours may dispel the gloom of fanaticism, and teach mankind whatever the Almighty has permitted them to know.—Here, while the delighted eye of presumption gazes with rapture, and pronounces the tablet perfect and eternal,—reverse the scene, and inscribe the mortifying lesson of human imbecility. Introduce commerce and prosperity spreading over the land, and enervating the minds of men with a secret, but swift infection. Let avarice and sensuality succeed to honor; faction and servitude invade the asylum of liberty; and manly reason, like a fettered lion, be dragged in triumph by fashion and caprice.—Such are the scenes I would present to my countrymen, could I boast an eloquence like your's, to explain the eternal principles which providence has decreed, shall influence the fate of nations; the causes which exalt them to security and dominion, or plunge them into that abyss of baseness and corruption, from whence they can no more emerge: such are the lessons for which you have been proscribed and persecuted by a world which you have enlightened. * * *

*   *   *

ARM'D with thy sad last gift—the pow'r to die,
Thy shafts, stern fortune, now I can defy;
Thy dreadful mercy points at length the shore,
Where all is peace, and men are slaves no more;
—This weapon, ev'n in chains, the brave can wield,   5
And vanquish'd, quit triumphantly the field:
—Beneath such wrongs let pallid Christians live,
Such they can perpetrate, and may forgive.

    Yet while I tread that gulph's tremendous brink,
Where nature shudders, and where beings sink,   10
Ere yet this hand a life of torment close,
And end by one determin'd stroke my woes,
Is there a fond regret, which moves my mind
To pause, and cast a ling'ring look behind?
—O my lov'd bride!—for I have call'd thee mine,   15
Dearer than life, whom I with life resign,
For thee ev'n here this faithful heart shall glow,
A pang shall rend me, and a tear shall flow.—
How shall I soothe thy grief, since fate denies
Thy pious duties to my closing eyes?   20

I cannot clasp thee in a last embrace,
Nor gaze in silent anguish on thy face;
I cannot raise these fetter'd arms for thee,
To ask that mercy heav'n denies to me;
Yet let thy tender breast my sorrows share,   25
Bleed for my wounds, and feel my deep despair.
Yet let thy tears bedew a wretch's grave,
Whom fate forbade thy tenderness to save.
Receive these sighs—to thee my soul I breathe——
Fond love in dying groans is all I can bequeathe.   30

   Why did I, slave, beyond my lot aspire?
Why didst thou fan the inauspicious fire?
For thee I bade my drooping soul revive;
For thee alone I could have borne to live;
And love, I said, shall make me large amends,   35
For persecuting foes, and faithless friends:
Fool that I was! enur'd so long to pain,
To trust to hope, or dream of joy again.

                    *   *   *

   And better in th'untimely grave to rot,
The world and all its cruelties forgot,   60
Than, dragg'd once more beyond the Western main,
To groan beneath some dastard planter's chain,
Where my poor countrymen in bondage wait
The slow enfranchisement of ling'ring fate.
Oh! my heart sinks, my dying eyes o'erflow,   65
When mem'ry paints the picture of their woe!
For I have seen them, ere the dawn of day,
Rouz'd by the lash, begin their chearless way;
Greeting with groans unwelcome morn's return,
While rage and shame their gloomy bosoms burn;   70
And, chiding ev'ry hour the slow-pac'd sun,
Endure their toils 'till all his race was run;
No eye to mark their suff'rings with a tear,
No friend to comfort, and no hope to chear;
Then like the dull unpitied brutes repair   75
To stalls as wretched, and as coarse a fare;
Thank heav'n one day of misery was o'er,
And sink to sleep, and wish to wake no more.—
Sleep on! ye lost companions of my woes,
For whom in death this tear of pity flows;   80
Sleep, and enjoy the only boon of heav'n
To you in common with your tyrants giv'n!
O while soft slumber from their couches flies,

Still may the balmy blessing steep your eyes;
In sweet oblivion lull awhile your woes,   85
And brightest visions gladden the repose!
Let fancy then, unconscious of the change,
Thro' our own fields, and native forests range;
Waft ye to each once-haunted stream and grove,
And visit ev'ry long-lost scene ye love!   90

—I sleep no more—nor in the midnight shade,
Invoke ideal phantoms to my aid;
Nor wake again, abandon'd and forlorn,
To find each dear delusion fled at morn;
A slow-consuming death let others wait,   95
I snatch destruction from unwilling fate:—
Yon ruddy streaks the rising sun proclaim,
That never more shall beam upon my shame;
Bright orb! for others let thy glory shine,
Mature the golden grain and purple vine,   100
While fetter'd Afric still for Europe toils,
And Nature's plund'rers riot on her spoils;
Be theirs the gifts thy partial rays supply,
Be mine the gloomy privilege to die.

                      *   *   *

In vain Heav'n spread so wide the swelling sea,   125
Vast wat'ry barrier, 'twixt thy world and me;
Swift round the globe, by earth nor Heav'n controul'd,
Fly stern oppression, and dire lust of gold.
Where-e'er the hell-hounds mark their bloody way,
Still nature groans, and man becomes their prey.   130
In the wild wastes of Afric's sandy plain,
Where roars the lion thro' his drear domain,
To curb the savage monarch in the chace,
There too Heav'n planted Man's majestic race;
Bade Reason's sons with nobler titles rise,   135
Lift high their brow sublime, and scan the skies.
What tho' the sun in his meridian blaze
Dart on their naked limbs his scorching rays?
What tho' no rosy tints adorn their face,
No silken tresses shine with flowing grace?   140
Yet of ethereal temper are their souls,
And in their veins the tide of honour rolls;
And valour kindles there the hero's flame,
Contempt of death, and thirst of martial fame:
And pity melts the sympathising breast,   145
Ah! fatal virtue!—for the brave distrest.

*   *   *

When crimes like these thy injur'd pow'r prophane,   370
O God of Nature! art thou call'd in vain?
Did'st thou for this sustain a mortal wound,
While Heav'n, and Earth, and Hell, hung trembling round?
That these vile fetters might my body bind,
And agony like this distract my mind?   375
On thee I call'd with reverential awe,
Ador'd thy wisdom, and embrac'd thy law;
Yet mark thy destin'd convert as he lies,
His groans of anguish, and his livid eyes,
These galling chains, polluted with his blood,   380
Then bid his tongue proclaim thee just and good!
But if too weak thy vaunted power to spare,
Or suff'rings move thee not, O hear despair!
Thy hopes and blessings I alike resign,
But let revenge, let swift revenge be mine!   385
Be this proud bark, which now triumphant rides,
Toss'd by the winds, and shatter'd by the tides!
And may these fiends, who now exulting view
The horrors of my fortune, feel them too!
Be theirs the torment of a ling'ring fate,   390
Slow as thy justice, dreadful as my hate;
Condemn'd to grasp the riven plank in vain,
And chac'd by all the monsters of the main;
And while they spread their sinking arms to thee,
Then let their fainting souls remember me!   395

*   *   *

OLAUDAH EQUIANO

Olaudah Equiano (1745–1797) was born in Nigeria and enslaved as a child. Near the start of his memoir, *The Interesting Narrative of the Life of Olaudah Equiano* (1789), he describes being sold to Michael Henry Pascal, lieutenant of the British Royal Navy, then commander of a trade ship, who gave Equiano the name Gustavus Vassa. After purchasing his freedom in 1766, Equiano gained fame as an author, orator, and abolitionist. His memoir sold well, with nine editions published in his lifetime.

From The Interesting Narrative of the Life of Olaudah Equiano[†]

Chapter 6[1]

Some account of Brimstone-Hill in Montserrat—Favourable change in the author's situation—He commences merchant with three pence—His various success in dealing in the different islands, and America, and the impositions he meets with in his transactions with Europeans—A curious imposition on human nature—Danger of the surfs in the West Indies—Remarkable instance of kidnapping a free mulatto—The author is nearly murdered by Doctor Perkins in Savannah.

In the preceding chapter I have set before the reader a few of those many instances of oppression, extortion, and cruelty, which I have been a witness to in the West Indies: but, were I to enumerate them all, the catalogue would be tedious and disgusting. The punishments of the slaves on every trifling occasion are so frequent, and so well known together with the different instruments with which they are tortured, that it cannot any longer afford novelty to recite them; and they are too shocking to yield delight either to the writer or the reader. I shall therefore hereafter only mention such as incidentally befel myself in the course of my adventures.

In the variety of departments in which I was employed by my master, I had an opportunity of seeing many curious scenes in different islands; but, above all, I was struck with a celebrated curiosity called Brimstone-Hill, which is a high and steep mountain, some few miles from the town of Plymouth in Montserrat.[2] I had often heard of some wonders that were to be seen on this hill, and I went once with some white and black people to visit it. When we arrived at the top, I saw under different cliffs great flakes of brimstone, occasioned by the steams of various little ponds, which were then boiling naturally in the earth. Some of these ponds were as white as milk, some quite blue, and many others of different colours. I had taken some potatoes with me, and I put them into different ponds, and in a few minutes they were well boiled. I tasted some of them, but they were very

---

[†] From *The Interesting Narrative of the Life of Olaudah Equiano, or Gustavus Vassa, the African*, vol. 1 (London: T. Wilkins, 1789), pp. 228–74.

1. This is the final chapter of vol. 1. Preceding chapters describe Equiano's enslavement, his travel from Africa through the Caribbean to the Virginia colony and to England, and his many experiences aboard the ships on which he traveled.

2. Part of the Leeward Islands in the West Indies and the site of a failed rebellion by enslaved persons in 1768. Now a British Overseas Territory, the island at the time of Equiano's writing was heavily populated by Irish settlers, many of whom held political sympathies with France.

sulphurous; and the silver shoe buckles, and all the other things of that metal we had among us, were, in a little time, turned as black as lead.

Some time in the year 1763, kind Providence seemed to appear rather more favourable to me. One of my master's vessels, a Bermudas sloop, about sixty tons burthen was commanded by one Captain Thomas Farmer, an Englishman, a very alert and active man, who gained my master a great deal of money by his good management in carrying passengers from one island to another; but very often his sailors used to get drunk and run away from the vessel, which hindered him in his business very much. This man had taken a liking to me; and many different times begged of my master to let me go a trip with him as a sailor; but he would tell him he could not spare me, though the vessel sometimes could not go for want of hands, for sailors were generally very scarce in the island. However, at last, from necessity or force, my master was prevailed on, though very reluctantly, to let me go with this captain; but he gave him great charge to take care that I did not run away, for if I did he would make him pay for me. This being the case, the captain had for some time a sharp eye upon me whenever the vessel anchored; and as soon as she returned I was sent for on shore again. Thus was I slaving as it were for life, sometimes at one thing, and sometimes at another; so that the captain and I were nearly the most useful men in my master's employment. I also became so useful to the captain on shipboard, that many times, when he used to ask for me to go with him, though it should be but for twenty-four hours, to some of the islands near us, my master would answer he could not spare me, at which the captain would swear, and would not go the trip; and tell my master I was better to him on board than any three white men he had; for they used to behave ill in many respects, particularly in getting drunk; and then they frequently got the boat stove, so as to hinder the vessel from coming back as soon as she might have done. This my master knew very well; and at last, by the captain's constant entreaties, after I had been several times with him, one day to my great joy, told me the captain would not let him rest, and asked me whether I would go aboard as a sailor, or stay on shore and mind the stores, for he could not bear any longer to be plagued in this manner. I was very happy at this proposal, for I immediately thought I might in time stand some chance by being on board to get a little money, or possibly make my escape if I should be used ill: I also expected to get better food, and in greater abundance; for I had oftentimes felt much hunger, though my master treated his slaves, as I have observed, uncommonly well. I therefore, without hesitation, answered him, that I would go and be a sailor if he pleased. Accordingly I was ordered on board directly. Nevertheless, between the vessel and the shore, when she was in port, I had little or no rest, as my master always wished to have me along with him. Indeed he was a very pleasant gentleman, and but for my expectations on shipboard I should not have thought of leaving him. But the captain liked me also very much, and I was entirely his right-hand man. I did all I could to deserve his favour, and in return I received better treatment from him than any other I believe ever met with in the West Indies in my situation.

After I had been sailing for some time with this captain, at length I endeavoured to try my luck and commence merchant. I had but a very small capital to begin with; for one single half bit, which is equal to three pence in England, made up my whole stock. However I trusted to the Lord to be with me; and at one of our trips to St. Eustatia, a Dutch island,[3] I bought a glass tumbler with my half bit, and when I came to Montserrat I sold it for a bit, or sixpence. Luckily we made several successive trips to St. Eustatia (which was a general mart for the West Indies, about twenty leagues from Montserrat)[4] and in our next, finding my tumbler so profitable, with this one bit I bought two tumblers more; and when I came back I sold them for two bits equal to a shilling sterling. When we went again I bought with these two bits four more of these glasses, which I sold for four bits on our return to Montserrat; and in our next voyage to St. Eustatia, I bought two glasses with one bit, and with the other three I bought a jug of Geneva, nearly about three pints in measure. When we came to Montserrat, I sold the gin for eight bits, and the tumblers for two, so that my capital now amounted in all to a dollar, well husbanded and acquired in the space of a month or six weeks, when I blessed the Lord that I was so rich. As we sailed to different islands, I laid this money out in various things occasionally, and it used to turn to very good account, especially when we went to Guadaloupe, Grenada,[5] and the rest of the French islands. Thus was I going all

3. St. Eustatius, small island in the northern part of the Lesser Antilles. During the 1600s and 1700s, the island changed hands twenty-two times during constant conflict between the Dutch, English, and French. During the American War of Independence, most American guns and gunpowder were purchased in St. Eustatius, and all correspondence and mail to Europe from the colonies passed through the island.
4. For an account of the February 1781 arrival in St. Eustatius of the British admiral George Brydges Rodney (1718–1792), see Victor Enthoven, "'That Abominable Nest of Pirates': St. Eustatius and the North Americans, 1680–1780," Early American Studies 10.2 (2012): 239–301. Enthoven notes that, for crews aboard the twelve English merchant ships unloading their cargoes on his arrival, "it could not have been far from their thoughts that the seizure of their own vessels and impressment into Her Majesty's navy would follow in short order" (240). Rodney deported the island's Jewish residents, an action criticized by Edmund Burke (1729–1797). Rodney's account of the island's vast riches is echoed by many throughout the period: "beyond all comprehension," he wrote, "one hundred and thirty sail ships in the road," besides the navy vessels. Enthoven adds that, "[a]ll together, the value of the loot was estimated by sober authorities at more than three million pounds sterling" (241).
5. Through her brothers Austen had connections to both of these locations. As Sheila Johnson Kindred notes, John Shortland (1769–1810), a British naval captain who worked with Charles Austen in 1808–09, died on Guadaloupe after a skirmish with

about the islands upwards of four years, and ever trading as I went, during which I experienced many instances of ill usage, and have seen many injuries done to other negroes in our dealings with whites: and, amidst our recreations, when we have been dancing and merry-making, they, without cause, have molested and insulted us. Indeed I was more than once obliged to look up to God on high, as I had advised the poor fisherman some time before. And I had not been long trading for myself in the manner I have related above, when I experienced the like trial in company with him as follows: This man being used to the water, was upon an emergency put on board of us by his master to work as another hand, on a voyage to Santa Cruz; and at our sailing he had brought his little all for a venture, which consisted of six bits' worth of limes and oranges in a bag; I had also my whole stock, which was about twelve bits' worth of the same kind of goods, separate in two bags; for we had heard these fruits sold well in that island. When we came there, in some little convenient time he and I went ashore with our fruits to sell them; but we had scarcely landed when we were met by two white men, who presently took our three bags from us. We could not at first guess what they meant to do; and for some time we thought they were jesting with us; but they too soon let us know otherwise, for they took our ventures immediately to a house hard by, and adjoining the fort, while we followed all the way begging of them to give us our fruits, but in vain. They not only refused to return them, but swore at us, and threatened if we did not immediately depart they would flog us well. We told them these three bags were all we were worth in the world, and that we brought them with us to sell when we came from Montserrat, and shewed them the vessel. But this was rather against us, as they now saw we were strangers as well as slaves. They still therefore swore, and desired us to be gone, and even took sticks to beat us; while we, seeing they meant what they said, went off in the greatest confusion and despair. Thus, in the very minute of gaining more by three times than I ever did by any venture in my life before, was I deprived of every farthing I was worth. An insupportable misfortune! but how to help ourselves we knew not. In our consternation we went to the commanding officer of the fort, and told him how we had been served by some of his people; but we obtained not the least redress: he answered our complaints only by a volley of

---

the French involving his first frigate, HMS *Junon*. (See *Jane Austen's Naval World*, sheilajohnsonkindred.com.) General Edward Mathew (1729–1805), who fought as a British colonel in the American War of Independence and served as commander-in-chief of the West Indies and governor of Grenada beginning in 1782, was also father-in-law to Jane Austen's clergyman brother, James (1765–1819), who was briefly married to Mathew's daughter Anne, who died in 1785. Mathew purchased for his son-in-law the higher-salaried rank of chaplain in the 86th Regiment and was instrumental in the Austen brothers' naval advancements.

imprecations against us, and immediately took a horse-whip, in order to chastise us, so that we were obliged to turn out much faster than we came in. I now, in the agony of distress and indignation, wished that the ire of God in his forked lightning might transfix these cruel oppressors among the dead. Still however we persevered; went back again to the house, and begged and besought them again and again for our fruits, till at last some other people that were in the house asked if we would be contented if they kept one bag and gave us the other two. We, seeing no remedy whatever, consented to this; and they, observing one bag to have both kinds of fruit in it, which belonged to my companion, kept that; and the other two, which were mine, they gave us back. As soon as I got them, I ran as fast as I could, and got the first negro man I could to help me off; my companion, however, stayed a little longer to plead; he told them the bag they had was his, and likewise all that he was worth in the world; but this was of no avail, and he was obliged to return without it. The poor old man, wringing his hands, cried bitterly for his loss; and, indeed, he then did look up to God on high, which so moved me with pity for him, that I gave him nearly one third of my fruits. We then proceeded to the markets to sell them; and Providence was more favourable to us than we could have expected, for we sold our fruits uncommonly well; I got for mine about thirty-seven bits. Such a surprising reverse of fortune in so short a space of time seemed like a dream, and proved no small encouragement for me to trust the Lord in any situation. My captain afterwards frequently used to take my part, and get me my right, when I have been plundered or used ill by these tender Christian depredators; among whom I have shuddered to observe the unceasing blasphemous execrations which are wantonly thrown out by persons of all ages and conditions, not only without occasion, but even as if they were indulgences and pleasure.

At one of our trips to St. Kitt's I had eleven bits of my own; and my friendly captain lent me five more, with which I bought a Bible. I was very glad to get this book, which I scarcely could meet with any where. I think there was none sold in Montserrat; and, much to my grief, from being forced out of the Ætna in the manner I have related, my Bible, and the Guide to the Indians, the two books I loved above all others, were left behind.[6]

While I was in this place, St. Kitt's, a very curious imposition on human nature took place:—A white man wanted to marry in the church a free black woman that had land and slaves in Montserrat: but the clergyman told him it was against the law of the place to

6. Equiano writes in his *Narrative* that it was aboard the *Ætna* that the captain's clerk taught him to write along with basic arithmetic, and where he met Daniel Queen, a man who befriended and educated him and about whom Equiano writes, "I almost loved him with the affection of a son." In February 1763, rather than being allowed to return with the ship to England, Equiano was sold in Montserrat to a Philadelphia Quaker merchant named Robert King.

marry a white and a black in the church. The man then asked to be married on the water, to which the parson consented, and the two lovers went in one boat, and the parson and clerk in another, and thus the ceremony was performed. After this the loving pair came on board our vessel, and my captain treated them extremely well, and brought them safe to Montserrat.

The reader cannot but judge of the irksomeness of this situation to a mind like mine, in being daily exposed to new hardships and impositions, after having seen many better days, and having been as it were in a state of freedom and plenty; added to which, every part of the world I had hitherto been in seemed to me a paradise in comparison of the West Indies. My mind was therefore hourly replete with inventions and thoughts of being freed, and, if possible, by honest and honourable means; for I always remembered the old adage; and I trust it has ever been my ruling principle, that "Honesty is the best policy;" and likewise that other golden precept—"To do unto all men as I would they should do unto me." However, as I was from early years a predestinarian, I thought whatever fate had determined must ever come to pass; and therefore, if ever it were my lot to be freed nothing could prevent me, although I should at present see no means or hope to obtain my freedom; on the other hand, if it were my fate not to be freed I never should be so, and all my endeavours for that purpose would be fruitless. In the midst of these thoughts I therefore looked up with prayers anxiously to God for my liberty; and at the same time used every honest means, and did all that was possible on my part to obtain it. In process of time I became master of a few pounds, and in a fair way of making more, which my friendly captain knew very well; this occasioned him sometimes to take liberties with me; but whenever he treated me waspishly I used plainly to tell him my mind, and that I would die before I would be imposed on as other negroes were, and that to me life had lost its relish when liberty was gone. This I said although I foresaw my then well-being or future hopes of freedom (humanly speaking) depended on this man. However, as he could not bear the thoughts of my not sailing with him, he always became mild on my threats. I therefore continued with him; and, from my great attention to his orders and his business, I gained him credit, and through his kindness to me I at last procured my liberty. While I thus went on, filled with the thoughts of freedom, and resisting oppression as well as I was able, my life hung daily in suspense, particularly in the surfs I have formerly mentioned, as I could not swim. These are extremely violent throughout the West Indies, and I was ever exposed to their howling rage and devouring fury in all the islands. I have seen them strike and toss a boat right up an end, and maim several on board. Once in the Grenada islands, when I and about eight others were pulling

a large boat with two puncheons[7] of water in it, a surf struck us, and
drove the boat and all in it about half a stone's throw, among some
trees, and above the high water mark. We were obliged to get all the
assistance we could from the nearest estate to mend the boat, and
launch it into the water again. At Montserrat one night, in pressing
hard to get off the shore on board, the punt[8] was overset with us
four times; the first time I was very near being drowned; however
the jacket I had on kept me up above water a little space of time,
while I called on a man near me who was a good swimmer, and told
him I could not swim; he then made haste to me, and, just as I was
sinking, he caught hold of me, and brought me to sounding, and
then he went and brought the punt also. As soon as we had turned
the water out of her, lest we should be used ill for being absent, we
attempted again three times more, and as often the horrid surfs
served us as at first; but at last, the fifth time we attempted, we
gained our point, at the eminent hazard of our lives. One day also,
at Old Road in Montserrat, our captain, and three men besides
myself, were going in a large canoe in quest of rum and sugar, when
a single surf tossed the canoe an amazing distance from the water,
and some of us near a stone's throw from each other: most of us were
very much bruised; so that I and many more often said, and really
thought, that there was not such another place under the heavens
as this. I longed therefore much to leave it, and daily wished to see
my master's promise performed of going to Philadelphia.

While we lay in this place a very cruel thing happened on board
of our sloop which filled me with horror; though I found afterwards
such practices were frequent. There was a very clever and decent
free young mulatto-man who sailed a long time with us: he had a
free woman for his wife, by whom he had a child; and she was then
living on shore, and all very happy. Our captain and mate, and other
people on board, and several elsewhere, even the natives of Bermudas, all knew this young man from a child that he was always free,
and no one had ever claimed him as their property: however, as
might too often overcomes right in these parts, it happened that a
Bermudas captain, whose vessel lay there for a few days in the road,
came on board of us, and seeing the mulatto-man, whose name was
Joseph Clipson, he told him he was not free, and that he had orders
from his master to bring him to Bermudas. The poor man could not
believe the captain to be in earnest; but he was very soon undeceived,
his men laying violent hands on him; and although he shewed a cer-
tificate of his being born free in St. Kitt's, and most people on board
knew that he served his time to boat building, and always passed

7. Barrels or casks, often containing West Indian spirits like rum.
8. Small, flat-bottomed boat used in shallow water.

for a free man, yet he was taken forcibly out of our vessel. He then asked to be carried ashore before the secretary or magistrates, and these infernal invaders of human rights promised him he should; but, instead of that, they carried him on board of the other vessel: and the next day, without giving the poor man any hearing on shore, or suffering him even to see his wife or child, he was carried away, and probably doomed never more in this world to see them again. Nor was this the only instance of this kind of barbarity I was a witness to. I have since often seen in Jamaica and other islands, free men, whom I have known in America, thus villainously trepanned and held in bondage. I have heard of two similar practices even in Philadelphia: and were it not for the benevolence of the quakers in that city, many of the sable race, who now breathe the air of liberty, would, I believe, be groaning indeed under some planter's chains. These things opened my mind to a new scene of horror to which I had been before a stranger. Hitherto I had thought only slavery dreadful; but the state of a free negro appeared to me now equally so at least, and in some respects even worse, for they live in constant alarm for their liberty; which is but nominal, for they are universally insulted and plundered without the possibility of redress; for such is the equity of the West Indian laws, that no free negro's evidence will be admitted in their courts of justice. In this situation is it surprising that slaves, when mildly treated, should prefer even the misery of slavery to such a mockery of freedom? I was now completely disgusted with the West Indies, and thought I never should be entirely free until I had left them.

> "With thoughts like these my anxious boding mind
> Recall'd those pleasing scenes I left behind;
> Scenes where fair Liberty in bright array
> Makes darkness bright, and e'en illumines day;
> Where nor complexion, wealth, or station, can
> Protect the wretch who makes a slave of man."[9]

9. Compare these lines to those in Byron's *The Corsair* (1814), included in this volume, and to "Ode to the Nightingale" by English poet Mary Darby Robinson (1758–1800):

> When to my downy couch remov'd,
> FANCY recall'd my wearied mind
> To scenes of FRIENDSHIP left behind,
> Scenes still regretted, still belov'd!
> Ah, then I felt the pangs of Grief,
> Grasp my warm Heart, and mock relief;
> My burning lids Sleep's balm defied,
> And on my fev'rish lip imperfect murmurs died.
> Restless and sad—I sought once more
> A calm retreat on BRITAIN's shore;
> Deceitful HOPE, e'en there I found
> That soothing FRIENDSHIP's specious name
> Was but a short-liv'd empty sound,
> and LOVE a false delusive flame.

In Mary Darby Robinson, *Poems* (J. Bell, 1791), p. 31.

I determined to make every exertion to obtain my freedom, and to return to Old England. For this purpose I thought a knowledge of navigation might be of use to me; for, though I did not intend to run away unless I should be ill used, yet, in such a case, if I understood navigation, I might attempt my escape in our sloop, which was one of the swiftest sailing vessels in the West Indies, and I could be at no loss for hands to join me: and if I should make this attempt, I had intended to have gone for England; but this, as I said, was only to be in the event of my meeting with any ill usage. I therefore employed the mate of our vessel to teach me navigation, for which I agreed to give him twenty-four dollars, and actually paid him part of the money down; though when the captain, some time after, came to know that the mate was to have such a sum for teaching me, he rebuked him, and said it was a shame for him to take any money from me. However, my progress in this useful art was much retarded by the constancy of our work. Had I wished to run away I did not want opportunities, which frequently presented themselves; and particularly at one time, soon after this. When we were at the island of Guadeloupe there was a large fleet of merchantmen bound for Old France; and, seamen then being very scarce, they gave from fifteen to twenty pounds a man for the run. Our mate, and all the white sailors, left our vessel on this account, and went on board of the French ships. They would have had me also to go with them, for they regarded me; and they swore to protect me, if I would go: and, as the fleet was to sail the next day, I really believe I could have got safe to Europe at that time. However, as my master was kind, I would not attempt to leave him; and, remembering the old maxim, that "honesty is the best policy," I suffered them to go without me. Indeed my captain was much afraid of my leaving him and the vessel at that time, as I had so fair an opportunity: but, I thank God, this fidelity of mine turned out much to my advantage hereafter, when I did not in the least think of it; and made me so much in favour with the captain, that he used now and then to teach me some parts of navigation himself: but some of our passengers, and others, seeing this, found much fault with him for it, saying it was a very dangerous thing to let a negro know navigation; thus I was hindered again in my pursuits. About the latter end of the year 1764, my master bought a larger sloop, called the Prudence, about seventy or eighty tons, of which my captain had the command. I went with him into this vessel, and we took a load of new slaves for Georgia and Charles Town. My master now left me entirely to the captain, though he still wished for me to be with him; but I, who always much wished to lose sight of the West Indies, was not a little rejoiced at the thoughts of seeing any other country. Therefore, relying on the goodness of my captain, I got ready all the little venture I could; and, when the

vessel was ready, we sailed to my great joy. When we got to our des-
tined places, Georgia and Charles Town, I expected I should have
an opportunity of selling my little property to advantage: but here,
particularly in Charles Town, I met with buyers, white men, who
imposed on me as in other places. Notwithstanding, I was resolved
to have fortitude; thinking no lot or trial is too hard when kind
Heaven is the rewarder.

We soon got loaded again, and returned to Montserrat; and there,
amongst the rest of the islands, I sold my goods well; and in this
manner I continued trading during the year 1764; meeting with various scenes of imposition, as usual. After this, my master fitted out
his vessel for Philadelphia, in the year 1765; and during the time we
were loading her, and getting ready for the voyage, I worked with
redoubled alacrity, from the hope of getting money enough by these
voyages to buy my freedom, in time, if it should please God; and also
to see the town of Philadelphia, which I had heard a great deal about
for some years past; besides which, I had always longed to prove my
master's promise the first day I came to him. In the midst of these
elevated ideas, and while I was about getting my little merchandize
in readiness, one Sunday my master sent for me to his house. When
I came there I found him and the captain together; and, on my going
in, I was struck with astonishment at his telling me he heard that I
meant to run away from him when I got to Philadelphia: 'And therefore,' said he, 'I must sell you again: you cost me a great deal of
money, no less than forty pounds sterling; and it will not do to lose
so much. You are a valuable fellow,' continued he; 'and I can get any
day for you one hundred guineas, from many gentlemen in this
island.' And then he told me of Captain Doran's brother-in-law, a
severe master, who ever wanted to buy me to make me his overseer.
My captain also said he could get much more than a hundred
guineas for me in Carolina. This I knew to be a fact; for the gentleman that wanted to buy me came off several times on board of us,
and spoke to me to live with him, and said he would use me well.
When I asked what work he would put me to, he said, as I was a
sailor, he would make me a captain of one of his rice vessels. But I
refused: and fearing, at the same time, by a sudden turn I saw in
the captain's temper, he might mean to sell me, I told the gentleman I would not live with him on any condition, and that I certainly
would run away with his vessel: but he said he did not fear that, as
he would catch him again; and then he told me how cruelly he would
serve me if I should do so. My captain, however, gave him to understand that I knew something of navigation: so he thought better of
it; and, to my great joy, he went away. I now told my master I did not
say I would run away in Philadelphia; neither did I mean it, as he
did not use me ill, nor yet the captain: for if they did I certainly

would have made some attempts before now; but as I thought that if it were God's will I ever should be freed it would be so, and, on the contrary, if it was not his will it would not happen; so I hoped, if ever I were freed, whilst I was used well, it should be by honest means; but as I could not help myself, he must do as he pleased; I could only hope and trust to the God of Heaven; and at that instant my mind was big with inventions and full of schemes to escape. I then appealed to the captain whether he ever saw any sign of my making the least attempt to run away; and asked him if I did not always come on board according to the time for which he gave me liberty; and, more particularly, when all our men left us at Guadeloupe and went on board of the French fleet, and advised me to go with them, whether I might not, and that he could not have got me again. To my no small surprise, and very great joy, the captain confirmed every syllable that I had said: and even more: for he said he had tried different times to see if I would make any attempt of this kind, both at St. Eustatia and in America, and he never found that I made the smallest; but, on the contrary, I always came on board according to his orders; and he did really believe, if I ever meant to run away, that, as I could never have had a better opportunity, I would have done it the night the mate and all the people left our vessel at Guadeloupe. The captain then informed my master, who had been thus imposed on by our mate, (though I did not know who was my enemy,) the reason the mate had for imposing this lie upon him; which was, because I had acquainted the captain of the provisions the mate had given away or taken out of the vessel. This speech of the captain was like life to the dead to me, and instantly my soul glorified God; and still more so on hearing my master immediately say that I was a sensible fellow, and he never did intend to use me as a common slave; and that but for the entreaties of the captain, and his character of me, he would not have let me go from the stores about as I had done; that also, in so doing, he thought by carrying one little thing or other to different places to sell I might make money. That he also intended to encourage me in this by crediting me with half a puncheon of rum and half a hogshead of sugar at a time; so that, from being careful, I might have money enough, in some time, to purchase my freedom; and, when that was the case, I might depend upon it he would let me have it for forty pounds sterling money, which was only the same price he gave for me. This sound gladdened my poor heart beyond measure; though indeed it was no more than the very idea I had formed in my mind of my master long before, and I immediately made him this reply: 'Sir, I always had that very thought of you, indeed I had, and that made me so diligent in serving you.' He then gave me a large piece of silver coin, such as I never had seen or had before, and told me to get ready for the voyage, and he would credit me with a tierce of sugar, and another of rum; he also said that he had two amiable sisters in Philadelphia, from whom I might get some necessary things. Upon this my noble captain desired me to go aboard; and, knowing the African metal,[1] he charged me not to say any thing of this matter to any body; and he promised that the lying mate should not go with him any more. This was a change indeed; in the same hour to feel the most exquisite pain, and in the turn of a moment the fullest joy. It caused in me such sensations as I was only able to express in my looks; my heart was so overpowered with gratitude that I could have kissed both of their feet. When I left the room I immediately went, or rather flew, to the vessel, which being loaded, my master, as good as his word, trusted me with a tierce of rum, and another of sugar, when we sailed, and arrived safe at the elegant town of Philadelphia. I soon sold my goods here pretty well; and in this charming place I found every thing plentiful and cheap.

While I was in this place a very extraordinary occurrence befell me. I had been told one evening of a *wise* woman, a Mrs. Davis, who revealed secrets, foretold events, &c. I put little faith in this story at first, as I could not conceive that any mortal could foresee the future disposals of Providence, nor did I believe in any other revelation than that of the Holy Scriptures; however, I was greatly astonished at seeing this woman in a dream that night, though a person I never before beheld in my life; this made such an impression on me, that I could not get the idea the next day out of my mind, and I then became as anxious to see her as I was before indifferent; accordingly in the evening, after we left off working, I inquired where she lived, and being directed to her, to my inexpressible surprise, beheld the very woman in the very same dress she appeared to me to wear in the vision. She immediately told me I had dreamed of her the preceding night; related to me many things that had happened with a correctness that astonished me; and finally told me I should not be long a slave: this was the more agreeable news, as I believed it the more readily from her having so faithfully related the past incidents of my life. She said I should be twice in very great danger of my life within eighteen months, which, if I escaped, I should afterwards go on well; so, giving me her blessing, we parted. After staying here some time till our vessel was loaded, and I had bought in my little traffic, we sailed from this agreeable spot for Montserrat, once more to encounter the raging surfs.

We arrived safe at Montserrat, where we discharged our cargo; and soon after that we took slaves on board for St. Eustatia, and from thence to Georgia. I had always exerted myself and did double work, in order to make our voyages as short as possible; and from thus overworking myself while we were at Georgia I caught a fever and ague.

---

1. Presumably, "mettle," meaning spirit or strength of character.

I was very ill for eleven days and near dying; eternity was now exceedingly impressed on my mind, and I feared very much that awful event. I prayed the Lord therefore to spare me; and I made a promise in my mind to God, that I would be good if ever I should recover. At length, from having an eminent doctor to attend me, I was restored again to health; and soon after we got the vessel loaded, and set off for Montserrat. During the passage, as I was perfectly restored, and had much business of the vessel to mind, all my endeavours to keep up my integrity, and perform my promise to God, began to fail; and, in spite of all I could do, as we drew nearer and nearer to the islands, my resolutions more and more declined, as if the very air of that country or climate seemed fatal to piety. When we were safe arrived at Montserrat, and I had got ashore, I forgot my former resolutions.—Alas! how prone is the heart to leave that God it wishes to love! and how strongly do the things of this world strike the senses and captivate the soul!— After our vessel was discharged, we soon got her ready, and took in, as usual, some of the poor oppressed natives of Africa, and other negroes; we then set off again for Georgia and Charlstown. We arrived at Georgia, and, having landed part of our cargo, proceeded to Charlstown with the remainder. While we were there I saw the town illuminated; the guns were fired, and bonfires and other demonstrations of joy shewn, on account of the repeal of the stamp act. Here I disposed of some goods on my own account; the white men buying them with smooth promises and fair words, giving me, however, but very indifferent payment. There was one gentleman particularly who bought a puncheon of rum of me, which gave me a great deal of trouble; and, although I used the interest of my friendly captain, I could not obtain any thing for it; for, being a negro man, I could not oblige him to pay me. This vexed me much, not knowing how to act; and I lost some time in seeking after this Christian; and though, when the Sabbath came (which the negroes usually make their holiday) I was much inclined to go to public worship, I was obliged to hire some black men to help to pull a boat across the water to God in quest of this gentleman. When I found him, after much entreaty, both from myself and my worthy captain, he at last paid me in dollars; some of them, however, were copper, and of consequence of no value; but he took advantage of my being a negro man, and obliged me to put up with those or none, although I objected to them. Immediately after, as I was trying to pass them in the market, amongst other white men, I was abused for offering to pass bad coin; and, though I shewed them the man I got them from, I was within one minute of being tied up and flogged without either judge or jury; however, by the help of a good pair of heels, I ran off, and so escaped the bastinadoes[2] I should

---

2. Punishment by caning the soles of the feet.

have received. I got on board as fast as I could, but still continued in fear of them until we sailed, which I thanked God we did not long after; and I have never been amongst them since.

We soon came to Georgia, where we were to complete our lading;[3] and here worse fate than ever attended me: for one Sunday night, as I was with some negroes in their master's yard in the town of Savannah, it happened that their master, one Doctor Perkins, who was a very severe and cruel man, came in drunk; and, not liking to see any strange negroes in his yard, he and a ruffian of a white man he had in his service beset me in an instant, and both of them struck me with the first weapons they could get hold of. I cried out as long as I could for help and mercy; but, though I gave a good account of myself, and he knew my captain, who lodged hard by him, it was to no purpose. They beat and mangled me in a shameful manner, leaving me near dead. I lost so much blood from the wounds I received, that I lay quite motionless, and was so benumbed that I could not feel any thing for many hours. Early in the morning they took me away to the jail. As I did not return to the ship all night, my captain, not knowing where I was, and being uneasy that I did not then make my appearance, he made inquiry after me; and, having found where I was, immediately came to me. As soon as the good man saw me so cut and mangled, he could not forbear weeping; he soon got me out of jail to his lodgings, and immediately sent for the best doctors in the place, who at first declared it as their opinion that I could not recover. My captain on this went to all the lawyers in the town for their advice, but they told him they could do nothing for me as I was a negro. He then went to Doctor Perkins, the hero who had vanquished me, and menaced him, swearing he would be revenged of him, and challenged him to fight.—But cowardice is ever the companion of cruelty—and the Doctor refused. However, by the skilfulness of one Doctor Brady of that place, I began at last to amend; but, although I was so sore and bad with the wounds I had all over me that I could not rest in any posture, yet I was in more pain on account of the captain's uneasiness about me than I otherwise should have been. The worthy man nursed and watched me all the hours of the night; and I was, through his attention and that of the doctor, able to get out of bed in about sixteen or eighteen days. All this time I was very much wanted on board, as I used frequently to go up and down the river for rafts, and other parts of our cargo, and stow them when the mate was sick or absent. In about four weeks I was able to go on duty; and in a fortnight after, having got in all our lading, our vessel set sail for Montserrat; and in less than three weeks we arrived there safe towards the end of the year. This ended my adventures in 1764; for I did not leave Montserrat again till the beginning of the following year.

3. Loading a ship or other vessel with cargo.

EDMUND BURKE

Edmund Burke (1729–1797), Irish-born philosopher, author, and politician, published the pamphlet *Reflections on the Revolution in France* in 1790, offering a strident defense of the conservative principles of heredity and inherited rights, the monarchy, and national and cultural traditions.

From Reflections on the Revolution in France[†]

* * *

* * * [T]he age of chivalry is gone. That of sophisters, economists, and calculators has succeeded; and the glory of Europe is extinguished forever. Never, never more, shall we behold that generous loyalty to rank and sex, that proud submission, that dignified obedience, that subordination of the heart, which kept alive, even in servitude itself, the spirit of an exalted freedom! The unbought grace of life, the cheap defence of nations, the nurse of manly sentiment and heroic enterprise, is gone! It is gone, that sensibility of principle, that chastity of honor, which felt a stain like a wound, which inspired courage whilst it mitigated ferocity, which ennobled whatever it touched, and under which vice itself lost half its evil by losing all its grossness!

This mixed system of opinion and sentiment had its origin in the ancient chivalry; and the principle, though varied in its appearance by the varying state of human affairs, subsisted and influenced through a long succession of generations, even to the time we live in. If it should ever be totally extinguished, the loss, I fear, will be great. It is this which has given its character to modern Europe. It is this which has distinguished it under all its forms of government, and distinguished it to its advantage, from the states of Asia, and possibly from those states which flourished in the most brilliant periods of the antique world. It was this, which, without confounding ranks, had produced a noble equality, and handed it down through all the gradations of social life. It was this opinion which mitigated kings into companions, and raised private men to be fellows with kings. Without force or opposition, it subdued the fierceness of pride and power; it obliged sovereigns to submit to the soft collar of social esteem, compelled stern authority to submit to elegance, and gave a domination, vanquisher of laws, to be subdued by manners.

† From *The Works of the Right Honourable Edmund Burke*, vol. 3 (London: John C. Nimmo, 1887), pp. 331–37. Unless otherwise indicated, notes are by the editor of this Norton Critical Edition.

But now all is to be changed. All the pleasing illusions which made power gentle and obedience liberal, which harmonized the different shades of life, and which by a bland assimilation incorporated into politics the sentiments which beautify and soften private society, are to be dissolved by this new conquering empire of light and reason. All the decent drapery of life is to be rudely torn off. All the superadded ideas, furnished from the wardrobe of a moral imagination, which the heart owns and the understanding ratifies, as necessary to cover the defects of our naked, shivering nature, and to raise it to dignity in our own estimation, are to be exploded, as a ridiculous, absurd, and antiquated fashion.[1]

On this scheme of things, a king is but a man, a queen is but a woman, a woman is but an animal,—and an animal not of the highest order. All homage paid to the sex in general as such, and without distinct views, is to be regarded as romance and folly. Regicide, and parricide, and sacrilege, are but fictions of superstition, corrupting jurisprudence by destroying its simplicity. The murder of a king, or a queen, or a bishop, or a father, are only common homicide,—and if the people are by any chance or in any way gainers by it, a sort of homicide much the most pardonable, and into which we ought not to make too severe a scrutiny.

On the scheme of this barbarous philosophy, which is the offspring of cold hearts and muddy understandings, and which is as void of solid wisdom as it is destitute of all taste and elegance, laws are to be supported only by their own terrors, and by the concern which each individual may find in them from his own private speculations, or can spare to them from his own private interests. In the groves of *their* academy, at the end of every visto, you see nothing but the gallows. Nothing is left which engages the affections on the part of the commonwealth. On the principles of this mechanic philosophy, our institutions can never be embodied, if I may use the expression, in persons,—so as to create in us love, veneration, admiration, or attachment. But that sort of reason which banishes the affections is incapable of filling their place. These public affections, combined with manners, are required sometimes as supplements, sometimes as correctives, always as aids to law. The precept given by a wise man, as well as a great critic, for the construction of poems,

1. Mary Wollstonecraft (1759–1797), novelist and essayist and the mother of Mary Shelley (1797–1851), published her *Vindication of the Rights of Men* the same year as Burke's pamphlet and in direct response to it. She accuses Burke of letting his emotions run away with his reason, writing, "all your pretty flights arise from your pampered sensibility; and that, vain of this fancied preeminence of organs, you foster every emotion till the fumes, mounting to your brain, dispel the sober suggestions of reason": "reflection inflames your imagination, instead of enlightening your understanding" (*Vindication*, 2nd ed. [J. Johnson, 1790], p. 6). She later published *An Historical and Moral View of the Origin and Progress of the French Revolution* (1795) and her most well-known work, *A Vindication of the Rights of Woman* (1792).

is equally true as to states:—"*Non satis est pulchra esse poemata, dulcia sunto.*"[2] There ought to be a system of manners in every nation which a well-formed mind would be disposed to relish. To make us love our country, our country ought to be lovely. But power, of some kind or other, will survive the shock in which manners and opinions perish; and it will find other and worse means for its support. The usurpation, which, in order to subvert ancient institutions, has destroyed ancient principles, will hold power by arts similar to those by which it has acquired it. When the old feudal and chivalrous spirit of *fealty*, which, by freeing kings from fear, freed both kings and subjects from the precautions of tyranny, shall be extinct in the minds of men, plots and assassinations will be anticipated by preventive murder and preventive confiscation, and that long roll of grim and bloody maxims which form the political code of all power not standing on its own honor and the honor of those who are to obey it. Kings will be tyrants from policy, when subjects are rebels from principle.

When ancient opinions and rules of life are taken away, the loss cannot possibly be estimated. From that moment we have no compass to govern us, nor can we know distinctly to what port we steer. Europe, undoubtedly, taken in a mass, was in a flourishing condition the day on which your Revolution was completed. How much of that prosperous state was owing to the spirit of our old manners and opinions is not easy to say; but as such causes cannot be indifferent in their operation, we must presume, that, on the whole, their operation was beneficial.

We are but too apt to consider things in the state in which we find them, without sufficiently adverting to the causes by which they have been produced, and possibly may be upheld. Nothing is more certain than that our manners, our civilization, and all the good things which are connected with manners and with civilization, have, in this European world of ours, depended for ages upon two principles, and were, indeed, the result of both combined: I mean the spirit of a gentleman, and the spirit of religion. The nobility and the clergy, the one by profession, and the other by patronage, kept learning in existence, even in the midst of arms and confusions, and whilst governments were rather in their causes than formed. Learning paid back what it received to nobility and to priesthood, and paid it with usury, by enlarging their ideas, and by furnishing their minds. Happy, if they had all continued to know their indissoluble union, and their proper place! Happy, if learning, not debauched by ambition, had been satisfied to continue the instructor, and not aspired to be the master! Along with its natural protectors and guardians,

---

2. From the Roman lyric poet Horace's *Ars Poetica*, written in 19 B.C.E.: "It is not enough that poems be beautiful; they should be pleasant, too" (Latin).

learning will be cast into the mire and trodden down under the hoofs of a swinish multitude.[3]

If, as I suspect, modern letters owe more than they are always willing to own to ancient manners, so do other interests which we value full as much as they are worth. Even commerce, and trade, and manufacture, the gods of our economical politicians, are themselves perhaps but creatures, are themselves but effects, which, as first causes, we choose to worship. They certainly grew under the same shade in which learning flourished. They, too, may decay with their natural protecting principles. With you, for the present at least, they all threaten to disappear together. Where trade and manufactures are wanting to a people, and the spirit of nobility and religion remains, sentiment supplies, and not always ill supplies, their place; but if commerce and the arts should be lost in an experiment to try how well a state may stand without these old fundamental principles, what sort of a thing must be a nation of gross, stupid, ferocious, and at the same time poor and sordid barbarians, destitute of religion, honor, or manly pride, possessing nothing at present, and hoping for nothing hereafter?

I wish you may not be going fast, and by the shortest cut, to that horrible and disgustful situation. Already there appears a poverty of conception, a coarseness and vulgarity, in all the proceedings of the Assembly and of all their instructors.[4] Their liberty is not liberal. Their science is presumptuous ignorance. Their humanity is savage and brutal.

It is not clear whether in England we learned those grand and decorous principles and manners, of which considerable traces yet remain, from you, or whether you took them from us. But to you, I think, we trace them best. You seem to me to be *gentis incunabula nostræ*.[5] France has always more or less influenced manners in England; and when your fountain is choked up and polluted, the stream will not run long or not run clear with us, or perhaps with any nation. This gives all Europe, in my opinion, but too close and connected a concern in what is done in France. Excuse me, therefore, if I have dwelt too long on the atrocious spectacle of the sixth of October, 1789,[6] or have given too much scope to the reflections

---

3. [See the fate of Bailly and Condorcet, supposed to be here particularly alluded to. Compare the circumstances of the trial and execution of the former with this prediction —*Burke*.] French intellectuals Jean Sylvain Bailly (1736–1793) and Nicolas de Condorcet (1743–1794). Bailly was guillotined during the Reign of Terror, and Condorcet died of poisoning in prison two days after having been captured by French authorities.

4. The French National Assembly and, by implication, the British House of Commons, both portrayed as fractious and corrupt.

5. "The cradle of our nation" (Latin), a phrase drawn from Roman poet Virgil's *Aeneid*, an epic poem of political and national tradition and destiny.

6. Date of the Women's March on Versailles (also known as the October March), involving women shoppers in the Paris markets protesting food scarcity and the high cost of

which have arisen in my mind on occasion of the most important of all revolutions, which may be dated from that day: I mean a revolution in sentiments, manners, and moral opinions. As things now stand, with everything respectable destroyed without us, and an attempt to destroy within us every principle of respect, one is almost forced to apologize for harboring the common feelings of men.

*　*　*

JAMES STEPHEN

From The Crisis of the Sugar Colonies†

The Crisis of the Sugar Colonies is a treatise in four letters by James Stephen (1758–1832), English Member of Parliament, lawyer, and abolitionist, and great-grandfather of Virginia Woolf. Stephen's time in Trinidad and Barbados led him to despise slavery. Returning to London, he joined William Wilberforce and became known as the architect of the 1807 Act for the Abolition of the Slave Trade in the British Empire. The Advertisement to this treatise states that the arguments therein were printed before "the news lately received from St. Domingo" involving the arrival of a large French naval fleet in San Domingo (or Saint-Domingue, now Haiti) sent to disarm the forces of Toussaint L'Ouverture, who had proclaimed himself governor of the island for life. Formerly enslaved himself, L'Ouverture had fought on the side of France but became the leader of the Haitian Revolution (1791–1804), a successful insurrection of enslaved persons.

*　*　*

That the true nature of West India slavery is very imperfectly understood in this country, may appear a bold proposition; but is one, which, from personal and long acquaintance with that system, and from ample opportunities of hearing the opinions prevalent in England on the subject, I am led with some confidence to affirm.

Neither the friends nor the enemies of the slave trade, seem to me to have attended sufficiently to that feature, which is in truth the most essential characteristic of colonial bondage, and chiefly distinguishes it from every other state of man, that is known to the traveller, or the historian.

---

bread. The crowd grew to include citizens with prerevolutionary sentiments, who marched to the Palace of Versailles to demand reform. The event was widely seen as depriving King Louis XVI, and thus the monarchy itself "thereafter referred to as the ancien régime," of absolute power. The storming of the Bastille had occurred three months earlier, on July 14, 1789.

† From *The Crisis of the Sugar Colonies; Or, An Enquiry into the Objects and Probable Effects of the French Expedition to the West Indies* (London: J. Hatchard, 1802), pp. 7–9, 13, 17–19. Unless otherwise indicated, notes are by the editor of this Norton Critical Edition.

"Are we then," it may be asked with alarm, "are we to have new facts disclosed; and new contradictions to decide upon, between Abolitionists and the Planters?" By no means. The misapprehension I allege, arises neither from the want nor the inconsistency of evidence; but from inattention to facts perfectly notorious, and never controverted or denied.

That West India slaves, whether French or English, are the property of their master, and transferrable by him, like his inanimate effects; that in general he is absolute arbiter of the extent and the mode of their labour, and of the quantum of subsistence to be given in return for it; and that they are disciplined and punished at his discretion, direct privation of life or member excepted; these are prominent features, and sufficiently known, of this state of slavery. * * *

* * * *The negroes were the absolute, vendible property of the master, were worked and maintained at his discretion,[1] and were driven at their labours in the field.* * * *

*   *   *

As the new state of the negroes both at Guadalupe and Cayenne[2] was introduced by the government, it was also defined by positive law, at the time of its introduction.* * *

The negroes were by this law expressly released from slavery, and invested with all the rights of French citizens, and though industry was enjoined as a duty, the declared objects of that duty were themselves, their families, and the state, and not any particular master or employer. If it was intended that the new relations of stipendiary servant and master, should be formed between them and the same planters whose property they formerly had been, which does not clearly appear, the latter were at least required to give them a competent salary in return for their work.

In a word, they were placed, as far as an express law could place them, in the condition of English labourers; though perhaps obliged to work on a particular estate.[3]

1. [The regulation of the *Code noir* which went partly to restrain the abuse of this power and that of punishment were almost wholly neglected in practice —*Stephen.*] The *Code Noir* or "Black Code" refers to a May 1687 edict by King Louis XIV that expelled all Jews from French Caribbean colonies and prohibited them from owning property, including enslaved persons; defined slavery as heritable from the mother; dictated that enslaved persons be instructed in Catholicism; and enforced the rightlessness of enslaved persons. While the murder of enslaved persons by their enslavers was illegal under British law, such acts occurred and were irregularly punished, as Stephen's note makes clear. See *Édit du Roi, Touchant la Police des Isles de l'Amérique Française* (Paris, 1687), ll. 28–58.

2. Following the French Revolution, France tried to reinstate enslavement in the empire in 1802, prompting a rebellion in Guadeloupe led by Louis Delgrès, a freeborn officer of France born in Martinique. Cayenne is the capital of French Guiana.

3. If reports prevalent in the Leeward Islands soon after this revolution were accurate, the limitation to a particular estate was the rule only in respect of such negroes as either could not or would not employ themselves industriously upon some other plantation of their own choice. But the fact is not very material to my argument, and I wish

From the language of the French government in 1794, it would I admit be rash to infer its real and permanent designs. But Victor Hugues[4] was not in a condition to violate with impunity his engagements to the negroes of Guadaloupe: By the sole aid of these newly-created citizens and soldiers, he was enabled to re-conquer that valuable colony; and solely by their fidelity and zeal could he hope to defend it during the war, against the unresisted masters of the seas. He was obliged therefore by political necessity to adhere to the promises on the faith of which they had joined him; and that he did in good earnest establish and maintain their freedom was well known, to the terror of the British planters in adjacent islands.

It was, indeed but too manifestly proved by the astonishing effects which followed; especially in the disastrous era of the insurrections in St. Vincent's and Grenada[5]. The freedom of the negroes alone, and their zealous attachment to the government, not only made this little territory impregnable, but enabled Victor Hugues to pour from it, as a volcano, terror and devastation around him.

*   *   *

GEORGE GORDON, LORD BYRON

George Gordon, Lord Byron (1788–1824) was an English poet and author who fought for and died in the Greek War of Independence, which culminated in the 1830 formation of the modern Greek state. According to Hazel Jones, Byron's "account in *The Corsair* of a seagoing life rang true among those, like James Stanier Clarke, who saw naval experience as heroic." The poem's opening five lines were reprinted on the cover of the July–December 1814 issue of the *Naval Chronicle*, the same year that Jane Austen wrote to her sister Cassandra that she had "read the Corsair, mended my petticoat, & have nothing else to do" (March 5–8, 1814). See Jones, "She Had Only Navy-Lists and Newspapers for Her Authority," *Persuasions* 39.1 (2018), n. p.

---

not to overstate the extent of this revolution in any point, but rather where the case is doubtful, to lean to the other side [*Stephen's note*].

4. Jean-Baptiste Victor Hugues (1762–1826), French officer and governor of Guadeloupe and (later) Cayenne who had emancipated the enslaved persons of Guadeloupe in 1794.

5. Two of the Windward Islands, a grouping created by the 1763 Treaty of Paris and located in the eastern Caribbean.

From The Corsair[†]

Canto the first

"——nessun maggior dolore,
Che ricordarsi del tempo felice
Nella miseria,——"[1]
        Dante, *Inferno*, v. 121

I.

"O'er the glad waters of the dark blue sea,
Our thoughts as boundless, and our souls as free,
Far as the breeze can bear, the billows foam,
Survey our empire, and behold our home![2]
These are our realms, no limits to their sway—   5
Our flag the sceptre all who meet obey.
Ours the wild life in tumult still to range
From toil to rest, and joy in every change.
Oh, who can tell? not thou, luxurious slave!
Whose soul would sicken o'er the heaving wave;   10
Not thou, vain lord of Wantonness and Ease!
Whom Slumber soothes not—Pleasure cannot please—
Oh, who can tell, save he whose heart hath tried,
And danced in triumph o'er the waters wide,
The exulting sense—the pulse's maddening play,   15
That thrills the wanderer of that trackless way?
That for itself can woo the approaching fight,
And turn what some deem danger to delight;
That seeks what cravens shun with more than zeal,
And where the feebler faint can only feel—   20
Feel—to the rising bosom's inmost core,
Its hope awaken and its spirit soar?
No dread of Death—if with us die our foes—
Save that it seems even duller than repose;
Come when it will—we snatch the life of Life—   25
When lost—what recks it by disease or strife?
Let him who crawls, enamoured of decay,
Cling to his couch, and sicken years away;

---

† From *The Works of Lord Byron*, vol. 3, ed. Ernest Hartley Coleridge (London: John Murray, 1900 [1814]), pp. 227–31. Unless otherwise indicated, notes are by the editor of this Norton Critical Edition.
1. The epigraph from *Inferno* (written ca. 1308–21) by Italian vernacular poet Dante Alighieri (1265–1321) reads, "There is no greater pain than to recall a happy time in the midst of misery."
2. Compare—"Survey the region, and confess her home." *Windsor Forest*, by (Alexander) Pope, line 256 [*Coleridge's note*].

Heave his thick breath, and shake his palsied head;
Ours the fresh turf, and not the feverish bed,— 30
While gasp by gasp he falters forth his soul,
Ours with one pang—one bound—escapes control.
His corse may boast its urn and narrow cave,
And they who loathed his life may gild his grave:
Ours are the tears, though few, sincerely shed, 35
When Ocean shrouds and sepulchres our dead.
For us, even banquets fond regret supply
In the red cup that crowns our memory;
And the brief epitaph in Danger's day,
When those who win at length divide the prey, 40
And cry, Remembrance saddening o'er each brow,
How had the brave who fell exulted *now*!"

II.

Such were the notes that from the Pirate's isle
Around the kindling watch-fire rang the while:
Such were the sounds that thrilled the rocks along, 45
And unto ears as rugged seemed a song!
In scattered groups upon the golden sand,
They game—carouse—converse—or whet the brand;
Select the arms—to each his blade assign,
And careless eye the blood that dims its shine; 50
Repair the boat, replace the helm or oar,
While others straggling muse along the shore;
For the wild bird the busy springes set,
Or spread beneath the sun the dripping net:
Gaze where some distant sail a speck supplies, 55
With all the thirsting eye of Enterprise;
Tell o'er the tales of many a night of toil,
And marvel where they next shall seize a spoil:
No matter where—their chief's allotment this;
Theirs to believe no prey nor plan amiss. 60
But who that Chief? his name on every shore
Is famed and feared—they ask and know no more.
With these he mingles not but to command;
Few are his words, but keen his eye and hand.
Ne'er seasons he with mirth their jovial mess, 65
But they forgive his silence for success.
Ne'er for his lip the purpling cup they fill,
That goblet passes him untasted still—
And for his fare—the rudest of his crew
Would that, in turn, have passed untasted too; 70
Earth's coarsest bread, the garden's homeliest roots,
And scarce the summer luxury of fruits,

His short repast in humbleness supply
With all a hermit's board would scarce deny.
But while he shuns the grosser joys of sense,   75
His mind seems nourished by that abstinence.
"Steer to that shore!"—they sail. "Do this!"—'tis done:
"Now form and follow me!"—the spoil is won.
Thus prompt his accents and his actions still,
And all obey and few inquire his will;   80
To such, brief answer and contemptuous eye
Convey reproof, nor further deign reply.

III.

"A sail!—a sail!"—a promised prize to Hope!
Her nation—flag—how speaks the telescope?
No prize, alas! but yet a welcome sail: 85
The blood-red signal glitters in the gale.
Yes—she is ours—a home-returning bark—
Blow fair, thou breeze!—she anchors ere the dark.
Already doubled is the cape—our bay
Receives that prow which proudly spurns the spray.   90
How gloriously her gallant course she goes!
Her white wings flying—never from her foes—
She walks the waters like a thing of Life![3]
And seems to dare the elements to strife.
Who would not brave the battle-fire, the wreck,   95
To move the monarch of her peopled deck!

IV.

Hoarse o'er her side the rustling cable rings:
The sails are furled; and anchoring round she swings;
And gathering loiterers on the land discern
Her boat descending from the latticed stern.   100
'Tis manned—the oars keep concert to the strand,
Till grates her keel upon the shallow sand.
Hail to the welcome shout!—the friendly speech!
When hand grasps hand uniting on the beach;
The smile, the question, and the quick reply,   105
And the Heart's promise of festivity!

V.

The tidings spread, and gathering grows the crowd:
The hum of voices, and the laughter loud,

3. Compare *The Isle of Palms*, by John Wilson, Canto I. (1812, p. 8)—"She sailed amid the loveliness / Like a thing with heart and mind" [*Coleridge's note*].

And Woman's gentler anxious tone is heard—
Friends'—husbands'—lovers' names in each dear word: 110
"Oh! are they safe? we ask not of success—
But shall we see them? will their accents bless?
From where the battle roars, the billows chafe,
They doubtless boldly did—but who are safe?
Here let them haste to gladden and surprise,   115
And kiss the doubt from these delighted eyes!"

*   *   *

ROBERT HAY

Robert Hay was a Scottish seaman. First published in 1953, *Landsman Hay: The Memoirs of Robert Hay* was written in 1820–21, with parts published in *Paisley Magazine* under the pen name "Sam Spritsail." According to Vincent McInerney, the memoir offers "an account of service on the lower deck of the Royal Navy during the great French wars"—Hay was at sea from 1803 to 1811—"with a narrator coming from a more humble background, Hay's family being essentially Scottish weavers and textile workers" (p. 1). Though Hay volunteered for the British Royal Navy, he twice deserted, once climbing down a rope into dark water and "steering by the great comet of 1811," but was pressed back into service (pp. 21–22). These acts were not prosecuted since, during the peace, "the Navy had more voluntary recruits than it needed," but also because "the sheer scale of desertion in the wartime Navy made concerted legal action beyond contemplation. One contemporary pamphlet calculated that in two years alone from May 1803 to June 1805, at a time when the Navy's nominal strength was around 90,000 seamen, over 12,000 deserted" (p. 24).

From Landsman Hay: The Memoirs of Robert Hay, 1789–1847[†]

As those who were of the regular ship's crew were but few in number, and chiefly employed manning officers' boats, it might be thought [the] lower deck a desirable berth, but as the greater number kept their wives and families on board, it was pretty much crowded day and night.[1] The middle and upper decks were set aside

---

[†] From *Landsman Hay: The Memoirs of Robert Hay, 1789–1847*, ed. Vincent McInerney (Barnsley: Seaforth Publishing, 2010), pp. 52–53, 139, 194–201. Reprinted by permission of the publisher. Notes are by the editor of this Norton Critical Edition.

1. Hay's description, dated August 1803, is of the *Salvador del Mundo*, "a three-deck ship taken from the Spaniards during the preceding war and which now lay as a guard ship in the [Plymouth] harbour, a guard ship being usually an obsolete vessel permanently anchored for the reception and temporary accommodation of seaman" (p. 50).

for the supernumeraries, the general name for those not yet allotted to any ship.

It would be difficult to give any adequate idea of the scenes these latter two decks presented: complexions of every varied hue, and features of every cast, from the jetty face, flat nose, thick lips and frizzled hair of the African, to the more slender frame and milder features of the Asiatic; the rosy complexion of the English swain, and the sallow features of the sunburnt Portuguese; people of every profession and of the most contrasted manners, from the brawny ploughman to the delicate fop; the decayed author and bankrupt merchant who had eluded their creditors; the apprentice who had run from servitude; the improvident and impoverished father who had abandoned his family, and the smuggler who had escaped by flight the vengeance of the laws. Costumes ranged from the kilted Highlander, to the shirtless sons of the British prison house, to the knuckle ruffles of the haughty Spaniard, to the gaudy and tinselled trappings of the dismissed footman, to the rags and tatters of the city beggar. Here, a group of half-starved and squalid wretches, not eating, but devouring with rapacity, their whole day's provisions at a single meal; there, a gang of sharpers at cards or dice, swindling some unsuspecting booby out of his remaining pence. To the ear came a hubbub little short of Babel: Irish, Welsh, Dutch, Portuguese, Spanish, French, Swedish, Italian, together with every provincial dialect prevailing between Land's End and John O'Groats. There was poetry being recited; failed thespians with their mutterings; songs, jests, laughter, while the occasional rattle of the boatswain's cane, and the harsh voices of his mates, blended with the shrill and penetrating sound of their whistles, served at once to strike terror into the mind, and add confusion to the scene.

*   *   *

The cargoes of these vessels[2] consisted of an extensive quantity of goods for Europe from the Chinese markets: boxes of hardware, jewellery and porcelain, bales of silk, hogsheads of tobacco, indigo, gum, cochineal, packages of opium, sacks of yams, bales of cotton, bars of copper, steel, and iron, cases of ivories, elephants' teeth, cases and bales and casks the contents of which were unknown. All were thrown relentlessly overboard, and although strict watch was kept to prevent any articles from being brought aboard our ship, yet a considerable number of sailors made some valuable prizes, not least in their eyes being the extensive and variegated assortment of

---

2. Describing an 1807 encounter involving Dutch coasting vessels. Assigned to HMS *Culloden*, a ship-of-the-line or gunship, at the time, Hay writes that the sailors were dumping cargo "preparatory to us stowing our guns and other heavy articles in these craft, that by this means we might be sufficiently lightened to float over the shallows" (p. 139).

spiritous liquors they had on board, including a great number of cases containing one dozen square half-gallon bottles of rum, brandy, wine, gin, and arrack of excellent quality.[3]

*   *   *

* * * We reached the metropolis [of London] next morning at eight o'clock, my feelings being considerably different from what they were when entered by the same way (Hyde Park Corner) twenty-five months before, when I was still in naval bondage.[4] Now my thoughts were raised by the idea of freedom, and my hopes excited at the prospect of embracing in a week or two those from whom I had long been separated. But if my hopes were high, so were my fears. One of my fellow passengers, hearing I was a stranger to London and intending to visit Scotland, offered to conduct me to the wharves where Scotch vessels lay. But I did not like his looks and, as civilly as I could, declined his offer.

Without stopping to breakfast, or to examine a single curiosity, I pressed forward in as straight a line as possible for the river. I had gained sight of the vessels' masts, and in imagination had procured a passage when, crossing Tower Hill, I was accosted by a person in seaman's dress who tapped me on the shoulder, enquiring in a familiar and technical strain, 'What ship?'

I assumed an air of gravity, and surprise, and told him I was not connected with shipping. At this he gave a whistle, and in a moment I was in the hands of six or eight ruffians whom I soon found to be a press gang. They dragged me hurriedly through several streets, amid bitter execrations bestowed on them from passers-by and expressions of sympathy directed towards me, until they landed me in one of those houses of rendezvous. Here I was carried into the presence of a lieutenant who questioned me as to my profession, and whether I had ever been to sea, and what business had taken me to Tower Hill. I made some evasive answers, but on my hands being

3. On "news of naval battles and prize taking" in relation to *Persuasion*, see Hazel Jones, "She Had Only Navy-Lists and Newspapers for Her Authority," *Persuasions* 39.1 (2018). Jones notes for instance that, as captain of the *Laconia*, Wentworth "could expect his success off the Western Islands to be published in the same source and read by Anne Elliot." Similarly, Jane Austen, while visiting Ashe Park, had "read of [her brother] Frank's capture of a Turkish ship in the paper belonging to her neighbor Mr. Holder and wrote to [her sister] Cassandra at Godmersham Park, 'You will see the account in the Sun I dare say' (8–9 November 1800). The report came three months behind the event, so it is likely that Mr. Holder's was a local newspaper. *The London Gazette* made no mention of this particular exploit; neither did the [*Naval*] *Chronicle*, perhaps because the Turkish vessel was deliberately destroyed to prevent its cargo falling into enemy hands. In the summer of the same year, the *Chronicle* published a letter written by Sir Thomas Williams, Lieutenant Charles Austen's captain on the *Endymion*, itemizing the prizes taken that spring. . . . The proceeds from one of these prizes—and there were several relatively minor captures that year—paid for Jane and Cassandra's topaz crosses and gold chains."
4. From an entry dated September–October 1811. The parenthetical interpolation is Hay's.

examined, and found hard with work, and discoloured with tar, I was remanded for further examination.

Some of the gang then offered me spirits, while the scoundrel who had first laid hold of me put on a sympathising look, and observed what a pity it was to be pressed when almost within sight of the Scottish smacks.[5] Such sympathy was well calculated to exasperate my feelings, but to think of revenge was folly. I was more concerned they would examine my small bundle, for in it there were a pair of numbered naval stockings, purser's issue, which would not only have made them suppose I had been at sea, but that I had been in a warship. I contrived to hide these, unobserved, behind one of the benches.

In a short time I was re-conducted for further examination before the lieutenant, who told me I might as well make a frank confession of my circumstances as it would save time and ensure me better treatment. What could I do? I might indeed have continued solid and silent, but whether or not such a procedure might have procured me worse treatment, the one thing would not do was restore me to liberty. I therefore acknowledged I had made a voyage to the West Indies as carpenter.[6] His eyes brightened at this.

'I am glad of that, my lad,' said he, 'We are very much in need of carpenters. Step along with these men and they will give you a passage on board.'

I was then led back the way I came by the fellow who first seized me, put aboard a pinnace at Tower wharf, and by midday was lodged securely on board the *Enterprise*, where I was immediately sent down into the great cabin. Here there were tables covered in green cloth, loaded with papers, and surrounded by well-dressed and powdered men. Such silence prevailed, and such solemn gravity was displayed, I was struck with awe and dread. No sooner did I enter the door than every eye started on me, and as there might be some there who knew me, I scarcely dared raise my eyes. A short sketch of what had passed between the press officer and myself had been communicated to the examining officer, who thus addressed me.

'Well, young man, I understand you are a carpenter by trade?'

'Yes, sir.'

'And you have been at sea?'

---

5. Large, single-masted vessels.
6. Hay sailed to the West Indies as carpenter aboard the *Edward*, a merchant ship. As McInerney notes, "The *Edward* lay near the wreck of the *Amethyst*, and every boat that approached put Hay on tenterhooks in case it contained one of the *Amethyst*'s officers who might recognise him." (See Hay's account in chapter 17: "HMS *Amethyst*—we are wrecked and I run away: 7 December 1809–16 February 1811.") Accustomed only to "heavy dockyard work," Hay and others aboard the *Edward* faced the threat of impressment on the approach to Jamaica. Because the press targeted professional seamen, Hay disguised himself in the clothes of a footman to avoid impressment. Nearly all of the *Edward*'s crew deserted at Jamaica.

'One voyage, sir.'

'Are you willing to join the King's service?'

'No, sir.'

'Why?'

'Because I get much better wages in the merchant service and, should I be unable to agree with the captain, I am at liberty to leave at the end of the voyage.'

'As to wages,' said he, 'the chance of prize money is quite an equivalent, and if you are obedient and respect your officers, that is all that is necessary to ensure you good treatment. Besides,' continued he, 'you may in time be promoted to carpenter of a line-of-battle ship, when your wages will be higher than in the merchant service, and should any accident happen to you, you will be provided for.' I argued, but under great disadvantage. My interrogator was like a judge on the bench; I like a criminal at the bar.

'Take my advice, my lad,' continued he, 'Enter the service cheerfully, then you will have a bounty, and be in a fair way to promotion. If you continue to refuse, remember you are aboard, and you will be kept as a pressed man and treated accordingly.' I falteringly replied I could not think of engaging in any service voluntarily when I knew of a better situation elsewhere. He said no more, but making a motion with his hand, I was seized by two marines with these words ringing in my ears, 'A pressed man to go below!'

My doom now being fixed, I was thrust down among five or six score miserable beings who like myself had been kidnapped and immured in the unwholesome dungeon of the press room. Such is the blindness of human nature! We are so often on the very brink of a precipice, when we think ourselves in the utmost safety, and dream not of impending danger.

By some mismanagement on the part of the purser's steward, I was left all day without food and water and would have been the second day also, but that two or three of the most humane of the seamen took me into their mess and applied for my allowance of provisions. With the exception of these few, I was generally treated with ridicule and contempt. Seamen who have been pressed together into one ship usually have a great affection for one another. Their trade, their habits, and their misfortune are all the same and they become endeared by similarity of suffering. But my landward appearance placed me in some measure beyond the pale of sympathy. I was styled by way of distinction 'the gentleman', and considered a butt for their shafts of nautical wit and banter. This did not affect me greatly as I knew I myself had often joined in the same strain of irony against those being brought on board the *Salvador del Mundo* in landsmen's clothes. I was now merely being paid in my own coin.

Once or twice a day, a limited number of us were permitted on deck to breathe fresh air, but from the surly manner in which we were treated, it was easy to observe that this was not for our pleasure, but to preserve our health, which would have soon been greatly endangered with the pestiferous breaths and pestilential vapours of the press room. I remained in the ship something more than a week, when she became so crowded as to render the removal of a considerable number of us as a measure of necessity. I, among others, was put aboard a cutter,[7] closely confined, never seeing anything in our passage down river but the sky divided into minute squares by the gratings which covered our dungeon.

We arrived at the Nore shortly after dusk and were immediately put on board the *Ceres*, guard ship.[8] I rejoiced at its being so dark, because I thereby escaped the prying gaze of four or five hundred pairs of eyes, among whom some might have known me. The following day I blended in properly with this motley crowd, thinking it folly to dress any longer in landsman's clothing. I therefore purchased a second-hand jacket, trousers, and check shirt, and packed up my long coat, breeches, vest, white neck cloth, etc. lest I should need them on some future occasion.

Next morning, my acquaintances were greatly surprised to see how completely I had been metamorphosed, not only in my external appearance, but even more so in my manners. Hitherto I had preserved the greatest taciturnity. I knew that had I talked too much, sea phrases would have slipped out. Hence credit was given me for far more wisdom, learning and politeness than I possessed. How easy is it to be thought wise? It is merely to preserve silence and though we may not thereby give an opportunity of displaying our wisdom and wit, we can, with greater ease, conceal our ignorance and folly. Now, being seen to be able to string together the technical terms of seamanship, I was on a footing with the rest. None of my shipmates knew my name except one, pressed shortly after myself, and who called to me as soon as he came aboard. This was one of the sailors in the *Edward*, one of those who had seized the boat in the West Indies and pulled ashore in spite of the captain's threats.[9] Bill, Tom, Dick, Bob, Jack came all alike familiar to me, and when I knew I was spoken to I answered to all of them promiscuously.

In the ship we had liberty to go on deck at all hours, and were thus much more comfortable than on the *Enterprise*. Our distance

---

7. A small, fast, single-mast ship, initially used by smugglers or in pursuit of them.
8. A Royal Navy anchorage at the narrowing of the Thames Estuary. The Nore was the site of one of two 1797 mutinies (the second was at Spithead, an anchorage near Portsmouth). Among the Nore mutineers' demands were better pay and an end to the war with France.
9. McInerney notes that "the leaky state of the *Edward* was a major factor in the desertions" that took place at Jamaica: "food was often poor, and the crew were still at the mercy of an arbitrary, and sometimes tyrannical, master" (p. 18).

from shore being only about six or eight miles, the land was seen very clearly, and many an anxious, earnest look did I take of it, forming in my imagination schemes how to gain it. The distance from the shore itself was no small barrier, but what made the attempt truly hazardous was that there was only one point where there was any probability at all of making a landing: the Isle of Grain.[1] But how was this to be gained in the dark? And even suppose it gained, how could I escape observation in wet seaman's clothes? How could I travel anywhere without being intercepted? But even if these obstacles were surmountable—how was it possible to escape from a ship guarded by midshipmen, quartermasters, ships' corporals and marines? Even though any attempt to escape seemed impractical, I was constantly mediating upon the subject.

❉   ❉   ❉

CAPTAIN A. T. MAHAN, U.S.N.

Alfred Thayer Mahan (1840–1914) was an American naval officer and historian and president of the Naval War College of Rhode Island. Mahan's writings, including *The Influence of Sea Power upon History, 1660–1983* (1890), were influential in positing that Britain's control of the seas was responsible for its global economic, military, and political dominance. Published at a time of economic depression in the U.S., his arguments were applied to U.S. foreign policy and were instrumental in developing American economic expansion overseas.

From The Influence of Sea Power upon the French Revolution and Empire, 1793–1812[†]

The ten years following the Peace of Versailles, September 3, 1783, coming between the two great wars of American Independence and of the French Revolution, seem like a time of stagnation.[1] The muttering and heaving which foretold the oncome of the later struggle were indeed to be heard by those whose ears were open, long before 1793.[2] The opening events and violences which marked the political

1. At the Hoo Peninsula in Kent.
† From "Outline of Events in Europe, 1783–1793," in *The Influence of Sea Power upon the French Revolution and Empire, 1793–1812*, vol. 1, 4th ed. (Boston: Little, Brown, and Company, 1894), pp. 1–6. First published in 1892. Unless otherwise indicated, notes are by the editor of this Norton Critical Edition. Some of Mahan's notes have been omitted.
1. More commonly called the Peace of Paris, marking the end of the American Revolution.
2. The French Revolutionary Wars lasted from 1792 to 1802. In 1793, France declared war on Great Britain; King Louis XVI of France and his wife, Marie Antoinette, were guillotined; and the Reign of Terror began, though the starting point of the latter remains in dispute.

revolution were of earlier date, and war with Austria and Prussia began even in 1792; but the year 1793 stands out with a peculiar prominence, marked as it is by the murder of the king and queen, the beginning of the Reign of Terror, and the outbreak of hostilities with the great Sea Power, whose stubborn, relentless purpose and mighty wealth were to exert the decisive influence upon the result of the war. Untiring in sustaining with her gold the poorer powers of the Continent against the common enemy, dogged in bearing up alone the burden of the war, when one by one her allies dropped away, the year in which Great Britain, with her fleets, her commerce, and her money, rose against the French republic, with its conquering armies, its ruined navy, and its bankrupt treasury, may well be taken as the beginning of that tremendous strife which ended at Waterloo.

To the citizen of the United States, the war whose results were summed up and sealed in the Treaty of Versailles is a landmark of history surpassing all others in interest and importance. His sympathies are stirred by the sufferings of the many, his pride animated by the noble constancy of the few whose names will be forever identified with the birth-throes of his country. Yet in a less degree this feeling may well be shared by a native of Western Europe, though he have not the same vivid impression of the strife, which, in so distant a land and on so small a scale, brought a new nation to life. This indeed was the *great* outcome of that war; but in its progress, Europe, India, and the Sea had been the scenes of deeds of arms far more dazzling and at times much nearer home than the obscure contest in America. In dramatic effect nothing has exceeded the three-years' siege of Gibraltar, teeming as it did with exciting interest, fluctuating hopes and fears, triumphant expectation and bitter disappointment.[3] England from her shores saw gathered in the Channel sixty-six French and Spanish ships-of-the-line,—a force larger than had ever threatened her since the days of the Great Armada, and before which her inferior numbers had to fly, for the first time, to the shelter of her ports. Rodney and Suffren had conducted sea campaigns, fought sea fights, and won sea victories which stirred beyond the common the hearts of men in their day, and which still stand conspicuous in the story of either navy.[4] In one respect above all, this war was distinguished; in the development, on both sides, of naval power. Never since the days of De Ruyter and Tourville had so close a balance of strength been seen upon the seas. Never

3. In June 1779 (on King George III's birthday), the French and Spanish, allied with the Americans in declaring war on Britain, sought to capture Gibraltar, planning to then invade mainland Britain. The siege lasted for three years and seven months and was the longest in British military history.
4. Decorated naval officers George Rodney (1718–1792) of Britain and Pierre André de Suffren de Saint Tropez (1729–1788) of France.

since the Peace of Versailles to our own day has there been such an approach to equality between the parties to a sea war.

The three maritime nations issued wearied from the strife, as did also America; but the latter, though with many difficulties still to meet, was vigorous in youth and unfettered by bad political traditions. The colonists of yesterday were thoroughly fitted to retrieve their own fortunes and those of their country; to use the boundless resources which Divine Providence had made ready to their hands. It was quite otherwise with France and Spain; while Great Britain, though untouched with the seeds of decay that tainted her rivals, was weighed down with a heavy feeling of overthrow, loss and humiliation, which for the moment hid from her eyes the glory and wealth yet within her reach. Colonial ambition was still at its loftiest height among the nations of Europe, and she had lost her greatest, most powerful colony. Not only the king and the lords, but the mass of the people had set their hearts upon keeping America. Men of all classes had predicted ruin to the Empire if it parted with such a possession; and now they had lost it, wrung from them after a bitter struggle, in which their old enemies had overborne them on the field they called their own, the Sea. The Sea Power of Great Britain had been unequal to the task laid upon it, and so America was gone. A less resolute people might have lost hope.

If the triumph of France and Spain was proportionate to their rival's loss, this was no true measure of their gains, nor of the relative positions of the three in the years after the war. American Independence profited neither France nor Spain. The latter had indeed won back the Floridas and Minorca; but she had utterly failed before Gibraltar, and Jamaica had not even been attacked. Minorca, as Nelson afterwards said, was always England's when she wanted it.[5] It belonged not to this power or that, but to the nation that controlled the sea; so England retook it in 1798, when her fleets again entered the Mediterranean. France had gained even less than Spain. Her trading posts in India had been restored; but they, even more than Minorca, were defenceless unless in free communication with and supported by the sea power of the mother-country. In the West Indies she returned to Great Britain more than the latter did to her. "France," says a French historian, "had accomplished the duties of her providential mission" (in freeing America); "her moral interests, the interests of her glory and of her ideas were satisfied. The interests of her material power had been badly defended by her government; the only solid advantage she had obtained was

---

5. British navy admiral Horatio Nelson (1758–1805), who died in the Battle of Trafalgar.

depriving England of Minorca, that curb on Toulon, far more dangerous to us when in their hands than is Gibraltar."[6]

Unfortunately at this moment France was far richer in ideas, moral and political, and in renown, than in solid power. The increasing embarrassment of the Treasury forced her to stay her hand, and to yield to her rival terms of peace utterly beyond what the seeming strength of either side justified. The French navy had reaped glory in the five years of war; not so much, nearly, as French writers claim for it, but still it had done well, and the long contest must have increased the efficiency of its officers along with their growing experience. A little more time only was wanted for France, allied to Spain, to gain lasting results as well as passing fame. This time poverty refused her.

Spain, as for centuries back, still depended for her income almost wholly upon her treasure ships from America. Always risked by war, this supply became more than doubtful when the undisputed control of the sea passed to an enemy. The policy of Spain, as to peace or war, was therefore tied fast to that of France, without whose navy her shipping lay at England's mercy; and, though the national pride clung obstinately to its claim for Gibraltar, it was forced to give way.

Great Britain alone, after all her losses, rested on a solid foundation of strength. The American contest by itself had cost her nearly £100,000,000, and rather more than that amount had during the war been added to the national debt; but two years later this had ceased to increase, and soon the income of the State was greater than the outgo. Before the end of 1783, the second William Pitt, then a young man of twenty-four, became prime minister. With genius and aims specially fitted to the restorative duties of a time of peace, the first of British finance ministers in the opinion of Mr. Gladstone,[7] he bent his great powers to fostering the commerce and wealth of the British people. With firm but skilful hand he removed, as far as the prejudices of the day would permit and in the face of much opposition, the fetters, forged by a mistaken policy, that hampered the trade of the Empire. Promoting the exchange of goods with other nations, simplifying the collection of taxes and the revenue, he added at once to the wealth of the people and to the income of the State. Although very small in amount, as compared with the enormous figures of later years, the exports and imports of Great Britain increased over fifty per cent between the years 1784 and 1792. Even with the lately severed colonies of North America the

6. [(Henri) Martin, *Histoire de France*, vol. xix. p. 370 —Mahan.] *Histoire de France* was published in fifteen volumes (1833–36), with a revised fourth edition, consisting of sixteen volumes and index, in 1861–65.
7. Francesco Nobili-Vitelleschi, "Upper Houses in Modern States," *The Nineteenth Century: A Monthly Review*, ed. James Knowles, vol. 34 (July–December 1893): 922–31.

same rate of gain, as compared with the trade before the war, held good; while with the old enemy of his father and of England, with France, there was concluded in 1786 a treaty of commerce which was exceedingly liberal for those days, and will, it is said, bear a favorable comparison with any former or subsequent treaty between the two countries. "In the course of little more than three years from Mr. Pitt's acceptance of office as First Lord of the Treasury," says the eulogist of his distinguished rival, Fox, "great commercial and financial reforms had been effected. . . . The nation overcoming its difficulties, and rising buoyant from depression, began rapidly to increase its wealth, to revive its spirit, and renew its strength."[8]

* * *

C. L. R. JAMES

First published in 1938, *The Black Jacobins* analyzes the Haitian Revolution (1791–1803), which C. L. R. James calls "the only successful slave revolt in history." James (1901–1989), a Trinidadian scholar, playwright, and novelist with firsthand experience of British colonial rule, argued that Britain's abolition of the slave trade was driven less by philosophical or moral ideals than by economic and political interests, specifically against France, which relied on the labor of enslaved persons in its colonies.

From The Black Jacobins: Toussaint L'Ouverture and the San Domingo Revolution[†]

Prosperity is not a moral question and the justification of San Domingo was its prosperity. Never for centuries had the western world known such economic progress. By 1754, two years before the beginning of the Seven Years' War,[1] there were 599 plantations of sugar and 3,379 of indigo. During the Seven Years' War (1756–1763) the French marine, swept off the sea by the British Navy, could not bring the supplies on which the colony depended, the

---

8. *The Life and Times of Charles J. Fox*, 3 vols. (London: Richard Bentley, 1859–66). Russell served as British prime minister from 1846 to 1852.
† From *The Black Jacobins: Toussaint L'Ouverture and the San Domingo Revolution*, 2nd ed. (New York: Vintage, 1989), pp. 45–46, 269–71, 289–90. Reprinted with permission. Unless otherwise indicated, notes are by the editor of this Norton Critical Edition.
1. The Seven Years' War was the first global war, involving five continents and centered on colonial and territorial disputes. The considerable debt France incurred during the war was a major factor in the subsequent Napoleonic conflict. Notably, seven years is also the duration of Anne Elliot's separation from Captain Wentworth.

extensive smuggling trade could not supply the deficiency, thousands of slaves died from starvation and the upward rise of production, though not halted, was diminished. But after the Treaty of Paris in 1763 the colony made a great stride forward. In 1767 it exported 72 million pounds'[2] weight of raw sugar and 51 million pounds of white, a million pounds of indigo and two million pounds of cotton, and quantities of hides, molasses, cocoa and rum. Smuggling, which was winked at by the authorities, raised the official figures by at least 25 percent. Nor was it only in quantity that San Domingo excelled but in quality. * * *

If on no earthly spot was so much misery concentrated as on a slave-ship, then on no portion of the globe did its surface in proportion to its dimensions yield so much wealth as the colony of San Domingo.

And yet it was this very prosperity which would lead to the revolution.

* * *

Toussaint was perfectly right in his suspicions [about Napoleon's move to restore slavery in San Domingo]. What is the régime under which the colonies have most prospered, asked Bonaparte, and on being told the *ancien régime* he decided to restore it, slavery and Mulatto discrimination.

Bonaparte hated black people. The revolution had appointed that brave and brilliant Mulatto, General Dumas,[3] Commander-in-Chief of one of its armies, but Bonaparte detested him for his colour, and persecuted him. Yet Bonaparte was no colonist, and his anti-Negro bias was far from influencing his major policies. He wanted profits for his supporters, and the clamorous colonists found in him a ready ear. The bourgeoisie of the maritime towns wanted the fabulous profits of the old days. The passionate desire to free all humanity which had called for Negro freedom in the great days of the revolution now huddled in the slums of Paris and Marseilles, exhausted by its great efforts and terrorised by Bonaparte's bayonets and Fouché's police.[4]

But the abolition of slavery was one of the proudest memories of the revolution; and, much more important, the San Domingo blacks had an army and leaders trained to fight in the European manner.

2. Gaston-Martin, *L'Ère des Négriers (1714–1774)*, Paris, 1931, p. 424 [*James's note*].
3. [Father of Alexandre père and grandfather of Alexandre fils. France has erected a monument to these three in the Place Malesherbes, Paris —*James.*] Thomas-Alexandre Dumas Davy de la Pailleterie (1762–1806) of San Domingo (now Haiti) was mixed-race and the first Black man to earn the rank of general in France. His son (especially) and grandson were successful French novelists and authors.
4. Joseph Fouché (1759?–1820), French statesman, minister of the police, and deputy to the National Convention (1792–95) tasked with drafting a new constitution after the overthrow of the French monarchy.

These were no savage tribesmen with spears, against whom European soldiers armed with rifles could win undying glory.

Occupied with his European campaigns, Bonaparte never lost sight of San Domingo, as he never lost sight of anything. His officers presented plan after plan, but the British fleet and the unknown strength of the blacks prevented action. Yet early in March 1801, a shift in his policy nearly compelled him to leave Toussaint in complete charge of San Domingo.[5]

*   *   *

* * * [T]he British bourgeoisie, driven out of America, now fully realised the importance of India. Pitt, in collusion with Paul's son Alexander, organised the murder of the pro-French Paul.[6] Seven days after the letter to Toussaint was written, Paul was strangled, and on the following day the British fleet sailed into the Baltic.[7] When Bonaparte heard he knew at once that Pitt had beaten him, and the Indian raid was off. The letter and instructions to Toussaint were never sent, and Bonaparte prepared to destroy Toussaint. It is Toussaint's supreme merit that while he saw European civilisation as a valuable and necessary thing, and strove to lay its foundations among his people, he never had the illusion that it conferred any moral superiority. He knew French, British, and Spanish imperialists for the insatiable gangsters that they were, that there is no oath too sacred for them to break, no crime, deception, treachery, cruelty, destruction of human life and property which they would not commit against those who could not defend themselves.

*   *   *

The defeat of Toussaint in the War of Independence and his imprisonment and death in Europe are universally looked upon as a tragedy. They contain authentic elements of the tragic in that even at the height of the war Toussaint strove to maintain the French

5. In *Persuasion*, Captain Wentworth is introduced in Chapter IV as having been "made commander in consequence of the action off San Domingo, and not immediately employed, ha[ving] come into Somersetshire, in the summer of 1806." That year also saw the opening of the original seawater bathhouse at Lyme Regis.
6. [Eugene Tarlé, *Bonaparte,* London, 1937, pp. 116–17 —*James.*] William Pitt (1759–1806), British statesman and prime minister. Of the murder of Tsar Paul of Russia (1754–1801) in March 1801, Tarlé writes that "no one had the least doubt that it was the English who had organised the assassination" (p. 117).
7. See Sudhir Hazareesingh, *Black Spartacus: The Epic Life of Toussaint Louverture* (Farrar, Straus and Giroux, 2020). Hazareesingh details how, in early 1801, Bonaparte wrote a letter appointing L'Ouverture as "capitaine-général" of the San Domingo colony and naming him the "principal representative of the Republic." The letter was never sent and, by late March, L'Ouverture was "secretly struck off the register of French military officials." If any single event could be said to have "provoked Bonaparte's ire," it may have been L'Ouverture's "take-over of the Spanish territory of Santo Domingo," which Bonaparte viewed "as an act of insubordination."

connection as necessary to Haiti in its long and difficult climb to civilisation. Convinced that slavery could never be restored in San Domingo, he was equally convinced that a population of slaves recently landed from Africa could not attain to civilisation by "going it alone." His tergiversations, his inability to take the firm and realistic decisions which so distinguished his career and had become the complete expression of his personality, as we watch his blunders and the inevitable catastrophe, we have always to remember that there is no conflict of the insoluble dilemmas of the human condition, no division of a personality which can find itself only in its striving for the unattainable. Toussaint was a whole man. The man into which the French Revolution had made him demanded that the relation with the France of liberty, equality, and fraternity and the abolition of slavery without a debate, should be maintained. What revolutionary France signified was perpetually on his lips, in public statements, in his correspondence, in the spontaneous intimacy of private conversations. It was the highest stage of social existence that he could imagine. It was not only the framework of his mind. No one else was so conscious of its practical necessity in the social backwardness and primitive conditions of life around him. Being the man he was, by nature, and by a range and intensity of new experiences such as is given to few, that is the way he saw the world in which he lived. His unrealistic attitude to the former masters, at home and abroad, sprang not from any abstract humanitarianism or loyalty, but from a recognition that they alone had what San Domingo society needed. He believed that he could handle them. It was not improbable that he could have done it. He was in a situation strictly comparable to that of the greatest of all American statesmen, Abraham Lincoln, in 1865: if the thing could be done at all, he alone could do it.[8] Lincoln was not allowed to try. Toussaint fought desperately for the right to try.

8. Abraham Lincoln (1809–1865), American lawyer and statesman who served as president during the American Civil War (1861–65) from 1861 until his assassination in 1865. He issued the Emancipation Proclamation, which declared the enslaved persons of America legally free, in 1863.

Reception

[MARIA JANE JEWSBURY]

From Athenaeum[†]

In the slight sketches which will from time to time occupy a page of the *Athenaeum*, we shall alternate between the dead and the living, the past time and the present, and thus tincture criticism with biography. Would that the interesting and gifted woman whose name is prefixed to this paper, could be numbered among the living! Would that, instead of closing her works with the saddened feeling, that the source whence so much pure amusement emanated is sealed for ever, we could glance over the list of books "nearly ready for publication," and find another announced by the same author. Miss Austen, however, has been dead fourteen years; and from what has been laid before the public of a biographical nature, (slight as that is,) there seldom appears to have been a more beautiful accordance between an author's life and writings; in fact, in the life and education of Miss Austen, may be discerned many of the causes of the excellencies that mark her works. * * * Placed by Providence in easy and elegant circumstances—endowed preeminently with good sense, and a placid unobtrusive temperament, she passed unscathed through the ordeal of authorship, and, in addition to exciting enthusiastic affection in immediate friends, received the general good-will of all who knew her. This alone is a high tribute to the benevolence of her temper, and the polish of her manners in daily life; for in print, her peculiar forte is delineating folly, selfishness, and absurdity—especially in her own sex. In society, she had too much wit to lay herself open to the charge of being too witty; and discriminated too well to attract notice to her discrimination. She was, we suspect, like one of her own heroines, "incurably gentle,"[1] and acted on the principle of another, that "if a woman have the misfortune of knowing anything, she should conceal it as well as she

† From "Literary Women No. II. Jane Austen," *Athenaeum* 200 (Aug. 27, 1831): 553–54.
1. A reference to Fanny Price, in *Mansfield Park* (1814).

can."[2] Besides this, whilst literature was a delightful occupation, it was not a profession to Miss Austen; she was not irrational enough to despise reputation and profit when they sought her, but she became an authoress entirely from taste and inclination; and as her judgment made her severely critical before she published her works, her unambitious temper was amply satisfied with the attention bestowed upon them by the public.

Unlike that of many writers, Miss Austen's fame has grown fastest since she died; there was no *éclat* about her first, or second, or third appearance; the public took time to make up its mind; and she, not having staked her hopes of happiness on success or failure, and not being obliged by circumstances to stake something more tangible on these results, could afford to wait for the decision of her claims. Those claims have long been established beyond a question; but the merit of *first* recognizing them, belongs less to reviewers than to general readers.

The able article in the *Quarterly Review* for 1821, was founded on a posthumous work, when the praise or blame of ten thousand critics were equally unimportant to the author.[3] So retired, so unmarked by literary notoriety, was the life Miss Austen led, that if any likeness was ever taken of her, (and the contrary supposition would seem strange,) none has ever been engraved; and of no woman, whose writings are as numerous and distinguished, is there perhaps so little public beyond the circle of those who knew her when alive—

> A violet by a mossy stone
> Half hidden from the eye.[4]

With regard to her genius, we must adventure a few remarks. She herself compares her productions to a little bit of ivory two inches wide, worked upon with a brush so fine that little effect is produced after much labour.[5] It is so; her portraits are perfect likenesses, admirably finished, many of them gems, but it is all miniature-painting; and, satisfied with being inimitable in one line, she never

2. Slight misquotation of *Northanger Abbey* (1817).
3. A reference to a review essay by Richard Whately, who describes *Persuasion* as perhaps "superior to all" of Austen's novels: "it has more of that tender and elevated kind of interest which is aimed at by the generality of novels, and in pursuit of which they seldom fail of running into romantic extravagance: on the whole, it is one of the most elegant fictions of common life we ever remember to have met with." In "Modern Novels," *Quarterly Review* 24.48 (1821): 352–76, at 368.
4. From William Wordsworth's 1798 poem "She dwelt among the untrodden ways," published in *Lyrical Ballads*.
5. Austen wrote to her nephew, James Edward Austen-Leigh, in December 1816: "What should I do with your strong, manly, spirited Sketches, full of variety and Glow?—How could I possibly join them on to the little bit (two inches wide) of Ivory on which I work with so fine a Brush, as produces little effect after much Labour?" In William Austen-Leigh and Richard Arthur Austen-Leigh, *Jane Austen: Her Life and Letters* (Smith, Elder & Co., 1913), p. 378.

essayed canvas and oils—never tried her hand at a majestic daub.
Her "two inches of ivory" just describes her preparations for a tale
of three volumes. A village—two families connected together—three
or four interlopers, out of whom are to spring a little *tracasserie*—a
village or a country town, and by means of village and country town
visiting and gossiping, a real plot shall thicken, and its "rear of dark-
ness"[6] never be scattered till six pages off *Finis*. The plots are simple
in construction, and yet intricate in developement [*sic*];—the main
characters, those that the reader feels sure are to love, marry, and
make mischief, are introduced in the first or second chapter; the
work is all done by half a dozen people; no person, scene, or sentence,
is ever introduced needless to the matter in hand—no catastrophes,
or discoveries, or surprises of a grand nature are allowed—neither
children nor fortunes are lost or found by accident—the mind is never
taken off the level surface of life—the reader breakfasts, dines, walks,
and gossips, with the various worthies, till a process of transmutation
takes place in him, and he absolutely fancies himself one of the company. Yet the winding up of the plot involves a surprise; a few incidents are entangled at the beginning in the most simple and natural
manner, and till the close one never feels quite sure how they are to
be disentangled. Disentangled, however, they are, and that in a most
satisfactory manner. The secret is, Miss Austen was a thorough mistress in the knowledge of human character; how it is acted upon by
education and circumstance; and how, when once formed, it shows
itself through every hour of every day, and in every speech to every
person. Her conversations would be tiresome but for this; and her
personages, the fellows to whom may be met in the streets or drank
tea with at half an hour's notice, would excite no interest. But in Miss
Austen's hands we see into their hearts and hopes, their motives, their
struggles within themselves; and a sympathy is induced, which, if
extended to daily life and the world at large, would make the reader a
more amiable person. We think some of Miss Austen's works deficient
in delineations of a high cast of character, in an exalted tone of
thought and feeling, a religious bias that can be seen as well as understood; Miss Austen seemed afraid of imparting imagination to her
favourites, and conceived good sense the *ultima Thule*[7] of moral possessions. Good sense *is* very good, but St. Leon's Marguerite, and
Rebecca, and Desdemona, and many other glorious shadows of the
brain, possessed something more.[8] However, the author of 'Pride

---

6. See "L'Allegro" (1645), a pastoral poem by John Milton (1608–1674).
7. Highest degree or limit, often with a geographical valence: a place inaccessible and
   remote, the farthest of the faraway places (Latin).
8. References to heroines in William Godwin's *St. Leon: A Tale of the Sixteenth Century*
   (1799), Sir Walter Scott's *Ivanhoe: A Romance* (1819), and William Shakespeare's *Oth-
   ello* (1604).

and Prejudice,' &c., limited herself to this every-day world; and to
return to the point of view in which her books yield moral benefit,
we must think it a reader's own fault who does not close her pages
with more charity in his heart towards unpretending, if prosing
worth—with a higher estimation of simple kindness and sincere
good-will—with a quickened sense of the duty of bearing and forbearing in domestic intercourse, and of the pleasure of adding to
the little comforts even of persons who are neither wits nor
beauties—who, in a word, does not feel more disposed to be benevolent. * * * We sometimes feel that Miss Austen's works deal rather
too largely with the commonplace, petty, and disagreeable side of
human nature—that we should enjoy more frequent sketches of the
wise and high-hearted—that some of the books are too completely
pages out of the world. In the last posthumous tale ('Persuasion')
there is a strain of a higher mood; there is still the exquisite delin-
eation of common life, such life as we hear, and see, and make part
of, with the addition of a finer, more poetic, yet equally real tone of
thought and action in the principals. Miss Austen was sparing in
her introduction of nobler characters, for they are scattered sparingly in life, but the books in which she describes them most we like
most; they may not amuse so much at the moment, but they interest
more deeply and more happily. In many respects Miss Austen resem-
bled Crabbe:[9] she had not his genius for grappling with the passions,
and forcing them to pass before the reader in living, suffering, bodily
forms—but Crabbe in his lighter moods, unveiling the surface of
things, playing with the follies of man, and even dealing seriously
with such of his minor faults as all flesh is heir to. Crabbe himself,
when not describing the terrible, is scarcely superior to the accomplished subject of this article. Her death has made a chasm in our
light literature, the domestic novel with its home-born incidents, its
"familiar matter of to-day,"[1] its slight array of names and great cog-
nizance of people and things, its confinement to country life, and
total oblivion of costume, manners, the great world, and "the mirror of fashion."[2] Every species of composition, is, when good, to be
admired in its way; but the revival of the domestic novel would make
a pleasant interlude to the showy, sketchy, novels of high life. * * *

9. English poet George Crabbe (1754–1832), noted for his realistic portraits of village life
   and the hardship of poverty.
1. From William Wordsworth's poem "The Solitary Reaper" (1807).
2. A general term describing fashionable subjects, the "mirror" or "glass of fashion" refers to
   newspaper and journal reportage on the events, dress, and gatherings of high society, as
   in La Belle Assemblée, or, Bell's Court and Fashionable Magazine Addressed Particularly to
   the Ladies, a British women's magazine that ran from 1806 to 1837 and also published
   literary works, including a March 1818 review of Mary Shelley's Frankenstein (1818).

MARGARET OLIPHANT

Margaret Oliphant (1828–1897) was a prolific Scottish author and novelist. Using the name Mrs. Oliphant, she published frequently in *Blackwood's Edinburgh Magazine*, as well as supernatural fiction and ghost stories, and historical fiction, including *Magdalen Hepburn: A Story of the Scottish Reformation* (1854). Financial uncertainty is frequently cited as a factor in Oliphant's literary career.

From The Literary History of England in the End of the Eighteenth and Beginning of the Nineteenth Century[†]

It is curious to note the difference between their contemporary Mrs. Inchbald and these ladies of the new light.[1] The *Strange Story*, with its graceful talent and individuality, belongs to the eighteenth century altogether.[2] It deals with no definable development of human nature, and has in it no real study of life. It is a surprise to us to realise that *Pride and Prejudice* was actually written earlier than that curious romance, though it did not till some time after see the light. Mrs. Inchbald is of the past, and her production is almost archaic; but Jane Austen belongs to humanity in all periods, and Miss Edgeworth is even more clearly natural and practical.[3] The life of average human nature swept by no violence of passions, disturbed by no volcanic events, came suddenly uppermost in the works of these women as it had never done before. Miss Austen in particular, the greatest and most enduring of the three, found enough in the quiet tenor of life which fell under her own eyes to interest the world. Without ever stepping out from the shelter of home, or calling to her help a single incident that might not have happened next door, she held the reader, if not breathless, yet in that pleased and happy suspension of personal cares and absorption of amused interest, which is the very triumph of fiction. She had not even a new country to reveal like Miss Edgeworth, or a quaint and obscure region of odd manners and customs like Miss Ferrier.[4] She

---

[†] From *Literary History of England in the End of the Eighteenth and Beginning of the Nineteenth Century*, vol. 3 (London: Macmillan & Co., 1882), pp. 205–07, 221–22.
1. Elizabeth Inchbald (1753–1821), English author, novelist, and actor. Inchbald's translation of *Lovers' Vows* (*Das Kind der Liebe*, 1791) by the German dramatist August von Kotzebue (1769–1817) made famous the play that features centrally in Austen's *Mansfield Park* (1814).
2. Oliphant presumably has in mind *A Simple Story* (1791).
3. Maria Edgeworth (1768–1849), Irish novelist and author of *Belinda* (1801) and *Castle Rackrent* (1800).
4. Susan Edmonstone Ferrier (1782–1854), Scottish novelist, the author of *Marriage* (1818) and other novels of manners and Scottish life.

had nothing to say that England did not know, and no exhibition of highly-wrought feeling, or extraordinary story to tell. The effect she produced was entirely novel, without any warrant or reason, except the ineffable and never-to-be-defined reason of genius which made it possible to turn all those commonplace events into things more interesting than passion. It would be difficult to find anything nearer witchcraft and magic. Why we should be so amused and delighted by matters of such ordinary purport, and why a tiresome old woman or crotchety old man, whom, in real life, we would avoid, should become in print an exquisite diversion, is one of the most unaccountable of literary phenomena. But so it is. And as we mark the growth and rise of the new flood of noble poetry at the meeting-point of the two centuries, we should be negligent of one of the first duties of a historian if we did not note likewise the sudden development of purely feminine genius as the same great era. Female writers have never been wanting. In the dimmest ages there has always been one here and there adding a mild, often a feeble, soprano to the deeper tenor of the concert. How it is that these have never risen to the higher notes and led the strain, as the feminine voice does in music, we need not inquire. Women are very heavily weighted for any race, but it can scarcely be that circumstances account for an inferiority so continual. But the opening of an entirely feminine strain of the highest character and importance—a branch of art worthy and noble, and in no way inferior, yet quite characteristically feminine, must, we think, be dated here in the works of these three ladies. Women's books before had either been echoes of those of men, or weakly womanish, addressed to "the fair" like so many productions of the eighteenth century. The three sister novelists who came to light in the beginning of the nineteenth were, in their own way, as remarkable and individual as Scott or Fielding,[5] and opened up for women after them a new and characteristic path in literature.

*   *   *

*** [Jane Austen] was only about twenty in her sheltered and happy life at home in the end of the old century, when she wrote what might have been the outcome of the profoundest prolonged observation and study of mankind—what is, we think, the most perfect of all her works—*Pride and Prejudice*. It must have been in her father's parish, in the easy intercourse of village or rural life, that she saw, probably without knowing she saw, so many varieties of human nature. No feasible inducement was before her to bring this strange endowment to life; no hothouse training in moralities and the creed

5. Sir Walter Scott (1771–1832), best-selling Scottish novelist and poet who favorably reviewed Austen's *Emma* in the *Quarterly Review* in 1815; Henry Fielding (1707–1754), English novelist, playwright, and satirist.

of universal instructiveness; no restless literary papa to set her an example; no unknown society or manners to reveal. An excellent ordinary strain of honest gentlefolks, peaceably tedious and undistinguished, and anxious to make it apparent that their Jane knew nothing of literary people, and was quite out of any possibility of association with such a ragged regiment, was the family that gave her birth. She wrote—no one can tell why—out of native instinct, preferring that way of amusing herself to fine needlework, telling stories, as Burns rhymed, "for fun," with no ulterior views.[6] She was pretty, sprightly, well taken care of—a model English girl, simple, and saucy, and fair. It is almost impossible to imagine that she who traced all the vicissitudes of long and faithful love in the delicate and womanly soul of Anne Elliot can have been entirely without such experiences in her own person; but if so, her life shows no trace of the hidden episode, and all is plain and unexciting and matter-of-fact in the little record.[7] * * *

CHARLES BEECHER HOGAN

From Jane Austen and Her Early Public[†]

During her lifetime Jane Austen was scarcely known; her six novels crept forth unnoticed; interest in her work came very slowly. . . .

So, at least, we have been told.[1]

Jane Austen died in 1817, and her novels had begun to "creep forth" only six years earlier. Between 1811 and 1816 she published four books; two were published posthumously.

To say that these books received the instantaneous welcome accorded to *Waverley* or to *Childe Harold*[2] would be preposterous, but to accept as definitive any notion that Jane Austen's novels were

6. Robert Burns (1759–1796), Scottish poet and author of "Epistle to James Smith" (1786), addressed to his friend "Dear Smith, the sleek'st, pawkie [cunning] thief / That e'er attempted stealth or rief [plunder]!" (lines 1–2). Smith, a draper, died in Jamaica (ca. 1823), a site Burns contemplates emigrating to in several of his writings, including "On a Scotch Bard, Gone to the West Indies" (1786). In *The Complete Works of Robert Burns*, ed. Allen Cunningham (Philips, Sampson, and Co., 1855).

7. Oliphant later characterizes *Persuasion* as "the least amusing of Miss Austen's books, but perhaps the most interesting, with its one *motif* distinct and fine, the thread that runs through all." By "motif" she means the love story, that "most momentous of human sentiments," coupled with Anne's "wistful wonder whether all is over, continually about her in the very air," and a "sense of suppressed anxiety and mute fear and hope" (p. 235).

† From *Review of English Studies* 1.1 (1950): 39, 41, 43, 51. Used with permission of Oxford University Press, conveyed through Copyright Clearance Center, Inc. Unless otherwise indicated, notes are by Hogan.

1. As the opening lines make clear, Hogan is, in 1950, working to revise critical truisms about Austen's early readership and reception [*Editor's note*].

2. *Waverley; or, 'Tis Sixty Years Since* (1814), a novel by Sir Walter Scott (1771–1832), and *Childe Harold's Pilgrimage* (1812–18), a long narrative poem by George Gordon, Lord Byron (1788–1824), were best-sellers in their day [*Editor's note*].

obliged to creep forth, or were scarcely known, would be not only equally preposterous but in every way misleading.

Jane Austen was a modest woman; she was more interested in writing a good book than in enjoying good publicity. Her novels were very dear to her: she wanted them to succeed, and they did succeed. Before she died two of them had gone into second editions, and one into a third. Her total profits were approximately £700. By the standards of today, and perhaps by those of 1817 as well, this sum may appear to be extremely small. But because Jane Austen herself made no effort to capitalize on this unostentatious success, and because her books were unostentatious in and of themselves, it by no means follows that a generation had to pass before anybody knew anything at all about her or cared to buy what she had to offer. Indeed, as Mr. Chapman points out, her fame "must have been in a way to dwindle from malnutrition, when in 1832 Bentley decided to restore it by including her works in his series of Standard Novels."[3] Malnutrition implies a wish to be fed. From 1811 to the late 1830's how urgent, then, was this wish?

* * *

* * * *Pride and Prejudice* * * * was first advertised in the *Morning Chronicle* of 28 January 1813, and was reviewed promptly, and at length, by the faithful *British Critic*.[4] The character of Elizabeth [Bennet] was found to be "supported with great spirit and consistency throughout"; Mr. Collins was pronounced "excellent"; and in Mr. Bennet was discovered "some novelty of character." The reviewer also remarked that

> We had occasion to speak favourably of the former production of this author or authoress, . . . and we readily do the same of the present. It is very far superior to almost all the publications of the kind which have lately come before us. . . . We entertain very little doubt that their [these volumes'] successful circulation will induce the author to similar exertions.

The Critical Review gave its usual lengthy exegesis of the plot, and then continued:

> We cannot conclude, without repeating our approbation of this performance, which rises very superior to any novel we have lately met with in the delineation of domestic scenes. . . . There is not one person in the drama with whom we could readily

3. R. W. Chapman, "Jane Austen and Her Publishers," *London Mercury* 22 (August 1930): 342. [Richard Bentley (1794–1871), prominent English publisher who produced and sold cheap, single-volume editions of popular novels, including Austen's —*Editor*.]
4. [*British Critic*] xli (Feb. 1813), 189–90.

dispense; they . . . fill their several stations, with great credit to themselves, and much satisfaction to the reader.[5]

Interest was at once aroused—and in a man whose influence was very great. The editor of the *Quarterly Review*[6] told the leading publisher of London that he had

> for the first time looked into "Pride and Prejudice"; and it is really a very pretty thing. No dark passages; no secret chambers; no wind-howlings in long galleries; no drops of blood upon a rusty dagger—things that should now be left to ladies' maids and sentimental washerwomen.[7]

Ground was evidently broken here. Two years later William Gifford made the arrangements for the famous review of *Emma* by Sir Walter Scott, at the very time that John Murray had taken over from Egerton (beginning with the second edition of *Mansfield Park*) the publication of Jane Austen's novels.

* * *

* * * The first announcement of publication [of *Mansfield Park*] is to be found in the *Star* of 9 May 1814, the edition consisting of about as many copies as did the first edition of *Pride and Prejudice*.[8]

Interest among the early readers of the book was keen, save among the reviewers, by whom it was totally ignored. It was ignored even by Scott, when, in his review of *Emma*, he undertook to speak of its author's previous novels. Jane Austen herself, whose opinion of *Mansfield Park* was high, wondered why this should have been so. On 1 April 1816 she wrote to John Murray, "I cannot but be sorry that so clever a man as the Reviewer of 'Emma' should consider [*Mansfield Park*] as unworthy of being noticed."[9]

Be that as it may, its admirers were numerous. A month after its publication, Lady Vernon was recommending it to Mrs. Frampton in lieu of Madame d'Arblay's recently published *The Wanderer*, as "very natural, and the characters well drawn."[1] The Earl of Dudley was

---

5. [*Critical Review*] iii, 4th ser. (March 1813), 324.

6. The *Quarterly Review* was founded by the London publishing house of John Murray (1737–1793), a Scottish officer of the Royal Marines, and edited by William Gifford (1756–1826) from 1809 to 1824. Murray's son John (1778–1843) was responsible for publishing works by Scott, Byron, and Austen [*Editor's note*].

7. Samuel Smiles, *Memoir and Correspondence of the Late John Murray* (London, 1891), i. 282. [The quotation is from an 1812 letter from William Gifford to John Murray —*Editor.*]

8. Geoffrey Keynes, *Jane Austen: A Bibliography* (London, 1929), p. 12. [The estimate for both books is about 1,500 copies —*Editor.*]

9. Jane Austen, *Letters*, ed. R. W. Chapman (Oxford, 1932), ii, 453.

1. *The Journal of Mary Frampton*, ed. Harriot Georgiana Mundy (London, 1885), p. 226. Lady Vernon to Mrs. Frampton (June 1814). [Madame d'Arblay is Frances (Fanny) Burney (1752–1840), English novelist, satirist, and playwright. *The Wanderer; or, Female Difficulties* (1814) was her final novel —*Editor.*]

equally enthusiastic. On 11 August 1814 he told Mrs. Dugald Stewart[2]
that he was "a great admirer of the two other works by the same
author."

> She has not so much fine humour as your friend Miss Edge-
> worth [he continued], but she is more skilful in contriving a
> story, she has a great deal more feeling, and she never plagues
> you with any chemistry, mechanics, or political economy.[3]

✳   ✳   ✳

[In the 1830s, a] clear indication of how familiar Jane Austen's
characters already were to the general public comes from Lockhart
himself. In referring to these personages in his *Letter to the Right
Hon. Lord Byron*,[4] he plainly infers that no identification of who
they were or where they came from was necessary.

> Now, tell me, Mrs. Goddard, now tell me, Miss Price, now tell
> me, dear Harriet Smith, and dear, dear Mrs. Elton, do tell me,
> is not this just the very look, that one would have fancied for
> Childe Harold? . . . Poor Lord Byron! who can say how much
> he may have been to be pitied? I am sure I would; I can bear
> with all Mr. E.'s eccentricities. . . . What think you of that
> other [passage] we were talking of on Saturday evening at Miss
> Bates's?
> —"Nay, smile not at my sullen brow,
> Alas! I cannot smile again."
> I forget the rest;—but nobody has such a memory as Mrs. E.

Scott, Miss Edgeworth, Jeffrey, Miss Ferrier, Miss Mitford, Lockhart, Whately. . . . Jane Austen's name was, to the literary world of
her day, a familiar one, and one that was held in esteem and affection. In 1835 Coleridge's "high commendation of Miss Austen's
novels, as being in their way perfectly genuine and individual productions" was made public.[5] Bulwer-Lytton wrote to his mother to
reprove her for disliking

> *Emma* and the other books. They enjoy the highest reputa-
> tion, and I own, for my part, I was delighted with them. . . .
> Their charm is in being so natural and simple. At all events,

2. Dugald Stewart (1753–1828), Scottish philosopher and historian. His wife, Helen
   D'Arcy Stewart (1765–1838), was a Scottish poet and author [*Editor's note*].
3. S. H. Romilly, *Letters to "Ivy" from the first Earl of Dudley* (London, 1905), p. 250.
4. John Bull, *Letter to the Right Hon. Lord Byron* (London, 1821), pp. 29–31. The identity
   of "John Bull" has been established by Alan Lang Strout in his edition of the pamphlet
   (Norman, Oklahoma, 1947).
5. *Specimens of the Table Talk of the Late Samuel Taylor Coleridge* [ed. Henry Nelson
   Coleridge] (London, 1835), i. 112.

they are generally much admired, and I was quite serious in my praise of them.[6]

*   *   *

IAN WATT

Ian Watt's highly influential study focuses primarily on the three British authors named in the subtitle but devotes a final coda, "Realism and the Later Tradition: A Note," pp. 290–302, to Austen along with two other prominent British female novelists, Frances (Fanny) Burney (1752–1840) and George Eliot (1819–1880).

From The Rise of the Novel[†]

* * * Jane Austen was the heir of Fanny Burney, herself no inconsiderable figure in bringing together the divergent directions which the geniuses of Richardson and Fielding[1] had imposed upon the novel. Both women novelists followed Richardson—the Richardson of the less intense domestic conflicts of *Sir Charles Grandison*—in their minute presentation of daily life. At the same time Fanny Burney and Jane Austen followed Fielding in adopting a more detached attitude to their narrative material, and in evaluating it from a comic and objective point of view. It is here that Jane Austen's technical genius manifests itself. She dispensed with the participating narrator, whether as the author of a memoir as in Defoe,[2] or as a letter-writer as in Richardson, probably because both of these roles make freedom to comment and evaluate more difficult to arrange; instead she told her stories after Fielding's manner, as a confessed author. Jane Austen's variant of the commenting narrator, however, was so much more discreet that it did not substantially affect the authenticity of her narrative. Her analyses of her characters and their states of mind, and her ironical juxtapositions of motive and situation, are as pointed as anything

---

6. The Earl of Lytton, *The Life of Edward Bulwer First Lord Lytton* (London, 1913), i. 457 (Edward Bulwer to Mrs. W. E. Bulwer, 23 Oct. 1834).

† From *The Rise of the Novel: Studies in Defoe, Fielding, and Richardson* (Berkeley: University of California Press, 1957), pp. 296–99. Used with permission of University of California Press, conveyed through Copyright Clearance Center, Inc. Unless otherwise indicated, notes are by Watt.

1. Samuel Richardson (1689–1761) and Henry Fielding (1707–1754), English novelists [*Editor's note*].

2. Daniel Defoe (1660–1731), English writer, merchant, and spy. Defoe's *Robinson Crusoe* (1719) is heralded as among the earliest examples of what would become the modern Anglophone novel [*Editor's note*].

in Fielding, but they do not seem to come from an intrusive author but rather from some august and impersonal spirit of social and psychological understanding.

At the same time, Jane Austen varied her narrative point of view sufficiently to give us, not only editorial comment, but much of Defoe's and Richardson's psychological closeness to the subjective world of the characters. In her novels there is usually one character whose consciousness is tacitly accorded a privileged status and whose mental life is rendered more completely than that of other characters. In *Pride and Prejudice* (published 1813), for example, the story is told substantially from the point of view of Elizabeth Bennet, the heroine; but the identification is always qualified by the other role of the narrator acting as dispassionate analyst, and as a result the reader does not lose his critical awareness of the novel as a whole. * * *

Jane Austen's novels, in short, must be seen as the most successful solutions of the two general narrative problems for which Richardson and Fielding had provided only partial answers. She was able to combine into a harmonious unity the advantages both of realism of presentation and realism of assessment, of the internal and of the external approaches to character; her novels have authenticity without diffuseness or trickery, wisdom of social comment without a garrulous essayist, and a sense of the social order which is not achieved at the expense of the individuality and autonomy of the characters.[3]

*   *   *

Jane Austen's novels are also representative in another sense; they reflect the process whereby * * * women were playing an increasingly important part in the literary scene. The majority of eighteenth-century novels were actually written by women, but this had long remained a purely quantitative assertion of dominance; it was Jane Austen who completed the work that Fanny Burney had begun, and challenged masculine prerogative in a much more important matter. Her example suggests that the feminine sensibility was in some ways better equipped to reveal the intricacies of personal relationships and was therefore at a real advantage in the realm of the novel. The reasons for the greater feminine command of the area of personal relationships would be difficult and lengthy to detail; one of the main ones is probably that suggested by John Stuart Mill's statement that "all the education that women receive from society inculcates in them the feeling that the individuals connected with them are the

---

3. Watt distinguishes between a realism of presentation, privileging technical and accurate (historical or experiential) detail, and realism of assessment, focused on evaluation and judgment, usually moral in nature [*Editor's note*].

only ones to whom they owe any duty."[4] As to the connection of this with the novel, there can surely be little doubt. Henry James, for example, alluded to it in a tribute which is characteristic in its scrupulous moderation: "Women are delicate and patient observers; they hold their noses close, as it were, to the texture of life. They feel and perceive the real with a kind of personal tact, and their observations are recorded in a thousand delightful volumes."[5] More generally, James elsewhere linked the "immensely great conspicuity of the novel" in modern civilization to the "immensely great conspicuity of the attitude of women."[6]

In Jane Austen, Fanny Burney, and George Eliot, the advantages of the feminine point of view outweigh the restrictions of social horizon which have until recently been associated with it. At the same time it is surely true that the dominance of women readers in the public for the novel is connected with the characteristic kind of weakness and unreality to which the form is liable—its tendency to restrict the field on which its psychological and intellectual discriminations operate to a small and arbitrary selection of human situations, a restriction which, since Fielding, has affected all but a very few English novels with a certain narrowing of the framework of experience and permitted attitude.

＊　＊　＊

4. *The Subjection of Women* (London, 1924), p. 105. [Originally published in 1869, John Stuart Mill's (1806–1873) defense of the rights and equality of women was cowritten with his wife Harriet Taylor Mill, who died in 1858 —*Editor.*]

5. Anthony Trollope, *Partial Portraits* (London, 1888), p. 50. One comparative study of conversations showed that 37 per cent of women's conversations were about persons as against 16 per cent of men's (M. H. Landis and H. E. Burtt, "A Study of Conversations," *J. Comp. Psychology*, IV (1924), 81–89).

6. "Mrs. Humphry Ward," *Essays in London* (London, 1893), p. 265.

CRITICISM

SUSAN MORGAN

From Captain Wentworth, British Imperialism and Personal Romance†

In his fascinating book on *Jane Austen and Representations of Regency England*, Roger Sales opens his chapter on *Persuasion* with the claim that "*Persuasion* debates the question of who will, and who deserves to, win the peace after the ending of the Napoleonic Wars."[1] One evocative power of this claim for me is that it emphasizes approaching the novel within the framework of British military interests at the beginning of the nineteenth century.[2] I want to extend Sales's point by saying that to talk about British military interests is also to talk about its imperial interests. Moira Ferguson and Edward Said have published critiques of *Mansfield Park* as a novel which, at least implicitly, supports the British government's policies of conquering and economically exploiting other countries.[3] Although I don't agree with their readings, I do agree with their premise: that it is important to consider Austen's work in the light of larger British international policies. Other critics, and I think of Frank Gibbon and, more recently, Joseph Lew, have looked in detail at the West Indian and anti-slavery allusions in *Mansfield Park* to argue that the book does not support British imperial enterprise.[4] But what about *Persuasion?* In *Persuasion* Captain Wentworth and his fellow officers in the Royal Navy are presented as an admirable and desirable group. Yet it is undeniable that throughout the nineteenth century the Navy would make possible the expansion of the empire. Is *Persuasion*, then, a novel which in some implicit ways supports British imperialism? And even if we decide that the answer is no, I think we must still ask the question of the political significance of the Royal Navy's presence in Austen's novel.

* * *

† From *Persuasions* 18 (1996): 88–91, 92–94, 95–97. Reprinted by permission of Susan Morgan. Unless otherwise indicated, notes are by Morgan. Page numbers in brackets are to this Norton Critical Edition.
1. Roger Sales, *Jane Austen and Representations of Regency England* (London: Routledge Press, 1994) 170.
2. For a book-length discussion of Austen's links to the French Revolution see Warren Roberts, *Jane Austen and the French Revolution* (New York: St. Martin's Press, 1979).
3. Moira Ferguson, "*Mansfield Park*: Slavery, Colonialism and Gender," *Oxford Literary Review* 13, 1–2 (1991): 118–39; Edward Said, *Culture and Imperialism* (New York: Alfred A. Knopf, 1993).
4. Frank Gibbon, "The Antiguan Connection: Some New Light on *Mansfield Park*," *The Cambridge Quarterly* Xl, 2 (1982): 298–305; Joseph Lew, "'That Abominable Traffic': *Mansfield Park* and the Dynamics of Slavery," *History, Gender and Eighteenth-Century Literature*, ed. Beth Fowkes Tobin (Athens: U of Georgia P, 1994).

* * * [T]here are two major reasons why it is important to think about *Persuasion* in terms of British imperialism. The first is that the topic *is* in the book. I think Jane Austen's readers have long since abandoned the portrait of the novels and their author as small gems about a very small world, written by a spinster of great genius but little or no experience or larger historical and political awareness. It is not enough to conclude that *Persuasion* is concerned with discussions about and portraits of the Royal Navy because Austen had two brothers in the navy and she loved them. I need only recall the explicit reference to how Captain Wentworth exerts himself at the end of the novel to make sure that Mrs. Smith will receive the income from her property in the West Indies. *Persuasion* seems to me very clearly to take as one of its major themes a representation of the navy as a national institution. Through its portraits of Admiral Croft, Captains Harville and Benwick, and Captain Wentworth, the novel offers some eloquent and complex arguments about what that navy should be like.

The second reason why I believe *Persuasion* should be looked at in terms of what it has to say about the British navy and thus about its nation's relations to other nations is that not to do so is to miss a whole dimension of what makes this novel so brilliant. *Persuasion* is a story of heterosexual love, not in some universal way but very much according to the possibilities and limitations of men and women of Austen's social class at the beginning of the nineteenth century. The novel offers a vision, as public and political as it is personal and romantic, in ways for nations as well as lovers to exist in the world. To read *Persuasion* as simply about a couple rather than about a couple and a country is to fall back on an approach that would leave out much of Austen's achievement.

The Royal Navy

During the nineteenth century the Royal Navy was crucial to British takeovers of states and regions around the world, from the West Indies to Singapore and the Malay Peninsula.[5] Seapower was why the British East India Company could pursue a very profitable policy of exporting opium to China in spite of the strict laws of the government of China.[6] And when that government finally moved in 1839 to stop the flow of smugglers bringing this illegal and debilitating

---

5. See J. R. Hill, ed., *The Oxford Illustrated History of the Royal Navy* (New York: Oxford UP, 1995); Lieut.-Cmdr. P. K. Kemp, ed., *History of the Royal Navy* (New York: G. P. Putnam's Sons, 1969); Fletcher Pratt, *Empire and the Sea* (New York: Henry Holt & Company, 1946).
6. For a discussion of the Opium Wars, see J. R. Hill, ed., *The Oxford Illustrated History of the Royal Navy*. See also Nicholas Tarling, ed., *The Cambridge History of Southeast Asia, Vol. Two: The Nineteenth and Twentieth Centuries* (Cambridge: Cambridge UP, 1992).

drug into their country by confiscating the supplies, it was the Royal Navy that attacked China's coast cities, blew away its fragile navy and much of its gathered army, and forced China's surrender. It was the threatening guns of the Royal Navy that forced China in 1842 to accept the appalling terms that England would not only have the right to export opium into China but would even get to keep the island of Hong Kong as a port for its ships and a depot for their cargoes of opium. And it was Royal Navy guns again at the end of the second Opium War that forced an extremely reluctant Chinese government in 1858 to accept British terms and sign the Treaty of Tiensin, actually legalizing opium in China.

The Chinese Opium Wars are only one historic moment where the navy was brought in to protect the profits, no matter how unjust or immoral, of British business. But the Opium Wars happened twenty to forty years after Austen was dead and on the opposite side of the earth. Does that make them irrelevant to a discussion of *Persuasion*? Why bring them up at all? Part of what I will be suggesting is that later international events such as the Opium Wars are not at all irrelevant to reading Austen.

But closer to home, both in time and space, were the navy's activities in the Caribbean. When we look at the activities of the Royal Navy in the later decades of the eighteenth century and during the first two decades of the nineteenth, in Austen's lifetime, their ships were everywhere. The wars with the French were fought almost all around the globe, as much through control of territories and trade routes as through battles. There were British fleets in the Mediterranean, the Baltic, the Indian Ocean and Far East, North America and the Atlantic, and the West Indies.[7] The West Indies was a major site of the ongoing battles with Napoleon throughout the first decade of the nineteenth century, both because neither the French nor the British were able to control the region and because its islands were so profitable.[8] Indeed, the West Indian planters formed a powerful block, referred to as the plantocracy, in the British parliament.

The reference in *Persuasion* to Mrs. Smith's property in the West Indies and the possible income from it, almost certainly refers to a plantation, probably sugar, with the income probably gained from crops produced by slave labor. On the other hand, references to West Indian plantations were not automatically associated with support for slavery. On the contrary, in that first decade of the century, after the March 1802 Treaty of Amiens and the brief peace it brought, a standard argument in parliament against the planters' block was

---

7. See G. J. Marcus, *Heart of Oak: A Survey of British Seapower in the Georgian Era* (London: Oxford UP, 1975), 20–28. See also N. A. M. Rodger, *The Wooden World: An Anatomy of the Georgian Navy* (London: Collins, 1986).

8. P. K. Kemp, ed., *History of the Royal Navy*, 150.

that, even leaving aside any moral question, West Indian businesses would improve their profits by replacing slaves with wage labor. Henry Brougham's 1803 pamphlet, *Inquiry into the Colonial Policy of the European Powers*, explicitly opposed the argument of the West Indian planters' lobby that slavery was good for business, by claiming that in the West Indies abolition would help rather than hinder British business interests.[9] This extremely popular pamphlet influenced the successful vote in the British Commons in 1804 to abolish the British slave trade (though a vote in the combined houses would not happen until 1807). The relations of slavery to British West Indian agricultural profits were a matter of visible public debate in the first decade of the nineteenth century. Austen's references to West Indian properties simply do not mean an acceptance of slave labor there.

In fact, it is more plausible that Austen's references imply the opposite. Another famous pamphlet was James Stephen's 1802 *The Crisis [of] the Sugar Colonies*:[1] Stephen argued that the slave revolution on the French held island of St. Domingue not only "showed the inherent fragility of the slave systems of the West Indies." He predicted that "Napoleon would be defeated by black insurgency." For Stephen, not only was West Indian slavery associated with that wicked Napoleon and the French. His greater claim was that winning the coming war against Napoleon actually depended on the British choosing to reform their own West Indian practices. For this abolitionist, the war with Napoleon would be won or lost in the West Indian theatre. Beating the French required eliminating an evil system employed by the French and establishing in its stead a British system of hired workers, thus removing "the motive for slave insurrection."[2]

Stephen's argument was based on his reference to the island known on its west side as French Saint Domingue and on its east side as San Domingo, now Haiti and the Dominican Republic.[3] One

9. I am indebted throughout this discussion to Robin Blackburn, *The Overthrow of Colonial Slavery, 1776–1848* (London: Verso, 1988, particularly the chapter "British Slave Trade Abolition: 1803–14"). See also James Walvin, *England, Slaves and Freedom, 1776–1823* (Jackson: U of Mississippi P, 1986); and Clare Midgley, *Women Against Slavery: The British Campaigns, 1780–1870* (London: Routledge, 1992).
1. Excerpted in this volume [*Editor's note*].
2. Robin Blackburn, *The Overthrow of Colonial Slavery*, 300–01. For an extended discussion of British tracts about San Domingo see Moira Ferguson, *Subject to Others: British Women Writers and Colonial Slavery, 1670–1834* (New York: Routledge, 1992).
3. As Morgan notes elsewhere (p. 92), the island had personal significance for Austen. Her sister Cassandra's fiancé, Rev. Thomas Fowle, died in San Domingo in 1792, and Frank Austen, their brother, fought in the 1806 Battle of San Domingo. That Wentworth earns the rank of commander there, in a conflict "particularly linked for British audiences with arguments for the cause of liberty," indicates Austen's awareness of the political significance of the site as well: his "enemies were explicitly the French, but also—as inextricably tied with the French through the mere mention of San Domingo—the cruelties of the slave trade and of the plantation slavery system" [*Editor's note*].

of the largest islands in the West Indies, Saint Domingue was generally also considered the richest. The successful slave revolts against the French in Saint Domingue from 1791 through 1802, along with a few bungled British attempts to control the island in 1795 and 1796, had made it the most highly visible former possession of the French in the West Indies to the British public.[4] Just to mention St. Domingue was to invoke tales of enormous cruelty to slaves, loathing and contempt for their French masters, and a general anxiety that slaves, meaning British-owned slaves, might rise up in similar successful rebellions. The Rebellion in Saint Domingue, which included several takeovers of San Domingo, functioned not only in Stephen's pamphlet but in the opinion of many in England as an event which argued for the practicality and patriotism as well as the humanity of abolishing slavery.

* * *

Remaking Captain Wentworth

Captain Wentworth is an action hero, returning in victory from a noble war. Nonetheless, in Austen's narrative that role does not absolve him, or the Royal Navy, of the need for change now that the war is over. I return to Roger Sales's remark that *Persuasion* is about who should win the peace after the Napoleonic wars. It will be England, of course, for Napoleon had already suffered his final defeat at Waterloo when Austen was writing *Persuasion*. But what kind of England will it be? Surely that question must have fascinated Austen during the summer of 1815, as she, and everyone around her, saw the end of a war that had lasted, with the brief official respite in 1802 and 1803, almost continuously from 1792 to 1815. Peace, and what it might mean, needed to be defined and constructed anew. The opening premise of *Persuasion* is precisely that Captain Wentworth, and the values he represents at the beginning of the book, would be the wrong choice, indeed are not fit, to win that peace.

* * *

At the end of the novel Captain Wentworth is himself eloquent on his mistakes, when he describes himself as having been "proud, too proud" to have proposed again after the first two years of separation. He goes on to say that "I have been used to the gratification of believing myself to earn every blessing that I enjoyed. I have valued myself on honourable toils and just rewards" (247)[5] [176].

---

4. Fletcher Pratt, *Empire and the Sea*, 108–26.
5. Jane Austen, *Northanger Abbey* and *Persuasion*. Ed. R. W. Chapman. 3rd ed. (Oxford UP, 1954).

One way to explain Captain Wentworth's inability to appreciate Anne is that his values and principles were those of a man at war and he must change them to fit the peace. Captain Wentworth has seen the world according to a concept of fixed justice, a world of clarity where there is a correspondence between what you are, what you do, and what happens to you. Thus who you are, and who anyone else is, is a measurable and an observable quality. Like so many of Austen's characters who need to be educated, Captain Wentworth understands the world in simple terms, and his version is a duller, more rigid, and more schematic universe than the one the narrative offers.

Captain Wentworth not only understands the world in fixed terms which make it easy for him to evaluate and judge. He absolutely insists on that fixity. During the long autumn walk from Uppercross to Winthrop, Captain Wentworth explains his philosophy to Louisa Musgrove. Character should above all be firm, not "yielding and indecisive" (88) [64], qualities which for him are indistinguishable. A person, in his famous metaphor, should be a "Beautiful glossy nut," completely and permanently encased in its hard shell, "blessed with original strength," and "not a puncture, not a weak spot anywhere." For Captain Wentworth change is understood as damage, a loss of "original" strength, happiness is stasis, and other people are threats which may puncture your glossy shell.

These are the beliefs of the man who reacted to Anne's being persuaded against an official engagement before he went to sea with opinions "totally unconvinced and unbending" and with the choice of a "final parting" (28) [21–22]. Captain Wentworth is a man who believes himself to shun compromise, and in that belief broke off all connection with the woman he loved. He refused to allow himself to be persuaded. But we could also say that Captain Wentworth's anger at Anne was caused not because she was too persuadable but because she was not persuadable enough, because, finally, she kept to what she believed to be right rather than succumbing to his persuasions. Captain Wentworth may admire firmness, but not as a quality in others which interferes with him arranging the world his way. His own firmness looks awfully like willfulness or, to paraphrase Austen's line about Emma Woodhouse, like the power of having rather too much his own way, and a disposition to think a little too well of himself.[6]

* * *

6. Emma Woodhouse, of *Emma* (1815) [*Editor's note*].

Love and the Royal Navy

If I may rephrase Roger Sales's point, *Persuasion* is a novel about what kind of qualities its people will need if England is to be as victorious in peace as the nation has been in war. Admiral Croft represents an earlier naval generation, and his friendliness and straightforwardness function in the novel as a tribute to the retiring sailors who had fought so long in the wars against the French. Captains Harville, Benwick and Wentworth are the new generation, part of the final decade of the long struggle against Napoleon, but also the generation which will shape the future. And it is through the story of Captain Wentworth that the desirable qualities of that generation are presented.

The argument of the novel is that England's future, which is to say Captain Wentworth and Anne's future, requires those qualities of flexibility and openness to different and even opposing points of view which Captain Wentworth has learned this second time with Anne. The national future requires a vision of the nation not as a hardshelled glossy nut committed to battling and repelling external influences. It requires a vision of international relations perceived not as a balance of hostile powers but as an interdependence of nations who are capable of acknowledging shared as well as opposing purposes. It requires a navy capable of the kind of practical decision-making which comes from a spirit of compromise rather than a rigid adherence to self-images of dominance or to internal rules.

Understanding *Persuasion* as at least in part a vision of relations between nations as well as between two young people who have taken it "into their heads to marry" (248) [176] illuminates for me that last, and somewhat odd, sentence of the novel. The ending offers more than a sentimental tribute to the sailor's profession and to Anne's being a "sailor's wife" (252) [180]. Rather, [it] summarizes the kind of navy the novel has been arguing for: one "which is, if possible, more distinguished in its domestic virtues than in its national importance." The point is not that British sailors are good husbands and fathers. Austen's claims are much greater: that the Royal Navy, precisely because it is distinguished by values usually considered to be domestic—the values of flexibility and understanding and tolerance—is also distinguished as of invaluable national and international importance.

Which brings me back to the Chinese Opium Wars. Finally I would say that *Persuasion*, an alluring love story, is also an alluring vision of the future of the Royal Navy and of a nation whose warriors will have learned the strength in bending as well as the strength in standing fast. But that future did not come to pass. In Austen's novel, the kind of self-satisfied aggressiveness which made Captain

Wentworth believe that he knew best and which led to blindness and intolerance, was a quality he learned to turn away from. As a lover and an officer, Captain Wentworth came to understand the satisfactions and the real practical usefulness of a mind and heart more attuned to the rights and needs of others, more open to outside influences and possibilities. In the novel learning that lesson is the requirement for winning the peace, for directing England toward the future. But historically that was not the lesson the officers in the Royal Navy would learn. The navy which fought so long to stop Napoleon's bid for domination in the Napoleonic Wars would go on fighting in other wars, often not against the aggressor, all too often as the aggressor. Less than twenty years after Austen wrote *Persuasion*, British admirals would order a fleet to sail to the coast of China and bombard its boats and its coastal cities to force its people to allow the trade in opium. I would hardly call that "the profession more distinguished in its domestic virtues than in its national importance." The Royal Navy, indeed the British nation, should have learned from *Persuasion*.

ADELA PINCH

From Lost in a Book: Jane Austen's *Persuasion*[†]

Persuasion's ambivalent explorations of the powers of books might be situated within the context of debates that take place in England from the mid-eighteenth century on, especially debates about women and reading: about whether and in what ways women are particularly susceptible to the effects of reading, and the extent to which this susceptibility can be either dangerous or beneficial to women's minds. This is an issue that Austen explores, of course, in *Northanger Abbey*. In that novel, the reading of gothic romances often laughably exaggerates Catherine Morland's perceptions of reality, but it also renders her highly sensitive to some real social difficulties. I would like to argue that Austen takes up this issue in *Persuasion* as well, though in more oblique and phenomenological ways. *Persuasion* explores what it feels like to be a reader. It does so by connecting this feeling to what the presence of other people feels like. It explores, that is, the influence reading can have on one's mind by exploring the influence of one person's mind over another's.

The question of the influence of other minds figures most centrally in Anne Elliot's great act of submission to duty and propriety,

† From *Strange Fits of Passion: Epistemologies of Emotion, Hume to Austen* (Stanford: Stanford University Press, 1997), pp. 137–63. Used with permission of Stanford University Press, conveyed through Copyright Clearance Center, Inc. Unless otherwise indicated, notes are by Pinch. Page numbers in brackets are to this Norton Critical Edition.

her refusal of Captain Wentworth. She refuses him, persuaded that her "engagement [was] a wrong thing—indiscreet, improper, hardly capable of success, and not deserving it" (27) [21].[1] The duties to which Anne submits herself belong to the scheme of things outlined in the Baronetage her father loves to read—the preservation and per-petuation of the landed gentry through marriage. Anne submits, however, under no terrors, no parental threats and prohibitions. She gives in under the gentler ministrations of a friend, Lady Russell, who compensates for her family's indifference to her. Devoted to reg-istering the repercussions of Anne's act of renunciation, *Persuasion* is about what it is like to be subject to the influences of others, and the novel conceives of this as particularly a women's predicament. (Indeed, one critic has argued that for contemporary readers the word "persuasion" would have resonated specifically with the ques-tion of parents' rights over the marriage of daughters.)[2] Concerned with the emotional repercussions of a woman's submission to duty, *Persuasion* thus continues the late eighteenth century's investigation of the origins and meanings of women's feelings. It ends with a famous debate between Anne Elliot and Captain Harville over the comparative strengths of men's and women's feelings, in which Anne links the strength of "woman's feelings" (233) [167] to their social posi-tion. "It is, perhaps, our fate rather than our merit" to feel, she says: "We cannot help ourselves. We live at home, quiet, confined, and our feelings prey upon us. You are forced on exertion. You have always a profession, pursuits, business of some sort or other, to take you back into the world immediately, and continual occupation and change soon weakens impressions" (232) [166]. Both Anne's argument and her language—as she speaks of women's "fate" to feel, of feel-ings that "prey"—place this conversation squarely in the tradition of debates over women's feelings in the late eighteenth century, in particular the sensibility debates of women's sentimental poetry.

Austen's interest in the subjects that Anne and Harville debate, however, derives most particularly from the concerns that her genre, the novel of manners, has with the traffic in men's and women's feel-ings. Austen's novels would seem to announce themselves as ene-mies of the emotional extravagances of the gothic. * * * Sir Walter Scott, whose 1816 essay on Austen did much to define the novel of manners by heralding a new "style of novel," distinguished the new style from the old romance by contrasting "the difference . . . of the sentiments." While the romance novel propelled its hero or heroine

---

1. Jane Austen, *Persuasion*, ed. R. W. Chapman, 3rd. ed. (London: Oxford UP, 1933) 3, vol. 5 of *The Novels of Jane Austen*.
2. Kenneth Moler, *Jane Austen's Art of Allusion* (Lincoln: U of Nebraska P, 1968) 187–223; see also Claudia Johnson, *Jane Austen: Women, Politics, and the Novel* (Chicago: U of Chicago P, 1988) 149–50.

through a series of outlandish adventures and vicissitudes of emotions never found in "ordinary life," the new kind of novel "affords" its readers "a pleasure nearly allied with the experience of their own social habits." For the "excitements" of the "pure, elevated, and romantic" sentiments of the romance, the new novel substitutes "the art of copying from nature as she really exists in the common walks of life, and presenting to the reader, instead of the splendid scenes of an imaginary world, a correct and striking representation of that which is daily taking place around him."[3]

The novel of manners, as Scott intimates, is crucially concerned with the pleasures of its readers' "social habits." The genre's innovation is its microscopic and seemingly realistic attention to behaviors, bodies, and signs of feeling. It imagines a world in which social habits—rather than power, rank, or class—themselves define and delimit the social order. Feelings are the social noise of the novel of manners: they are the environment that makes possible the commerce between people and the relationships that constitute society. This vision of feelings' role in society-making is reminiscent of [David] Hume's essay "Of the Delicacy of Taste and Passion," [wherein] Hume encouraged his readers to manage their emotions by channeling a "delicacy of passion," which heightens the emotional vicissitudes of an ungoverned life, into a "delicacy of taste" in which the emotions are roused strongly only by the beauties of art and manners.[4] For Hume, such exercise of the passions improves society by weaning the individual from vulgar passions. An extravagant emotional sensitivity is thus made socially productive, and thus allows society itself to be conceived in a restrictive sense; "society" designates a polite community of people who appreciate manners. The "society" that novelists like Austen, Edgeworth, Inchbald, Brunton, and Burney imagine is often similarly restrictive.[5] That Scott—and other readers after him—takes Austen's novels to be representing "ordinary life" and its "common walks" indicates that he has already assented to the novels' aesthetic and political claims: to make the romantic lives of young women of the lower gentry seem ordinary and common. The promise of such an "ordinary life," in which style and morality come together, was surely an attractive one in early nineteenth-century England, when in public life * * * style and morality often seemed at odds. In the novel of manners as in Hume's vision, emotion improves polite society not principally by being

---

3. Sir Walter Scott, *Quarterly Review*, XIV (1816), pp. 188–201.
4. David Hume, "Of the Delicacy of Taste and Passion" (1742), in *Essays, Moral, Political, and Literary*, vol. 1 (1741), pp. 3–7 [*Editor's note*].
5. Maria Edgeworth (1768–1849), Elizabeth Inchbald (1753–1821), Mary Brunton (1778–1818), and Frances (Fanny) Burney (1752–1840), prominent British female authors [*Editor's note*].

restrained but by being trained to flourish in certain domains. In
the novel that domain is, above all, romantic love.

*   *   *

For Scott as for Hume, a passion is a social good—even when it
ends miserably; for Scott the place where the benefits of romantic
love are best exhibited is the novel. If the novels of manners of
Scott's contemporaries are concerned with calibrating feelings to
"social habits," then, they do so not by discouraging extravagant
feelings but by routing them along improving paths. Thus while it
may be tempting to stress the "difference of sentiments" between
the gothic novel and the Regency novel of manners, both genres—in
spite of their different emotional registers—do similar work. If the
gothic novel's emotional excesses are linked * * * to its philosophical accounting for feelings' origins, the social form of feeling in the
novel of manners is inseparable from those feelings' place at the
center of the novels' epistemological dramas. For the novel of manners puts feelings into motion by making them difficult to know.
The subject of Austen's novels, for example, is the arduousness of
knowing both one's own feelings and the feelings of others—of
knowing, as Anne Elliot wonders about Captain Wentworth, "how
were his sentiments to be read?" (60) [44]. Austen's novels thus put
the drive to know feelings * * * into social circulation.

*   *   *

Persuasion is striking for the ways in which the presences of other
people are apprehended as insistently sensory phenomena. Anne
Elliot's sister, Mary Musgrove, who has more of the "Elliot pride" (88)
[64] than does Anne, and who is constantly fretting that her in-laws
do not give her the "precedence" that is due to her, registers their
claims as a physical pressure. She complains after a dinner party:

> It is so very uncomfortable, not having a carriage of one's own.
> Mr. and Mrs. Musgrove took me, and we were so crowded! They
> are both so very large, and take up so much room! And Mr. Mus-
> grove always sits forward. So, there was I, crowded into the
> back seat with Henrietta and Louisa. And I think it very likely
> that my illness today may be owing to it. (39) [30]

Mary feels the Musgroves' proximity to be a threat, their bodily presence capable of making her ill. Anne, however, also frequently finds
herself crowded in by other people, in rooms, on furniture. She feels
"astonishment" at finding herself, at the Harvilles' house in Lyme,
in "rooms so small as none but those who invite from the heart could
think capable of accommodating so many" (98) [71]. She is crowded
on a sofa by Wentworth and the "substantial" Mrs. Musgrove.

Perhaps the best emblem for Anne's tendency to be swamped by family duties is the moment in chapter 9 * * * in which, as she busily attends to one of her nephews, another one fixes himself upon her back. Her family is literally crawling all over her. * * *

It is not simply other people's bodily presence that conditions mental life in this novel; mental life seems crowded in by bodily life in general. In chapter 8, we find the estranged lovers Anne and Wentworth, divided from each other by the physical form— "no insignificant barrier"—of Mrs. Musgrove, whose body, Austen declares, "was of a comfortable substantial size, infinitely more fitted by nature to express good cheer and good humour, than tenderness and sentiment" (68) [50]. Anne and Wentworth are listening to her "large fat sighings over the destiny of a son, whom alive nobody had cared for." Austen comments: "Personal size and mental sorrow have certainly no necessary proportions. A large bulky figure has as good a right to be in deep affliction, as the most graceful set of limbs in the world. But, fair or not fair, there are unbecoming conjunctions, which reason will patronize in vain,—which taste cannot tolerate,— which ridicule will seize" (68) [50]. This passage has baffled readers as a piece of gratuitous viciousness. It is vicious; Austen applies the language of neoclassical aesthetic judgment ("unbecoming conjunc- tions . . . taste cannot tolerate") to Mrs. Musgrove's expressive body, as if she were a bad poem or book. The result is not far from the physical snobbery of Sir Walter Elliot: deeply offended and disgusted by the weatherbeaten looks of Navy men, Sir Walter deems them "not fit to be seen," and to spare the world the sight of them, opines, "It is a pity they are not knocked on the head at once, before they reach Admiral Baldwin's age" (20) [16]. But if extreme physical snob- bery has already been represented and ridiculed *within* the novel in the characters of Sir Walter and Elizabeth Elliot, finding the narra- tor raising similar questions suggests that a serious inquiry of some kind about the relationship between personal form and mental life is taking place here. In spite of the rational disclaimers of the first two sentences, the last seems to be admitting that there are, in fact, "necessary proportions" between body and mind.

* * *

In *Persuasion,* the realm of feelings is the realm of repetitions, of things happening within a strong context of memory. Revising the plot of the origin of romance, Austen's novel also revises an empir- icist account of the experience of sensation. The sensational quality of Anne's and Wentworth's encounters arises not from the newness of stimuli but rather from stimuli that work on a consciousness already prepared by memories of earlier sensations. * * * As the novel progresses, Anne's moments of shock and inundation increasingly take a typically sublime turn: a trauma from without is parried and inverted to become part of a power within. What before seemed to bring an inundation by the outside world now becomes part of her resistance to it. In the Octagon Room at the concert hall in Bath, a wash of noise signals her subjectivity's dominion over the outside world: "in spite of the agitated voice in which [Wentworth's speech] had been uttered, and in spite of all the various noises of the room, the almost ceaseless slam of the door, and ceaseless buzz of persons walking through, [Anne] had distinguished every word" (183) [131]. Here too, heightened awareness of Wentworth's presence ushers in as well a heightened awareness of all that is not Wentworth, a room full of persons and voices. As is often the case in *Persuasion,* sensory experience is rendered primarily in terms of aural interference. But here, the narrator impresses these noises upon us in order to assert that Anne can subordinate them. The sounds of the room are reduced to ceaseless (the word is repeated), abstract, continuous sound, affirming the capacity of mind, even as it has been traumatized by the rushing in of sensations, to reduce the external world to a blur. These moments of shock suggest that the more Anne appears resistant to the outside world, the more she knows: these moments are crucial to her reunion with Wentworth. The outside world, however, never goes entirely away. When, reunited at last, Anne and Wentworth retire to the gravel walk, it might seem that the outside world intrudes into the text only to affirm the characters' absorption in each other:

> And there, as they slowly paced the gradual ascent, heedless of every group around them, seeing neither sauntering politicians, bustling housekeepers, flirting girls, nor nursery maids and children, could they indulge in those retrospections and acknowledgments . . . which were so poignant and so ceaseless in interest. (241) [172]

Anne and Wentworth are no longer in a crowded concert room but rather in a more expansive public space: the outside world gets bigger and more populous even as they become more enclosed in each other. The list of urban characters here is reminiscent of Austen's earlier urban pastoral of the sounds of Bath (135) [96]. The listing serves to stress that a sense of the presence of other people does not go away: it maintains * * * its continuous, one-thing-after-another form. The progress that organizes the list—from politicians to housekeepers to flirting girls to infants—might seem to follow a descending scale of political importance, though from an early nineteenth-century woman's perspective, this list may not be descending in its claims to attention. The appearance here, however, of the word "ceaseless,"

previously linked to the "white noise" of the world, signals the inver-
sion that has occurred. Here, what is "ceaseless" are not the noises of
the outside world but the absorptions of love.

DEIRDRE LYNCH

From Jane Austen and the Social Machine[†]

* * *

* * * I aim here to demonstrate how Austen's novels position interiority at a relay point that articulates the personal with the mass-
produced.

Compare the mental life of an Elinor Dashwood (*Sense and
Sensibility*) or an Anne Elliot (*Persuasion*) to that of Burney's Wanderer, a misunderstood loner. The comparison casts into relief one
measure Austen adopts to register her insight into the embarrassing
sociability of her readers' rites of introspection and to give us the
wherewithal to manage that embarrassment. In contrast to Burney's
protagonists, an Austen heroine is never precisely in a position to be a
"female Robinson Crusoe" and have her thoughts as her sole companions.[1] Characters who are rarely alone with their thoughts—characters
who instead are perpetually anxious about keeping the lines of communication open and the wheels of conversation turning—are precisely those whom Austen chooses for her heroines. At the same time
that Austen mobilizes the hallmarks of literary psychology to endow
her heroine with an inner life, she also depicts her (to adopt a locution
the novelist favors throughout her oeuvre) as conscientiously "mindful" of "the feelings of others." Her "mind filled," this heroine has a
head supplied with emotions that belong to other people, a mental life
that unfolds in what accordingly is at once an interior and a social
space. In *Sense and Sensibility* and *Persuasion* especially, Austen
handles point of view so that listening in on the self-confirming language of depth that endows a heroine with an inner life consistently
involves hearing in the background the murmurs of a crowd.

* * * I will, accordingly, treat not just Austen's interest in individualizing her characters and readers; I will also treat her interest in

† From *The Economy of Character: Novels, Market Culture, and the Business of Inner
Meaning* (Chicago: University of Chicago Press, 1998), pp. 210–13, 214–16, 239–40,
241–42. Used with permission of University of Chicago Press, conveyed through
Copyright Clearance Center, Inc. Unless otherwise indicated, notes are by Lynch. Page
numbers in brackets are to this Norton Critical Edition.
 1. Frances (Fanny) Burney (1752–1840), English writer, playwright, diarist, and social
satirist and the author of successful epistolary novels including *Evelina, or the History
of a Young Lady's Entrance into the World* (1778) and *Camilla, or a Picture of Youth*
(1796). *The Wanderer; or, Female Difficulties* (1814), featuring the social fall and rise of
a woman seeking to hide her identity, is set during the Reign of Terror [*Editor's note*].

crowding. Even as Austen equips novel readers to participate in a psychological culture's rites of distinction, she also has us contemplate copying as she archly goes through the motions of writing women's fiction and as she adds more texts to an overcrowded novel market, and she makes us contemplate how a commercial culture renders people copies of one another. In the latter vein, she offers crowd portraits of the sort that the narrator of *Persuasion* puts together as she introduces the women who are Anne Elliot's neighbors for Volume 1, Henrietta and Louisa Musgrove. Thinking of these particular two young ladies prompts the narrator to think of vast numbers and so dislocate the question of individual particularity: "Henriette and Louisa, young ladies of nineteen and twenty, . . . had brought from a school at Exeter all the usual stock of accomplishments, and were now, like thousands of other young ladies, living to be fashionable, happy, and merry."2 * * * Such portraits of copycats, whose characterization is exhausted in a single sentence, indulge novel readers with the pleasure of instant legibility—the pleasure of character *types*. Another way to say this * * * is that throughout her work Austen is concerned not just with the sound of the round character's inner voice, but also with noise. She concerns herself with the noise emitted by what I call her culture's copy machines—a label I use to underline how frequently Austen confronts us with the mechanized aspects of social life (and of literature). In Austen's novels, complying with fashion and the demands of what the Dashwood sisters call "general civility"—writing bread-and-butter letters, talking about the weather—involves recycling the commonplaces that everybody uses and accommodating oneself to customs and linguistic forms that, machinelike, have an impersonal logic of their own. Thus to depict social transactions such as epistolary exchanges and polite conversations—transactions in which, as with the character type, meaningfulness is sacrificed to repetition—Austen will use language we more often associate with a machine and its clatter. In *Persuasion*, rooms filled with people are experienced by Anne Elliot as stages for unintelligible sound: the fashionable world's "nothing-saying" (178) [135] is apprehended less often as an aggregate of distinct voices, more frequently as a "ceaseless buzz" or a hum (173) [131]. * * *

Noise in Austen registers the ubiquity of the social.3 By directing attention to it, Austen reveals the mechanisms of transmission that compose a society and the networks for mechanical repetition that

2. Jane Austen, *Persuasion*, ed. John Davie (Oxford: Oxford University Press, 1971), 42–43. * * *

3. The only other discussion of noise and Austen with which I'm acquainted occurs in Adela Pinch's account of the lyricism of *Persuasion*: "Lost in a Book," chap. 5 of *Strange Fits of Passion: Epistemologies of Emotion, Hume to Austen* (Stanford: Stanford University Press, 1996). * * * [Pinch's essay is excerpted in this volume —*Editor*.]

sustain mass communications. She directs attention to the circuits of exchange that underwrite the inside stories of romantic fiction—that give that fiction's deep meanings their currency in the book market. Paying attention to the busy, prosy hum of her crowds dislocates our sense of what Austen's priorities are. Customarily, Austen's position within histories of the novel is pinpointed by relating her to a concept of "romantic individualism." Either she is against it, as we are told by the scholarship associating her with an anti-Jacobin recoil from the cult of sensibility and the moral claims of individual feeling,[4] or she finds in her novels the means—specifically, her use of free indirect discourse[5]—of bringing about an ideal blend of the individual and the social, rehabilitating sensibility for the nineteenth-century novel's sociocentric world. As *The Rise of the Novel* put it in a now somewhat notoriously androcentric statement, Austen combines into "a harmonious unity" the subjective narrative mode cultivated by the domestic Samuel Richardson and the objective mode cultivated by the public man Henry Fielding and thereby makes Henry James possible.[6] These ways of relating Austen to literary history converge insofar as each preempts consideration of how a self-society opposition is constructed and how it is naturalized. They preempt consideration of how Austen's novels, in bringing impersonal discourses into dynamic exchange with the feeling-filled language of inside views, help to establish the staging and management of that opposition as the special social office of "the" novel, an office that endows the genre with its authority among the disciplines.[7] * * * I will show how Austen stages and manages that exchange between the impersonal and personal in ways that recast the emergent romantic protocols for reading: she supplements the opportunities her readers have for practice in sympathetic feeling by inviting them to partake in lighthearted games of stereotype-recognition and cliché-busting. I will also suggest that for Austen self-expression and the rite of self-culture prosper truly only when sheltered by the whir and hum of the run-of-the-mill.

*   *   *

4. For example, for Marilyn Butler (*Jane Austen and the War of Ideas* [Oxford: Clarendon, 1975], 274), Austen "masters the subjective insights that help to make the 19th-century novel what it is, and denies them validity."
5. See n. 9, p. xviii in this volume [*Editor's note*].
6. Ian Watt, *The Rise of the Novel: Studies in Defoe, Richardson, and Fielding* (1957; reprint, Harmondsworth: Pelican, 1972), 338 [excerpted in this volume —*Editor*].
7. See David Kaufmann's pithy comments on novels' disciplinary distinction (*The Business of Common Life: Novels and Classical Economics Between Revolution and Reform* [Baltimore: Johns Hopkins University Press, 1995], 63): "[Political economics and the novel] show the relation of the part to the whole, the individual to the alien totality that appears to stand over and against that individual. Nevertheless, they are not redundant. Economics began by looking at the general and inferred the individual; the novel began with the individual and allegorized the general."

In *Persuasion*, the "little history of sorrowful interest" (31) [22] that relates how in 1806 Anne Elliot was persuaded out of her engagement with Captain Wentworth is framed [as] * * * the basis for a * * * reading situation in which readers can measure their sympathies against the characters' and in which the true story, played against a publicly apprehended story, seems more possessible [*sic*] because it seems possessed exclusively. When in *Persuasion* the action of the novel proper begins, as peace turns the navy ashore and Anne and Wentworth find themselves reunited by chance eight years after their first separation, no one but the reader is aware of this prior narrative. This "little history of sorrowful interest" is, in effect, off the record. At this point, Anne, at Uppercross with her younger sister Mary, is separated from Lady Russell, Sir Walter Elliot, and her elder sister Elizabeth, who are the "only three of her own friends in the secret of the past" and who have buried the episode in "oblivion" (33–34) [23–24]. Her consciousness of the past isolates her. Free indirect discourse reveals to readers how Anne copes alone with the shock of this reunion with Wentworth. Repeatedly following Anne as she retreats into the spaces of privacy that offer her intervals for reflection, it suggests that she savors this revival of bygone pains and pleasures, in the way that one savors a secret indulgence. Reading *Persuasion* is an experience of reading a narrative that, focusing on second chances even more than other Austen novels do, frames itself as "a second novel"—a successor narrative to that first novel that is off the record.[8] What enhances readers' intimacy with Anne is that the experience of living *Persuasion* feels like that too. * * *

Participating in Anne's point of view means being privy to another, secret story in a way that generates a constant awareness of the lacunae in what is being narrated. In such a context, innocuous-sounding statements—"'We are expecting a brother of Mrs. Croft's here soon; I dare say you know him by name'" (51) [37]—are laced

---

8. On *Persuasion* as a "second novel," see Tony Tanner, *Jane Austen* (Cambridge: Harvard University Press, 1986), 211. For the argument that almost all Austen's love stories are framed as repetitions of a prior narrative, see Daniel Cottom (*The Civilized Imagination: A Study of Ann Radcliffe, Jane Austen, and Sir Walter Scott* [New York: Cambridge University Press, 1985], 90): "There is no such thing as an original love in Austen's novels," Cottom writes. Another way to say this is to say that Austen's hero and heroine, who never fall in love at first sight, also never really see each other as strangers. The couple in Austen is the product of an erotic alchemy that affects, in Susan Morgan's words, "people who are already familiar to each other": Darcy may look perfect for the part of the glamorous stranger, "but the first movement of his feelings is a failure and he must return to propose again" (*In the Meantime: Character and Perception in Jane Austen's Fiction* [Chicago: University of Chicago Press, 1988], 187). The look of love is always a second glance at someone who is already known and remembered. When Elizabeth Bennet visits the picture gallery at Pemberley, she finds that there are "many family portraits, but they could have little to fix the attention of a stranger. Elizabeth walked on in quest of the only face whose features would be known to her. At last it arrested her—and she beheld a striking resemblance of Mr. Darcy, with such a smile over her face, as she remembered to have sometimes seen, when he looked at her" (*Pride and Prejudice*, eds. James Kinsley and Frank W. Bradbrook [Oxford: Oxford University Press, 1970], p. 220).

with ironies for the initiated reader; polite conversation has
unsuspected depths. Anne's absorption in her memories of how she
formerly stood with Wentworth, her engagement with the story
inside her head, has the effect of making her both thought-full and
wordless. She and Wentworth share the past but share it separately.
As a participant in the public life of the nation, Wentworth *can*
revert to the year of their engagement: "His profession qualified
him, his disposition led him, to talk; and '*That* was in the year six;'
'*That* happened before I went to sea in the year six,' occurred in the
course of the first evening they spent together" (63) [46]. By contrast, remembrance of the past—which for her is wholly defined in
terms of a private life spent either with or without Wentworth—
seems to bar Anne from speaking. Thus the interior animation that
makes *Persuasion* into the record of the "dialogue of Anne's mind
with itself" is also manifested as a form of privation, as if interiority
had as its necessary consequence an impassive, incommunicative
exterior.[9] *Persuasion* makes this dissociation between inner and
outer worlds into a principle of characterization. Describing the
reactions that Wentworth elicits from his female listeners as he
recounts his somewhat macho stories of disasters at sea, the narrator
separates Anne from the others: "Anne's shudderings were to herself
alone: but the Miss Musgroves could be as open as they were sincere,
in their exclamations of pity and horror" (66) [48]. The negative distinction here ascribed to Anne registers how Austen accommodates
her psychological culture's protocols for characterization. She is
enabling readers to practice feeling along with Anne, with a sympathy that feels more authentic, like a more immaculately personal
effect, because nobody within the novel, with the eventual exception
of Wentworth, is conscious of her story. With their exclamations, the
Misses Musgrove make too much noise for any one to notice it.

* * *

* * * Austen is interested in the nonsignificative aspects of language
because she understands the business of common life in the same
terms that Lionel Trilling does when, attempting to define *manners*
in the broad sense of the term, he uses words such as *hum* and *buzz*
and refers to "the voice of multifarious intention and activity . . . all
the buzz of implication which always surrounds us."[1] Austen understands social life, as Trilling, her reader, does, in terms of noise. She

---

9. Discussing how in *Persuasion*, more than in the other novels by Austen, the heroine's
   consciousness seems to monopolize the narrative voice, Elizabeth Deeds Ermarth
   characterizes the novel as the record of the conversation that Anne sustains with herself (*Realism and Consensus in the English Novel* [Princeton: Princeton University
   Press, 1983], 166).
1. Lionel Trilling, "Manners, Morals, and the Novel," in *The Liberal Imagination: Essays
   in Literature and Society* (New York: Harcourt Brace Jovanovich, 1979), 194.

often positions her heroines so that they are excluded from others' colloquies but unable to avoid overhearing information of unexpected interest to themselves. This measure makes readers conscious of the auditory contingencies that impinge on communications. *Persuasion* particularly, a novel notable for its poignant depiction of impasses in communications, is also a novel of noise. Like the works that precede it, it deals with chatter and records how people trade fatuities and re-urge "admitted truths" (218) [165], but it is also a book, as Adela Pinch notes, in which doors slam (173) [131] and fires roar, "determined to be heard" (127) [96], in which the "bawling . . . newsmen, muffin-men, and milkmen" (128) [96] of the Bath marketplace contribute to the cacophony, and in which individual characters are liable to be distinguished by their "taste in noise" (128) [96].[2] When she stages scenes of overhearing, Austen makes us conscious both of the ambient noise that frustrates the listener's efforts to hear and of the idle chatter that delays her receipt of a crucial piece of intelligence.

Thus *Sense and Sensibility* and *Persuasion* present the language of real feeling as a language of undertone, uttered under a blanket of noise. * * *

* * * Anne Elliot's place is * * * on the piano bench, and * * * mental activity has a pianoforte accompaniment. "Her fingers . . . mechanically at work, proceeding for half an hour together, equally without error, and without consciousness" (71) [53], Anne seems to find in her performances—in going through the motions of performances—a means of at once being alone with her thoughts and fulfilling her public duties. Evidence of how, with their "modern minds and manners [and] . . . usual stock of accomplishments," the daughters of the house cannot resist a trend, the piano at Uppercross Hall contributes to the crowdedness of an overfilled parlor (42) [31], but Austen shows how these noise machines give their female operators and auditors the space for private life.

*   *   *

* * * In the chapter * * * in which the Elliots attend an evening concert at Bath, and in which Anne has a conversation with Wentworth that encourages her to hope that he loves her once again, the narrator is very exact in the way she *places* her heroine's emotion of joy. "Anne saw nothing, thought nothing of the brilliancy of the room. Her happiness was from within" (175) [132]. At such moments, what Austen has us hear with Anne is a buzz of voices. Adopting Anne's point of view means experiencing what the people in this

2. Pinch, "Lost in a Book," *passim*. On overhearing and eavesdropping, see the discussions of *Persuasion* offered by Keith Thomas ("Jane Austen and the Romantic Lyric: *Persuasion* and Coleridge's Conversation Poems," *ELH* 54 [1987]: 893–924) and Cottom (*Civilized Imagination*, 119–20).

assembly room are saying not as a number of distinct utterances issuing from particular agents, but as a wash of noise. Here, for instance, is how, linking inwardness and noise, Austen records Anne's reception of the words Wentworth uses when he seems to be on the brink of renewing his former feelings. "[I]n spite of the agitated voice in which [his remarks] had been uttered, and in spite of all the various noises of the room, the almost ceaseless slam of the door, and ceaseless buzz of persons walking through, [Anne] had distinguished every word, was struck, gratified, confused, and beginning to breathe very quick, and feel an hundred things in a moment" (173) [131]. The process delineated in this passage, as Adela Pinch has argued, is one in which subjectivity has "dominion over the outside world": "the narrator impresses these noises upon us in order to assert that Anne can subordinate them . . . [and in order to affirm] the capacity of the mind, even as it has been traumatized by the rushing in of sensations, to reduce the external world to a blur."[3]

But the dilemma *Persuasion* confronts is that these internal resources—the capacities for thinking, feeling, and listening that enable her to close out the noise of social contingency and hear only words of love—are not enough for Anne. * * * *Persuasion* in its second half is preoccupied with the sort of repetitive sounds of polite "nothing-saying" we witness when Anne and Wentworth talk "of the weather and Bath and the concert" (171) [130] largely because it is addressing the question of whether something-saying is possible and whether Anne can say what she means.[4] If Wentworth indeed has a heart returning to Anne, how is the truth about her feelings to reach him? "How . . . would he ever learn her real sentiments?" (180) [136].

BARBARA M. BENEDICT

From Jane Austen and the Culture of Circulating Libraries: The Construction of Female Literacy[†]

* * *

In her fiction, Austen explores the uses of a variety of purchases to advertise the self, including not only books and clothes, but also accomplishments—skills or arts that displayed the woman for

---

3. Ibid., 155.
4. For an extended discussion of the barriers to communication in *Persuasion*, see [Tony] Tanner, *Jane Austen* [(Cambridge: Harvard UP, 1986), p. 236].
† From *Revising Women: Eighteenth-Century "Women's Fiction" and Social Engagement*, ed. Paula R. Backscheider (Baltimore: Johns Hopkins University Press, 2000), pp. 151–56, 256–57. © 2000 The Johns Hopkins University Press. Reprinted with permission of Johns Hopkins University Press. Unless otherwise indicated, notes are by Benedict.

purchase through marriage, such as singing, speaking in languages, drawing, dancing, and playing music. Parents bought these skills either through such schools as Frederica Vernon, Lady Susan's daughter, attends, or via such private governesses as Jane Fairfax in *Emma* will become.[1] Lady Susan cynically polishes Frederica for sale in the marriage market; Mrs. Elton similarly attempts to sell Jane to raise the cultural prestige of her acquaintances and, through the exchange, herself. These women are used by the consumer culture around them, yet Jane, at least, has also improved herself enough to become the wife of Frank Churchill, heir to a fortune, and even Frederica attracts Sir Reginald. It is the correct consumption of these commodities—be they skills or objects—that concerns Austen, a consumption that respects their social value and power to illustrate the self, yet preserves personal integrity. When Harriet Smith in *Emma* is distracted by all the different colored ribbons while looking for a hat, she is overcome by shopping and loses her sense of purpose to commercialism. Similarly, Lydia Bennet in *Pride and Prejudice*, entranced by shops, buys a hat she dislikes and must "pull it to pieces" to make it wearable (219).[2] Emma sneers at Harriet's indecision as a sign of mental weakness, but it is equally a sign of social ambiguity. Harriet does not know where she belongs, and therefore what to consume; she does not know who she is, and therefore what to wear. She cannot purchase the elegant thing. Lydia will take anything—or anyone, as her choice of elopement and Wickham proves. Similarly, Mary Bennet performs on the piano to "exhibit" herself, as her father remarks, whereas Anne Elliot in *Persuasion* plays to conceal herself, wholly for the amusement of others (*Pride and Prejudice*, 100). Elizabeth Bennet, who does not "perform to strangers," represents the golden mean (176).

*   *   *

Throughout the eighteenth century, cultural critics complained about female consumption in general, often linking moralistic objections to female appetite with attacks on women's reading, especially of circulating library fiction. George Colman's *Polly Honeycombe* bluntly identifies literary with other commodities. In recounting Polly's illicit love for the novelist Scribble instead of the approved Ledger, who reads only *The Daily Advertiser* and Lloyd's list,[3] the play roundly

---

1. In Austen's novels "Lady Susan" (written ca. 1794) and *Emma* (1815) [*Editor's note*].
2. Jane Austen, *Sense and Sensibility*, ed. R. W. Chapman (Oxford: Oxford University Press, 1978), 249. All citations to Austen's novels and juvenilia refer to this six-volume edition, in which *Northanger Abbey* and *Persuasion* are printed in one volume, but separately paginated. References to Austen's juvenile and minor works derived from volume six, Minor Works, are cited with that title.
3. *The Daily Advertiser* (1730–1807) was primarily an advertising paper with some news content. *Lloyd's Register* was begun in 1760 to fund the investigation of and publish

attacks women's literature for violating neoclassical dicta. In his preface, Colman ironically cites his mother's criticism that "the *Catastrophe* (that was really her word) is directly contrary to all known rules" and sarcastically lists female principles of good drama as valuing romantic love, "reconciliation," and moral "reformation" above satire.[4] As illustration, the play contains an "Extract" from an imaginary circulating library catalogue that subtitles Fielding's *Amelia* "The Distressed Wife"[5] to highlight its appeal to victimized women. * * *

Colman attacks circulating library literature for nourishing women's self-pity, secrecy, and self-importance. He also associates these with women's other appetites. As the play opens, Polly reads a passage from the novel that compares the dawn with "iced cream crimsoned with raspberries" (1). While burlesquing Fielding's own mock-heroic diction in *Tom Jones*, this analogy both derides romances' derivative style and satirizes the frothiness of feminine taste.[6] Furthermore, the supposedly licensed public fantasizing of circulating library fiction is depicted as stimulating women's self-display. The stage directions describe Polly as "acting it as she reads" and as "reading and acting" as she imagines accepting a marriage proposal (2). She is performing what should be private feelings to an imagined audience—as well as to the audience in the theater. According to Colman, romantic values breed artifice and exhibitionism. As Polly's father exclaims, "a man might as well turn his Daughter loose in Coventgarden, as trust the cultivation of her mind to A CIRCULATING LIBRARY" (31). He depicts female reading as a public display of the self that makes gender, class, and morality dangerously unreadable.

This distrust of staged female identity is a response to contemporary changes in the avenues and languages of self-representation, especially of female self-representation. Markedly, as the population of London grew and traditional social bonds loosened, city dwellers began to advertise their desires in newspapers. Typically, early advertising plagiarized literary texts, leveled traditional distinctions of value and provenance, and translated satire into enthusiasm in order to tout novelty; these techniques affected not only the style of popular novels but people's self-presentation in print.[7] The depiction of women and men as marriage commodities

lists of ships with descriptions of their safety records, cargo, and funding; it remains the oldest ongoing ship classification society in the world [*Editor's note*].

4. George Colman, "*Polly Honeycombe*, A Dramatic Novel in One Act" (Edinburgh: A. Kincaid & J. Bell, 1741 [misprinted for 1761]), iv. This epilogue was by Garrick. Subsequent citations in the text refer to this edition. [David Garrick (1717–1779), English actor, playwright, and theater manager —*Editor*.]

5. *Amelia* (1751), a novel by English satirist, novelist, and playwright Henry Fielding (1707–1754) [*Editor's note*].

6. Fielding, *The History of Tom Jones, a Foundling* (1749) [*Editor's note*].

7. See Francis Doherty, *A Study in Eighteenth-Century Advertising Methods: The Anodyne Necklace* (Lewiston: Edwin Mellen Press, 1992); also Peter M. Briggs, "'News from the

was commonplace in eighteenth- and early nineteenth-century printed culture, in which advertisements characteristically jumble the pecuniary and the moral. In 1785, *The Public Advertiser* rather hypocritically mocks the homogeneity advertising confers on commodities:

> The Advertising Age.
> "This is the Advertising Age," said a friend to me t'other day, as we were remarking the great number of advertisements in the news-papers.
> This is the *Age of Advertising*. If you want to buy an estate—
>
> > To sell an estate.
> > To get a place at Court.
> > To shew a comedy.
> > To shew a pig.
> > To make known your writings.
> > To teach turkeys to dance.
> > To procure charity.
> > To hire a house.
> > To marry a wife.
> > To keep a mistress.
> > To buy dogs.
> > To let horses.
> > To nurse children.
> > To vamp pamphlets.
> > To go up in a balloon.
> > To teach dancing.
> > Or
> > To sell hair-powder.
>
> In all these and many other cases, you will experience the good effects of *advertising*. . . . When we consider the language and artful manner of these advertisements, the lures they throw out, and the success they have, we may say, *lead us not into temptation*. (*Public Advertiser*, April 13, 1785)

Advertising equalizes things and services that traditionally occupy very different planes in a moral hierarchy.

The power of advertising to level traditional distinctions of value produces a conservative rhetoric of resistance, even while it shapes self-presentation in print. One man very like Sir Walter Elliot deplores his declassé "recourse to advertisement" in the news-papers, yet clearly requires it, since he reissues his 1790 plea for a wife or companion in 1791.[8] Another declares himself as a good

---

Little World': A Critical Glance at Eighteenth-Century British Advertising," *Studies in Eighteenth-Century Culture* 23 (1994): 29–45.

8. *The Daily Advertiser* 1790, 1791, in *Matrimonial Advertisements*, 1746–1862 (B.L. Cup 407 ff 43). Unless otherwise noted, all advertisements cited in the text can be found in this collection.

bargain in a long advertisement that echoes Mr. Collins's sycophantic bullying:

> No character in this kingdom can be more respectable than that of a clergyman; and yet how many worthy men are there of that profession whose incomes, barely sufficient for the present maintenance, afford them not the means of making the smallest provision for their children.—There are undoubtedly at this very instant several young ladies under this description, who, though accomplished both in mind and person, have no better prospect than the necessity of submitting to stations unworthy their birth and education.
>
> To the parents or near relations of any lady thus accomplished, the advertiser now addresses himself. He is a gentleman of easy fortune, and can provide for a wife in case of death. He presumes to say, that the offer of his hand in marriage would be both honourable and advantageous to a lady of little or no fortune; nor could she miss of happiness if her temper and inclinations dispose her to search for it within the circle of domestic enjoyments. Nevertheless he had not the vanity to suppose that a handsome and accomplished lady would make him the object of her choice.—That his good temper, indulgence, and attention to her would secure her esteem he had not the least doubt. But he is at the time same [sic] conscious, that her consent to receive his addresses must take its rise from an honest pride wishing for independence, and from a laudable ambition which she feels to move in a station for which both nature and education seem to have intended her.
>
> Charles Winterton, Esq. (*Whitehall Evening*, 1771)[9]

Accomplished women with "a laudable ambition" like Charlotte Lucas, conventionally trained in religious principles, whose poverty and plainness situate them below companionate marriage, have the opportunity of selling themselves to Mr. Winterton, and hoping to feel "esteem" from his "indulgence." Women did indeed so sell themselves, and marriage was not their only venue, albeit the only one Austen openly acknowledges:

> A Young Gentlewoman, by birth unexceptionable of good character, solicits the friendship of a Gentleman who answers the following delineation: Free from every incumbrance, in the enjoyment of a good fortune, independent, possessed of sense, sentiment, delicacy, and humanity, in short, she wishes him to possess the endowments of the heart to an eminent degree,

9. *The Whitehall Evening Post* (1718–1801) was a London paper founded by English novelist and author Daniel Defoe (ca. 1660–1731). It contained the *London Gazette*'s list of insolvencies, bankruptcies, and debtors, legal and political news, poetry, shipping news, and birth, marriage, and death announcements [*Editor's note*].

those permanent, and would sufficiently compensate for age, or the want of personal qualifications; let him have stability too, and be divested of hypocrisy. Letters to be left at a snuff shop. . . . High Holborn, for R. S. T. (1771)

The language of such advertisements elides marriage and prostitution.

One publication, specifically directed to subscribers, illustrates the terms in which people were advertised to prospective purchasers. This "Matrimonial Plan," entitled *The Imprejudicate Nuptial Society; or, Grand Matrimonial Intercourse Institution*, separates its entries by class: the first class holds "all parties, male and female, whose expectations exceed £5,000," the second contains those possessing between £5,000 and £500, and the third "or lowest Class comprehends all expectations from a Guinea up to £500."[1] This rhetoric leaves no room for moral claims: class is money. In the fictional examples, financial and aesthetic language mingles to objectify the commodity: "I am 19 years of age, heiress to a freehold estate, in Kent, of the value of £500 per annum, besides £15,000 in the Public Funds; I have lately lost my father, and am under a guardian; I am of the middle size, my eyes dark, my person agreeable, my temper and disposition gay, my religion of the Church of England, Etc." (2).[2] Like the opening sentences of *Mansfield Park* and *Emma*, this passage both sketches and links the physical appearance, the social identity, and the possible destiny of a young woman. In the papers, advertisers sell their own commodities by rhetorical packaging; if that commodity is themselves, they must present themselves in the conventional language of advertisement. Similarly, in Austen's novels, the narrator initially advertises the heroine, but she must also advertise herself.

*   *   *

1. *Matrimonial Advertisements*, 1746–1862 (B.L. Cup 407 ff 43), 1.
2. An entry in the British Masonic Society journal *Ars Quatuor Coronatorum* describes the mélange of some newspapers' contents: "excerpts on the newly imported Waltz [that] appear from the columns of the *Morning Post* during the year 1811" alongside news of "the discovery of the body of Charles I., at Windsor." Of the fourth volume, which is "lettered 'Wants and Wanted,'" the authors write: "In the very early years of the eighteenth century many Offices were in existence where single persons, 'whether Low, Middle, or Tall, Black, Brown, or Fair, Bachelors, Maids, or Widows' could by payment of small entrance fees and quarterages insure their meetings with a marriageable partner possessed of any required qualifications. Several advertisements of this nature are dated 1709. Private individuals afterwards took up this class of business." This entry also references "a four-page Prospectus" called "'Matrimonial Plan. A New and Original Imperial and Royal Plan, according to the Usage of the Potentates and Sovereign Princes of Europe, as well as in all the polished Courts throughout the known World, entitled The Imprejudicate Nuptial Society: or Grand Matrimonial Intercourse Institution. On a Scale of important Novelty and general Utility; established on the most impartial and liberal Terms, for the mutual Benefit and Advantage of Subscribers, at No. 32, Old Bond-Street, London.' We have not yet got rid of Matrimonial Agencies. We have within recent years heard of wives being sold, but raffling for mates is distinctly peculiar." *Ars Quatuor Coronatorum, Being the Transactions of the Quatuor Coronati Lodge* 28.207 (1915): 50–51 [*Editor's note*].

WILLIAM H. GALPERIN

From The Historical Austen[†]

*   *   *

In noting the prevalence of nostalgia as a reflexive element in the fictions prior to *Persuasion*, I am not minimizing the material and historical elements that * * * contributed to Austen's awareness of her particular agency in the novel's rise and in the social work to which domestic fiction and realistic writing were already conscripted. From her abiding allegiance to epistolary instability, and the particular reading habits that epistolary "silence" cultivated and served, to her awareness of the naturalizing, indeed regulatory, bent of any art that spoke in the name of either probability or nature, to her recognition that the subordinate status of women, especially women of privilege, attested to the equally conscribed status of men, to her uncanny alignment with her romantic contemporaries in locating horizons of possibility in quotidian life, Austen—or the "historical Austen"—is far from seamlessly aligned with the major developments with which her achievement is usually deemed synonymous. It is not that such developments as the rise of the novel and the continued rise of bourgeois domesticity are alien or irrelevant to Austen's accomplishment. It is more that her growing, and at times inchoate, unease over the disposition of her achievement—on which a variety of recoverable influences and developments conceivably bear—became, in the six years during which all six novels were either composed or revised for publication, more acute and * * * more knowing.

*   *   *

Both a critique and an instance of historical method, my [methodological] way with Austen takes seriously her function as an historian of her milieu, which takes seriously in turn both the milieu that her works attend to and the uncanny prospects to which that world, particularly in retrospect, had been surprisingly open. The "historical Austen," in other words, implicitly contests the assumption germane to historical method generally that the material and cultural circumstances of a given text, not to mention the novels at issue here, work somehow to divest the text of the awareness that

† From *The Historical Austen* (Philadelphia: University of Pennsylvania Press, 2003), pp. 216–27, 230–31, 236–38, 269–70. Reprinted with permission of the University of Pennsylvania Press. Unless otherwise indicated, notes are by Galperin. Page numbers in brackets are to this Norton Critical Edition.

has devolved most recently upon the historically minded reader. Critics may well have a point in arguing that Wordsworth's poems, to cite the most obvious contemporaneous example, are in a state of denial regarding both their motives and the history they put under erasure. Nevertheless, apart from the fact that such approaches merely recapitulate a way of reading Wordsworth practiced long before it was history or the French Revolution or the vagrant dwellers at Tintern Abbey that were an issue, it does not follow that every author is either disabled or sufficiently possessed of false consciousness to require the supplement of retrospective reading.[1]

Such circumspection is particularly relevant in the case of Jane Austen, who not only wrote at a moment of extraordinary transition in British life and letters but whose flailings in the welter of these changes, from developments in which she was instrumental to changes where she was merely powerless, were coordinated and given a second chance in the years that her novels achieved final form.[2] This interval, more than any other, remains the context par excellence where Austen is concerned. This is not because the years at Chawton supersede all other contexts and conditions to which her writing may be referred. It is because the extraordinary compression, under which twenty years of observation and struggle were suddenly available for reconsideration and revision, provided Austen with an aperture on her historicity as well as her grapplings with it that is fairly unique. We will never know at what point Colonel Brandon may have become a rigorously conceived figure for both narrative authority in *Sense and Sensibility* and the still larger cultural forces that governed it. But there is little doubt that by the time that *Sense and Sensibility* was forwarded to the printer Austen had come to know, better than she had initially, what she was in fact up to.

As the last of Austen's completed novels, not to mention one that followed in short order upon the two novels she had most recently published, *Persuasion* presents special problems along with special exegetical opportunities. While there is probably no novel by

---

1. For the "New Historical" approach to Wordsworth see especially Marjorie Levinson, *Wordsworth's Great Period Poems: Four Essays* (Cambridge: Cambridge University Press, 1986), and Alan Liu, *Wordsworth: The Sense of History* (Stanford, Calif.: Stanford University Press, 1989).

2. The question of change during the interval in which Austen was writing has come under scrutiny by David Spring who maintains that the "rural elite was neither going bankrupt in the early nineteenth century nor disintegrating spiritually and socially" and that there were "no winners or losers" in the ostensible rise of the "bourgeoise in which the landed class was equally involved and instrumental" ("Interpreters of Jane Austen's Social World: Literary Critics and Historians," in *Jane Austen: New Perspectives*, ed. Janet Todd [New York: Holmes and Meier, 1983], 53–72). This is not, however, what many other readers, including Southam *** believe, nor does it take into account the considerable changes in domestic life and in the lives of educated women that Austen effectively oversaw and documented. [The reference is to B. C. Southam, "*Sanditon*: The Seventh Novel," in *Jane Austen's Achievement*, ed. Juliet McMaster (London: Macmillan, 1976), 3–4 —*Editor.*]

Austen to which the adjective *nostalgic* has been assigned with greater regularity, the version of nostalgia that we have been exploring here, involving the temporalized character of hope itself, makes the insubstantiality of change, or the displacement of the conditions under which substantive change was once fathomable or a possibility, the basis in *Persuasion* for a perplexity at once limiting and enabling. The central theme in *Persuasion*—as its posthumously bestowed title suggests—remains the coercive reach of culture, or what amounts, in Austen's reckoning, to the likely indivisibility of the individual's wants and what ideology, for want of a better term, has already mandated. Where previously, and as recently as *Emma*, there was a sense that the world is still pervious to otherness and variation, from the shadow narrative of Frank and Jane to the poultry pilferage that not even Mr. Woodhouse can control successfully, such alterity comes mostly at a price in the last completed novel.

Anne Elliot's refusal of Capt. Frederick Wentworth in the prehistory of the narrative and the mysterious physical transformation that she experiences in aftermath are factors unquestionably in Anne's exertion of responsible, even progressive, agency at the moment we first encounter her. But even as there is a palpable link between the mysterious loss of bloom and the still unravished Anne's ability to make a difference, whether in securing the Elliots' removal from Kellynch or in the numerous services she performs at Uppercross, where domesticity and her sister's debility bear a similar connection, it is difficult to rejoice in the particular autonomy that the narrative, in recognition of Anne's agency, confers upon her.[3] I am only the umpteenth reader to remark on the sense of isolation in *Persuasion*, and on the sympathetic identification that separates this most subjective of Austen's texts from the novel that precedes it, where the narrator and her protagonist are—until the very end—never on the same page.[4] What must be stressed about this development, specifically the movement from a "heroine whom no one . . . will much like"[5] to one whom everyone must like, is not just the abiding melancholy or sense of loss that the heroine's dilemma instills in *Persuasion*. Even more important is the improvement that such sympathetic alignment with the heroine holds for a narrative practice—specifically

3. Stuart Tave, in particular, stresses Anne's "usefulness to others" and the "self-command and sense of duty that make [her] actions possible" (*Some Words of Jane Austen* [Chicago: University of Chicago Press, 1973], 286). In his view Anne is a paragon of agency, whose autonomy and judgment are never violated, not even in conjunction with Mrs. Smith, whom Tave regards as a merely clumsy addition.
4. On Anne's sense of isolation and the narrative's sympathetic identification with her, see especially A. Walton Litz, *Jane Austen: A Study of Her Artistic Development* (London: Chatto and Windus, 1965), 150–60.
5. James Edward Austen-Leigh, *Memoir of Jane Austen* (Oxford: Clarendon Press, 1926), 157.

the practice of free indirect discourse—that, by its regulatory bent, had been as much an achievement as a liability.

Unlike *Mansfield Park*, where a similar alignment of narrator and protagonist abides, *Persuasion* demonstrates that sympathy and judgment no longer need be mutually exclusive any more than an understanding of Anne's limitations, particularly as someone who cannot finally prevent herself from "fall[ing] into a quotation" (83) [62],[6] is reason to "like" her any less. It is more, in fact, that the otherness that had previously infiltrated Austen's novels in, for example, the practices of its less tractable or significant characters has been transferred willy-nilly to narrative practice itself, which tracks and even celebrates Anne's reunion with Wentworth while itemizing all that is lost in a trajectory where being in love also means being in language. Only by perplexity over the subject's fate, in other words, or by recognition that the body outside of quotation will be necessarily deformed in the same way that Anne's restored body is more nearly a simulacrum, is Austen in a position to liberate free indirect discourse from its directive or regulatory function. Although there may be a great deal left to lament in the world and in domestic life, it is the case in *Persuasion* that there is really nothing left, at least by way of opposition, to regulate and control.[7] After a relatively brief interval during which the Anne shorn of "bloom" enjoys success in resolving her family's fiscal difficulties and in helping to negotiate what, according to the novel's social allegory, involves a transfer of stewardship from the aristocracy to the professional classes, the novel's heroine undergoes a restoration that proves a precondition for her eventual marriage to a representative of the new order. Thus the rather bleak and dystopic future that *Mansfield Park* imagines and projects, moreover, under the nostalgic pressure of opportunities lost and possibilities foreclosed upon, is by *Persuasion* at any rate a done deal.

* * *

It is probably the case that *Persuasion* marks something of a change in Austen's outlook in its increased focus on the individual subject and in its endorsement of the individualism of which military professionalism is a projection even as the novel reflects an

6. References to *Persuasion* are to the text of the novel in *Persuasion*, ed. John Davie (Oxford: Oxford University Press, 1990).

7. Although Tara Ghoshal Wallace rightly emphasizes Anne's fallibility as a heroine, she construes the narrator's sympathy with Anne as a means by "which Austen deliberately compromises her own narrative authority and indeed questions the sources of any narrator's authority" (*Jane Austen and Narrative Authority* [New York: St. Martin's, 1995], 115). While the interrogation of narrative authority is a major element in Austen's writings, *Persuasion* is arguably the last place where it occurs, largely because the narrator is capable here of representing her heroine both sympathetically and judgmentally, which is continuous in turn with the narrator's perplexity over the constitution of human relations in general.

abiding conservatism of which the heroine's stoicism is merely one aspect.[8] At the same time, such controversies regarding *Persuasion*—and the social and political valences of Austen's project overall—are from the perspective of this study beside the point. They are of little use because they fail to explain how a novel so plainly inured to things as they are—on which the aforementioned ideologies presumably bear—is also capable of marshaling that resignation to ends that are oppositional, or again nostalgic, in the way that Anne's progress, very much like Emma's, is readable as default, and as a falling away from the possibilities and practices that her restoration abruptly cancels.

I have already mentioned Anne's mysterious loss of bloom and the responsible, even progressive agency that she is capable of exerting in aftermath. What must be explored now is the novel's dilation on that connection. There is no question that Anne's father, Sir Walter Elliot, is among the most diminished and satirized of Austen's characters: a figure whose criteria of judgment—from birth to physiognomy—mark him as shallow and as representing a social order and its modes of discrimination that, beginning with Lady Catherine,[9] have long been a point of contention in Austen. Nor is there any question that Anne's mysterious transformation in the years following her rejection of Captain Wentworth would seem to serve the antiaristocratic argument in showing the denaturing effects of her refusal, which we are given to believe was offered in deference to her family's values. Still, a closer look at the brief summary of Anne's past at the beginning of *Persuasion* suggests that, however much the refusal of Wentworth redounds on Anne's family in the unhappiness it provokes, Anne's recourse to her family's claims, and to the advice in particular of Lady Russell, in rejecting Wentworth is more a measure of her resourcefulness than the result

---

8. For readings of the novel as a progressive statement in support of the developing culture of individualism or as a meditation on the dissolution of the old order, see especially Nina Auerbach, "O Brave New World"[: Evolution and Revolution in *Persuasion*," in *Romantic Imprisonment: Women and Other Glorified Outcasts* (New York: Columbia University Press, 1985), 38–54]; Julia Prewitt Brown, *Jane Austen's Novels: Social Change and Literary Form* (Cambridge, Mass.: Harvard University Press, 1975), 128–50; Marvin Mudrick, *Jane Austen: Irony as Defense and Discovery* (Princeton, N.J.: Princeton University Press, 1952), 207–40; Tony Tanner, *Jane Austen* (Cambridge, Mass.: Harvard University Press, 1986), 208–49; and despite his conservative reading, [Alistair] Duckworth, *The Improvement of the Estate* [(Baltimore: Johns Hopkins University Press, 1971), 179–208]. Those who regard *Persuasion* as supporting tradition and the landed order as part of England's future as well as its past include David Spring, "Interpreters of Jane Austen's Social World," and John Wiltshire, *Jane Austen and the Body* (Cambridge: Cambridge University Press, 1992), 155–96. David Monaghan, by contrast, sees the novel as "fractured into two contradictory halves" that support the old and new orders respectively (*Jane Austen: Structure and Social Vision* [London: Macmillan, 1980], 162).

9. Lady Catherine de Bourgh, of *Pride and Prejudice* (1813) [*Editor's note*].

of what Wentworth, in decrying her "feebleness of character," later terms "over-persuasion" (62) [45].

In describing the early attachment that Anne is obliged to sever, the narrator offers a description of the relationship that, with the weight of information that has accumulated and will continue to accumulate, suggests that "over-persuasion" is far from the one-way street that Wentworth's condemnation implies. It is more that persuasion, or again "over-persuasion," is omnipresent and that even Anne's very personal recollections of Wentworth bear the marks of outside influence:

> He was, at that time, a remarkably fine young man, with a great deal of intelligence, spirit and brilliancy; and Anne an extremely pretty girl, with gentleness, modesty, taste, and feeling.—Half the sum of attraction, on either side, might have been enough, for he had nothing to do, and she had hardly any body to love; but the encounter of such lavish recommendations could not fail. They were gradually acquainted, and when acquainted, rapidly and deeply in love. It would be difficult to say which had seen highest perfection in the other, or which had been the happiest; she, in receiving his declarations and proposals, or he in having them accepted. (29–30) [20]

In the method of narration that we have come to associate with Austen, it is often difficult to distinguish a character's internal representation of her thoughts and feelings and the narrator's interpretation of them. Never is this difficulty more to the point than here. Although hardly rife with Austen's customary irony, the detachment essential to irony reasserts itself in a remembrance that teeters precariously on the brink of cliché of which Anne, as much as the narrator, is the presumable author.[1] The normative scenario, where Wentworth and Anne dissolve effortlessly into "he" and "she" roles, coupled with the rapid and by no means unorthodox acceleration of their mutual attraction into declarations of love has a certain girlish charm, particularly as a retrospection susceptible to idealization. But there lurks within this storybook scenario a more severe recognition of the flattening and depersonalizing effects of normative relations, not to mention the lop-sidedness of gender relations, that bears as much on the present—or on what, from the narrator's perspective, may be a gentle criticism of such arrangements—as it does on the past and on Anne's initial refusal.

That rejection, to which the narrative immediately and characteristically turns its attention, is understood in retrospect to have

---

1. Tara Ghoshal Wallace also stresses the "prosaic," hence ironic, nature of Anne's remembrance of the courtship (*Jane Austen and Narrative Authority*, 101).

been the result of family pressure and of the influence of Lady Russell, who—whatever her lapses—is certainly a less toxic and ridiculous figure of traditionalism than Anne's father. Nevertheless the actual influences driving Anne's decision are represented, or again recollected, in a way that clearly complicates this interpretation of events, which is also Wentworth's interpretation:

> She was persuaded to believe the engagement a wrong thing—indiscreet, improper, hardly capable of success, and not deserving it. But it was not a merely selfish caution, under which she acted, in putting an end to it. Had she not imagined herself consulting his good, even more than her own, she could hardly have given him up.—The belief of being prudent, and self-denying principally for *his* advantage, was her chief consolation, under the misery of a parting—a final parting; and every consolation was required, for she had to encounter all the additional pain of opinions, on his side, totally unconvinced and unbending, and of his feeling himself ill-used by so forced a relinquishment. (31) [21–22]

Although the specter of "persuasion" is raised for the first time in the novel in describing Lady Russell's influence, it is not many sentences before the importance of that inaugural appearance (and the coercive force it designates) is compromised by other disclosures, notably the influence of Anne's altruism. While such self-denial is instrumental in marking Anne as an ethically informed subject, it is equally important in showing her resourcefulness. We see Anne's ability to marshal the coercive weight of class and family interests, along with the moral imperative to disinterestedness, in the service of *still other interests* that, while not strictly selfish, are directed toward an autonomy that Wentworth's obduracy (as revealed here) would likely stifle. It is unclear whether it is Anne herself or Anne according to the narrator who is protesting too much on the question of her selfishness. But the point to stress is that while it is presumably the narrator's purpose to introduce Anne's capacity for self-deception, if only to make her rejection of Wentworth vaguely tolerable, it is done less with the aim of criticizing Anne (in the manner, say, of *Emma*'s narrator) than with the object of showing Anne's remarkable ability to hold persuasion at bay *even by capitulation*. While autonomy and selfishness are not exactly one and the same, it is the case still that the *effect* of Anne's refusal, and of the persuasions she internalizes, is to escape persuasion along with the oppressive shape of life to come.[2]

---

2. In a related reading that deals similarly—that is, dialectically—with the dynamic of persuasion here, Adela Pinch argues that *Persuasion* "present[s] us with a heroine who seems to resist knowing what she doesn't already know, and who experiences knowledge

What follows from here is the memorably cryptic account of Anne's physical transformation in the wake of her rejection, beginning with her sustained suffering and culminating in the "early loss of bloom" (31) [22] that has not abated. And it remains an account, where Anne's demonstrable self pity is dutifully rendered by the narrator, making their apparent consensus on the cause of Anne's facial transformation a little suspect. In fact just as Anne is able to secure a space for herself amid the persuasions of family and moral authority, so it is the case here that, with the sudden agreement over its apparent cause, the "lasting effect" of Anne's early decision to remain single is readable in other ways. Anne's "loss of bloom," to put it bluntly, seems more a cause in its own right: an initiative that, as future events will shortly clarify, is remarkably on a continuum with the rejection that supposedly precipitated it.

The events to which I am referring involve the famous walk at Lyme later in volume 1, where Anne's miraculous restoration is as much an effect, or the result of persuasion, as it is apparently the cause of two men's admiration. But before we get to Lyme, and to the various persuasions that succeed in restoring Anne to desirability at the very moment they imbue Wentworth with a renewed desire for her, it must be emphasized that in the seven years that Anne has remained bloomless, she has also remained quietly autonomous and, in consequence, an effective agent. Readers are free to debate the extent of Anne's agency, including the political yield of getting her father and sister to lease their ancestral home and relocate to Bath. Yet despite the decidedly incremental nature of Anne's various interventions, which accords in any case with Austen's abiding fascination with the local as a site of possibility or difference, both the bricolage of Anne's overpersuasion and the loss of bloom that ensues follow her rejection of Wentworth in continuing to pave her egress from the heteronormative economy and its strictures.

Much of Anne's resistance is in the past, and by the time we rejoin Anne in the present she is of a different mind regarding her previous decision. Not only is she "persuaded" now that "she should yet have been a happier woman in maintaining the engagement" (32–33) [23]; she is also convinced at this point that in breaking the

---

of others' wishes and desires as a form of oppressive persuasion" (*Strange Fits of Passion: Epistemologies of Emotion, Hume to Austen* [Stanford, Calif.: Stanford University Press, 1996], 44–45 [excerpted in this volume —*Editor*]). Although my reading credits Anne with knowing, at least intuitively, what Pinch claims "she doesn't already know," so much so that much of the novel is about "disowning knowledge" (to borrow Stanley Cavell's term), my approach is also proximate to Pinch's in weighing the tension "between pressures from without and internal desires." We differ primarily in our conceptions of how that "conflict" is resolved. For Pinch the resolution is poised between a subscription to "outside influence" *and* by "a kind of consciousness that is constituted as resistance to outside influence" (154) whereas I argue that such resistance dissipates in the welter of outside influence.

engagement she was simply following Lady Russell's advice and adhering to her family's wishes. The memory of her former altruism or self-denial has apparently receded along with any sense of the complex of influences that just two pages earlier had made it clear that however much Anne may have acceded to Lady Russell her decision to break the engagement was also linked to something that might be confused with selfishness. The narrator's explanation for the transformation in Anne's thinking is both simple and suggestive. Although Anne, she observes, "had been forced into prudence in her youth, she learned romance as she grew older—the natural sequence of an unnatural beginning" (33) [23].

The narrator's point may seem obvious enough, but it is scarcely removed from perplexity. Beginning with the forces behind Anne's early prudence, which are notably opaque, the narrator's observation is additionally vexed by the continued interchangeability of the "natural" and the "learned." Where Anne is simply convinced that she made a mistake, even as she will expend a good deal of effort making the same mistake in continuing to resist Wentworth, the rather ironic notion of "learned romance" complicates the complexion of Anne's development. Is Anne's prudence less natural than her current discovery that romance and love truly matter? Or is it a question of her having assimilated different lessons and discourses? In either case there is a problem in determining the naturalness of Anne's early self-regard, where prudence is surely a factor, in conjunction with the concomitant, and presumably greater, naturalness of heterosexual desire. The particular difficulty in differentiating the natural from the discursive, which is registered in the oxymoron "learned romance" (not to mention the notion of "romance" itself), owes in no small measure, then, to Anne's earlier and continued imperative to self-preservation, where prudence—and the multiple forces that provoke it—is obviously a factor.

Much of what follows in *Persuasion* involves the competition between the impulses—or as the case may be, discourses—of romance and prudence. And while it may seem altogether churlish to reduce love and romance to a pedagogical or disciplinary instrument, we are given, in Anne's continued resistance to Wentworth upon his reappearance in her life, some hint that her continued prudence—following her mysterious but equally innate loss of bloom—may well be the more "natural," or the more sustaining, of the two. It is not that the narrative is necessarily averse to erotic feeling, or that Anne is not plainly moved by desire, particularly when Wentworth comes to her assistance in relieving her of little Charles Musgrove or in "assist[ing] her into the carriage" (89) [66]. It is rather that such impulses are continually met by countervailing impulses, including the "pain" that immediately compounds

Anne's "pleasure" in being helped into the carriage, that, however inflected by the past or by the still gloomy trajectory of heterosexual love into married life, are impulses nonetheless.

It is surely no accident that much of the circumstantial detail in *Persuasion*, particularly at the moment when Wentworth and Anne are brought into close proximity upon his return from the war, is taken up with issues of domesticity and marriage. These issues include the debility of Anne's sister, Mary, and the particular imbalance it demonstrates and serves, along with the marriage of Captain and Mrs. Harville, which is marked similarly by asymmetry. There is also, of course, Wentworth's sister and her husband, Admiral Croft. Their childless and companionate marriage is more than simply the exception that proves the rule here. It is a union, importantly, whose nearly cartoonish ecumenicism proves the backdrop for a rather heated debate over the appropriateness of having wives aboard ship where Wentworth typically takes the negative and customary position. Wentworth's position regarding women makes him, as Claudia Johnson has observed, the author of his own disappointment since the feebleness and fussiness that render women constitutionally unsuited for naval life in his view are the very aspects of femininity that make Anne culpable, as he sees it, in earlier rejecting him (*Jane Austen*, 149–57).[3] Wentworth is wrong in accusing Anne of feebleness. But right or wrong, his endorsement of domestic ideology, and the imbalance it creates in its divisions of labor and ability, is sufficient to make desire and discourse coterminous in the same way that Anne's prudence remains—now as before—the comparatively natural response to an unnatural and regulated social world.

The impulsiveness peculiar to Anne's reticence regarding Wentworth, which is often construed as stoicism on her part, is evident from the moment of their reunion, where Anne's repeated observation to herself—"It is over! It is over. . . . The worst is over!" (60) [44]—plainly oscillates between embarrassment at encountering Wentworth after so long a duration, where sexual desire no doubt figures prominently, and an equally spontaneous sense of relief over the termination of their attachment. And the tension continues in a variety of forms. In noticing, at one point, that Wentworth is looking at her, Anne speculates that he is "observing her altered features, perhaps, trying to trace in them the ruins of the face which had once charmed him" (71) [53]. The "perhaps" or caesura that intrudes upon Anne's fantasy undoubtedly looks toward erotic closure, but not without a certain apprehension over the prospect of Wentworth's picking up where he left off.

---

3. Claudia Johnson, *Jane Austen: Women, Politics, and the Novel* (Chicago: U of Chicago P, 1988) [*Editor's note*].

Several chapters later, in a conversation with the lovelorn, hope-lessly romantic Captain Benwick, who is still pining for his recently departed fiancée, Anne is only too willing make her interlocutor privy to a future that, for her part, seems impossible. Recurring, once again, to the imbalance of gender relations against which her prudence has been arguably a defense, Anne reflects on her differ-ences from Benwick: "'And yet,' said Anne to herself, as they moved forward to meet the party, 'he has not, perhaps, a more sorrowing heart than I have. I cannot believe his prospects so blighted for ever. He is younger than I am; younger in feeling, if not in fact; younger as a man. He will rally again, and be happy with another'" (95) [71]. Apart from the recurrence of "perhaps," which again marks a nearly instinctive mitigation of the subject's normative yearning, the pro-jection of the courtship plot onto some other figure looks in two directions simultaneously: to a desire for union whose projection is more properly a confession (much as Emma's matchmaking initia-tives are often taken to signify her own desire to be married) as well as to another future, in this case to Anne's continued autonomy, for which the gender differences that she rehearses remain a powerful incentive.

Anne's resistance to imagining herself in a courtship narrative is also, of course, a means of steeling herself against Wentworth's suspi-ciously overt dalliances with the Musgrove sisters, Henrietta and Louisa. Nevertheless the substance of Anne's resistance—particularly as it stands distinct from mere denial—is given succinct if ultimately ironic confirmation in the scene that follows almost immediately upon the conversation with Benwick. This is Anne's memorable walk at Lyme, where she is "caught" in the triangulated—and reciprocally entrapped—gaze of two admiring men:

> When they came to the steps, leading upwards from the beach, a gentleman at the same moment preparing to come down, politely drew back, and stopped to give them way. They ascended and passed him; and as they passed, Anne's face caught his eye, and he looked at her with a degree of earnest admiration, which she could not be insensible of. She was looking remarkably well; her very regular, very pretty features, having the bloom and freshness of youth restored by the fine wind which had been blowing on her complexion, and by the animation of eye, which it had also produced. It was evident that the gentleman, (com-pletely a gentleman in manner) admired her exceedingly. Cap-tain Wentworth looked round at her instantly in a way which shewed his noticing of it. He gave her a momentary glance,—a glance of brightness, which seemed to say, "That man is struck with you,—and even I, at this moment, see something like Anne Elliot again." (101) [76]

Although Anne is necessarily mindful of the first admiring glance directed at her, it is not at all clear that the ventriloquism performed on Wentworth is anyone's doing but the narrator's. It makes sense that this is the case. Beyond the fact that Anne's fantasies of Wentworth are invariably fraught by some hesitation or impulse to self-preservation, the narrator's assumption of omniscience in surveying all three figures simultaneously is consistent with her perplexity throughout the novel over the constitution of sexual relations in general.

This perplexity, in which sexual desire and desirability are suspended somewhere between the natural and the discursive, or between the natural and the *naturalized*, is registered in the ambiguity of Anne's sudden restoration. Although we have only the narrator's word that Anne was aware of the gentleman's admiring look, it is significant that Anne's constitution as an object of desire is prior, in the narrator's accounting, to the otherwise natural explanation for her transformation. There is no reason to suppose that Anne was not already the beneficiary of the elements at the moment that her cousin William Walter Elliot (as it turns out) is disposed to take notice of her. Yet even as the narrator allows for this interpretation, it is an interpretation vexed by questions of causality or, again, issues of persuasion.

It is not enough for the narrator to observe that Anne was aware of the gentleman's glance for which the play of wind and physiognomy were chiefly responsible. The narrator makes a point of giving his glance an equal, if not greater, role in the *effect* of beauty, whose priority in turn, in this case as a discourse or desideratum, supersedes its immediate manifestation. If Anne is rendered beautiful by the animation of eye that she produces, it is because that "eye" (and the mind behind it) is already "caught" by an abstraction that Anne merely renders concrete. And were there any doubt of this "overpersuasion"—or of the interpellation, to be precise, that makes "internal persuasio[n]" (207) [157] a register of coercion from without—there is the fortuitous addition here of Wentworth. Wentworth's renewed appreciation of Anne is more than the result of the triangulation that Mr. Elliot's admiration "instantly" adds to the scene. It is the effect as well of a mediation so pervasive that his designation of the object of beauty as "something like Anne Elliot" nearly beclouds the fact that, in becoming beautiful in the way that she has, Anne is more properly "like something" else here. Anne has become, thanks chiefly to a gaze that is *itself* an effect of discourse, the very simulacrum or type that her loss of bloom had earlier vitiated and on whose suppression her autonomy has depended.[4]

4. In a variant reading of this scene that also focuses on questions of spectation and the so-called male gaze, Robyn R. Warhol seeks to differentiate the male way of looking and the narratological practice it figures from Anne's, and by implication Austen's, way

The perplexity on which the Lyme scene devolves entails more than the recognition that the natural or spontaneous is sufficiently adulterated that any opposition of the natural and the artificial, including the social artifice that the novel begins by excoriating, is already compromised. This perplexity also involves the alternative to persuasion, from the self-determination in which being Anne Elliot is a stay against being "something" desirable to other versions of autonomy or exteriority, where the body removed from quotation is reciprocally prone to abjection or degradation. The "autumnal" readings of *Persuasion*, that Claudia Johnson shrewdly cautions against, wherein the novel's tenderness on "romantic subjects" issues primarily from a "wistful and romantically unfulfilled" author "in the twilight of her life" (*Jane Austen*, 144), are perhaps not so wide of the mark after all. This is not so because Austen, or her narrator, has finally relented amid her own debility and personal disappointment. It is that Anne's capitulation to desire or to what, in the above scene, is transparently the desire of the other, bifurcates in two directions that are basically dead ends. First, Anne's persuasion provides the occasion to reflect on what is lost by her capitulation and by the consignment to domesticity and married life that must follow. Second, Anne's metamorphosis at Lyme proves an occasion to parse the increasingly abstract or utopian comedy of Anne's opposition to normativity, and the actual ravages, beginning with her own defacement, that being out of quotation effectively mandates. All of this bespeaks a resignation quite different from the wish fulfillment [born] of disappointment and terminal illness. For in the manner of virtually every other novel by Austen, *Persuasion* is affected still by the prospect of a different configuration among humans, or what amounts here to a tertium quid,[5] to which the present dialectic of being in and out of discourse is simply inadequate.

*   *   *

Anne's transformation at Lyme, which is both documented and deconstructed in the two critical scenes there, marks a turning point in the narrative that is irreversible. Despite some clumsy complications in volume 2 involving Mr. Elliot's interest in Anne and her family's efforts in persuading her to marry him, the end of *Persuasion*, no less than the resolution of *Pride and Prejudice* following Darcy's declarations in the second volume, is entirely a foregone

---

of both seeing and narrating, which looks beyond the object to the interior of the subject ("The Look, the Body, and the Heroine: A Feminist-Narratological Reading of *Persuasion*," *Novel* 26 [1992]: 5–19).

5. The Latin term implies both opposition or oppositeness and intermediateness (a "third" way or thing). The *Oxford English Dictionary* defines it as "something (indefinite or left undefined) related in some way to two (definite or known) things, but distinct from both" [*Editor's note*].

conclusion. And like *Pride and Prejudice*, whose final volume assumes a nearly metafictional status in exposing (with an assist from Lydia) the cultural work that the Darcy–Elizabeth coupling otherwise mystifies, the second half of *Persuasion* follows upon the nodal scenes at Lyme in making Anne's inevitable fate as Mrs. Wentworth an object of sharply critical attention.

The only difference between the critical machinery in *Persuasion* and the critical machinery in Austen's other novels * * * is that it no longer operates at the cost of narrative authority. With the scenes at Lyme as a model, in fact, the coincidence of sympathy and judgment, particularly as Anne is conscripted and rehabilitated within the economy of the gaze, makes it clear that however much Anne is coopted or persuaded, this is not necessarily the narrator's wish. Rather, Anne's progress en route to becoming a captain's wife demarcates an inevitable course to which the narrator lends a critical eye simply by recounting. As a result the oppositional elements of Austen's previous novels, from the practices of seemingly marginal characters to the practices of those who are either directly derogated or, in the case of Catherine Morland, misunderstood,[6] are incorporated to the narrator's perspective in *Persuasion* rather than becoming aspects of the novel against which narrative authority must be mobilized. It is not that Austen's narrator is without opinions in *Persuasion*, or that she fails to render judgments on, among other matters, Anne's family and their values. It is that with Anne as the focus here the narrator can engage in the business of criticism, which is also the business of disappointment, merely by attending to her subject.

We see this understanding quite clearly in the sequence of events at Lyme. Where the first scene demonstrates the persuasive effects of the male gaze and the persuasion in turn to which that gaze refers in always seizing, regardless of who is looking, on the object of beauty, the second scene explores the consequences of that demonstration.[7] It is only after being transported back to the economy of normative relations by the gaze and by the discursive field it denotes that Anne can assist Wentworth in ways that, however called for by the situation at hand, have the additional, and readable, effect of papering over his default and failure to do as he "ought." This save is equally true of Anne's internal actions. Confronted with the decidedly specular and unforgettable image of the debased Wentworth, Anne mentally retrieves him from a position, which is the very one she had earlier occupied outside of quotation, by imagining a

---

6. Catherine Morland, protagonist of *Northanger Abbey* (1817) [*Editor's note*].
7. The "second scene" and the "debased Wentworth" referenced later in this paragraph refer to the walk along the Cobb, where Wentworth fails both to persuade Louisa against jumping and to catch her when she falls, exclaiming: "Oh God! that I had not given way to her at the fatal moment! Had I done as I ought! But so eager and so resolute! Dear, sweet Louisa!" [85] [*Editor's note*].

recognition on his part that is in fact a recent, and tentatively held, awareness of her own.

*   *   *

The bearing of the quotable on Anne's renewed love, which is really a new or "learned" love, is further reflected in the extended dialogue with Harville that ensues [in Chapter XXIII]. This dialogue on the essential differences of men and women, which has no counterpart in the original ending, is important now for several reasons. In emphasizing the imbalance that currently characterizes gender relations, where women are neurotically "confined" and men are happily "forced on exertion" (219) [166], the dialogue both punctuates *and* punctures the marriage plot in *Persuasion* by exposing the false symmetry and the false democracy that sexual difference, and the marital ideal it serves, continues to uphold. More important, the dialogue also shows that even as Anne is sufficiently in quotation that she must confuse the material bases of a woman's disposition with what she and Harville repeatedly regard as natural and innate to women, she retains a sense, or more properly a memory, that something is not quite right or as it should be.

This recognition cum recollection figures most prominently in Anne's reminder to Harville that the many encomiums on male constancy over time owe to the fact that "the pen," as Anne nicely puts it, "has been in their hands" (221) [167]. It is manifest in other forms as well, from Anne's reprisal of the naturalized division of labor prescribed in the conduct manuals of Thomas Gisborne and others[8] to her overdetermined insistence, in ostensible defense of women's loyalty, of "loving longest, when existence or when hope is gone" (222) [168]. While this concluding maxim confuses Anne's early love for Wentworth, which *was* resistible, with the "learned" and irresistible "romance" that currently governs her affections, the insistence on loving in the absence of *both* hope and existence has a curiously transhistorical reach. Although apposite to her revised sense of the past, in which she never stopped loving Wentworth, Anne's clinching claim on behalf of women's constancy bears powerfully and skeptically on her present and future condition, where marriage and the loss of existence—or such existence as Anne has known—maintain some relation.

None of this awareness, of course, is sufficient to prevent, or to delay beyond this point, the narrative's now inevitable movement to

---

8. Thomas Gisborne the Elder (1758–1846), English Anglican priest and abolitionist. Galperin has in mind works such as *Enquiry into the Duties of Men* (1795) and *Enquiry into the Duties of the Female Sex* (1797), which advocate for the rightness of sexual difference and a social hierarchy given by divine law [*Editor's note*].

marital closure. But the dialogue on the sexes is sufficient to shadow this otherwise gratifying close and its attendant eclaircissement in ways that are palpable and evidently to the narrator's purpose. The letter to Anne, for example, that Wentworth has been composing during her debate with Harville, and which results immediately in their reunion as lovers, is not only filled with enough cliché and quotation to suggest that loving and learning are necessarily synonymous. Wentworth's letter reveals, more important—and by jointure of the hackneyed and coercive—that the "pen" is still in the hands of men. Thus while Anne's response to Wentworth's initiative is notably yielding, even as it is judged by the narrator to be something from which she must "recove[r]" (224) [170], it is insufficient in dispelling a sense of the sacrifice or loss that marriage to Wentworth will entail.

Such loss emerges in *Persuasion*'s concluding sentences, where the "dread of a future war" and the "glor[y]" of "being a sailor's wife" are inextricably and pathetically yoked, never more perhaps than in the ironic designation of wifehood as a "profession" (237) [180]. But the real sense of loss, which is a reminder at the same time that the pen is not always in the hands of men, even if the prerogatives of professionalism are, comes in the two interrogatives that inaugurate the final chapter in both the original and published versions:

> Who can be in doubt of what followed? When any two young people take it into their heads to marry, they are pretty sure by perseverance to carry their point, be they ever so poor, or ever so imprudent, or ever so little likely to be necessary to each other's ultimate comfort. This may be bad morality to conclude with, but I believe it to be truth; and if such parties succeed, how should a Captain Wentworth and an Anne Elliot, with the advantage of maturity of mind, consciousness of right, and one independent fortune between them, fail of bearing down every opposition? (233) [176–77]

This is hardly the first time that Austen's narrator reverts to the first person in her fictions, or the first time that such reversion is an invitation to regard the narrator as a character with opinions of her own.

Still, without exaggerating what might also have been an oversight or simply a shift that did not, in Austen's view, compromise the formal rigor of her achievement, the narrator's position seems largely descriptive of, even hostile to, its subject rather than supportive. The "bad morality," to which the narrator confesses yet assigns the mantle of "truth," may simply be the success with which young couples routinely meet at a time when "affective individualism" rather than "parental tyranny" increasingly governs relational decisions.[9] But the "truth" of the narrator's convictions bears as much on this particular observation as it does on the horizon of disappointment to which marriage, in general, appears to give access. The two questions here, which are about resistance to marriage and about the sites from which either "opposition" or "doubt" may be registered, are not simply rhetorical. They are, like so many interrogatives in Austen, remarkably open-ended. They are questions, in other words, directed to a readership whose exposure to the prerogatives of the pen involves two things. It involves the ability to witness what the reader, no less than the writer, is also incapable of changing *and* the *inability* to resist what, for the reader no less than for Anne, is too imitable in the end to be opposed.

MARY A. FAVRET

From Everyday War[†]

* * *

* * * In bringing her military men home, and in fashioning a wide-ranging conversation between Anne's situation and the situation of these sailors, Austen explores an alternative but no less risky grounding for wartime: the everyday. Through her novelistic construction of the everyday, she composes a negative history of wartime—built less of rousing fortification than of rejection, unspoken pains, and unaccountable failings and fallings. This chapter takes up the everyday, our legacy from Romanticism, as another structure of modern wartime, indeed as a structure of feeling akin to trauma, conveying in its gaps and silences an unrecoverable, absent sense of suffering.

---

9. Affective individualism is a concept defined by the historian Lawrence Stone as the modern cultural valuation of marriage as a union of choice, formed on the basis of personal sentiment, intellectual match, and individual attraction, rather than of custom or economic or political arrangement (*The Family, Sex and Marriage in England, 1500–1800* [New York: Harper & Row, 1977]). Galperin references this concept in relation to Stone and Randolph Trumbach, who argue (in his words) that it "both accompanied and abetted the family's atomization into smaller and more modern units" (p. 260, n. 3) [*Editor's note*].

† From *War at a Distance: Romanticism and the Making of Modern Wartime* (Princeton, NJ: Princeton University Press, 2009), pp. 145–49, 151, 162–63. Used with permission of Princeton University Press, conveyed through Copyright Clearance Center, Inc. Unless otherwise indicated, notes are by Favret. Page numbers in brackets are to this Norton Critical Edition.

A History of Suffering

The traumatized, we might say, carry an impossible history within them, or they become themselves the symptom of a history that they cannot entirely possess.[1]

In her novel *Persuasion*, Jane Austen offers up symptoms of a history not entirely possessed. The past presented in the novel is incomplete, interrupted. Over the narrative hangs the unaccountable weight of "eight years and a half ago," a period of romance which the novel conjures only to dismiss in a few paragraphs. "A short period of exquisite felicity . . . and but a short one.—Troubles soon arose" (26) [20].[2] The narrator emphasizes the brevity of a lost love which, now in the form of enduring pain, possesses her heroine, Anne Elliot. "A few months had seen the beginning and the end of their acquaintance"—already the narrator diminishes the affair:

> but, not with a few months ended Anne's share of suffering from it. Her attachment and regrets had, for a long time, clouded every enjoyment of youth; and an early loss of bloom and spirits had been their lasting effect. (*P* 28) [22]

Loss of bloom, loss of spirits, loss of money, loss of status: characters in *Persuasion* are variously in danger of having the present slip away. "Tell me not that I am too late, that such precious feelings are gone for ever," Captain Wentworth writes desperately, and he too uses the language of pain to underscore his own share of suffering: "You pierce my soul. I am half agony, half hope" (*P* 237) [169]. In the end the novel, like Shakespeare's *A Winter's Tale*, reassures us that love can, magically, come back to life.[3] But even that resuscitation remains tenuous, and not without the threat of further pain. The narrator closes the novel by reminding us that the moment of happiness may not last and troubles may arise again. United with her love, Anne Elliot "gloried in being a Sailor's wife," but had to "pay the tax of quick alarm"—dread of his being called back to war (*P* 252) [180]. What does endure, filling most of the narrative and more than eight years, testifying to love and loss, is suffering. One name for that history of suffering is the everyday, a term often invoked to characterize the world of Austen's novels. Another name for that history, which cannot be possessed but possesses the novel, is war.

---

1. Cathy Caruth, *Trauma: Explorations in Memory* (Baltimore: Johns Hopkins UP, 1995), 5.
2. Jane Austen, *Persuasion*, *The Novels of Jane Austen*, vol. 5, 3rd ed. (Oxford: Oxford UP, 1993, 1988) ***. All references to this text will be cited parenthetically by page number and abbreviated *P*.
3. In *The Winter's Tale* (the title preferred by the Folger Shakespeare Library) (1623), a statue of the dead Hermione returns to life [*Editor's note*].

Like other versions of the everyday constructed in the Romantic period, Austen's in *Persuasion* emerges from the reality of worldwide war. Reading these unaccountable histories of pain and loss confirms the thought that the everyday is another form of wartime. This chapter thus extends claims made at the end of the previous chapter: in tracking the itinerary of pain and suffering into the realm of Austen's novel, it tracks anew the mediation of distant war, this time * * * through the narrative structures of domestic realism. Sending my argument about modern wartime into what might be called the romantic home of everydayness, the chapter also pursues a distinct strand of thinking about the everyday, from its philosophical and aesthetic roots in Romanticism into twentieth-century critical theory. Throughout I find the everyday informed by the language, the features, and the affective resonance of wartime. Austen and her contemporaries allow us to see with specificity how modern war—with its national armies, its tendency to erase the line between combatants and noncombatants, its global reach—is the history that possesses, perhaps determines our own current thinking about the everyday. At moments when war appears to have no horizon, it seems appropriate to acknowledge, as Austen's *Persuasion* does, this marriage of war and the everyday, but also to call into question, as the best romances do, the inevitability of this marriage.

For Austen, the everyday is the elastic form in which she tries to hold the recent history of the Napoleonic wars; by understanding the everyday as a record of pain and alienation, as Anne's story, Austen makes it permeable to the suffering of war. The everyday, with its rhythms of routine and accident, of endless waiting and unforeseen returns, provides a chronotope[4] for Austen's novels; in *Persuasion* it reveals itself to be as well the register, the telling surface, on which to read traces of nearly ineffable loss. Distressed, anxious, and punctuated by confusion and pain, the everyday Austen creates for *Persuasion* is, I want to argue, another form of wartime; more and less than a container, it is the medium through which she evokes the costs of prolonged war.

Like the wartime of [William] Cowper's influential poem,[5] Austen's everyday composes itself of uncertainties and gaps of time; his lost hour grows into her lost years, increasing the historical burden of Cowper's "unceasing lapses." Shadowing Anne's history, and even

---

4. The chronotope, conceptualized in 1937 by Russian scholar Mikhail Bakhtin, conceives of time and space as inseparable and the core concept that "defines genre and generic distinctions." "Forms of Time and of the Chronotope in the Novel," in *The Dialogic Imagination*, ed. Michael Holquist, transl. Caryl Emerson and Michael Holquist (Austin: U of Texas P, 1981), p. 85 [*Editor's note*].
5. From *The Task: A Poem, in Six Books* (1785) by English poet William Cowper (1731–1800), hymnist and abolitionist who also wrote "The Negro's Complaint" (1788) [*Editor's note*].

more sketchy in its details, is Frederick Wentworth's naval service in Britain's wars with Napoleon. Much of the drama of the novel depends on the reader—and Anne—not having access to Wentworth's "share of suffering" during those years. Even the Musgrove sisters' eager reading about his ships and postings in the Navy List merely points to the scarcity of information. With danger apparently behind him, Wentworth can now affect a nonchalance, who knows how hard-won, and joke about the less than seaworthy ship that was his first command. The satisfaction later afforded by his love letter to Anne, which arrives at the climax of the novel, rests in part in its revelation of how much pain he has borne. Here Austen seems to eclipse the sufferings of warfare with the trials of love, and wipe away both with the romance of her ending. But why then does she leave the novel with the "dread of a future war" and that nagging tax of quick alarm? And why does she set her novel so carefully in 1814, the year known as the False Peace,[6] after which "troubles soon arose" and Europe found itself again at war?

When the Duke of Wellington wrote that "The history of the battle [Waterloo] is not unlike the history of a ball," he was not being flippant: both, he went on to insist, are histories impossible to grasp.[7] Despite their seeming punctuality (one can usually assign them a date), both ball and battle are composed as much of eventlessness (a fraught waiting-for-something-to-happen, or meantime) or unfelt, mechanical behavior (repeated recourse to one's equipment) as distinct event. Beyond these similarities stretches the ineffable affect of each occasion, which leaves its representation open to the seemingly disaffected modes of formality, mockery, or understatement. Thus a British sailor, recording in his diary the "dreadful massacre" of his companions that took place in November 1803, provides a characteristic account of how much cannot be told:

> Wilkinson [the captain] makes his appearance at the entrance of the gangway and salutes his bleeding[,] partly exhausted first lieutenant in this manner[:] "Well, Pridham, you have had a fine

---

6. The False Peace refers to the period following the Treaty of Paris of May 30, 1814, before Napoleon Bonaparte's escape from Elba, the Hundred Days of his restoration to power, and his eventual defeat at the Battle of Waterloo of June 18, 1815, which ended twenty-three years of intermittent war between France and other allied European nations [Editor's note].

7. Qtd. in John Keegan, *The Face of Battle* (Harmondsworth, UK: Penguin, 1976), 117. Compare Walt Whitman, writing fifty years later, during the American Civil War:

   Such was the war. It was not a quadrille in a ball-room. Its interior history will not only never be written—its practicality, minutiae of deeds and passions, will never be even suggested. The actual soldier of 1862–'65, North and South, with all his ways, . . . will never be written—perhaps must not and should not be.

   "The Real War Will Never Get in the Books," in *Prose Works 1892, Vol. 1: Specimen Days*, ed. Floyd Stovall (New York: New York UP, 2007).

night's diversion. What the devil were you all about to let the damn'd Croppoes[8] [the French] give you such an infernal drubbing? Why you must have been all asleep along side her." "Capt. Wilkinson," answered Mr. Pridham, "Sir, had you been there perhaps you might have done some great exploit, and as for sleeping we are all convinced you would not have found much opportunity to sleep, there was quite the contrary sort of employment."[9]

When, in her last complete novel, Jane Austen, that great historian of the ballroom, attempts something "not unlike" a history of war, she does so precisely by calling the reader's attention to a negative sort of history, a lost history, a history of what seems unable to be told. Through this untold and nearly eventless history—so laden with silence, litotes, and negation that her first draft of the final chapter had at its heart a series of pronounced "No's"—she demonstrates another crucial way modernity binds together the structures of military violence and the everyday.[1] In following William Galperin's recent suggestion that Austen writes as a conscious historian of the fate of the everyday during those tumultuous years in Great Britain and drawing out, as he advises, the possible histories "that are always close at hand" if left unwritten in her novels, I hope to call forth Austen's history of everyday war along with the everydayness of modern war.[2]

In doing so, I will also draw out a barely submerged preoccupation with the troubling but enduring marriage of the everyday with war shared by twentieth-century theory. The everyday emerges as an object of significant historical and theoretical interest in the wake of the Second World War. Signaling the shift from wartime to its aftermath, attention to the everyday appears to demonstrate an ability to situate oneself at a distance from wartime itself; it takes the survivor's perspective. And yet twentieth-century theorists of the everyday seem eager to hold on to or perpetuate war, to realize in the everyday what Michel Foucault calls "the continuation of war by other means," a reformulation of what Joseph Fawcett * * * had identified in 1803 as "inactive war."[3] From this point of view, the

8. From the French *crapaud*, or toad [*Editor's note*].
9. John Wetherell, *The Adventures of John Wetherell*, ed. C. S. Forester (London: Michael Joseph, 1994), 78. * * *
1. The canceled chapters 10 and 11 of an earlier draft of *Persuasion* are reprinted in Appendix A of Bree's edition [and on pp. 180–90 of this volume —*Editor*]. In a remarkable passage, Austen finally reunites her lovers precisely through a negative truth: "'No Sir. . . . There is no message. . . . —There is no Truth in any such report.' 'No Truth in any *part* of it?'—'None.'" The two subsequently share "a silent, but a very powerful Dialogue" (263) [184]. The entire chapter 10 abounds in negatives, double negatives, and silences. Austen, *Persuasion*, ed. Linda Bree (Peterborough, Ont.: Broadview, 1998).
2. William Galperin, *The Historical Austen* (Philadelphia: U of Pennsylvania P, 2003), 12. See esp. chap. 1 and 8.
3. Michel Foucault, *"Society Must Be Defended": Lectures at the Collège de France, 1975–76*, ed. Mauro Bertani and Alessandro Fontana, trans. David Macey (New York: Picador,

postwar everyday maintains under the veneer of peace the work of war even after its formal end.

As a philosophical pivot point, however, the everyday had emerged earlier, during those world wars preceding and concurrent with the Napoleonic period, where reflection back upon war was barely imaginable. "Long months of peace . . . / Are mine in prospect," Wordsworth writes tentatively at the outset of the 1805 *Prelude*; but he has to admit the fantasy of this view, inserting the parenthetical, "(if such bold word [peace] accord / With any promises of human life)."[4] This earlier everyday understood itself from within wartime, absorbing, if not embracing, war and its pains. Comparing romantic representations with twentieth-century discussions of everyday war calls into question not the operations of war, which are in both cases almost always assumed; rather it calls into question peace. Romantic writers found it nearly impossible to imagine any space or time free from the pains—Austen's "tax"—of warfare. Many twentieth-century theorists, by contrast, find it not impossible, but rather undesirable or disadvantageous, to conjure peace. The twenty-first century, with its promise of enduring global warfare, invites us to review the romantic position and reconsider our subscription to a critical practice that relies upon, elaborates, and promotes the logic of war.

❋   ❋   ❋

No Peace

For all its spectacular trappings, modern warfare rarely escapes intimacy with the prosaic everyday. Historians have argued that the concept of the everyday arose when the military enterprise of the early modern nation-state "faded as the preeminent activity of elites" and court life replaced camp life as a social and political ground.[5] The ideal of military heroism, so much at odds with the everyday, yielded to the ideal of leisurely gentlemanliness. "There was a 'place' now . . . to notice how pleasant ordinary occupations might be" (Kinser 79). The everyday became charming—witness the paintings of Chardin or Greuze[6]—when warfare was put aside; indeed, it

---

2003), 48 and following. On these issues, I have profited from Chris J. Cuomo, "War Is Not Just an Event: Reflections on the Significance of Everyday Violence," *Hypatia* 11.4 (Autumn 1996): 30–45.

4. William Wordsworth, *The Prelude, 1799, 1805, 1850*, ed. Jonathan Wordsworth, M. H. Abrams, and Stephen Gill (New York: Norton, 1979), I: 26–29.

5. Samuel Kinser, "Everyday Ordinary," *diacritics* 22.2 (Summer 1992): 79. For a parallel thought about the historiographical shift from accounts of battles to accounts of social interaction and everyday experience, see Mark Salber Phillips, *Society and Sentiment: Genres of Historical Writing in Britain, 1740–1820* (Princeton: Princeton UP, 2000).

6. Jean Siméon Chardin (1699–1779) and Jean-Baptiste Greuze (1725–1805), French painters known for their domestic, sentimental, and genre scenes [*Editor's note*].

suggested that warfare could be put aside. For the now genteel, no longer warrior classes, the everyday could be cultivated as a reward for such putting aside, a transition repeatedly inscribed in [Sir Walter] Scott's *Waverley* novels.[7] But by the time of the Revolutionary and Napoleonic wars, when ordinary men rather than battle-trained elites assembled on ship and in camp, the quotidian redefined itself both as the goal of warfare, what one was fighting for; and as the very practice of waging war, the daily routine of ordinary men.[8]

*   *   *

Diverting Away the Time

*   *   *

Try as she might, Anne Elliot cannot find peace in peacetime; the peace she thinks she has achieved during her nearly eight years of limbo is too fragile, too easily broken, and, as events in the novel prove, too illusory to count as true peace. Thus, following her first meeting with Wentworth after his return from the navy, Anne Elliot aims to flee the turbulence:

> [S]he began to reason with herself, and try to be feeling less. Eight years, almost eight years had passed, since all had been given up. How absurd to be resuming the agitation which such an interval had banished to distance and distinctness! What might not eight years do? Events of every description, changes, alienation, removals,—all, all must be comprised in it; and oblivion of the past—how natural, and how certain too? It included nearly a third part of her own life. (*P* 60) [44]

Like Anne's sense of peace, the clock time of historicism, with its clear divisions and oblivions, falls apart through the uncertain chronology of affect: "Alas! with all her reasonings, she found, that to retentive feelings eight years may be little more than nothing" (*P* 60) [44]. Anne's love for Wentworth, in fact, has to break through such false peace and tidy chronology into the stir and roar of a messier, potentially traumatic history. If we recall Walter Scott's 1816 assessment of Austen's accomplishment in the novel, we might hear the agitation of that history in his very description of "ordinary life"

---

7. Sir Walter Scott (1771–1832), Scottish author and historian. The *Waverley* novels, published between 1814 and 1832, helped to inaugurate the historical novel in Britain [*Editor's note*].

8. Austen stages set pieces of a national everyday in her other novels: Henry Tilney's outraged (or facetious?) speech to Catherine Morland in *Northanger Abbey*; Emma's relieved reflection upon Donwell Abbey's "Englishness"—different tonal shading, but a similarly nationalized frame for the everyday. See Kinser and Deidre Lynch's helpful insights in "Homes and Haunts: Austen's and Mitford's English Idylls," *PMLA* 115.5 (October 2000): 1103–8.

with its "*striking* representation of that which is daily taking place around [one]" (emphasis added).[9] What is daily taking place all around *Persuasion*, prior to 1814 and afterward, is not at all peaceful; the pains of war overflow into the supposed idyll that is 1814 as they flow into the domestic novel.

Designed to register precisely that overflow are Anne Elliot's consciousness, her affective state of simultaneous belatedness and anticipation[,] * * * and her refined sensibility. Locked within Anne is the history of a war no one around her seems to acknowledge. Indeed after keeping her heroine silent for the opening two chapters, while detailing her thoughts, Austen makes these nearly the first words that Anne utters, nearly despite herself: "He [Admiral Croft] is rear admiral of the white. He was in the Trafalgar action . . ." (her very first utterance is "The Navy, I think . . .") (*P* 21–22) [17].[1] The repeated bouts of vertigo and dislocation Anne suffers in Wentworth's presence can be read, then, as a record of the sort of profound *vertige* Paul de Man diagnoses as the sign of self-alienation within history.[2] For de Man, such *vertige* discloses "a truly temporal predicament" or "temporal void" (222) that collapses the sequence and priorities of chronological time so that, in this case, the temporality of the past (the wartime of 1806 and after) and the present (the peacetime of 1814) are not at all given or distinct; and, as Anne recognizes, "eight years away may be little more than nothing" (*P* 60) [44]. In this sense, the novelist situates Anne and *Persuasion* within history, suffering history * * *. Even after Waterloo, Austen refuses to let the noise and dust of wartime settle into a clear structure of before and after, now and then. What James Chandler says about vertiginous states and the history of war in W. G. Sebald's novel *Vertigo* (1990) applies directly to Anne's predicament: in the flux of powerful emotions, "[i]t is seldom an easy matter . . . to tell whether one is moving in the direction of remembering or of forgetting."[3]

* * *

9. [Walter Scott], "Unsigned review of *Emma*," *Quarterly Review*, 14 March 1815. Rpt in *Jane Austen: Critical Assessments,* ed. Ian Littlewood, vol. 1 (Mountfield, UK: Helm Information, 1998), 290–91.
1. "Rear admiral of the white" refers to a senior rank in the British Royal Navy. The Battle of Trafalgar (October 21, 1805), in which allied French and Spanish fleets attempted to seize control of the English Channel, marked a victory for the British navy under Admiral Horatio Nelson (1758–1805) in fending off Napoleon Bonaparte's efforts to invade the English mainland (though Nelson perished as a result of injuries sustained in the battle) [*Editor's note*].
2. Paul de Man, "The Rhetoric of Temporality," *Blindness and Insight,* intro. Wlad Godzich, 2nd ed. (Minneapolis: U of Minnesota P, 1983).
3. James Chandler, "About Loss: W. G. Sebald's Romantic Art of Memory," *South Atlantic Quarterly* 102.1 (Winter 2003): 245.

GILLIAN DOW

From Uses of Translation: The Global Jane Austen[†]

* * *

Thanks to the research of many Austen scholars in recent decades, the story of her comparative [scholarly] neglect in Britain in the nineteenth century is now a familiar one. The transition to an author with broad appeal in Anglo-American circles moves through polite interest within Austen's own lifetime to the early control of the author's literary reputation by her brothers' descendants, to increasing and discerning enthusiasm through the early and mid-twentieth century, to a veritable explosion of interest in "popular culture" from the mid-1990s, the moment of the appearance of the influential film and television adaptations of *Pride and Prejudice* and *Sense and Sensibility*. * * * In the nineteenth century, there were French translations of all six of Austen's novels, German translations of *Persuasion* and *Pride and Prejudice*, Swedish translations of *Persuasion* and *Emma* and a Danish translation of *Sense and Sensibility*.[1] If Austen's British compatriots were somewhat slow to appreciate her talents, this was much more the case on the Continent. European languages such as Spanish and Italian translated selected novels in the 1920s and 1930s, but it was not until the 1980s, 1990s and early 2000s that all of Austen's six novels were translated into mainstream European languages, and minority languages started to translate her work. * * * [T]here is concrete evidence of increased European reception in translations of *Pride and Prejudice* into Catalan (1985), Basque (1996), Lithuanian (1997), Latvian (2000) and Galician (2005). In Japan, the picture is similar: polite interest in translating Austen in the early twentieth century has now led to a veritable translating industry. In the last ten years, Japanese translators have translated all of Austen's major novels and the unfinished work and juvenilia, and have also set to work translating related texts: Austen's letters, biographies and companions, and even Emma Tennant's sequels.[2]

* * *

[†] From *Uses of Austen: Jane's Afterlives*, ed. Gillian Dow and C. Hanson (London: Palgrave Macmillan, 2012), pp. 156–61, 172–73. Reproduced with permission of SNCSC. Unless otherwise indicated, notes are by Dow.

1. See *The Reception of Jane Austen in Europe*, ed. by Anthony Mandal and Brian Southam (London, Continuum, 2007), [p. 8].

2. Emma Tennant (1937–2017), English-Scottish novelist and author of prequels and sequels such as *Pemberley Revisited* (1994) [*Editor's note*].

That "Jane Austen does not travel well" stands as a truism in studies of translations of her novels.[3] For translators themselves, there are linguistic challenges. Soya Michiko, the translator of Austen's *Lady Susan*, sees the family-based and codified world of Austen's fiction as particularly hard to translate into Japanese. In that language, a word such as cousin cannot be translated unless the translator knows whether the cousin is older or younger, male or female. Add to that the fact that Japanese has around ten different words for each of "I" and "you," and that the correct one must be selected according to both the situation and the relationship between those who are speaking, and one gets a sense of the intricacies of the work of translating any English novel into Japanese. Soya points out, furthermore, that Austen's syntax presents a particular challenge, since her rhetorical style depends frequently on anticlimax, understatement and overstatement in the narrative voice; according to this translator, once rendered into Japanese, Austen can lose a great deal of her charm.[4] It is clear that Austen's style is seen to be "beyond emulation" by many contemporary specialists in literary translation who engage with comparative readings of her novels and their translations into other languages, and that many translators themselves are acutely aware of the challenges, even where these challenges apply to novels by her contemporaries.

Yet there is an additional complicating layer of interpretive material for foreign readers and translators of Austen to navigate. Her presumed inability to "travel" into other languages is felt to be due to her inherent Englishness, and seems, moreover, to be linked to biographical certainties about the author herself. The portrait of the quiet Hampshire-loving spinster who never left the southern counties of England in life, or in her fiction, has had a lasting legacy. The result is the assumption that if she is "at home" in Chawton (or Steventon, or even, less frequently, in Bath or Southampton), she cannot possibly be "at home" in Madrid, or Tokyo, or Alexandria.

* * * The production of Austen as a national canonical author has its roots much earlier than the establishment of the museum in her home village, of course[5]—the late nineteenth century was already casting her as a novelist of green and pleasant England. Now, in the 1940s, the foreigner had a logical destination to enable them to "enter into the spirit" of her novels, just as educational visits might be taken to Stratford or the Lake District to further understanding

3. Andrew Wright, "Jane Austen Abroad," in *Jane Austen: Bicentenary Essays*, ed. by John Halperin (Cambridge: Cambridge University Press, 1975), pp. 298–317 (p. 298).
4. I am extremely grateful to Soya Michiko, who in February 2011 provided me with careful notes on the challenges of translating Austen into Japanese.
5. The Jane Austen House Museum at Chawton was formally opened by the Duke of Wellington in July 1949 [*Editor's note*].

of Shakespeare or Wordsworth. Equipped with such "insider knowl-edge" as a visit to Chawton was presumed to provide, the teacher could return to her home country and instruct her charges accordingly.

An approach to the study of any author that requires a visit to the settings of the novels for a true understanding of them has far-reaching implications for translations of the texts. Is it possible to "translate" Austen's characters from their spatial and temporal locations in late eighteenth-century England? Should one even try? Here, the twenty-first-century scholar of Austen holds a different viewpoint to his or her nineteenth-century predecessors. Transla-tion theorists tend to view the purpose of translation as to provide a guide to the original, by which I mean an accurate sense of the "foreignness" of the source text. The "foreignizing translation" eth-ics of the influential scholar Lawrence Venuti insist on a model of translation that preserves the "strangeness" of the source language: to adopt any other model, Venuti argues, is to commit ethnocentric violence * * *.[6]

Nineteenth-century practitioners—the first translators of Aus-ten's novels—saw things somewhat differently. Early translations adopted the domesticating model of translation, in which the source text is made to fit the horizon of expectations of the reader in the target language. Through this translation model, Austen's characters become less English and more like characters who would be known to readers in the literatures of their own countries. The best-known expression of this practice for the Anglo-American reader is [John] Dryden's famous assertion, in his *Dedication of the Aeneis* (1697), that he has "endeavoured to make Virgil speak such English as he would himself have spoken, if he had been born in England, and in this present age."[7] Similarly, Isabelle de Montolieu[8]— the Franco-Swiss translator of *Sense and Sensibility* (*Raison et sensibilité, ou les deux manières d'aimer*, 1815) and *Persuasion* (*La Famille Elliot*, 1821)—made Austen speak such French as she would have spoken had she been born in Geneva in the early nineteenth century.

Montolieu's popularity as an author in the late eighteenth and nineteenth centuries was Europe-wide. She was the author of a novel, *Caroline de Litchfield* (1786), that met with considerable success in translation, and she published many translations or

---

6. Lawrence Venuti's translation ethics are set out in the polemical *The Translator's Invis-ibility: A History of Translation* (London: Routledge, 1995) and in the subsequent *The Scandals of Translation: Towards an Ethics of Difference* (London: Routledge, 1998).
7. Quoted in *Translation—Theory and Practice: A Historical Reader*, ed. by Daniel Weiss-bort and Astradur Eysteinsson (Oxford: Oxford University Press, 2006), p. 150.
8. (1751–1832) [*Editor's note*].

adaptations of English and German novels. In continental Europe, the taste for the romantic, rather than the realist, novel was still at its height in this period. Montolieu's sentimentality was both very much of its time and extremely popular: in the mid-nineteenth century, her books were the third most borrowed in French circulating libraries, after Stéphanie-Félicité de Genlis and Walter Scott.[9]

In her translation of *Sense and Sensibility*, Montolieu recasts Austen's Marianne as Maria, a true creature of *sensibilité* in the vein of Marivaux's Marianne and Rousseau's Julie, both heroines of best-selling and influential early and mid-eighteenth-century novels in the sentimental tradition.[1] The change is significant. The name Marianne had peculiarly French, and Revolutionary, connotations by 1815, and was synonymous with Revolutionary excess from the 1790s on.[2] An allusion to the bare-breasted warrior woman, a symbol of the Revolution and of the new Republic, and indeed of the lower orders, was surely something that Montolieu wanted to avoid when she targeted the Franco-Swiss reading public with her version of an apolitical "English" novel. Montolieu's translation of *Persuasion, La Famille Elliot*, also adds a sentimental vein to this novel, making Austen's novel longer with additional passages of the translator's own invention. Changes of this nature are the translator's prerogative in the period; although we see them as travesties, the original readers would not have done so. Indeed, Montolieu's reworkings had considerable success throughout Europe: it was her *La Famille Elliot* that was used as the source language for the 1836 Swedish translation of *Persuasion, Familjen Elliot: skildringar af engelska karaterer* (The Elliot family: description of English characters), and the French translation of *Mansfield Park* was erroneously attributed as an original novel by Montolieu by the French bibliographer Marc in 1819.[3]

9. Stéphanie-Félicité de Genlis (1746–1830) and Sir Walter Scott (1771–1832), popular authors and novelists. Jane Austen's letters contain references to her reading of Genlis's *Alphonsine; ou, La tendresse maternelle* (1805) and "Olympe et Théophile" (1784), and *Emma*'s Emma Woodhouse comments that Mrs. Weston has had practice at raising a daughter "like La Baronne d'Almane or La Comtesse d'Ostalis in Madame de Genlis's Adelaide and Theodore" [*Editor's note*].
1. Pierre Carlet Chamberlain de Marivaux's *La Vie de Marianne* was published between 1731 and 1742. Jean-Jacques Rousseau's *Julie, ou La Nouvelle Héloïse* was first published in 1761.
2. Maurice Agulhon's *Marianne into Battle: Republican Imagery and Symbolism in France, 1789–1880*, trans. by Janet Lloyd (Cambridge: Cambridge University Press, 1981) gives an excellent account of Marianne in the popular arts, alongside which Montolieu's rejection of the name Marianne can be usefully read.
3. For an excellent and detailed reading of the early translations of Austen in Switzerland, see Valérie Cossy, *Jane Austen in Switzerland: A Study of the Early French Translations* (Geneva: Éditions Slatkine, 2006).

ROBERT D. HUME

From Money in Jane Austen[†]

A great deal has been written about the socio-economic identities and circumstances of Jane Austen's characters. Until quite recently, however, few critics have paid much attention to the particulars of money and the relative buying power of money in Austen's novels, despite the fact that Austen specifies many sums, particularly 'fortunes' and annual incomes. Happily some very fine scholarship has been published on Austen and money in the last two decades. I am indebted to the work of Edward Copeland and Alan Downie, both of whom have done much to clarify the importance and meaning of economic issues in the fiction.[1] Downie's lucid demonstration that Austen is *not* writing about a 'bourgeois' world significantly changes the way we should approach her work.[2] Austen's concern with money and income permeates her novels. I shall try to show that we cannot read them competently if we do not fully comprehend the economic circumstances of both the author and her characters.

* * * [E]ach of her six major novels poses an explicit or implicit question about money, concerning which Austen's views are consistently anxious and glum, her fairy-tale endings to the contrary notwithstanding. Examining Austen's own finances emphasizes a hard fact: she lived at the bottom margin of gentility. I want to suggest that reading the novels in the context of their author's circumstances underlines a brutal contrast between the tiny sums that were painfully important in Austen's own life and the giant sums that we find in her fiction. In reading these texts, we should be aware of Austen's

---

† From *Review of English Studies* 64.264 (April 1, 2013): 289–93, 296, 299, 301. Used with permission of Oxford University Press, conveyed through Copyright Clearance Center, Inc. Unless otherwise indicated, notes are by Hume. Page numbers in brackets are to this Norton Critical Edition.

1. See especially Edward Copeland, *Women Writing about Money: Women's Fiction in England, 1790–1820* (Cambridge, 1995); Copeland's chapters on 'Money' in Copeland and Juliet McMaster (eds.), *The Cambridge Companion to Jane Austen* (Cambridge, 1997), 131–48, and Janet Todd (ed.), *Jane Austen in Context* (Cambridge, 2005), 317–26; and J. A. Downie, 'Who Says She's a Bourgeois Writer? Reconsidering the Social and Political Contexts of Jane Austen's Novels', *Eighteenth-Century Studies*, 40 (2006), 69–84.

2. Reading the novels in economic terms has become much easier since the publication of the Cambridge edition, whose editors systematically provide assistance with the interpretation of particular sums, large and small. References to Austen's texts are to Janet Todd, gen. ed., *The Cambridge Edition of the Works of Jane Austen*, 9 vols. (Cambridge, 2005–2008). This edition comprises *Sense and Sensibility*, ed. Edward Copeland (2006); *Pride and Prejudice*, ed. Pat Rogers (2006); *Mansfield Park*, ed. John Wiltshire (2005); *Emma*, ed. Richard Cronin and Dorothy McMillan (2005); *Northanger Abbey*, ed. Barbara M. Benedict and Deirdre Le Faye (2006); and *Persuasion*, ed. Janet Todd and Antje Blank (2006). The massive and helpful 'Annotated Edition' of *Pride and Prejudice* recently published by Harvard and edited by Patricia Meyer Spacks (Cambridge, MA, 2010) does offer some statements of equivalency in 2010 dollars, though without explaining how the numbers have been calculated or pursuing their implications.

penchant for contrasts, not only in character but in money matters and their implications. We need to comprehend the magnitude of fortunes and incomes, both in their own context and from the sometimes startling perspective of equivalent present-day buying power. * * *

I. Money in Jane Austen's Life

Jane Austen was the daughter of the Rev. George Austen (1731–1805), a Church of England parish clergyman who had a wife, six sons, two daughters, and an income in the vicinity of £600 a year in the latter part of his career.[3] As of 1779 part of his earnings came from tutoring boys at £35 per annum for tuition, board, and lodging (Le Faye, 42). Roughly £100 derived from investments. About 1784 he bought a small 'chariot' but he had to put it into storage in 1798 as too expensive a luxury (Le Faye, 50, 112). This sounds like a fairly modest lifestyle, but the Rev. George Austen had a decidedly good income for a man in his position. Williamson states the 'Nominal Annual Earnings' of clergymen in England and Wales as £238 in 1797.[4] A 'reasonable income in 1810' for a clergyman was reportedly £150 a year.[5] As of 1794 at age 19, Jane Austen was getting a £20 annual allowance from her father for personal expenses, paid in quarterly instalments (Le Faye, 87). When George Austen died in 1805, however, he left his wife and daughters in dire straits, heavily dependent upon the generosity of the Austen sons (Le Faye, 146–7). We cannot tell how typical Jane's budget for 1807 was—it survives in a unique manuscript for which we have no comparative data—but it is a revealing document.[6] She started the year with £50 15s 6d[7] * * * and wound up with £6 4s 6d. Her principal expense was £13 19s 3d for 'Cloathes & Pocket'. Washing consumed £9 5s 11½d. 'Presents' totaled £6 4s 4d; alms-giving was £3 10s 3½d. 'Letters and Parcels' came to £3 17s 6½d. Her one great extravagance, as Le Faye notes, was £2 13s 6d for 'Hire Piano Forte' (Le Faye, 163). Keeping annual records to the halfpenny seems suggestive.

3. Figures are from Deirdre Le Faye, *Jane Austen: A Family Record*, 2nd edn (Cambridge, 2004). George junior, the second son (1766–1838), was deaf and apparently 'mentally abnormal'; he 'had to be boarded out . . . with a respectable village family' (22).
4. Jeffery G. Williamson, 'Structure of Pay in Britain, 1710–1911,' *Research in Economic History*, 7 (1982), 1–54 at 48.
5. W. M. Jacob, *The Clerical Profession in the Long Eighteenth Century, 1680–1840* (Oxford, 2007), 116. [Hume relies on a "100/150 multiplier" to calculate, with "at least a crude sense of equivalency," Regency-era sums into contemporary equivalents, circa 2010: "if £150 is a reasonable income for a Church of England pastor in 1810," for instance, then that figure suggests "a present-day income for a minister of £15,000–22,500 (with housing suppled in both cases)" (302–03) —*Editor*.]
6. Reproduced from the manuscript in the Pierpont Morgan Library by Patrick Piggott, 'Jane Austen's Southampton Piano,' *Collected Reports of the Jane Austen Society 1976–1985* (1989), 146–9.
7. Fifty pounds, fifteen shillings, and six pennies, or pence [*Editor's note*].

Austen's letters are a fertile source of financial information, liberally studded with references to gowns, shopping, balls, and dancing. The difficulties of dressing satisfactorily for social occasions on a pinched budget are a recurrent theme, early and late. About lace for a cloak for her sister: 'If you do not think it wide enough, I can give 3*d* a yard more . . . & not go beyond the two Guineas'.[8] This is an altogether exceptional purchase for the Austen girls, but there is definitely a budget cap, and the extra 3*d* a yard is an issue to be worried about. Earnings loosen pocketbooks. Writing in 1811 (the year in which *Sense and Sensibility* was published), Austen admits to being 'very extravagant' and buying 'check'd Muslin' at 7*s* a yard, and ten yards of 'coloured muslin' at half that price (*Letters*, 179). She has a straw hat made for a guinea, and is thrilled enough not to begrudge the price, but 'Pelisses' for the two of them at 17*s* each come to a sum that clearly bothers Austen: the maker 'charges only 8/ for the making, but the Buttons seem expensive;—*are* expensive' (*Letters*, 180). Jane is excited to find decent gloves for 'only four Shillings' (209). Acting on instructions, she buys a locket set in gold on Cassandra's behalf in 1813, but winces at having had to spend 18*s*—'which must be rather more than you intended' (*Letters*, 212). The same year she buys herself a fancy cap: 'white sattin and lace, and a little white flower perking out of the left ear . . . I have allowed her to go as far as £1–16' (*Letters*, 220).

*   *   *

What is perhaps most striking is that apparently small or even insignificant amounts of money produced anxiety and stress. Austen was addicted to correspondence, but intensely aware of the cost of sending and receiving mail. As John Wiltshire notes, paper was disturbingly expensive—sufficiently so that when Austen was drafting her novels she rarely began a paragraph on a new line.[9] Writing a thank-you note to Cassandra in 1798 she says, 'I have taken a long sheet of paper to shew my Gratitude' (*Letters*, 15). When a friend borrows two sheets of 'Drawing paper' she is upset until the friend returns 'two of superior size & quality' (*Letters*, 28, 35). In 1801 she tells her sister, in response to a letter, 'I thank you for yours, tho' I should have been more grateful for it, if it had not been charged 8*d* instead of 6*d*' (*Letters*, 74).[1] As late as 1815, making significant sums of money as a published novelist, she breaks off a letter to Cassandra,

8. Deidre Le Faye (ed.), *Jane Austen's Letters*, 3rd edn (Oxford, 1995), 42.
9. *Mansfield Park*, xl.
1. Recipients of letters paid the postage. For the postal rates established in 1797, see Howard Robinson, *The British Post Office* (Princeton, 1948), 154. A single-sheet letter going less than 15 miles cost 3*d*; for 15–30 miles, 4*d*; 30–60 miles, 5*d*; 60–100 miles, 6*d*; 100–150 miles, 7*d*; to Edinburgh, 8*d* (37 George III, c.18). Rates were hiked in 1801 and again in 1805, when a single letter under 15 miles was raised to 4*d* with

saying, 'I must finish it now, that I may save you 2*d*' (*Letters*, 304).[2] Paying for incoming mail, she is exquisitely sensitive to how many lines get written on a page, exclaiming with pleasure over a missive with 'Two & forty Lines in the 2*d* Page' (*Letters*, 234). Acknowledging an expensive overseas letter from her brother, Frank, in 1813 she says, 'I assure you I thought it very well worth its 2*s* 3*d*' (*Letters*, 229). Incidentals are a constant worry. Reporting attendance at a ball in 1808, she notes that 'We paid an additional shilling for our Tea' (*Letters*, 157). Even in her father's lifetime, the family was bothered by sums we might not notice but which make them cringe. Austen reports her father's unhappiness in 1800 over a 3*s* 6*d* charge for a packing box for stockings (*Letters*, 51). She is triumphant that she can get her hair dressed for 2*s* 6*d* rather than 5*s*, though not sure whether the moderate charge is in consideration of 'Youth or our poverty' (*Letters*, 108). Meticulous track is kept of small debts within the family. In 1811 3*s* 6*d* are duly dispatched to Edward to pay off her 'debt' to her brother (*Letters*, 191), and in 1813 she tells Cassandra, 'I enclose the Eighteen pence due to my Mother' (*Letters*, 223).

＊　＊　＊

II. The Economic Basis of the Novels

As W. H. Auden long ago observed, Austen 'frankly' reveals 'the economic basis of society'.[3] The foundational reality underlying all of Austen's novels is painfully simple: a genteel woman *must* either *have* money or *marry* money. As Charlotte Lucas understands, 'marriage . . . was the only honourable provision for well-educated young women of small fortune' (*P&P*, 138). Pat Rogers observes in his note on this passage in the Cambridge edition that although 'a young woman who took up a career as a governess (about the only occupation which fitted the specified terms) did not lose her respectability, she sacrificed any claim she might have had to gentility, simply by virtue of taking paid employment' (*P&P*, 494). For women, working to support themselves was incompatible with genteel social position: they could inherit money or marry it; there were no other options. The economic facts of genteel female life being what they were, Austen builds into each novel explicit or implicit money issues

---

corresponding increases for longer distances. For details, see J. C. Hemmeon, *The History of the British Post Office* (Cambridge, MA, 1912), 148–52.

2. John Murray offered £450 this year for the copyright of *Emma*, *Mansfield Park*, and *Sense and Sensibility*. Austen refused and published *Emma* at her own risk. By the time of her death in 1817 her profit on it was £372 12*s* 11*d*, though much of this was lost on the second edition of *Mansfield Park* (*E*, xxvii–viii).

3. Auden, 'Letter to Lord Byron', in *Letters from Iceland* (London, 1937), Part 1, stanza 17.

and income contrasts that invite the reader to reflect on the brutal constraints on women.

*   *   *

Persuasion occupies a curious position in Austen's fiction. It offers an acid commentary on Sir Walter Elliot's fecklessly spending beyond his income: seven years of economical living will be required to clear the debts he has run up (13) [10]—and he cannot sell his estate.[4] Anne Elliot is an older and more battered Elizabeth Bennet, but in no danger of penury. She will get £10,000 from her mother's marriage portion after Sir Walter's death (270) [177], and 'she might always command a home with Lady Russell' (158) [104]. Unlike Elizabeth, Anne can afford to refuse Charles Hayter because she is assured of an income on which a single lady can live a genteel life. To accept Captain Wentworth when he 'had no fortune' (29) [21] would have been imprudent. Would she have taken him in 1808 'with a few thousand pounds' (268) [176]? Yes indeed. But now, with £25,000 in prize money plus Anne's £10,000 'hereafter' (270) [177] they will have an income not far short of Mr. Bennet's £2,000, and they will presumably get it by investing in very safe 'Navy five percents' (available as of 1810).[5] Anne emerges as a triumphant embodiment of wish-fulfillment, but we should perhaps remember that while Jane Austen was writing *Persuasion* Henry Austen's bank failed (March 1816) and her brothers Francis and Charles were soon out of work on half pay at the end of the Napoleonic wars.[6] Henry and Francis could not continue their £50 annual allowances to their mother and sisters (Le Faye, 246–7). Jane Austen was making some money from writing, but this was not an assured or stable income. * * *

*   *   *

IV. Fortunes and Income Calculations

When Austen reports that Colonel Brandon has an income of £2,000 a year (*S&S*, 223) there is no particular reason that the reader should

4. Austen is less than fully explicit about property right issues in this novel. Janet Todd and Antje Blank (the Cambridge editors) devote an extensive footnote to 'the entail' (339), but I believe that word never appears in the text. Clearly there is a settlement agreement giving the Kellynch property to the male heir to the baronetcy. What Austen actually tells us is that 'There was only a small part of his estate that Sir Walter could dispose of' (10) [9].
5. Navy annuities, from British navy debts, were a popular form of investment during the period 1810–1821 [*Editor's note*].
6. Hume notes that, with Mrs. Austen's "bit of capital" and the interest Cassandra received from a £1,000 bequest, the Austen women's combined income "was apparently about £210, plus whatever the brothers could supply" (308, n. 41). By comparison, Edward and Elinor in *Sense and Sensibility* will live on £850 per annum, and Edmund and Fanny in *Mansfield Park* on £700. £350 is the annual income that "Edward and Elinor are not sufficiently in love to find bearable" (298) [*Editor's note*].

wonder what it derives from. Likewise when she says that Miss Morton has a fortune of £30,000 (S&S, 255), we do not stop to ask exactly what this means or what income this capital generates, whatever form it may be in. But such questions are not frivolous. Both income and 'fortune' may derive from land. Alternatively, the capital might be in either what we would now call common stock investments or income-yielding bonds. At the time of a woman's marriage, her fortune might be in cash, or in stocks or bonds. Of course landed estates must be managed (well or ill): someone has to oversee farming or collect rents, and only a rather substantial estate could make a professional manager affordable. We may presume that Darcy can well afford the Steward who succeeded Wickham's father, but does Longbourn yield a significant part of Mr. Bennet's £2,000 a year, and if so, how much management does he do himself and how much does he entrust to a bailiff? Austen does not tell us, and perhaps she did not care, but for a reader of the time applying the circumstances of the novel to real life, this would have been an obvious question.

When Austen says '£2,000 a year', are we entitled to assume that the person or the family have that to spend? She does not specify 'net after taxes', but Napoleonic-era taxes were steep (and a very sore subject). Income tax was reimposed in 1803 when hostilities were resumed, and was increased from 5% to 6½% in 1805 and further to 10% in 1806 (2s in the pound). Taxes were levied on all sorts of things.[7] As of 1808, the tax on windows, for example, started at 6s 6d for houses with not more than six windows and under the value of £5 per annum; jumped to £1 for houses with no more than seven, and escalated rapidly thereafter. A house with not more than ten paid £2 16s; with forty to forty-four windows the tax was £28 17s 6d—and rose yet further beyond that.[8] Income derived from land is far from stable, even before one factors in taxes and inflation: weather and agricultural prices vary erratically, with net profits wobbling unpredictably and occasionally soaring or crashing.

* * *

A daring speculator might have made a fat capital gains profit buying and selling at the right times: consols were transferable securities.[9] One could also, of course, lose one's shirt that way. In the period

7. For a lucid summary of the bewilderingly varied and ever-changing taxes in the period 1802–1815, see Stephen Dowell, *A History of Taxation and Taxes in England*, 4 vols, 3rd edn (London, 1965), II, 229–45. Direct taxes, stamp duties, and taxes on articles of consumption are covered in volumes III and IV.
8. See Andrew E. Glantz, 'A Tax on Light and Air: Impact of the Window Duty on Tax Administration and Architecture, 1696–1851,' *Penn History Review*, 15.2 (2008), article 3.
9. Hume explains that consols (derived from "Consolidated Annuities") refers to "a class of security created by Act of Parliament in 1751 to consolidate all existing government debt into a single issue of what we now call bonds with a fixed interest rate of 3%," adding that

when Austen was publishing novels, a return on consols of 4–5% is a reasonable estimate. By no means, however, can one safely assume that a 5% return on capital represents a stable, reliable, never-changing fact of life. If Captain Wentworth invested his £25,000 in 3% consols at the lowest price in 1814 he would have netted a very nice 5.49% (£1,372 p.a.), but at the highest price in 1815 the rate would have been 4.48% (£1,120 p.a.). If he had cautiously waited until 1818 to invest, he might have got a rate of only 3.66% (£915 p.a.). Probably he would, like Austen, have invested in the 'Navy 5 per cents', which were selling almost at par in 1810 (as opposed to the 3 per cents, which were discounted by 40%). Then again, in 1822 his income would have taken a 20% hit when the government replaced 5% securities with 4% (reduced further to 3.5% in 1824).[1] What all this means is that a 'fortune' of however many thousand pounds (whether in land or investments) did not in fact translate into a stable income from year to year.

DEVONEY LOOSER

From Breaking the Silence: Exploring the Austen Family's Complex Entanglements with Slavery[†]

When it comes to probing the politics of Jane Austen's family, we may need to put reproach and recuperation alongside pride and prejudice. The question of how culpable the Austens were in the support and perpetuation of slavery—or how much they benefited from what Jane Fairfax in *Emma* calls the sale of human flesh—should remain an open one. But new information, which I've discovered through digital and archival research, makes it clear that, over the course of eighty years, the family's commitments and actions changed profoundly, from known complicity in colonial slavery to previously unnoticed anti-slavery activism.

The complicity of Austen's father in the legacy of British slave ownership in Antigua was first described fifty years ago. It's hardly breaking news * * *.[1]

"as of 1751 the safest investment for generating income was government 3% consols, which remained the foundation of public debt until the 1880s" (300) [*Editor's note*].

1. [Sidney Homer and Richard Sylla, *A History of Interest Rates*, 4th edn (Hoboken, NJ, 2005),] Table 18.

† From the *Times Literary Supplement* 6164 (May 21, 2021): 3–4. © TLS / News Licensing. Notes are by the editor of this Norton Critical Edition.

1. See Martin Ivens, "Jane Austen and Abolition: Devoney Looser on the Part Played by the Novelist's Family," *Times Literary Supplement* 6164 (May 21, 2021). "It has long been known that the novelist's father, the Revd George Austen, was a co-trustee for a marriage settlement financed by slavery. A close friendship may have overcome his qualms. Austen's naval brothers, Francis and Charles, however, policed the newly

There is no shortage of research. As Manu Samriti Chander and Patricia A. Matthew argue, "It should no longer be possible to read" literary works from this period "without attending to the geopolitics of slavery, especially as it is reflected in diverse literary forms."[2] Some teachers now assign *Mansfield Park* (1814) and *Emma* (1816) alongside the anonymously authored *A Woman of Colour: A tale* (1808), as well as poems, plays and essays, creating new opportunities for layered and nuanced conversations in classrooms. Popular commentary on these subjects has increased, too, following the ITV series *Sanditon* (2019), based on Austen's last unfinished novel, which features a mixed-race West Indian heiress named Miss Lambe, not to mention the success of the Regency romance-inspired Netflix series, *Bridgerton*.

It is no surprise that today's visitors to Austen museums and cultural sites might show up with pressing questions about the history of race, colonialism and slavery. These questions deserve answers, even if they sometimes prove difficult or uncomfortable, and even if some of the information is necessarily speculative or provisional. What exactly were the Austen family's ties to the institution of slavery?

The short answer, perhaps predictably, is that it's complicated. It is made even more complicated, however, by errors and misinterpretations that have crept into peer-reviewed scholarship and popular commentary alike. Some sources will tell you that the Revd George Austen, Jane's clergyman father, was the principal trustee in an Antiguan sugar plantation. That's not quite true, although his connections to that plantation's owners turn out to be more significant than previously thought.

Another misinterpretation that is often repeated is that Austen's fiction is silent on the subject of slavery and colonialism. This misleading claim comes from the work of Edward Said, who misconstrued one line in *Mansfield Park*.[3] The novel's heroine, Fanny Price, says that she asked her uncle, Sir Thomas Bertram, a question about the slave trade—since he owns an estate in Antigua—which he is said to have answered. The conversation comes to a halt, however, when the exchange is met by "such a dead silence" from most of Fanny's Bertram cousins, who are ignorant and arrogant characters.

---

outlawed slave trade after its abolition in 1807 (in his unpublished diaries Francis declared his detestation of the institution), and Looser has found evidence that a third brother, Henry Thomas Austen, was a staunch opponent too. She reveals that the Revd H. T. Austen (Jane's first biographer) was a delegate at the opening of the first World Anti-Slavery Convention, held in London in 1840 at Freemason's Hall."

2. Manu Samriti Chander and Patricia A. Matthew, "Introduction: Abolitionist Interruptions: Romanticism, Slavery, and Genre," *European Romantic Review* 29.4 (2018): 431–34.

3. Edward W. Said, "Jane Austen and Empire," *Culture and Imperialism* (Knopf, 1994), pp. 80–96.

That line about their silence may be an indictment, not an endorsement, of privileged whites who remain incurious about racism and
injustice.

Even if readers continue to disagree about what that "dead silence"
signals in *Mansfield Park*, there are some questions about the Austen family's attitudes towards slavery that may be met with new facts.
Two of Austen's siblings declared slavery to be repugnant. It has long
been known that one of her brothers thought so privately. What
hasn't been noticed before is that another Austen brother became
publicly involved in anti-slavery activism.

Austen's father's economic ties to a West Indian sugar plantation
are very real ties, but they've been both under-described and over-
stated. George Austen's connection to James Langford Nibbs's
plantation-owning Antiguan family is a direct, personal one. The
Nibbses were a white settler family whose accumulated wealth
derived from the labour of enslaved people.

The Revd George Austen is said to have first met James Langford
Nibbs at Oxford, where the clergyman may have served as the
younger man's tutor or proctor. Later, Austen made Nibbs the god-
father of his eldest son, James. Nibbs sent his second son, George,
to be educated by Austen at the school he ran out of his home in
Steventon, in Hampshire, where Jane Austen was raised. It is possible that George Nibbs and James Austen were both named after their
father's friend. There was apparently a portrait of a Mr Nibbs—or a
portrait that went by that nickname, seriously or in jest—in the Austen household.

It is not accurate to say that George Austen was either a principal
or sole trustee for an Antiguan sugar plantation. He was, instead, a
co-trustee in a marriage settlement that involved the dispersal of the
plantation and its profits. He pledged to serve as one of two trustees
named to ensure the conveyance of the plantation to Nibbs's heir or
heirs, along with an annuity of [£]500 to Nibbs's wife, Barbara Langford, his first cousin and an heiress of [£]10,000.

Austen must have understood that he was being asked to play a role,
potentially, in extracting some of the plantation's ill-begotten profits.
What has gone unnoticed until now is that he may have been named
a co-trustee for a very particular reason. Austen married James Langford Nibbs and Barbara Langford at St. Clement Danes church in
London, on February 12, 1760. This newly unearthed fact matters,
because it shows an even closer connection between Nibbs and Austen, reaching beyond their university ties in Oxford. It was the only
wedding that Austen performed at that London church that year.

Placing George Austen at St. Clement Danes, close by the Royal
Courts of Justice, is important for another reason. The co-trustee
named with him in Nibbs's marriage settlement was a far more

experienced and important man called Morris Robinson. While Robinson's name has appeared in Austen scholarship, what others have not noted is that he was employed in the Six Clerks' Office in the Court of Chancery at the time of the Nibbses' marriage. As a solicitor, Robinson would have been highly familiar with marriage settlements. He, not Austen, would have been selected as a co-trustee for expertise and experience with the law and estate management.

Morris Robinson is a fascinating person to be able to tie to the Austens. He was the brother of Elizabeth Robinson Montagu, the so-called Queen of the Bluestockings, one of the most important figures in British women's intellectual circles. (Mrs. Montagu's husband, meanwhile, was a wealthy coalmine owner.) Mrs. Montagu was close to her brother and later informally adopted one of his sons. It has been known that the Austens and the extended Robinson family had social ties, but it was assumed they came through a path more distant from Montagu. George Austen's connection to Morris Robinson through Nibbs may put Jane in closer social proximity to the Bluestocking Circle than has been formerly thought.

The most interesting fact about Morris Robinson's connection to George Austen for our purposes is that his work at the Six Clerks' Office locates him half a mile from St. Clement Danes church, where the Nibbses' wedding was performed. It was customary then for marriage settlements to be finalized before the wedding. (This one was drawn up on February 8 and 9, 1760, three days before the ceremony.) Such agreements named at least two trustees.

Knowing this might expand the ways we imagine George Austen's becoming a co-trustee for these complicit-in-slavery assets. He may have been asked due to his proximity to the couple at the time the contract was drawn up. It is true that he could have refused to serve in this way. He didn't. He could have cut close ties with Nibbs after that. He didn't. But the idea that the Revd Austen, in 1760, would have imagined himself signing on to manage a West Indian sugar plantation, if Nibbs should die, exaggerates his role and fails to capture the complexity of this responsibility. It should be emphasized that, under a strict settlement, the plantation was settled in the name of the life tenant, who had full powers to manage it; it was not in the name of the trustees.

Morris Robinson and George Austen would have understood that their duties as co-trustees meant transferring the plantation's ownership from Nibbs to his heir or heirs, in accordance with the terms of the settlement. George Austen was legally implicated, then, in conveying the ownership of a plantation estate in Antigua. But the co-trustees would not have been responsible for managing the estate itself. In later years, when Nibbs's financial and familial situation became more complicated, he directly assigned management of the plantation to another man.

George Austen's entanglement with Nibbs does seem to have had an effect on Jane's fiction writing. The Nibbs family ended up being involved in domestic conflicts that are likely to have influenced the plot of *Mansfield Park*, as previous scholars have noted. The fate of James Langford Nibbs and his son, also named James Langford Nibbs, closely resembles that of Sir Thomas Bertram and his wastrel son, Tom Bertram. Both young men, real and imagined, went deeply into debt and dug into the family fortunes, as each father took steps to stop the son's extravagances and protect the family's Antiguan plantation fortunes. In neither case, the real or the fictional, does one come away feeling much sympathy for the morally corrupt colonial rich.

Further details about the relationship between the Austens and the Nibbses must continue to emerge, and will no doubt be better described by those with expertise in the history of English and Antiguan property law. What literary historians can agree on is that the novelist's attitudes towards the institution of slavery, like the mentions of it in her fiction, are difficult to unravel. Her 161 surviving letters don't give us much hard information, other than telling us that she was "much in love" with the writings of the white abolitionist Thomas Clarkson.[4] Those who generalize out from the George Austen–James Langford Nibbs connection to conclude that the Austen family was unreflectively pro-slavery don't have the full picture.

We know that Austen's naval brothers, Francis and Charles, would have policed the newly outlawed slave trade as part of their duties, after 1807. Francis Austen privately recorded his disgust with slavery in his still-unpublished diaries, which were first quoted in a family biography. "Slavery however it may be modified is still slavery," he wrote, "and it is much to be regretted that any trace of it should be found to exist in countries dependent on England, or colonised by her subjects."[5] This statement was not made public until 1906.

What has not been previously noted is that another Austen brother, Henry Thomas Austen—a failed banker turned clergyman and Jane's first biographer—became publicly involved in the anti-slavery movement. The Revd H. T. Austen (as he was then calling himself) was named as a delegate to the World Anti-Slavery Convention, held in London from June 12 to 23, 1840, more than two decades after Jane's death, and seven years after slavery was supposedly on a path

---

4. Thomas Clarkson (1760–1846), abolitionist and founder, with Granville Sharpe, of the Society for Effecting the Abolition of the African Slave Trade, established in 1787.

5. See J. H. and Edith Hubback, *Jane Austen's Sailor Brothers* (John Lane, 1906), p. 192.

to being dismantled in the British colonies. Henry Austen was one of two delegates representing Colchester, where he was a clergyman. He sat among the nearly 500 delegates who travelled from around the world to seek an end to slavery.

The Convention, despite its ambitions, did not run smooth. The racism, sexism and exclusion found within the nineteenth-century anti-slavery movement continue to be documented and interpreted—even interrogated—as well they should be. At the Convention, Henry Austen would have heard the address of its frail, elderly president: the Thomas Clarkson whose abolitionist writings his late sister Jane had so admired. The Convention prevented the white women who had been sent as delegates from being seated on the floor with the men, and just a handful of Black men were so seated. The famous painting that immortalized the Convention, by Benjamin Robert Haydon, includes 130 figures and provides a key to them by name. Henry Austen is not among them.

It is not clear how actively Henry participated in the Convention. He had a reputation for excellent public speaking, having delivered sermons of great eloquence and animation, in a style that was said to rouse fellow clergy, families of the first distinction, farmers and the poor alike. Whether he spoke or not, his presence as a Convention delegate is notable. Eighty years after his father signed on as a co-trustee to convey the ownership and proceeds of an Antiguan plantation, Henry became a next-generation Austen publicly supporting a political commitment to abolish slavery across the globe.

For readers today who might resist reading Jane Austen's fiction in a political framework, these newly unearthed facts about her family ought to serve as a wake-up call. The years 1760 to 1840 were transformational for the institution of slavery, in terms of laws, activism, literature, visual representations and popular opinion. It stands to reason that the Austen family's politics would have changed, too, even if we can't know the extent to which Jane Austen shared the opinions of her father or brothers, during the half of this period that she was alive.

With this new information, it is now possible to understand that Austen's beloved brother Henry—"Oh! what a Henry!," Jane once said of him—did not, in the end, sit idly by in the face of racial injustice. One may rightly say that it took too long for someone in the Austen family to stake out such a public position. It is also true that it has taken too long for those of us who study literature in a social context to notice it.

If we are asked to determine whether the Austen family was pro-slavery or anti-slavery, then the best answer to that question is both. We can't take up one half of the facts and ignore the other. We ought to continue to engage directly with these matters as they arise in her writings and to investigate them further in the cataclysmic times in which she wrote. To respond to today's conversations about Austen and race with dead silence is to join the rest of the Bertram cousins. Scrutinizing the past in these ways ought to prompt a reckoning in fandoms and readerships, as well as better museum labels.

Jane Austen: A Chronology

1775   Jane Austen born on December 16 at Steventon, Hampshire, UK, the seventh of eight children of the Rev. George Austen and Cassandra Leigh. George III is king of England. In April, the American Revolutionary War begins, lasting until September 1783.

1784   Austen's formal education begins at age 9 at a school in Reading.

1786   Francis (Frank) Austen, Jane's brother, joins the British navy, where he would fight in the French Revolutionary and Napoleonic Wars and be promoted to admiral of the fleet, the highest naval rank, in 1863.

1789–91   Between the ages of 14 and 16, Austen writes a novel called "Love and Freindship" [*sic*], a "History of England," and the stories "Lesley Castle" and "A Collection of Letters."

1789   The French Revolution occurs, overthrowing the monarchy and establishing the French Republic. A constitutional monarchy is established under King Louis XVI of France, but it is short-lived.

1790–96   The French Assembly votes to maintain slavery in the colonies; uprisings occur in Martinique, Mauritius, San Domingo, Guadeloupe, and French Guinea. Rioting across France.

1791   The event known as the Haitian Revolution begins, led by Toussaint L'Ouverture, born enslaved on the French colony of San Domingo (now Haiti) and later serving as general in the French army. Austen's youngest brother, Charles John Austen, joins the British navy. Like Frank Austen, he would participate in the French Revolutionary and Napoleonic Wars, and he would be promoted to his highest rank, rear admiral, in 1846.

1792–96   The French Revolutionary Wars begin, lasting until 1802. The Reign of Terror begins, 1793, with the executions by guillotine of King Louis XVI and Marie-Antoinette, along with members of his court, the military, and the aristocracy. In 1794 the French National Convention votes to abolish slavery in the colonies, only to reestablish the practice in 1802. Between 1794 and 1796, Austen writes "Lady Susan," an epistolary novella, and "Elinor and Marianne," an early version of what would become *Sense and Sensibility*.

1797–98   Austen writes "First Impressions," the earliest version of *Pride and Prejudice*, and rewrites "Elinor and Marianne" as *Sense and Sensibility* (which remains unpublished until 1811).

1798–99   Austen rewrites *Northanger Abbey*, which would be published posthumously in 1818. A coup d'état establishes Napoleon Bonaparte as first consul of France. Austen's brother Frank assumes command of HMS *Peterel*, a 16-gun warship.

1801   The Austen family moves to Bath. Using prize-money earned in capturing the French gunship *Scipio*, Charles Austen purchases topaz crosses and gold chains for his sisters Jane and Cassandra.

1802–03   The Treaty of Amiens between France and Britain is signed, bringing a period of peace following a decade of warfare in Europe. War resumes in May 1803, marking the beginning of the Napoleonic Wars.

1804–06   Austen's father dies, and the family moves to Southampton, where Austen writes "The Watsons," possibly an early version of *Emma*.

1804   In May, Napoleon declares himself emperor of France. The Haitian Revolution ends with the island achieving independence.

1805   Death of Admiral Horatio Nelson after defeating the French in the Battle of Trafalgar.

1806   The Battle of San Domingo occurs, and Frank Austen participates.

1807   Passage in Britain of the Slave Trade Abolition Act, banning the trade of enslaved persons in the British Empire; however, the banning of slavery did not occur until 1833.

1809   Austen rewrites "First Impressions" as *Pride and Prejudice* and revises *Sense and Sensibility* for publication.

1811–20   The Regency period in Britain. George, prince of Wales, takes over the powers of his father, King George III, until the latter's death in 1820.

1811   *Sense and Sensibility* published anonymously, as would be true of all of Austen's published works. Austen writes *Mansfield Park*.

1813   *Pride and Prejudice* published.

1814–15   Napoleon abdicates as emperor and retreats into exile on the Mediterranean island of Elba. He then escapes and marches toward Paris but is defeated and recaptured in the Battle of Waterloo, ending the Napoleonic Wars. Eruption of the Indonesian volcano Mount Tambora, leading to the "Year Without a Summer" of 1816.

1814   Austen writes *Emma* and publishes *Mansfield Park*.

1815   Austen writes the first draft of *Persuasion*. *Emma* is published.

1817   On July 18, Austen dies in Winchester, aged 42, likely of Addison's disease, leaving the unfinished novel "Sanditon," which remains unpublished until 1925.

1818   *Northanger Abbey* and *Persuasion* published.

1820–21   George IV crowned king of England on the death of his father, George III. Death of Napoleon in St. Helena.

Selected Bibliography

The first section of this bibliography lists the essential editions of Jane Austen's works. The second section includes works of biography and scholarship, with emphasis on more recent criticism, and excluding materials excerpted in the present volume.

Jane Austen: Works and Letters

Austen, Jane. *Emma*. Edited by Richard Cronin and Dorothy McMillan. *The Cambridge Edition of the Works of Jane Austen*. Cambridge UP, 2005.

———. *Jane Austen's Letters*, 4th ed. Edited by Deirdre Le Faye. Oxford UP, 2014.

———. *Juvenilia*. Edited by Peter Sabor. *The Cambridge Edition of the Works of Jane Austen*. Cambridge UP, 2006.

———. *Later Manuscripts*. Edited by Janet Todd and Linda Bree. *The Cambridge Edition of the Works of Jane Austen*. Cambridge UP, 2008.

———. *Mansfield Park*. Edited by John Wiltshire. *The Cambridge Edition of the Works of Jane Austen*. Cambridge UP, 2005.

———. *Northanger Abbey*. Edited by Barbara M. Benedict and Deirdre Le Faye. *The Cambridge Edition of the Works of Jane Austen*. Cambridge UP, 2006.

———. *Persuasion*. Edited by Janet Todd and Antje Blank. *The Cambridge Edition of the Works of Jane Austen*. Cambridge UP, 2006.

———. *Pride and Prejudice*. Edited by Pat Rogers. *The Cambridge Edition of the Works of Jane Austen*. Cambridge UP, 2006.

———. *Sense and Sensibility*. Edited by Edward Copeland. *The Cambridge Edition of the Works of Jane Austen*. Cambridge UP, 2006.

Chapman, R. W., editor. *The Novels of Jane Austen*, 3rd ed. Vols. 1–7. Oxford UP, 1933.

Biography and Criticism

Armstrong, Nancy. *How Novels Think: The Limits of Individualism from 1719–1900*. Columbia UP, 2005.

Austen-Leigh, J. E. *A Memoir of Jane Austen, and Other Family Recollections*. Edited by Kathryn Sutherland. Oxford UP, 2008.

Barchas, Janine. *Matters of Fact in Jane Austen: History, Location, and Celebrity*. Johns Hopkins UP, 2012.

Christmas, Danielle, and Susan Allen Ford, editors. "Beyond the Bit of Ivory: Jane Austen and Diversity." Special Issue of *Persuasions* 41.2 (2021).

Chwe, Michael. *Jane Austen, Game Theorist*. Princeton UP, 2013.

Copeland, Edward, and Juliet McMaster. *The Cambridge Companion to Jane Austen*, 2nd ed. Cambridge UP, 2011.

Dames, Nicholas. *Amnesiac Selves: Nostalgia, Forgetting, and British Fiction, 1810–1870*. Oxford UP, 2001.

Folsom, Marcia McClintock, and John Wiltshire, editors. *Approaches to Teaching Austen's Persuasion*. Modern Language Association, 2021.

Gallagher, Catherine. *The Body Economic: Life, Death, and Sensation in Political Economy and the Victorian Novel*. Princeton UP, 2008.

Harris, Jocelyn. *A Revolution Almost Beyond Expression: Jane Austen's Persuasion*. U of Delaware P, 2007.

———. *Satire, Celebrity, and Politics in Jane Austen*. Bucknell UP, 2017.

Johnson, Claudia L. *Jane Austen's Cults and Cultures*. U of Chicago P, 2012.

Le Faye, Deirdre. *A Chronology of Jane Austen and Her Family*. Cambridge UP, 2006.

Lanser, Susan S. "Second-Sex Economics: Race, Rescue, and the Heroine's Plot." *The Eighteenth Century* 61.2 (2020): 227–44.

Looser, Devoney. *The Making of Jane Austen*. Johns Hopkins UP, 2017.

Lynch, Deirdre, editor. *Janeites: Austen's Disciples and Devotees*. Princeton UP, 2000.

———. "The Unwritten History of the Woman of Genius (Austen, Staël, Siddons): What She Says, Goes." *Romanticism* 29.2 (2023): 165–76.

Markovitz, Stephanie. "Jane Austen, By Half." *Eighteenth-Century Fiction* 32.2 (2020): 297–315.

Miller, Andrew H. *The Burdens of Perfection: On Ethics and Reading in Nineteenth-Century British Literature*. Cornell UP, 2008.

Miller, D. A. *Jane Austen, or the Secret of Style*. Princeton UP, 2003.

Murphy, Olivia. *Jane Austen the Reader: The Artist as Critic*. Palgrave, 2013.

Nesbit, Kate. "'Taste in Noises': Registering, Evaluating, and Creating Sound and Story in Jane Austen's *Persuasion*." *Studies in the Novel* 47.4 (2015): 451–68.

Richardson, Alan. "Of Heartache and Head Injury: Reading Minds in *Persuasion*." *Poetics Today* 23.1 (2002): 141–60.

Todd, Janet, editor. *Jane Austen in Context*. Cambridge UP, 2020.

Wilson, Cheryl A., and Maria H. Frawley, editors. *The Routledge Companion to Jane Austen*. Routledge, 2021.

Woloch, Alex. *The One vs. the Many: Minor Characters and the Space of the Protagonist in the Novel*. Princeton UP, 2004.